RUSSIAN

CLASSICS

IVAN BUNIN

Light Breathing and Other Stories

Translated by *OLGA SHARTSE*

RADUGA
PUBLISHERS
MOSCOW

Translation from the Russian
Designed by *Vladimir Levinson*
Illustrated by *Alexander Valdman*

Иван Бунин

**ЛЕГКОЕ ДЫХАНИЕ
И ДРУГИЕ РАССКАЗЫ**

На английском языке

Printed in the Union of Soviet Socialist Republics

ISBN 5-05-001666-5

CONTENTS

IVAN BUNIN

Ivan Bunin (1870-1953) wrote his first story when he was only 15 and his last book, an unfinished work about Anton Chekhov, at 83. Thus, he enjoyed a remarkably long creative life of nearly 70 years.

The contribution Bunin made to Russian literature and Russian culture is invaluable and varied in form. There is his clear-cut, perfectly finished prose, now scathingly critical, now lyrically exalted or somberly philosophical. There is his poetry, done in the exacting traditions of Pushkin's school. And last but not least there are his translations which in a number of instances (such as Longfellow's *Song of Hiawatha*) remain unsurpassed to this day. Bunin's work, in fact, makes a whole chapter in the development of 20th century Russian literature.

* * *

Maxim Gorky, who knew Bunin intimately, wrote of him: "This most gifted of Russian writers who knows the very soul of each word, is a dry and not 'kind' person, he loves people not with his heart but with his head, and he is so parsimonious with his emotions that it is really comical. He knows his own worth, actually exaggerating it somewhat in his own estimation, he is vain, and hard to please, and he uses his nearest and dearest quite shamelessly." And the same Gorky said: "Take Bunin out of Russian literature, and it will grow dim without the live sparkle and stellar radiance of this wanderer's lonely soul..."

Nature, it is true, endowed Bunin very, very lavishly. Although his enormous, undisputed talent was not duly acclaimed at once by his contemporaries, it was appreciated more and more by the reading public with every year. His talent was likened to "matt silver", his language was called "brocaded", and his merciless psychological analysis was said to cut like an "icy razor". Anton Chekhov, shortly before he died, asked friends to tell Bunin that he had "the makings of a big writer"; Lev Tolstoy said of Bunin's descriptive skill: "Even Turgevev could not have written this so well, to say nothing of myself"; and Maxim Gorky called him "the best craftsman in modern Russian literature".

Bunin was born into the family of a country squire in the very heart of Russia, and his pride in his ancient lineage, in the gentry's way of life and culture, in the mores and manners that specifically belonged to his social layer that had been irrevocably swept away by time, naturally influenced his world outlook and were manifested in his writing. Life at his father's country estate, which was becoming hopelessly impoverished, nostalgia for the landed gentry's old mode of life and lingering traditions evoked such unambiguous confessions from Bunin as this (in a letter to Varvara Paschenko dated August 14, 1891): "Not only do the times of serfdom no longer seem hateful to me now, but in spite of myself I am even beginning to poeticize them... Honestly, I'd love to live like a country squire of old for a while."

However, poverty was knocking on his father's door and it compelled Bunin, when he was nineteen, to leave the family nest and learn at first hand the joys and sorrows of the less privileged classes. He changed a great many jobs—he was a proof reader, a librarian, a statistician, he once started a book shop, he called himself a "freethinker" and said that he was quite indifferent not only to having blue blood but also to losing everything connected with it. Such was the nature of Bunin's social duality: he was drawn to the traditions of the nobility and at the same time he wanted to alienate himself from them.

While he was living in Russia this duality largely determined the originality of his writing. But when he became estranged from Russian reality his class feeling awakened in him anew...

* * *

Whereas Bunin's traditionally 19th century poetry is mainly devoted to the Russian landscape, his pre-revolutionary prose deals above all else with the old countryside, starting with such turn-of-the-century stories about small impoverished country estates as "At the Homestead", "Apple Fragrance", to such "hits"—to use a modern expression—as "The Village" (1909-1910), "Zakhar Vorobyev" (1912), "A Jolly Place" (1911). In fact it was "The Village" and "Sukhodol" (1911) which promoted Bunin to the front ranks of the new century's Russian realist writers.

For a long time these stories were taken one-sidedly, as a harsh criticism of Russia's village world with its narrow-mindedness and barbarousness. But it was the village world and not the peasants that his accusations were aimed against. It would be only fair to say that when describing the darkest sides of Russian reality Bunin made no distinction between peasants and small landowners, and, what is more, he perceived these dark sides of life with pain and compassion, anger and pity, with what were truly filial emotions.

In developing the theme of Russia, Bunin presented to readers a number of national types, some purely Russian characters, such as the beautiful Youngbride, the senile Ivanushka, the book-lover Balashkin, and the Krasov brothers in "The Village", the meek labourer Averky in "Weeds", the giant Zakhar Vorobyev in the story of the same title, and others.

The best definition of Bunin's feelings for Russia's rural life, both the peasantry's and the landed gentry's, would be love-hate. Love for the beauty of old Russia that shone through all the social adversities, and hatred for all that was so barbarous and ignorant in that life.

In these years Bunin was perfecting his method of realistic writing. He took up various new themes and handled them with greater pliancy. He described the stifling world of smug philistinism ("The Cup of Life"), the urban lower depths ("Loopy Ears"), the charming image of a schoolgirl whose life was as short as a butterfly's ("Light Breathing"), and also drew a portrait of an extraordinarily sober-minded, smug German ("Otto Stein").

Life and death, and their constant confrontation, inevitably form the background against which the tragedies of Bunin's characters are played out.

Bunin examined the strange workings of the Russian soul in order to divine the "eternal" and "immobile" traits of the Russian character. Whoever he wrote about, he always seemed to see his heroes' countless forebears receding into the reverse perspective of generations. He discovered a lurking catastrophe in everyone's life, however secure and happy it would seem to be, and saw it as hanging over an abyss.

These seekings of his reflected in their own way the approaching great social upheavals in Russia.

* * *

Reflecting on Russia as a peasant country that was meek yet secreting the explosive power of revolt, Bunin tried to find the key to its future in its past. At the same time he pondered on the purpose of living, he tried to understand what made some people suddenly renounce the comforts of life and physical delights, and looked for an explanation now in Buddhism, now in the philosophy of Lev Tolstoy.

From the height of absolute moral criteria he examined "ordinary" life stories ("The Gentleman from San Francisco", "Brothers" and "Chang's Dreams"). He wanted to do more than simply tell readers about the vainness of mundane happiness, the onus of passions, the perishableness of everything human–fame, wealth, power, beauty and strength.

According to Bunin, happiness is given to a few, it is a sort of monopoly of the chosen in whom "breeding" has manifested itself as a physical and moral beauty and strength. These chosen ones do not have to be highly born, not at all. Everything is beautiful in the peasant Zakhar

Vorobyev, for instance, he is a model of health in body and mind, of moral integrity and strength. And Bunin's story "Youth and Senility" (1936) also affirms this principled stand of his.

In his 1936 treatise "The Liberation of Tolstoy" Bunin expressed his philosophical views on the role and mission of man. In addition to the thirty years of life granted him by God, man has wheedled another fifteen from an ass, fifteen from a dog, and fifteen more from a monkey. And so: "His own thirty years he lived like a man–he ate, drank, fought in wars, danced at weddings, and made love to married women and girls. During the fifteen ass's years he worked and amassed wealth. The fifteen dog's years he watched over his riches, yapping and snapping all the time, and staying awake at night. And then he became nasty and ugly like the monkey he had wheedled the last fifteen years from."

Thus, according to Bunin, only a man who is luckily spared the need to make and hoard money, and who is as luckily endowed with bodily health, beauty and valour, can remain a *man* after his allotted thirty years. Such was the Kurd chief in the story "Youth and Senility".

Zakhar Vorobyev is also a *man*, while the kulak Tikhon Krasov (in "The Village") who has wasted his whole life on senseless money-grubbing is an *ass*.

The Gentleman from San Francisco was also an *ass* and a *dog*, having squandered his whole life on making money, ruthlessly exploiting his slaves and not even sparing himself. He did not want to become a *man*, or perhaps he could not become one.

More and more sharply contrasting life and death, joy and horror, hope and despair, and pushing them closer and closer together, Bunin was not simply being pessimistic, as might be thought. The "sharpened feeling of death" which he discovered in himself was directly linked by him with as sharp a "feeling of life". These words are taken from his major work, the novel *The Life of Arseniev*, in which death and oblivion retreat before the power of love, before Arseniev's and the author's sharpened "feeling of life".

Bunin turned out to be the only emigrant writer who, though he had suffered a creative loss, got over the crisis and continued to perfect his artistic method in unusual and extremely unfavourable conditions. His talent revealed new facets, even on foreign soil, resulting in such important works as "Mitya's Love" (1927), "Sunstroke" (1925), the novel *The Life of Arseniev*, and the book of short stories *Shadowed Paths* (1946).

Always a patriot at heart, he could not but remain a profoundly national Russian writer, unlike the majority of Russian emigrant authors, who only mourned their loss or had changed the pen of a belletrist for the sting of a tendentious journalist. Though he lived far from Russia, it remained a part of him. Still, it was not the Russia that once began outside his window in a country house; it existed and yet it seemed unreal, and everything in it stood to doubt.

* * *

There was one theme, however, to which Bunin was devoted all his life, which he never doubted, and this was the theme of love.

In this sphere, abounding in unexpressed shades of feeling and understatements, his talent truly came to flower.

Love, in Bunin's description, is subservient to some inner laws unbeknown to man. These laws do not often come into the open, and most people now never experience their fatal influence. This attitude to love unexpectedly lends a romantic glow to Bunin's sober, "merciless" talent. However, this only seems unexpected. Bunin, who never forgave his characters the smallest vulgarity, weakness, or even physical imperfection, Bunin, if only driven by his inner logic, naturally had to give precedence to the ideal, cleansed of mundane "chaff".

Prosiness, as Bunin understands it, is just another form of ugliness, anti-beauty, disfigurement. In all his stories love is a passion that grips a person wholly, mentally, spiritually and physically. In this sense "The Grammar of Love" (1915) anticipates the theme developed in "Mitya's Love" (1927), while "A Small Love Affair" written in 1909 does not differ in principle from the much later "Sunstroke" (1925). Lovers have to part, and part forever, so that their love should not outlive itself and expire. If the lovers themselves do not do it, then fate intervenes, killing one of the lovers to save their love.

The passion common to Bunin's heroes and heroines is astounding in its strength and sincerity. Take "Sunstroke". The story we are told is surely not an ordinary shipboard romance? She says: "I give you my word of honour that I'm not at all what you might have thought me to be, nothing even remotely like this has ever happened to me before, nor will it ever happen again. I must have lost my senses... Or, rather, we both had something like a sunstroke..."

Bunin does not intend to justify the officer's lustful impulse with any high-sounding words, and on the contrary he actually emphasizes the "modesty" of his original wish to have a small amorous adventure. However, little by little and as if against the lovers' will, they enter an enchanted world of absolutely new feelings, which affect them powerfully and hurtfully, all the more hurtfully the more clearly do they realize that it is all over, that they are to part forever. The amorous adventure develops into a rare, noble and soul-shattering love, powerfully communicated to the reader. I can hardly find another story which in such concise form should render so convincingly the drama of a man who has suddenly come to know real love, a love too overwhelming and too happy; so happy, in fact, that if his intimacy with that little woman were to last one more day (and she knows it) this love which had illumined the whole of their drab lives would instantly forsake them.

Re-reading Maupassant, Bunin jotted down in his diary on August 3, 1917: "He is the only one who had the courage to go on saying that the life of a man is wholly ruled by his desire of a woman." An emotional, passionate nature, Bunin went through several profoundly shattering, dramatic love phases in the course of his long life. It may be said that four Muses accompanied him through life, inspiring, stimulating his urge to write, and either causing him suffering or bringing him joy. These were four different types of women, each one making an epoch in his life: Varvara Paschenko, Anna Tsakni, Vera Muromtseva, and Galina Kuznetsova.

The boyish, powerful and tragic love, so beautifully told in "Lika" (the fifth part of *The Life of Arseniev*) was painted from Bunin's remembrance of his love for Varvara Paschenko, a strong-willed, resolute young woman who had the courage to go against her parents' will and public opinion. In the photograph taken in 1892 she is sitting beside young Bunin and looks much his senior, perhaps because she is wearing a pince-nez. There is something in her of those women who, in the 1860's started their movement for equal rights in Russia–women who thirsted for emancipation and education, and despised middle-class conventions.

Bunin's love was profound and enthralling. It would be naive, of course, to see a portrait of Varvara Paschenko in Lika, but the autobiographical basis of the novel, and the pages devoted to Alexei Arseniev's infatuation with Lika were so unquestionable for the author's intimates, that shortly before his death Bunin said to a journalist half-jokingly: "I'm going to die soon ... and you'll see: my wife will write *The Life of Arseniev* anew."

He was quite right. In her book *The Life of Bunin*, his widow, Vera Nikolayevna Bunina-Muromtseva, stresses again and again the erroneousness of regarding the novel as an autobiography. "And Lika is not Varvara Paschenko, not in appearance and not in character," she writes. Thus, Bunin's wife, who was also his closest and truest friend, disputed not only a simplified interpretation of the novel *The Life of Arseniev* but even the fact of his infatuation.

One would think that Anna Tsakni, his first wife, was not the type of woman to leave a trace of any depth in Bunin's soul. On the photograph taken in 1898 we see a very young woman with regular and a bit heavy features–a woman quite different from Varvara Paschenko. She was a true *fin de siècle* lady, she adored noisy parties and musical soirées attended by everybody who was anybody in Odessa's artistic circles. What could she have in common with Bunin? "It pains me to remember," he once told his brother Yuly, "how many times I opened my heart out to her, a heart brimming with the purest tenderness–and it left her cold, she was as unfeeling as a block of wood ... she did not give a hang for a single *word* of mine, not for a single *opinion* of mine about anything." But when this marriage, unfortunate *a priori*, fell apart, Bunin was miserable and suffered a terrible sense of loss. At the end of 1899 he wrote to his brother: "You won't believe this, but if it were not for a faint glimmering of hope I'd kill myself without a quaver... I'm not going to describe my sufferings, and there's no sense in doing so. But I'm finished–it's an accomplished fact... Only this morning I lay on the ground in the steppe for three hours sobbing and screaming, for no man perhaps has ever suffered greater agony, greater despair and indignity from losing love, hope, everything... Think of me and remember that I'm dying, that I am perishing irresistibly... You can't imagine how I love her... There's no one dearer for me in the world." It must be remembered that this was written not by a lovesick boy, but by a man of thirty with a fully formed character and an established writer's career.

The lucky star in Bunin's life, his guardian angel and companion, was Vera Muromtseva. She was the daughter of a Moscow professor; self-possessed, reserved, rather cool perhaps, but devoted and considerate. The comfort with which she surrounded her husband was constant and steady, and little by little she made herself as necessary to him as the air he breathed.

There was one more Muse, the fourth Muse in Bunin's life who was wholly a creature of the 20th century. This was the writer Galina Kuznetsova, whose face with the large eyes and a slightly retroussée nose held a peculiar enchantment.

Four Muses–four epochs. However, Bunin himself once confessed that his ideal of a woman was different from all the four Muses, being a "swarthy, thin, Asiatic" type. This was the type of woman he described in "Rusya".

"Love, any love, is a great happiness, even if it is unrequited," we quote from the book *Shadowed Paths*, and these words could have been said by any of Bunin's lovers. The men and women in his stories, in spite of their different social standing and their vastly differing individualities, all live in expectation of love, they seek love and when they find it, they mostly perish in its flames.

Bunin was, I should say, the first of our Russian writers to let the theme of love play such an important role in his work.

In this mysterious sphere he has no equal. The idea of love as an evenly burning low flame, as contentment, is arrogantly rejected by Bunin and the heroes and heroines of his stories, as they also reject a love drama that is diffused and dissolved in prosiness (as in Chekhov's "Lady with a Dog"). Love fleetingly visits our sinful world, prepared to disappear at any moment. Bunin denies it the ability to last–in marriage, in the family, in the everydays. A brief, blinding flash, illumining the souls of the lovers to their very depths, brings them to the brink, beyond which awaits death, suicide, non-existence.

The closeness of love and death, their conjugation, is seen by Bunin as a manifestation of life's general calamitousness. Death and tragedy do not stem from love, they descend on the lovers from without. It is fate, rather than anything else. Here Bunin reveals his notion about the insecurity of everything which had heretofore appeared established and stable, and in the final count we hear in this, though only reflected and re-interpreted, an echo of the great social upheavals which the 20th century has brought mankind.

In all Bunin's work, and particularly in his stories of love, we see the best features common to classical Russian literature–active compassion ("Hotel Madrid"), a hymn to love ("Sunstroke", "Rusya"), protest against everything petty that stands in the way of love ("Shadowed Paths"). These stories, written many years ago, still stir and move us to compassion, because their subject, to quote Bunin, "is the eternal and forever the same love between man and woman, mother and child, the theme of man's eternal sorrows and joys, and the mystery of his birth, existence and death".

Oleg Mikhailov

Light Breathing and Other Stories

Apple Fragrance

1

...I remember a fine, early autumn. August was a month of soft, warm rains that seemed to fall specially for the sowing-rain just when it was needed, in the middle of the month, about St. Lawrence's Day. And the belief is that autumn and winter will get on well together if the waters are still and there's rain on St. Lawrence's Day. And then, in Indian summer, gossamer settled lavishly on the fields. That's a good sign too. I remember a crisp, clear morning... I remember a large, golden, rather dry, and thinning garden. I remember the walks lined with maples, the delicate fragrance of fallen leaves and the smell of Antonovka apples–a smell of honey and autumn freshness. The air was so pure it hardly seemed to be there, and the whole garden resounded with voices and the squeaking of cart wheels. That was the *tarkhane*, the trading gardeners who, with the help of hired peasants, were loading apples into carts to send to town that very night–at night it had to be, when it was so pleasant to lie on top of the load, gazing into the starry sky, smelling the tar in the crisp air and hearing the gentle creaking of the long train of carts along the dark road. A peasant loading the apples would eat one after another with a juicy crunch, but that was one of the unwritten laws–the employer would never stop him; on the contrary, he would say:

"Go ahead and eat your fill, there's nothing for it. Everyone drinks mead on barrelling day!"

All that disturbed the cool stillness of the morning was

the complacent clucking of thrushes in the coral-red rowans in the thickets of the garden, the sound of voices and the hollow thud of apples as they were poured into the measures and barrels. Through the thinning orchard you could see far down the straw-strewn road leading to a large tent, and the tent itself which the *tarkhane* had made quite a household during the summer months. The smell of apples was strong everywhere, particularly here. Inside the tent they had their pallets, a single-barrelled gun, a mouldy-green samovar, and some kitchen utensils in the corner. Mats and crates, rags and rubbish lay in a heap beside the tent, and a hearth for the fire had been dug in the ground. At midday a delicious millet stew was cooked there and in the evening the samovar was warmed up, and a long ribbon of bluish smoke trailed between the trees in the garden. But on holidays there was a regular fair round the tent and bright Sunday finery flickered behind the trees. There was a cluster of pert girls, the daughters of *odnodvortsi*,* dressed in sarafans that smelled strongly of dye; the gentry's servants came too, in their beautiful and crude, strange dress, and the young pregnant wife of the village elder, with a broad, sleepy face and the sedateness of a cow. She wore a head-dress known as "horns": the hair was parted in the middle, plaited and pinned up on each side, with several kerchiefs worn over it, making the head look enormous. Her feet in half-boots with steel-tipped heels were planted firmly, the toes turned in; her sleeveless jacket was of velveteen, her apron long, and her skirt of deep mauve with brick-red stripes had a wide gold braid trimming.

"That's the right sort of little woman!" the tradesman remarked, slowly shaking his head. "They're getting rare nowadays..."

Little boys in white homespun shirts and short trousers, with hair bleached white by the sun, kept coming up. They came in twos or threes, tripping along in their bare feet and darting wary glances at the shaggy watch-dog tied to an apple-tree. Only one of the group was a buyer, of

******Odnodvortsi***—families who in the 17th century were settled in "outlying" districts, mainly Tambov, Voronezh and adjacent gubernias. They claimed noble descent, some owned serfs, and all enjoyed certain special rights. —*Tr.***

course, as all the wealth they possessed was a kopek or a fresh egg to barter; but there were plenty of customers anyway, business was brisk, and the consumptive tradesman in a long frock-coat and yellow top-boots served them gaily. He and his brother, a lively, burring half-wit, whom he kept "out of charity", joked and clowned, and sometimes even played a tune on a Tula accordion as they sold their wares. And until late in the evening there was a crowd of people in the garden, there was laughter and talk close to the tent and sometimes the tap of dancing feet...

In fair weather it grew very cold and damp towards nightfall. After a day out on the threshing-floor, where you had breathed your fill of the scent of threshed rye and chaff, you briskly walked home to supper past the earthen bank at the bottom of the garden. Voices down in the village or the creaking of a gate rang with extraordinary clearness in the frosty evening air. Darkness fell. And then there was a new smell, that of a woodfire being lighted in the garden and the fragrant smoke of the burning cherry branches. The picture you saw at the bottom of the dark garden was like a scene from a fairy-tale: in the surrounding darkness, the crimson flames blazing close to the tent were like a corner of hell, with black shapes that seemed to be carved of ebony moving around the fire, while their monstrous shadows wavered over the apple-trees. A black arm, several yards in length, lay along the whole tree, or suddenly a pair of legs, like two black pillars, was etched very clearly. And suddenly, all these shadows slipped down from the tree and one long shadow fell on the path, from the tent to the very gate...

Late at night when the lights had gone out in the windows and the seven brilliant stars of the Pleiades shone high in the sky, you ran once again into the garden. With the dry leaves rustling underfoot, you groped your way blindly to the tent. It was a little lighter there in the clearing, with the Milky Way overhead.

"Is that you, young master?" someone's voice called softly from the darkness.

"Yes. Aren't you asleep yet, Nikolai?"

"We're not supposed to sleep. But it must be late, eh? There's the passenger train now, I think."

We listened long and hard, and caught a tremor running

along the ground. The tremor became a noise, it grew and grew until it seemed that wheels were beating time loudly and hurriedly just behind the garden; knocking and clamouring, the train came on ... closer and closer, louder and angrier... And suddenly the sound grew fainter and muffled as though it were vanishing into the ground...

"Where's your gun, Nikolai?"

"Why, here, beside the box."

You flung up the gun that was as heavy as a crowbar, and fired at random. A crimson spurt of flame shot up into the sky with a deafening report, blinding you for a moment and snuffing out the stars, and a cheerful echo roared and rolled towards the horizon, fading in the pure and keen air, far, far away.

"My, that was a good one!" the tradesman said. "Give them a scare, young master, give them a scare! The trouble they're giving us; they've shaken down all the pears by the wall again..."

Shooting stars streaked the black sky with fiery trails. You gazed so long into its dark blue depths thronged with constellations, that you felt the ground slipping away from under your feet. Then you got up and, hiding your hands in the sleeves of your coat, ran home quickly along the path... How cold and damp it was, but how good to be alive!

2

"If the apples are good, the year will be good." All's well in the village if the Antonovkas are good: it means the grain crop is a good one too. I remember a year of abundant crops.

At the break of day, when cocks were still crowing and black smoke was pouring from the chimneyless huts, I would throw open the window into the cool garden, filled with a lilac mist, through which the morning sun flashed brightly here and there, and the temptation would be so strong that I would order my horse to be saddled at once, while I hurried down to the pond to wash. The willows dipping to the water were almost stripped of their tiny leaves, and the bare branches were lacy against the turquoise sky. The water beneath the willows had grown transparent, icy, and heavy, as it were. It dispelled your drowsiness and lassitude at once, and when you had dressed and eaten your breakfast of hot potatoes and black bread sprinkled with damp coarse salt in the kitchen with the farm hands, you revelled in the feel of the slippery leather saddle as you rode out hunting through the village of Viselki. Autumn is the season of patron saint's days, and the people look trim and happy; the village itself has quite a different, festive air. If the crops were good that year and tall castles of pure gold rose from the threshing-floors, while the geese gabbled shrilly and clearly on the river of a morning, then life in the village was not bad at all. Moreover, our Viselki has always been known for a prosperous village since the beginning of time, since grandfather's day. Viselki people lived to a ripe old age—which is the first sign of a prosperous village—and all these old people were tall and big-boned, with hair as white as snow. You were always hearing someone say: "Look at Agafya there, she's eighty-three if she's a day!" Or conversations like this:

"And when are you going to die, Pankrat? You must be nearly a hundred?"

"What's that you say, Your Honour?"

"I'm asking how old you are."

"That I couldn't tell you, Your Honour."

"D'you remember Platon Apollonich?"

"Of course I do, I remember him well."

"You see! That means you can't possibly be less than a hundred."

The old man, standing rigidly before his master, would smile a humble and guilty smile. Was it his fault that he had outlived his day? And probably he would have outlived it even longer if he had not eaten too many onions on St. Peter's Day.

I remember his wife too. The old woman was always sitting on a bench on the porch, her back hunched, her head shaking, her hands clutching the edge of the bench, her breath coming in short gasps, and her mind busy on something. "Thinking of her wealth, I expect," the women used to say, because she really had a lot of "wealth" in her trunks. But she seemed not to hear; with fading eyes, she gazed from under her sadly raised eyebrows into the distance, shaking her head as though trying to remember something. She was a large woman, and everything about her was dark. The skirt she wore looked a hundred years old, her slippers were the kind they put on the dead, her neck was yellow and scraggy and her blouse, inset with dimity diamonds, was always very, very white—"good enough to bury her in", they said. There was a large stone slab lying close to the porch: she had bought it herself for her gravestone, as also her burial robe—a splendid shroud with angels, crosses and a prayer printed round the edges.

The houses at Viselki were in keeping with the old people. They were brick cottages built by their grandfathers. But the more prosperous peasants, like Savely, Ignat and Dron, had big cottages built in two or three sections, for in those days in Viselki when sons married they did not set up their own households. Families such as these kept beehives, took a pride in their steel-blue stallions, and looked after their property well. Hemp-fields, thick and lush, stretched beyond the threshing-floors; the sheds and barns were neatly thatched; store-rooms and cellars had strong, heavy doors, which guarded bolts of linen, spinning-wheels, new sheepskin coats, silver-chased harness, and measuring casks, hooped with copper. The top of the gates and the sledges had a cross burnt into the wood. I remember there were times when I thought it must be wonderful to be a peasant. As I rode through the village on a sunny morning I kept thinking how good it was to mow and thresh, to sleep in the strawstacks by the threshing-floor, and on holidays to rise with the sun to the deep, melodious pealing of church bells in the village, to wash from a water barrel, put on a clean twill shirt and trousers and a pair of indestructible hob-nailed top-boots. And if, in addition to this, you had a beautiful, healthy wife, dressed in holiday finery to drive to church with, the service followed by dinner at your bearded father-in-law's, a dinner of sizzling mutton served on wooden platters, fresh white bread, honey from the comb and homebrewed beer, you had nothing more to wish for.

Until very recently, already in my time, the mode of

life of most of the country squires bore a very strong resemblance to that of the wealthy peasants in its thriftiness and its rustic old-world prosperity. Such was the estate of my Aunt Anna Gerasimovna, for example, which was some twelve versts from Viselki. By the time you got there it would be quite light. You would be riding slowly if you had your dogs on leashes, and indeed, you would not want to hurry, for it was so nice to be out in the open on a cool, sunny morning. The plain was flat and you could see far into the distance. The sky was so light, so spacious and fathomless! The sun cast its brilliant slanting rays on the road, which had been rolled smooth by the carts after the rains and shone with the oily sheen of steel rails. Lush, green winter crops stretched far and wide. A young hawk would soar up into the crystalline air and hang poised there, fluttering its pointed wings. You could see the telegraph-poles running away into the bright distance, their wires like silver strings, gliding along the clear sky. Merlins perched on the wires—little black signs on a sheet of music.

I have neither known nor seen serfdom, but I remember I could sense it at Aunt Anna Gerasimovna's. The moment you rode through the gate you felt that here it was still in full sway. The estate was not large, but all of it was old, sturdy, and surrounded by century-old birches and willows. The outbuildings, though low-raftered, were convenient and numerous, and they all seemed to have been cast in the same mould—dark old logs and thatched roofs. Only the smoke-blackened servants' house stood out among them because of its size, or rather its length, with some ancient men and women, and a senile retired chef who looked like Don Quixote, peeping out of the door—the last of the mohicans of the house serfs. As you rode into the yard all of them would draw themselves up and bow very, very low. The grey-haired coachman, coming towards you from the coach-house to take your horse, would take his hat off at the coach-house door and walk across the yard bare-headed. He used to be Aunt's postillion, but now he drove her to church in a covered sledge in winter and in summer in a sturdy little trap reinforced with metal hoops, the type of cart popular among the priests. My aunt's garden was famous for its state of neglect, its nightingales, turtledoves and apples, and her house for its roof. The house stood at the entrance to the estate, with the garden close around it and the branches of lime-trees caressing it. It was squat and rather small, but its unusually steep, thickly thatched roof, blackened and hardened with time, gave it such a solid appearance that it looked as if it would last for ever. I always fancied its façade was a living thing, an old face that seemed to watch you from under a huge hat with deep-sunk eyes–window panes, iridescent like mother-of-pearl from the rain and the sun. There were two old, large, pillared porches–one on either side of this face. Plump, self-satisfied pigeons were always sitting in the gables, while thousands of sparrows scattered in a torrent from roof to roof. And a guest was snug and comfortable in this nest beneath the autumn skies of turquoise blue...

When you walked into the house you first noticed the fragrance of apples, then the smell of old mahogany furniture and of dried lime blossom that had lain on the window-sills since June... All the rooms–the front hall, the dining-room and the drawing-room–were cold and dark; that was because the house was surrounded by trees and the top panes of the windows were of coloured glass–blue or mauve. All was quiet and clean, though, I believe, the armchairs, the inlaid tables and the mirrors in their narrow, fluted gilt frames had never been moved from their places. And then you would hear a light cough, and Aunt Anna would come in. She was not a tall woman but, like everything about her, she looked sturdy. A large Persian shawl was draped round her shoulders. She entered the room with an air of solemnity but with a smile of welcome, too, and while keeping up an unstemmed flow of conversation about the old days, wills and inheritances, she would at once begin to treat her guest to various delicacies, such as pears and apples of four sorts, to be followed by a wonderful dinner: pink boiled ham with green peas, stuffed chicken, turkey, pickles and red kvas,* strong and very, very sweet... The windows into the garden would be left open so that the bracing coolness of autumn flowed into the room...

**Kvas*–a drink made, in this case, of fermented beetroot.–*Tr.*

3

In recent years the only thing that kept up the waning spirits of the landowners was hunting.

Estates such as our aunt's were no rarity in the old days. There were also those which, though going to rack and ruin, still clung to the standards of high living, maintaining their vast properties and fifty-acre gardens. And though some of these country seats have managed to survive to this day, all the life has gone out of them. There are no troikas, no Kirghiz riding horses, no hounds, no borzois, no serfs and even no owners of all this—no hunting country squires like my late brother-in-law Arseny Semyonich.

From the end of September our gardens and fields began to take on a desolate look, and the weather would change suddenly. The wind blustered and tore at the trees for days on end, and rain drenched them from morning till night. Occasionally the tremulous golden glimmer of the setting sun broke through the gloomy, low-hanging clouds in the west, the air turned pure and clear, and a ray of sunlight would flash blindingly on the leaves and branches as they moved against the sky in an animated network, stirred by the wind. The watery-blue sky gleamed coldly and brightly in the north above the dark, leaden clouds, while white clouds like snow-clad mountain ridges rose slowly behind them. You would stand by the window and think: "Let's hope it clears up." But the wind would not abate. It worried the garden, rent the column of smoke curling in an ininterrupted stream from the kitchen chimney, and drove the ominous, shaggy grey clouds together again. They sailed low and fast and soon enveloped the sun in a smoky shroud. Then the sunshine dimmed, the little window in the blue sky closed, and the garden became desolate and bleak; the drizzle started again, softly and gently at first, but growing in intensity until at last it became a downpour with storm and darkness. Night would fall, long and uneasy...

After a drubbing like this the garden emerged practically bare, subdued and humble, and strewn with wet leaves. But then how beautiful it looked when fair weather set in again, in those first days of October, transparent and cold—autumn's parting glory! And the leaves which had not fallen would remain upon the branches until the first frost. The black orchard, transparent against the cold blue sky, would meekly wait for winter now, finding what warmth it could in the shine of the sun. But already the patches of upturned soil were standing out blackly in the fields, and winter crops sprang up in a bright green carpet. Hunting time had come!

And now my memory takes me back to the country seat of Arseny Semyonich, to the hall of his large house, filled with sunlight and the smoke of many cigarettes and pipes. There were many people there—all sunburnt men with weatherbeaten faces, dressed in *poddyovkas** and top-boots. They had just finished a very rich dinner; they were flushed and excited with their loud discussion of the coming hunt, and although dinner was over they did not forget to refill their glasses with vodka. A hunting-horn blared in the yard and hounds wailed in various keys. A black borzoi, Arseny Semyonich's favourite, climbed on to the table and started guzzling away at the remains of the roast hare. Arseny Semyonich, coming out of his study armed with a hunting-crop and revolver, suddenly fired with a deafening report, and the dog, squealing horribly, bounded off the table, overturning plates and glasses. Smoke hung thicker than ever, but Arseny Semyonich just stood there laughing.

"Pity I missed," he said, his eyes flashing.

He was tall and lean, broad-shouldered and well-built. He had the face of a handsome Gipsy and a savage gleam in his eyes. He looked very smart in his raspberry-red silk shirt, velvet trousers and top-boots. Having given the dog and the company a scare with his gun, he recited in a baritone with comic solemnity:

The time has come to mount your eager
steed,
Across your shoulders sling the strident
horn...

**Poddyovka*—a Russian long, collarless coat, fitted and gathered at the waist, worn with a sash or belt.—*Tr.*

Then he shouted:

"Well then, don't let's waste precious time!"

I remember to this day how greedily and deeply my young lungs drank in the coolness of the clear, damp air of the late afternoon when I rode with Arseny Semyonich's noisy crowd, thrilling to the music of the hounds' excited baying in the thick woods somewhere in Krasny Bugor* or Gremyachy Ostrov,** whose names alone were exciting enough to the huntsman. I used to ride a stocky Kirghiz hunter, fierce and strong, and as I strained to hold it in I felt I was almost one with it. The horse snorted, impatient to go into a canter, its hoofs rustling noisily through the deep, brittle carpet of dead black leaves, and every sound echoed hollowly in the emptiness of the damp woods. A hound barked far away, another one responded plaintively and passionately, a third joined in, suddenly the whole forest was in an uproar, ringing as if it were all glass, with the furious barking and baying. A shot rang out sharply above the din—and the chase began, rolling and rumbling away into the distance.

"Tally-ho!" the forest rang with someone's desperate yell.

"I'll hold it!" the heady thought flashed through your mind. Whooping at your horse, you broke away and tore through the woods, no longer conscious of anything on the way. There was nothing but flickering trees before you and clots of mud, kicked up by the horse and flying into your face. You leapt out of the wood to see the motley pack strung out across the green fields, you spurred your horse on even harder to cut off the quarry, speeding across the fields, across ploughland and stubble, until at last you flew into the copse and the pack in full cry disappeared from view. And then, wet through and shaking with excitement, you reined your foaming, panting hunter and thirstily gulped in the icy dampness of the wooded dell. The shouts of the huntsmen and the baying of the hounds died away in the distance, and perfect silence dropped around you. There was no movement in the shrubless tall pine forest, and you seemed to be in some forbidden realm.

**Krasny Bugor*—Red Mound.—*Tr.*
***Gremyachy Ostrov*—Rumbling Island.—*Tr.*

The strong, dank smell of mushrooms, decayed leaves and sodden bark came from the gullies. And the dampness rising from the ravines could be felt more keenly, the forest grew colder and darker... It was time to call it a day. But it was not easy to get the pack together again. The huntsmen's horns rang through the forest with a hopeless wistfulness, for a long time you would hear shouting, swearing and the yelps of the hounds. Finally, when it was quite dark a crowd of huntsmen would invade the bachelor home of some gentleman, little known to any of them, and fill with a noisy din the whole yard, lighted by lanterns, candles and lamps brought out of the house to welcome the guests.

It sometimes happened that the hunt would stay for several days at some hospitable neighbour's. We would ride out into the woods and fields at the break of day, in the damp early snow and the icy wind, and towards nightfall we would be back again, our faces flushed, covered with dirt, and our clothes saturated with the stench of horse sweat and the hide of the run-down beast; and the night would be spent in drinking. The bright, crowded house seemed very warm after a day out in the icy air. Everyone wandered from room to room with his coat open, eating and drinking in a disorderly sort of way, discussing the day's run noisily over the body of the big wolf, which lay sprawled in the middle of the hall, staining the floor with pale congealed blood, its teeth bared and eyes rolled up, its fluffy tail flung out. After the vodka and the food you felt so deliciously tired, so sweetly drowsy, that the hum of voices seemed to come through a wall of water. Your chapped face stung, and if you closed your eyes the ground seemed to slip away from you. But when you retired and lay back in a soft feather bed in some old-world corner room with an icon stand and a sanctuary lamp before it, visions of fiery-coloured hounds would flash before your eyes; your whole body would ache with the sensation of galloping, and before you knew it you would plunge into a sweet and healthy sleep, forgetting all your visions and sensations, without even remembering that the room had once been the chapel of an old man around whose name sinister legends of serfdom days were woven, and that he had died in that very room and probably in that very bed.

If you happened to oversleep and miss next morning's hunt, your rest was particularly enjoyable. When you woke up you would lie in bed for a long time. The whole house would be locked in silence. You could hear the gardener treading carefully about the rooms lighting the stoves, and then the logs crackling and shooting. Ahead of you lay a whole day of leisure in a house already muffled up for winter. You dressed unhurriedly, wandered through the garden, found a cold, wet apple which had been overlooked among the wet leaves, and for some reason it seemed extraordinarily tasty and quite unlike other apples. Then you would settle down to the books of grandfather's day, volumes bound in thick leather, with golden stars on their morocco backs. There was a nice smell about those volumes, which looked like prayer-books with their rough, yellowed pages. A smell of old perfume clung to them, and a pleasant tang of mustiness. I liked the notes which had been made in the margins with a quill in a soft, rounded hand. I would open a book and read: "A thought worthy of ancient and modern philosophers, the light of reason and deep feeling." And you could not help becoming engrossed in the book itself. It was the *Nobleman-Philosopher*, an allegory, published some hundred years before at the expense of a "cavalier of many orders" and printed by the charity board printing press. It was the story of a "nobleman-philosopher who, having the time and aptitude for reflection, to which the mind of man might be elevated, one day conceived the desire of making an *Orbis mundi* on his spacious land". Then you would come across "The Satirical and Philosophical works of M. Voltaire", and for a long time you would revel in the charming and pretentious style of the translation: "Sires! It pleased Erasmus to compose a praise to buffoonery in the sixteenth century (an affected pause–semicolon); while you, sires, are commanding me to extol reason for you..." After that, from the ancient times of Catherine the Great you would pass on to the day of romance, to almanacs, to novels–sentimentally pompous and long... The cuckoo would hop out of the clock and in the empty house somewhere above your head, you would hear its sadly mocking call. And little by little a strange, sweet melancholy would creep into your heart.

Then you opened *The Secrets of Alexis*, then *Victor, or the Child in the Woods*, and you read: "The clock struck twelve. Inviolable silence replaced the noise of the day and the merry songs of the villagers. Sleep spread its sombre wing over the surface of our hemisphere; it scattered darkness and dreams... Dreams... How often are they simply the continuance of the sufferings of the wretched!" And beloved old words would flash before your eyes: rocks and groves, a pale moon and loneliness, ghosts and wraiths, Cupid's darts, roses and lilies, "the playful pranks of naughty youths", lily-white hands, Ludmilas and Alinas... And there were the periodicals with the names of Zhukovsky, Batyushkov, and Pushkin, the young Lycée student. And you'd wistfully recall Grandmamma, the polonaises she played on the clavichord, the languid way she read verses from *Yevgeny Onegin*. And the old, dreamy world rose before you... How lovely were the girls and women who once lived in these country homes! These beautiful, noble women with old-world coiffures looked down on me from their portraits on the wall and dropped their long eyelashes shyly and gracefully over their sad and gentle eyes...

4

The fragrance of Antonovka apples is disappearing from the country houses. Those days were such a short while ago and yet it seems to me that a whole century has passed since then. The old people of Viselki are all dead; Anna Gerasimovna is dead too, and Arseny Semyonich has shot himself... The reign of the small-estate owners, impoverished to a state of beggary, has now taken over. But even the beggarly life of the small estates is good.

I remember going back to the country late one autumn. The days were dimly blue and overcast. In the morning I mounted my horse, took but one dog along and rode out into the open, armed with a gun and a huntsman's horn. The wind sang in the barrel of the gun and blew hard into my face, sometimes bringing dry snow with it. I roamed the desolate plain all day long... Towards dusk I rode back to the house, hungry and frozen through, but what a warm and happy feeling I had when I saw the lights of Viselki flickering in the darkness ahead and caught the smell of smoke, of home, wafting towards me. I remember, our family were fond of the twilight hour, they would sit and converse softly without putting on the lights. When I walked into the house I found that the double windows had already been put in, and that, more than anything else, attuned me to the peaceful drowsiness of winter. One of the servants was lighting the fire in the hall and I, just as I did when I was a child, squatted beside the heap of straw, smelling sharply of what was already a wintry crispness, and gazed into the roaring fire or at the windows beyond which the twilight was sadly waning in the darkening blue. And then I went into the kitchen, brightly lit and crowded: kitchen maids were chopping cabbage for salting, and I listened to the vigorous, rhythmic tapping of their flashing knives and their voices, harmoniously blended in a wistfully-gay village song... Sometimes one of the neighbouring small-estate owners called on us and took me away for a long stay with him... The life of a small-estate owner is good too.

He rises early. After a good stretch he gets up and rolls himself a thick cigarette of cheap black tobacco. The pale light of an early November morning reveals a plain study with bare walls except for a couple of brittle yellow foxskins over the bed, a stocky man in Cossack trousers and a loose unbelted shirt, while the mirror reflects a face with a Tatar cast, heavy with sleep. Dead silence reigns in the warm dusky house. The old cook snores softly in the corridor; she has served in this house since she was a little girl, but this will not stop the master from shouting huskily at the top of his voice: "Lukerya! Samovar!"

And then, putting on his top-boots and throwing his coat over his shoulders, without buttoning the neck of his shirt, he goes out on to the porch. The entrance hall, which has been shut all night, reeks of dogs; they stretch lazily, yawn with little squeals and, smiling, cluster close to him.

"Get away!" he says slowly in a condescending, low-pitched voice, and walks through the garden to the threshing-floor. He breathes deeply of the biting early-morning air and the fragrance of the bare garden, chilled by the night. Autumn leaves, curled and blackened by the frost, rustle underfoot in the birch-lined walk, of which half the trees have already been felled. Ruffled jackdaws sleeping on the ridge of the barn roof stand out in sharp relief against the sombre, low skies. "A good day for hunting, today," he says to himself and, pausing in the middle of the walk, stands and gazes for a long time at this autumnal scene, across the bleak fields of green winter crisp with some calves wandering over them. Two hounds are already whimpering at his feet, while Zalivai has gone beyond the garden, and as he bounds across the prickly stubble-field, he seems to be calling to his master and begging to be allowed to run out into the open. "But what can you do with hounds now? The wolf is out in the open, it is on the black fields, frightened of the woods because the leaves rustle in the wind... Oh, if only I had some borzois!"

Threshing is under way in the barn. The threshing drum hums and drones as it slowly works up speed. Horses walk, swaying, round and round tugging lazily at their traces and thrusting their legs into a manure-strewn path. The driver sits on a little stool fitted on to the driving bar, and as he revolves he shouts monotonously at the horses, his whip falling on the brown gelding alone, the laziest of the lot, sleeping as it walks, since its eyes are blind-folded anyway.

"Come on, girls, get a move on!" the drum-operator, a sedate man, shouts sternly at the girls as he puts on his loose hempen shirt. The girls hastily sweep the threshing-floor and rush about with barrows and brooms.

"Godspeed!" he says and the first trial cluster of rye flies through the buzzing, squeaking drum and is tossed up in an untidy fan. The droning of the drum grows more and more insistent, work goes on apace and soon all the sounds merge in the one pleasant hum of threshing. The master stands at the barn door and watches the red and yellow kerchiefs, the hands, the forks and the straw flickering in the darkness within, all of it moving rhythmically and busily to the roaring of the drum, the monotonous shouts of the driver and the cracking of his whip. Clouds of chaff come flying to the door, and the master stands there getting covered with this grey dust. He keeps glancing out into the fields... Very, very soon they will be white, very soon they will be covered with the first frost...

The first frost, the first snow! He has no borzois to go hunting with in November, but winter is coming and then he can put his hounds to work. And once again, as in the old days, the small-estate owners go visiting one another, drinking away the last of their money, spending all their days in the snow-clad fields. And at night, in the darkness of winter, a light shines out from the hunting-lodge of some remote little estate, where in a room, filled with clouds of smoke, lighted with dimly burning tallow candles, a guitar is tuned up...

A blizzard fierce arose at night
And threw my gates wide open,

a deep tenor will begin, and the others will join in discordantly with sad and hopeless bravado, pretending this is nothing but fun:

It threw my gates wide open
And buried roads in snow-drifts
white...

1900

Sukhodol

1

What had always amazed us about Natalia, was her attachment to Sukhodol.

She was the daughter of Father's wet-nurse and was brought up in the house with him. She lived with us at Lunevo for eight years; we treated her as one of the family and not like a former serf at all. And all those eight years, as she herself used to say, she was recovering from Sukhodol and from all that the place had made her suffer. But evidently, what is bred in the bone, never gets out of the flesh: when she had raised us to adolescence she went back to Sukhodol once more.

I remember snatches of conversation we had with her when we were children.

"You're an orphan, aren't you, Natalia?"

"Yes, I take after my masters in this. Your grandmamma, Anna Grigoryevna, she closed her bonny eyes ever so early, too. Just like my father and mother."

"And they—why did they die young?"

"Their death came and so they died."

"But why so young?"

" 'Twas God's will. The masters punished my father by sending him off to be a soldier, and my mother didn't live her time on account of the turkey-poults. I don't remember, of course, I was too young, but they told me afterwards. She was a poultry-maid, and looked after ever so many turkey-poults, and then out in the meadow one day they got caught in a hail-storm and every one of them was struck down dead... She rushed out to the meadow, took one look—and gave up the ghost from fright."

"Why didn't you ever get married?"

"My betrothed hasn't been born yet."

"But really, why?"

"They say that the young lady, your auntie, ordered it so. That's why they call me 'miss', too."

"Oh, go on, what sort of a 'miss' are you?"

"A real and proper one," Natalia replied with a thin smile, pursing her lips and wiping them with her dark old hand. "You know I'm Arkady Petrovich's foster-sister, a second aunt to you..."

As we grew older we listened more attentively to everything that was being said in our house about Sukhodol, and whatever we had failed to understand before grew clearer now, so that the queer peculiarities of life at Sukhodol stood out more sharply. Who if not we should feel that Natalia, who had grown up with our father, almost sharing his life, was really one of us Khrushchovs, gentlefolk of ancient lineage! And now it appeared that these same gentlefolk had driven her father into the army and her mother into such terror of them that her heart had burst at the sight of the dead turkey-poults.

"But then a misfortune like that might kill anyone,"

Natalia said. "She'd have been packed off to some God-forsaken hole."

And then we learnt something even stranger about Sukhodol: that "in the whole wide world there were no masters kinder and simpler than theirs", but we also heard that none were "hotter" than they were either; we learnt that the old house had been dark and gloomy, that our insane Grandfather Pyotr Kirillich had been murdered there by his illegitimate son Gervaska (our father's friend and Natalia's cousin), that our Aunt Tonya had gone out of her mind long ago because of an unhappy love affair and was now living in one of the servants' old cottages close to the impoverished manor-house, rapturously playing écossaises on a piano which droned and jingled from old age; we learnt that Natalia, too, had once been insane, that as a very young girl she had fallen in love with our late Uncle Pyotr Petrovich once and for all time, but that he had banished her to the farmstead of Soshki... We were justified in weaving our exciting dreams about Sukhodol. To us it was nothing but a romantic memorial to the past. But what did it mean to Natalia? It was she who once uttered with great bitterness, as though in answer to some thought of her own:

"Well, there it was! At Sukhodol they even sat down to dinner armed with Tatar whips. Just thinking of it makes you shudder."

"You mean hunting-crops?" we asked.

"It's all one," she said.

"But what for?"

"In case they quarrelled."

"Did they all quarrel at Sukhodol?"

"Heaven save us! Never a day went by without a fight. They were all hot-tempered—proper fireworks."

We all but swooned at her words and exchanged ecstatic looks. And for a long time afterwards we would picture a huge garden, a huge estate, a house built of oak logs with a great thatched roof blackened with time; and then the dinner in the dining-hall where everyone sat round the table glaring at one another, eating and throwing the bones down to their hunting dogs, each man with a whip across his knees; we dreamed of the time when we, too, would be grown up and would also dine with whips across our knees.

We understood well enough, though, that it was not Natalia who got any pleasure out of those whips. And yet, she left Lunevo for Sukhodol, she went back to the source of her sinister memories. She had neither a corner of her own there nor any kin, and it wasn't her former mistress Aunt Tonya she served there, but Klavdia Markovna, the widow of the late Pyotr Petrovich. But there it was, Natalia could not live without Sukhodol.

"I can't help it, I'm used to it," she said humbly. "Where the needle goes, the thread must follow. Where you're born, there's your home..."

Neither was she the only one to be obsessed with this love for Sukhodol. All the other Sukhodolians were as ardently devoted to it, as passionately fond of its memory.

Aunt Tonya was living in misery, in a hovel. Sukhodol had deprived her of happiness, sanity and human dignity. Yet she never even entertained the thought of leaving her nest and settling at Lunevo, however much Father reasoned with her.

"Why, I'd rather break stones in a quarry," she'd say.

Father was a carefree man; he seemed to be above any kind of attachment. But his stories of Sukhodol, too, rang with a deep nostalgia. It was years and years since he had left it and settled down on our great-aunt Olga Kirillovna's estate at Lunevo, yet he brooded on it almost to the day he died:

"The last, the only Khrushchov left in the world! And even he is not at Sukhodol!"

And after saying this he would often grow thoughtful and stare through the window at the fields, then suddenly he would chuckle and, taking down his guitar from the wall, add just as sincerely as he had spoken but a minute before:

"Sukhodol's a fine one too, damn and blast it!"

But then his soul belonged to Sukhodol—the soul over which the sway of memories was so immeasurably strong, the sway of the steppe, its sluggish way of life, that ancient clannishness that united the village, the servants' hall and the manor-house into one. Of course, we Khrushchovs come of an old lineage; our name is entered in the Sixth Book of Noblemen, and many of our legendary ancestors were noblemen of old Lithuanian stock or Tatar princelings. But then, since time immemorial, the blood of the Khrushchovs was mingled with that of the servants and the villagers. Who fathered Pyotr Kirillich? History differs on this point. Who was the father of Gervaska, his murderer? Ever since we were little we always heard that it was Pyotr Kirillich. What caused the characters of our father and our uncle to be so sharply dissimilar? There were different explanations for this, too. And then Natalia and Father were suckled at the same breast, while Father and Gervaska exchanged baptismal crosses... It was certainly high time for the Khrushchovs to reckon up their relations with the servants and the villagers!

For many years my sister and I were entranced by our longing for Sukhodol and the attraction of its history. The servants' hall, the village and the manor-house there formed one family. Our forefathers ruled the family, and the consciousness of it lingered long in their descendants. The history of a family, a clan, is deep, tangled, mysterious and often gruesome. But its very strength lies in its dark depths, its legends and its past. As for written records or other memorials, Sukhodol is no richer in this than any *ulus** in the Bashkir steppe. In Russia, legend takes their place. But legends and songs are poison to the soul of a Slav. Our former serfs were passionate idlers and dreamers—where, if not in our house, could they have found such spiritual satisfaction? The only remaining representative of the Sukhodol masters was our father. The first language we learnt to speak was Sukhodol talk. The first stories and the first songs that moved us were Sukhodol ones, too—Natalia's and Father's. And I doubt if anyone could possibly sing the way our father, taught by the servants, sang of "his true and haughty love" with that carefree sadness, that tender reproach and weak-willed sincerity. Could anyone tell stories like Natalia? Was anyone closer to us than the Sukhodol peasants?

Like any other family which has long been living in close and isolated unity, the Khrushchovs were known since the beginning of time for their wrangles and their quarrels. The quarrel which took place between Sukhodol and Lunevo in our childhood was so bitter that for ten

Ulus*—a nomad tent village.—*Tr.*

years our father never crossed the threshold of his home. That was why we did not really know Sukhodol when we were little; we had only been there once and even then it was in passing on our way to Zadonsk. But sometimes dreams are apt to be stronger than reality. And that long summer day left an indelible though vague memory of undulating fields, a wide, neglected road which fascinated us with its spaciousness and the old, hollow willows which had survived here and there; we remembered a beehive on one of these stray willows far from the road, amid the corn—a beehive abandoned to its fate in fields bordering a desolate road; we also remembered a wide turning up a long slope, a barren common surrounded by wretched chimneyless huts, the yellow of the rocky gullies behind them and the white of the pebbles and broken stones lining the bottom of these gullies. The first event which struck terror into our hearts took place at Sukhodol, too, when Grandfather was murdered by Gervaska. And as we listened to the stories of this murder, we wove endless fancies round the yellow gullies which led we knew not where, believing that this was the way Gervaska had escaped, "dropping like a key to the bottom of the sea", after he had done his heinous deed.

The reasons that sent the Sukhodol peasants to call on us at Lunevo were different from those of the Sukhodol servants. The peasants mostly wanted a plot of land, but they, too, treated our home like their own. They would bow low to Father, kiss his hand and then, tossing their hair, kiss him thrice on the lips, after which they would kiss Natalia and the two of us. They brought us gifts of honey, eggs and homespun towels. And, reared as we were in the open, as conscious of scents and odours as we were of songs and legends, we forever remembered that peculiar and pleasant hempy smell we caught when we kissed the Sukhodol men. We remembered, too, the smell that clung to their gifts, the smell of an old village in the steppes: their honey smelt of buckwheat in flower and rotting oak-wood beehives, their towels smelt of hempen sacking and the smoky huts of our grandfather's day. The Sukhodol peasants told us no stories. And what did they have to tell? They had no legends to pass down. Their graves bear no names. And their lives are so like one another, so poor, that they leave no trace. For the fruit of their labour and endeavour is bread, just ordinary bread which is eaten up. They tried digging ponds in the stony bed of the little Kamenka River, long since exhausted. But there was no security in ponds—they dried up. They built dwellings. But their dwellings were not long-lived: they burnt down to the ground at the merest spark... Why then did all of us feel drawn to the barren common, to the huts, to the gullies, to the ruined Sukhodol estate?

2

We were already in our teens when we got the opportunity of staying at Sukhodol, the estate we had heard so much about, which had shaped Natalia's soul and ruled her entire life.

I remember it as if it were yesterday. Rain came pouring down in torrents, thunder crashed in deafening claps and lightning flashed blindingly in swift fiery snakes when, towards the end of the day, we drove up to Sukhodol. A violet thundercloud slumped heavily down towards the north-west, arrogantly blotting out half the sky. Against its vast background the green wheat field looked flat, clear and deathly pale, and the short wet grass on the highroad seemed bright and extraordinarily lush. The wet horses, which suddenly seemed to have grown lean, sloshed through the blue mud, their horseshoes sparkling, and there was a moist sound in the swish of the wheels... And all of a sudden, as we turned in towards the house, we saw a tall, strange figure, which might have been either an old man or an old woman, in a dressing-gown and hood, standing in the tall wet rye and whipping a hornless, skewbald cow with a switch. At our approach this old woman wielded the switch more fiercely, and the cow, twitching its tail, ran clumsily out on the road. Yelling something, the old woman made for the carriage and, coming up close, strained towards us with her pale face. Staring, terrified, into her black, mad eyes, and feeling the touch of her sharp cold nose, and shrinking from her strong musty smell, we exchanged kisses with her. Could it be Baba-Yaga the witch herself? But this Baba-Yaga had a tall hood made of a piece of dirty rag on her head, and her naked body was wrapped into a ragged dressing-gown, wet to the waist, that left her withered breasts uncovered. She screamed as though we were deaf or as though she were trying to start a vicious brawl. And from her screams we understood: this was Aunt Tonya.

Klavdia Markovna screamed too, but her scream was jolly, with a schoolgirlish excitement in it. She was a small fat woman with a little silver beard and unusually eager eyes. She was sitting at the open window of the house which had two imposing porches, knitting a cotton sock and, with her spectacles pushed up on her forehead, she looked out over the common which had merged with the yard. On the right-hand porch stood Natalia, wearing bast shoes, a red woollen skirt and a grey blouse cut low round her dark, wrinkled neck, and she welcomed us with a low bow and a soft smile on her kindly sunburnt face. I remember thinking as I looked at her neck, her jutting collar bones and her wearily sad eyes, that it was she who grew up with Father a very, very long time ago; and that it was here, on this very spot, where all that remained of Grandfather's oaken house, burnt down time and again, was this ugly building; and all that was left of the ancient garden were some shrubs and a few old birches and poplars; and all that remained of the outbuildings and the servants' quarters were a hut, a granary, a mud barn and the ice-house, overgrown with wormwood and goosefoot... We could smell the samovar being kindled, questions were showered on both sides, crystal jam bowls began to appear from the century-old sideboard, along with little golden spoons worn to maple-leaf thinness and some sugar biscuits, kept specially for unexpected guests. And while the conversation warmed up, intensely friendly after the long quarrel, we went wandering through the darkening rooms in search of a terrace or a door into the garden.

Everything was dark with age, plain and crude, in these low empty rooms, the arrangement of which was the same as in Grandfather's day, and which were actually built of what remained of those same rooms where he used to live. In the corner of the hall hung a large dark icon of St. Mercury of Smolensk, whose iron sandals and helmet repose on the dais in front of the iconostasis in the ancient Smolensk

Cathedral. We heard it said that St. Mercury had been a distinguished man, to whom the voice spoke from the icon of the Virgin Hodigitria the Guiding, summoning him to the rescue of the lands of Smolensk from the Tatars. When he had defeated the Tatars, the Saint fell asleep and his foes beheaded him. And then, carrying his head in his hands, he came to the town gate to tell the people of the happening... We had a creepy feeling as we looked at this ancient Suzdal painting of the decapitated man, holding in one hand his deathly livid, helmeted head and in the other the icon of the Holy Virgin. This painting of St. Mercury, cherished by Grandfather, so we were told, which had gone through several frightful fires and had split in the flames, was encased in heavy silver and bore on the back the genealogical table of the Khrushchovs, written in Church Slavonic. As though to match the icon, the heavy folding doors to the dining-hall were secured with heavy iron bars at top and bottom. The floorboards were inordinately broad, dark and slippery, and the windows were small. Though half the size, this was a replica of the dining-hall where the Khrushchovs had once sat down to dinner armed with hunting-crops. In the drawing-room, opposite the doors opening on to the terrace, had stood the piano, which Aunt Tonya used to play when she was in love with Voitkevich, Pyotr Petrovich's officer friend. As we went on, we saw the open doors into the sitting-room and the corner room where once our grandfather had his apartments...

It was a gloomy evening. Summer lightning flashed in the thunderclouds beyond the edge of the felled orchard, the half-dismantled barn and the stand of silvery poplars, and for a moment revealed mountains of a roseate gold in the clouds. The downpour had evidently passed by Troshin Wood, darkling far beyond the garden on the hills behind the gullies, for the dry, warm smell of oaks was wafted up, mingling with the fragrance of verdure and of the moist, mellow breeze that ran through the tops of the surviving birch-trees, the tall nettles, the burdock and the shrubs around the terrace. And the profound silence of the evening, of the steppe, of the depths of Russia reigned supreme...

"Tea is served, if you please," a voice called to us softly.

It was she, the participant and witness of all this life, its chief bard, Natalia. Her mistress appeared behind her, peering intently with her mad eyes, bending slightly forward and gliding ceremoniously across the dark smooth floor. She had not taken off her hood, but instead of the dressing-gown she now wore an old-fashioned *barège* dress with a silk shawl of faded gold thrown over her shoulders.

"*Où êtes-vous, mes enfants?*" she screamed with a prim smile, and her voice, clear and strident like a parrot's, echoed strangely in the dark, empty rooms...

3

The impoverished estate held the same charm as did Natalia in her peasant simplicity, in all the beauty and pathos of her soul, born of Sukhodol.

There was a smell of jasmine in the old drawing-room with its slanting floorboards. The greyish-blue terrace crumbling with age, from which you had to jump down because there were no steps, was submerged in a wild growth of nettles, elders and priest's-hoods. On hot days, when the sun blazed hard upon the terrace, when its warped glass doors were flung open and the merrily sparkling glass panels were reflected in the dim oval mirror on the opposite wall, we could not help thinking of Aunt Tonya's piano which had once stood under the mirror. There had been a time when she had played the piano, looking into her yellowed music with vignettes decorating the titles, while *he* stood behind her, his left hand on his waist, his jaws clamped tight and a frown upon his brow. Beautiful butterflies wearing bright cotton frocks, or Japanese kimonos, or black and mauve velvet shawls, flitted into the drawing-room. And just before he left, in a fit of anger he slapped one of them down as it alighted tremulously on the piano lid. Only a little silvery powder remained. But when a few days later the housemaids, in their stupidity, dusted it, Aunt Tonya had a fit of hysterics... We would come out on to the terrace through the drawing-room doors, and sit down on the warm boards to think and think. The wind running through the garden carried up the silky rustle of the birches—their trunks were white satin inlaid with niello, and their branches were green and spreading. It blew across the fields, rustling and swishing, and a green and golden oriole darted like an arrow over the white flowers with a shrill and joyous cry in pursuit of the chattering jackdaws that dwelt with their numerous relatives in the tumbledown chimneys and the dark attics that smelt of old bricks and were heaped with greyish purple ashes shot with streaks of golden light coming in through the dormer windows. The breeze died down, bees crawled sleepily over the flowers near the terrace performing their leisurely work—and in the silence all you could hear were the silvery poplar leaves murmuring softly, with a steady, dripping sound, like the incessant patter of a thin rain. We wandered through the garden and made our way into its remotest corners. There, where it merged into the cornfields, stood our great-grandfather's bath-house, the bath-house where Natalia had once kept the mirror she had stolen from Pyotr Petrovich. The ceiling had caved in, and white rabbits lived there now. They jumped out of the door very softly and, twitching their whiskers and their split lips, squinted queerly with wide-apart goggling eyes at the tall thistles, the henbane and nettles that choked the blackthorns and the cherry-trees. The half-dismantled barn was the home of a brown owl. Haystack poles stood up in a corner, and on the very top perched the owl, choosing a spot as gloomy as possible, sticking up its ears, bulging its blind yellow eyes and looking wild and fiendish. The sun sank far beyond the garden on to a sea of wheat, and evening fell, mellow and tranquil; a cuckoo called in Troshin Wood, and the old shepherd's pipe rang plaintively far out in the meadows... The brown owl sat and waited for night to come. Everything slept at night—the fields, the village and the house. But the brown owl sobbed and hooted. It rushed noiselessly round the barn and across the garden, it flew to Aunt Tonya's cottage, alighted softly on the roof and gave an agonizing shriek... Aunt Tonya, sleeping on a bench by the stove, would wake with a start.

"Gentle Jesus, save me," she whispered, sighing.

Flies buzzed sleepily and resentfully close to the ceiling of the hot, dark cottage. Something disturbed their sleep every night. It was either the cow rubbing her flanks against the wall, or a rat scurrying along the piano keys to make them ring with staccato notes until it lost its footing and fell with a clatter into the pile of broken crockery which Aunt Tonya stacked carefully in a corner; or else it was the black, green-eyed cat coming home late from his prowls and lazily begging to be allowed in; or again the brown owl would alight on the roof, presaging disaster with its screams. And Aunt Tonya, overcoming her drowsiness and beating off the flies which swarmed at her eyes in the darkness, would get up, grope over the benches, slam back the door and, standing on the threshold, fling her rolling-pin at random into the starlit sky. The brown owl would tear off the roof, rustling the straw with its wings, and drop down into the darkness far below. It almost touched the ground as it flew smoothly to the barn, and, soaring up, perched on the ridge of the roof. And once again the wind carried its sobs to the house. It sat there as though trying to remember something and, suddenly, it would let out a wail of amazement; then silence, and abruptly it started hooting hysterically, laughing and screeching; it would grow silent again for a moment and then burst out with groans, whimpers and sobs... But the nights, warm and dark, with little mauve clouds in the sky were so perfectly serene. The slumbering poplars murmured on sleepily and monotonously. Summer lightning flashed warily over Troshin Wood, and the air was filled with the dry, warm smell of oaks. In a gap between the clouds, over the sea of oats, close to the forest, the Scorpio shone in a triangle of silver, like a gravestone with a little roof over the cross...

We returned late. Having breathed our fill of the dew, of the freshness of the fields, of the wild flowers and grass, we made our way quietly up the porch steps and entered the dark hall. And often we came upon Natalia saying her prayers before the image of St. Mercury. She stood before the icon—slight, bare-footed, her hands folded—and whispered something, crossing herself and bowing low in the darkness to the invisible saint. And all of it was done so simply as if she were talking to one of her family, to another simple, kind and gracious soul.

"Natalia!" we called quietly.

"Yes?" she answered softly, breaking off her prayer.

"Why aren't you in bed yet?"

"I expect I'll sleep my fill in the grave."

We then sat down on the window-seat and opened the window, while she stood before us with her arms crossed. Summer lightning flickered mysteriously, brightening the dark rooms; far away in the dewy steppe a quail was crying, and on the pond a duck, awakening, quacked warningly in alarm...

"Been for a walk?"

"Yes, we have."

"Oh well, you're only young once... We used to stay out all night too... Sunset would send us out and sunrise drive us in..."

"Was life good in the old days?"

"Yes, it was good."

And a long silence followed.

"Tell us, nanny dear, why does the owl scream so?" my sister asked.

"He bodes no good with his screaming, curse him. Perhaps we should give him a scare with the shotgun, it makes you creepy, thinking some disaster might be coming. And it frightens Miss, too. She's scared to death of everything."

"How did she fall ill?"

"The usual way–crying and crying and grieving... And then she took to praying... And she grew fiercer and fiercer with us servants, and angrier and angrier with her brothers..."

And remembering the hunting-crops, we asked:

"You mean they didn't get on?"

"Heavens, did they get on! Especially after Miss fell ill and Grandfather died, the young gentlemen grew up and the late Pyotr Petrovich got married. They were a fierce lot–real gunpowder!"

"And did they often flog the servants?"

"No, that has never been the way here, never. Look what I did, for instance. And all the punishment I got was Pyotr Petrovich ordering my hair to be cropped with sheep shears, a shirt of ticking put on me and having me packed off to the farmstead..."

"But what had you done?"

A quick and straight answer did not always follow. At times Natalia told her stories with amazing frankness and punctiliousness, but at others she faltered and paused, thinking something over, then she sighed and, although we did not see her face in the dusk, we could tell by her voice that she was smiling mirthlessly.

"I did what I did. I've told you before, you know... I was young and stupid... 'To her woe and grief sang a nightingale...' And, of course, being a young girl..."

My sister begged her sweetly:

"Nanny dear, please tell us the rest of the verse."

This embarrassed Natalia.

"It's not a verse, it's a song... And I can't remember all of it now..."

"It's not true. You can."

"Oh well, have it your own way... Now how does it go?" and she finished off rapidly: " 'To her woe and grief sang a nightingale in the garden dark, and its song of love kept the foolish maid wide awake all night...' "

Fighting down her shyness, my sister asked:

"Were you very much in love with Uncle?"

And Natalia whispered curtly and flatly: "Very."

"D'you always remember him in your prayers?"

"Always."

"They say you fainted when they were taking you to Soshki?"

"That I did. We house servants were ever so delicate ... thin-skinned when it came to punishment ... no comparing us with those coarse-grained settlers. When Yevsey Bodulya started off with me, I went all numb with sorrow and fear... First time in town the dust all but choked me. But once we were out in the steppe, I felt so weak and sorry for myself. And suddenly there was an officer driving towards us who looked like the master. I cried out and fainted dead away! And when I came to, I lay in the cart and thought: I'm so happy now, like I'm in heaven."

"Was he fierce?"

"Heaven preserve us!"

"But still, Auntie was the most wilful, wasn't she?"

"She was, she was. But I'm telling you, they even took her to the saint. Oh, the time she's given us all! She could have lived in health and happiness, as is proper, but she scorned him and so she went off her head... And Voitkevich, he loved Miss so! But there you are."

"Well, and Grandfather?"

"Grandfather was different. He was feeble in his mind. But, of course, it happened with him too sometimes. Everyone was hot-tempered in those days... But then, the old masters were not squeamish about the likes of us... Sometimes your father would punish Gervaska at dinner—and he well deserved it too—and in the evening you'd see the two of them out in the yard, thrumming their balalaikas..."

"Tell us, was he good-looking, Voitkevich, I mean?"

Natalia grew pensive.

"No, I wouldn't tell a lie; he was like a Kalmyk. And he was ever so serious and stubborn, always reading poetry to Miss and scaring her that he'd die and come after her..."

"But it was love, too, that made Grandfather mad, wasn't it?"

"That was because of your grandmother. Quite a different thing. And then our house was so gloomy—it was never a cheery place, bless it. Well, listen to my foolish words if you please..."

Her voice low and unhurried, Natalia then began her long, long story...

4

If legend is to be believed, our great-grandfather, a wealthy man, only moved to Sukhodol from Kursk towards the end of his days: he did not care for the place with its remoteness and its woods. But then, it has come to be a saying now that "woods were everywhere in the old days". People walking our roads some two hundred years ago had to make their way through dense forests. Everything was lost in the forests then—the River Kamenka, the country up river, the village, the estate, and the undulating fields around it. But in Grandfather's time it was no longer the same. The scenery had changed—rolling steppe, bare hills, fields of rye, oats and buckwheat, straggling hollow willows lining the road, and nothing but white pebbles on the rise where the house now stands. All that remained of the forests was Troshin Wood. The garden was beautiful, of course. There was a broad walk lined with seventy spreading birches, cherry-trees submerged in nettles, a wilderness of raspberry, acacia and lilac bushes, and what was almost a grove of silver poplars at the bottom where it merged into the cornfields. The house was roofed with thick, dark, sturdy thatch. The windows faced a courtyard surrounded by outbuildings and the servants' quarters in long, many-sectioned timber buildings; and beyond the courtyard stretched a boundless green common and then the sprawling village which belonged to the estate, a large village, poor but carefree.

"Took after the masters, it did," Natalia said. "The masters were carefree, too, not good managers and not greedy either. Semyon Kirillich, your grandfather's brother, divided the property: he himself took the bigger and better part, the patrimonial estate he took, and he left us only Soshki, Sukhodol, and four hundred souls thrown in. But of the four hundred almost half ran away..."

Grandfather Pyotr Kirillich died when he was about forty-five. Father often said that he went out of his mind after a sudden hurricane had hurled a torrent of apples down upon him as he lay sleeping on a rug under an apple-tree. In the servants' hall, Natalia told us, Grandfather's insanity was explained differently. They said that Pyotr Kirillich went off his head from being lovelorn when our beautiful grandmother died, and that on the evening before a great thunderstorm had swept Sukhodol. And so Pyotr Kirillich—a dark, round-shouldered man with a tender, intent look in his black eyes, a little like Aunt Tonya, had ended his days in a state of mild insanity. According to Natalia, they had more money than they could spend in those days, and Grandfather, wearing morocco-leather boots and a florid house-coat, wandered anxiously and soundlessly from room to room and, glancing about him warily, thrust gold pieces into the cracks in the timber walls.

"It's Tonya's dowry I'm thinking of," he muttered when caught in the act. "It's safer, my friends, much safer ... but on the whole—it's up to you. If you don't want me to, I won't ..."

And he went thrusting them in again. Or then he started moving the heavy furniture about in the hall and in the drawing-room, for he was always expecting visitors, although his neighbours hardly ever came to Sukhodol at all; sometimes he complained that he was hungry and made some hash for himself, awkwardly chopping and mashing some green onions in a wooden bowl, shredding bits of bread in, pouring thick frothing *surovets** over it and sprinkling the whole with such a quantity of grey, coarse salt that it was bitter and quite inedible. And when there was an after-dinner lull in the house and everyone trailed away to his favourite corner for a good, long nap, Pyotr Kirillich, who slept very little even at night, did not know where to turn in his loneliness. When he could stand it no longer, he went peeping into the bedrooms and living-rooms and quietly called the sleeping:

"Arkasha, are you asleep? Sleeping, Tonya dear?"

And, rewarded with an angry shout: "Oh, leave me alone, for heaven's sake, Papa!" he mumbled hastily and placatingly: "Well, sleep, my dear, sleep. I shan't disturb you..."

And he continued on his way, only giving a wide berth to the servants' hall, for the footmen were a very rude lot. And within ten minutes he would be back at the bedroom doors, calling the sleeping with more caution than ever, inventing news of someone driving down the village road with jingling stage-coach bells—"It couldn't be Petenka coming on leave from the army, could it?"—or of great hailclouds gathering in the sky.

"The master, bless him, was ever so scared of storms," Natalia told us. "I was only a pigtailed chit at the time, but I remember it, too. Our house was so black somehow ... a cheerless place, so help me. And the summer days were so long. We had so many servants—footmen alone we had five. Well, the young masters would naturally go to sleep after dinner, and we, faithful servants, good serfs, would do the same. And then Pyotr Kirillich had better not come near us, especially Gervaska. 'I say, footmen, are you asleep?' he would ask. And Gervaska would raise his head from the coffer and growl: 'D'you want me to stuff your pants with stinging nettles right now?' 'Who d'you think you're talking to, you rascal?' 'To the house goblin, sir, in my sleep.' Well, then Pyotr Kirillich would go back to

**Surovets*—a beverage made by pouring warm water over flour and letting it ferment.—*Tr.*

the dining-hall and the drawing-room again, he'd look out of the windows and into the garden to see whether a thunderstorm was gathering. It's true, though, thunderstorms broke out ever so often in the old days. And what terrible thunderstorms they were! Soon after dinner an oriole would start crying, and clouds would creep up from behind the garden ... the house would grow dark, the grass and dead-nettles would start rustling, the turkey-hens and their chicks would all hide under the terrace ... real creepy it was. And he, the master, would sigh and cross himself, climb a chair to light a wax candle before the icons and hang up the sacred towel left over from your great-grandfather's funeral–I was scared to death of that towel. Or he'd throw a pair of scissors out of the window. That's the first thing you do, scissors I mean, it's very good against a thunderstorm..."

* * *

It had been jollier in the Sukhodol house when the French people were staying there. At first it was a certain Louis Ivanovich, a genleman with dreamy blue eyes and long moustaches, who wore exceedingly wide trousers narrowing down at the bottom and hair plastered across his bald pate from ear to ear. After that came an elderly Mademoiselle Zizi who was always shivering, and Louis Ivanovich's thundering voice could be heard in all the rooms as he yelled at Arkasha: "Go away and don't come back again!" From the classroom came: "*Maître corbeau sur un arbre perché*", and Miss Tonya would be heard practising on the piano. The French people remained at Sukhodol for eight years, staying on to keep Pyotr Kirillich company even after the children had been sent away to school in town, and they did not leave till the children came home for their third summer holidays. But after this, Pyotr Kirillich never sent either Arkasha or Tonya anywhere any more, for in his opinion it was enough if Petenka alone went to school. And so the children remained for ever untutored and uncared for.

Natalia used to say:

"I was the youngest of them all, you know. And since

Gervaska and your papa were almost the same age, they came to be the best of frinds. But it's a true saying that you can't put the wolves in with the sheep. Well then, they came to be friends, they swore eternal friendship, they even exchanged baptismal crosses, but Gervaska soon went and cut a caper: he almost drowned your papa in the pond. He was just a dirty brat, but already he was a great one for criminal pranks. He said to the young master one day, 'When you grow up are you going to flog me?' 'I am.' 'Oh no, you're not!' 'Why not?' 'Just because...' And he went and thought something up: we had a barrel standing on top of the hill above the pond, and it gave him an idea. He told Arkady Petrovich to get into it and roll down the hill. 'You get first chance, master, I'll do it after you.' Well, the young master did what he was told: he got into the barrel, pushed, and off he went clattering downhill and plopped straight into the water... Oh, Holy Mother of God! Nothing but dust whirling in a cloud. A good thing some shepherds happened to come along..."

The house had still looked habitable as long as the French people remained in it. Before Grandmother died Sukhodol had masters and owners, rule and obedience, state rooms and family rooms, holidays and weekdays. A semblance of this had been retained while the French people were there. But they went away and the house had no masters left at all. While the children were small, Pyotr Kirillich remained the head of the house to all appearances. But what could he do? Who ruled whom? Did he rule the servants or did the servants rule him? The piano was closed, the table cloth vanished from the oaken table, they ate without one at odd hours, and the front hall was always full of borzois. There was no one to care for the house, and the dark log walls, the dark floors and ceilings, the dark heavy doors and door-frames, the old icons with their Suzdal painted saints taking up a whole corner of the dining-hall, soon grew quite black. The house was frightening at night, especially if there was a thunderstorm when the garden became turbulent in the wind and rain, when lightning flashed across the faces of the saints in the corner, when the sky burst apart and the tremulous rosy-gold heavens opened wide above the trees and the thunder crashed mightily in the blackness. In the daytime it was sleepy, empty and dreary. Pyotr Kirillich grew feebler and feebler as the years went by, more and more insignificant, while the house was run by old Darya Ustinovna, Grandfather's wet nurse. But her power was almost equal to Grandfather's, and the bailiff Demyan did not meddle in the housekeeping. All he worried about was farm management, and he would sometimes say with a slow smile: "Why, I wouldn't wrong my masters!" My father, a youngster then, could not be bothered with Sukhodol: he was crazy about hunting, the balalaika, and about Gervaska who was supposed to be footman, but who spent whole days with him duck shooting on the Meshchera Marshes somewhere, or in the coach-house learning new tricks on the balalaika or the reed pipe.

"We got used to it," Natalia said. "The master only came home to sleep. And if he didn't even do that, it meant he was either in the village, or in the coach-house, or out shooting: hare in winter, fox in autumn, quail, duck or bustard in summer. He'd get on the racing droshky, sling his gun on his shoulder, whistle for Dianka, and off he'd go, to the Serednaya Mill one day, the Meshchera Marshes the next, or out into the steppe. And Gervaska was always with him; he was always the ringleader, but he pretended it was the young master who dragged him into things. And Arkady Petrovich loved him, this enemy of his, truly, like a brother, but Gervaska made ever nastier sport of him as time wore on. Master would say, 'Come on, Gervaska, let's play our balalaikas. For heaven's sake teach me to play "The sun went down beyond the trees..." ' And Gervaska would glance at him, blow some smoke out through his nostrils, and say with a smirk, 'First you kiss my hand.' Arkady Petrovich would turn deathly white, jump up and slap him on the cheek with all his might, but he'd only jerk his head and turn blacker still, scowling like some brigand. 'Get up, you scoundrel!' He'd stand up, stretching like a wolf-hound, his velveteen trousers hanging ... and he'd say nothing. 'Beg my pardon!' 'Beg your pardon, sir.' But the young master almost chocked with rage, he wouldn't know what to say next. 'Sir is right!' he'd shout. 'I'm trying to treat you like an equal, you scoundrel; at times I think I'd give my soul for you... And you? Trying to enrage me on purpose, are you?' "

"It's a funny thing," Natalia said. "The young master and Grandfather were mocked by Gervaska, and I was tormented by Miss Tonya. The young master and Grandfather too, if the truth be told, doted on him, and I on her ... when I came back from Soshki and got my senses back a bit after my crime..."

5

They did not begin to arm themselves with hunting-crops for dinner until after Grandfather had died, Gervaska had fled, Pyotr Petrovich had got married, Aunt Tonya, her mind deranged, had dedicated herself to be a bride of Christ, and until Natalia had returned from Soshki. And the reason why Aunt Tonya's mind was deranged and why Natalia had been in exile was love.

Now came the day of the young masters to replace the dull, shut-in life of Grandfather's time. Pyotr Petrovich, retiring from the army to everyone's surprise, came back to Sukhodol. And his arrival proved fatal for both Natalia and Aunt Tonya.

They both fell in love. Neither knew how it had happened. It seemed to them at first that "life had simply become more exciting".

At the outset Pyotr Petrovich steered the life at Sukhodol on a new course of glitter and leisure as befitting the gentry. He brought with him his friend Voitkevich and a chef, a clean-shaven drunkard who looked scathingly at the fluted jelly moulds green with age, and the crude knives and forks. Pyotr Petrovich wanted to appear hospitable, generous and prosperous before his friend, and he went about it in an awkward, boyish way. But he was, indeed, little more than a boy, very gentle and handsome to look at, but harsh and cruel by nature, a boy who seemed self-assured, yet was easily thrown into confusion almost to the point of tears, and nursed a grudge for a long time afterwards against the person who had caused his confusion.

"I seem to remember, Arkady," he said at dinner the very day he arrived home, "I seem to remember we had some Madeira that wasn't at all bad."

Grandfather blushed and tried to say something but, his courage failing him, he only tugged at the neck of his coat nervously and said nothing. Arkady Petrovich asked in surprise:

"What Madeira?"

And Gervaska threw Pyotr Petrovich a brazen look and smirked.

"You have forgotten, sir," he said to Arkady Petrovich without even trying to conceal his smirk. "We really did have any amount of this Madeira stuff, but it's all been pinched by us menials. It's a gentleman's wine, but we just guzzled it down instead of kvas."

"What's this I hear!" Pyotr Petrovich shouted, turning a dark red. "Silence!"

Grandfather joined in delightedly:

"That's the way, Petenka, that's the way! Bravo!" he cried joyfully in a thin voice and almost wept. "You can't imagine how he flouts me. If I've thought of it once, I've thought of it again and again. I'll steal up to him one day and crush his head with a bronze pestle. I swear I will! I'll stick a knife into his ribs to the very hilt!"

And Gervaska was quick to retort:

"I've heard the punishment for that is very severe, sir," he said with a frown. "Because I, too, can't drive the thought away that it's time the master went to heaven."

Pyotr Petrovich used to say that when he heard this unexpectedly insolent reply he only controlled himself because his guest was there. All he said to Gervaska was: "Get out this minute!" And afterwards he actually felt ashamed of his outburst and, making his hurried excuses to Voitkevich, he smiled and looked at him with those beautiful eyes of his which no one who had known him could ever forget.

With Natalia, too, the memory of those eyes lingered too long.

Her happiness was extremely short-lived—and who could have thought that it would end in her going to Soshki, which was the most outstanding event in her whole life?

Soshki exists to this day, although a Tambov merchant has owned it for some time now. It is a long timber cottage standing in a barren plain; there is a granary, a well with a long arm to let down the bucket, and a threshing barn with water-melon fields around it. All this was the same in Grandfather's time of course, and the town which lies halfway between Sukhodol and Soshki has not changed very much, either. Natalia's crime was that on a sudden impulse she stole Pyotr Petrovich's little folding mirror, framed in silver.

She saw the mirror and was so struck by its beauty (this, however, was the way she felt about all Pyotr Petrovich's things) that she could not resist the temptation of taking it. And for several days, until the mirror was missed, she lived dumbfounded by her crime, spellbound by her dreadful secret and her treasure, like the girl in the tale about the little scarlet flower.* Before she went to sleep she prayed for the night to be over soon and for morning to come quickly. There was a holiday atmosphere in the house which had come to life filled with something new and wonderful, brought to it by the handsome young master, smart and pomaded, with a high red collar to his tunic, and a face that was tanned but as delicate as a young lady's; even the corridor where Natalia slept on a trunk had a festive air, and when she woke at dawn she instantly remembered that there was joy in the world, because the pair of top-boots that stood waiting to be cleaned outside the door were so fine, they were fit for a prince to wear. But the most awesome and exciting place was behind the garden, in the neglected bath-house, where the folding mirror in its heavy silver frame was hidden—there, behind the garden, where Natalia hurried stealthily through the shrubbery, wet with dew, while everyone was still in bed, so she could revel in her possession of this treasure, take it to the door, open it out in the hot morning sunlight and stare at her reflection till her head reeled, and then hide it again concealing it carefully, and once more hurry back to the house to serve the one to whom she did not even dare to raise her eyes, and because of whom she stared at herself in the mirror with the mad hope that he might take a fancy to her.

But the tale of the little scarlet flower ended all too

**The Little Scarlet Flower* by Sergei Aksakov (1791-1859) in which the youngest daughter of a merchant wants him to bring her just a pretty scarlet flower from his travels, unlike her sisters who ask for costly gifts and the little scarlet flower he brings her turns out to be a magic one.—*Tr.*

quickly. It ended in disgrace and shame which words could not describe, or so thought Natalia. It ended with Pyotr Petrovich himself ordering her hair to be cropped, to make her ugly, while all the time she had been decking herself out, blackening her eyebrows in front of the little mirror, and creating some delicious secret, an imaginary intimacy between them. He had been the one to discover her crime and turn it into an ordinary case of theft, into the stupid escapade of a servant wench who, in a dress of ticking, her face swollen from weeping, was put on a manure cart in view of all the servants and disgraced, abruptly severed from all that was dear to her, driven to some strange and horrible farmstead, into the distant steppe. She knew beforehand: there, on the farm, she would have to tend the chickens, turkeys and melons; there, she would be scorched by the sun, forgotten by the whole world; there in the steppe, the days would drag like years, when a shimmering haze cloaked the horizon and all was so quiet, so sultry that you could sleep the sleep of the dead all day long if it were not that you had to listen to the gentle crackling of the dried-up pea-pods, the busy fussing of the brood-hens in the hot sand, the placidly sorrowful cries of the turkeys, to watch the sudden approach of the eerie shadow of a hawk and leap up, shouting in a thin, drawn-out voice, "Shoo-oo!" There at the farmstead was the terrible old Ukrainian woman who held Natalia's life and death in her hands, and who was certainly awaiting her victim with impatience. Natalia had but one advantage over those taken to their execution—she was free to hang herself. That was the only thought that sustained her on her way into exile—for ever, she believed.

There was much to see on this journey from one end of the district to the other. But she was in no state to see anything. All she thought of or, rather, felt was that her life was over, her crime and disgrace were much too great to leave her any hope of ever returning to it. So far she had one of her own people beside her, Yevsei Bodulya, but what was to come when he had handed her over into the keeping of the Ukrainian woman? He would sleep the night and depart, leaving her for ever in a strange land. When she could weep no longer she began to feel hungry. And to her amazement Yevsei seemed to consider this very natural, and as they ate he talked to her as if nothing had occurred. And then she fell asleep and did not waken until they had reached the town. And the town seemed to her bleak, dusty and oppressive, and something else that was vaguely terrifying and nostalgic, like a dream you could not relate. All the recollection she had of that day was that it was very hot in the steppe in summer, that there was nothing in the world more endless than a summer day, nothing longer than a highroad. She remembered that in the town the streets were cobbled in places, making the cart rumble strangely; she remembered that from afar the town smelt of iron roofing, while in the centre of the market square, where they took a rest and fed the horse, close to the eating-sheds which were empty at that hour, it smelt of dust, tar and rotting hay, tufts of which, stamped into the dung, are always left behind at peasants' halts. Yevsei unharnessed the horse and put it to the cart to feed; he pushed his hot cap to the back of his head, wiped his sweating brow with a sleeve and, looking black from the heat, made for the tavern. He gave Natalia very, very strict orders to keep an eye on things, and to yell at the top of her voice if something happened. And Natalia sat without moving, never taking her gaze off the dome of the newly built cathedral, which shone like a great silver star far behind the houses. She sat thus until Yevsei came back, looking merrier and chewing something. Holding a loaf of white bread in the crook of his arm, he began to lead the horse back between the shafts.

"We're a bit on the late side, my princess," he muttered happily, addressing either Natalia or the horse. "Let's hope they won't hang us for it. There's no fire, eh? And I won't break its wind on the way back either, the master's horse means more to me than your dirty mouth," he said, meaning Demyan now. "Bawling his mouth at me! 'Watch out! If you don't look sharp I'll see you with your pants down...' Oh you!... I thought. I felt sick at the stomach, it made me so mad. I'll have you know that even my masters never took my trousers down yet ... and you're no match for them, you foul mug... 'Look sharp!' he says. Why should I look sharp? I'm no more a fool than you are, I hope. If I feel like it, I won't come back at all. I'll deliver the wench and then I'll take to the open road and that's the last you'll ever see of me. I wonder at the wench too: what's the fool worrying about anyway? Has the end of the world come or something? There'll be wagoners or old folks coming past the farm—just say the word and you'll find yourself far beyond old Rostov in no time ... they can try and catch you then!"

And the thought "I'll hang myself" gave way in Natalia's sheared head to the thought of flight. The cart began to squeak and rock. Yevsei lapsed into silence and led the horse towards the well in the middle of the square. Over there, from where they had come, the sun was setting behind a large monastery garden, and the windows of the yellow prison, which stood across the road from the monastery, sparkled with gold. For a minute the sight of the prison stirred her thoughts of flight even more. "You can live even if you're a runaway. Only they say the old people blind the wenches and the children they steal by scalding their eyes with boiling milk, and then they make them beg for alms, and the wagoners whisk them away to the sea and sell them to the Nogais... Sometimes it happens that the masters catch their escaped servants, too, put chains on them and throw them into jail... But, as Gervaska was wont to say, here's hoping the warders are men and not beasts."

But the light reflected in the prison windows faded and her thoughts became confused—no, to run away was even more terrifying than to hang herself. And then Yevsei sobered up and turned moody.

"We're late, lass." He spoke uneasily now, jumping on to the edge of the cart.

And the cart, out on the highroad now, began to rock and jolt again, clattering loudly over the cobbles... Natalia felt rather than thought: "Ah, but anyway it would be better if the cart were turned back, if I could only fly to Sukhodol and fall at my master's feet." But Yevsei was whipping his horse on. She could no longer see the star behind the houses. Ahead lay nothing but the bare white street, the white road and white houses—and all of it terminated in the huge white cathedral with its new white metal dome and the sky above it looked a bleak, bluish white... Back home at this time the dew would already be falling, the garden would be sending up its cool fragrance and a warm smell would be coming from the kitchen; far beyond the sea of corn, beyond the silvery poplars on the edge of the garden, beyond the old bath-house, the glow of the sunset would be dying away, while in the drawing-room the terrace doors would be open, the crimson light merging with the shadows in the corners, and the sallow-skinned young lady with the black eyes, who looked both like Grandfather and Pyotr Petrovich, would be sitting with her back to the sunset, peering into her music, continually pulling down the sleeves of her light and loose gown of orange silk, striking the yellow keys and filling the drawing-room with the solemnly melodious, sweetly despairing strains of Oginsky's polonaise and appearing to take no notice at all of the officer—a stocky, dark-skinned man, who stood behind her, his left hand on his waist, watching her swift hands with concentration and gloom...

"She has hers, and I have mine," on evenings such as this Natalia felt rather than thought, with fluttering heart; and, running into the cool, dewy garden, deep into the wilderness of nettles and damp, strongly smelling burdocks, she would stand poised, waiting for the impossible—for the young master to come down the terrace steps, go into the garden, catch sight of her and, turning abruptly, come close to her with quick strides—and she would not have made a sound, numbed by fear and joy...

But the cart clattered on. The town was all round them, hot and fetid, the same town she used to imagine as a place enchanted. And Natalia gazed in painful surprise at the dressed-up crowds, walking up and down along the stone paving in front of the houses, at the gates and the wide-open doors of the shops... "And why did Yevsei have to go this way?" she mused. "How could he dare clatter along here with his cart?"

And now they were past the cathedral, driving down the humpy and dusty road to the shallow river, past smithies and the hovels of the workmen... Once again there was a familiar smell of fresh warm water, of silt and the evening coolness of the fields. The first to light its flickering lamp was a lonely little house by the barrier, far away on the opposite bank... Then they came to the open country, crossed the bridge, drove up to the barrier and saw, staring in their eyes, a stony desolate road, dimly white, that disappeared into the boundless distance, into the blue of the cool night. The horse began to jog along and once past the barrier it slowed down to a walk. And again you could hear how very, very still were the earth and the sky at night—only a tiny bell tinkled plaintively far away. The sound grew ever louder, ever more melodious, until at last it merged with the rhythmic thudding of a troika, the even beat of hoofs on the road, and with the swish of carriage wheels... A young freedman was driving the troika, while, in the carriage, his chin thrust into the collar of his hooded army coat, sat an officer. He raised his head for a moment when they passed the cart—and suddenly Natalia saw a red collar, black moustache, and young eyes flashing at her from beneath the bucketshaped helmet... She cried out, blanched and fainted.

A crazy thought flashed across her mind that it was Pyotr Petrovich, and from the pain and tenderness which pierced her nervous servant's heart she suddenly understood what it was she had lost—his nearness... Yevsei rushed to douse her cropped lolling head with water from his travelling can. And then a fit of nausea brought her back to her senses. She hastily thrust her head out over the edge of the cart. Yevsei quickly placed his palm beneath her icy forehead.

After that, relieved and shivering, the neck of her blouse wet, she lay on her back and gazed at the stars. The terrified Yevsei remained silent, thinking she was asleep—he merely shook his head and hurried his horse on and on. The cart jogged and sped away. And to the girl it seemed as though she had no body, that she had nothing but her soul. And this soul of hers felt as happy as though it were in heaven.

Her love was a little red flower blossoming in a fairytale garden. But it was into the steppe, into a remoteness even more forbidding than the remoteness of Sukhodol, that she carried her love, so that there, in silence and solitude, she could get over its first sweet and poignant torments, and afterwards for a long time to come, for ever, until the day she died, bury it in the depths of her Sukhodolian soul.

6

At Sukhodol they loved strangely. They hated strangely, too.

Grandfather, whose end was as ridiculous as that of his murderer or, for that matter, of anyone who met his end at Sukhodol, was killed that same year. The special holiday Intercession of the Holy Virgin was Sukhodol's, and Pyotr Petrovich invited a number of guests to dinner. He was very nervous, wondering if the marshal of nobility, who had promised to be there, would come. Grandfather was also excited, for no apparent reason. The marshal arrived and the dinner went off famously. It was both noisy and merry, Grandfather being the merriest of all. Early next morning, on the second of October, he was found dead on the drawing-room floor.

When he retired from the army, Pyotr Petrovich made no secret of the fact that he was sacrificing himself to save the Khrushchovs' honour, and the family estate. He made no secret of being "forced" to take up the reins of management. He was also "obliged" to make ties, to associate with the most enlightened and useful noblemen in the district, and as for the others—to avoid breaking off all relations with them. In the beginning he did exactly what he had planned; he called on all the small-estate owners; he even visited his Aunt Olga Kirillovna, a monstrously fat old woman who had the sleeping sickness and who cleaned her teeth with snuff. By autumn it did not surprise anyone any more that Pyotr Petrovich was ruling the estate like an autocrat. But then, he no longer looked the dandy young officer who had come home on leave, he was the master, a young landowner. He did not blush with embarrassment so easily now. He was perfectly groomed, he put on flesh, he wore expensive house-coats, pampered his small feet with soft red Tatar slippers, and adorned his small hands with turquoise rings. Arkady Petrovich shrank from looking into his brother's black eyes, he did not know what to talk to him about, and at first he gave way to him in everything and spent his days out shooting.

At this dinner of his, Pyotr Petrovich wanted to charm each of his guests with his hospitality, and show them, besides, that he was indeed the master of the house. But

Grandfather was a terrible nuisance. Grandfather was blissfully happy but he was tactless, garrulous and pathetic in his little velvet cap—a sacred relic—and his new and much too wide blue coat, made by the family tailor. He also fancied himself a good host and fussed since early morning, making some stupid ceremony of receiving the guests. Only one side of the folding doors from the dining-hall into the passage was ever opened. Yet he personally moved back the iron bolts at the top and bottom, brought up a chair himself and, shaking all over, climbed on to it. When he had thrown the doors wide open, he took his stand on the threshold and, taking advantage of Pyotr Petrovich's silence, who was numb with shame and rage but resolved to endure everything, never left his post until after the last guest had arrived. His eyes were glued to the front door, which had to be flung open as well in conformity with some ancient custom or other—he shuffled his feet in his excitement, and as soon as he sighted the next guest coming in, he rushed out to meet him, hastily made a *pas*, skipping and throwing one foot out across the other, bowed low to him and said to one and all, gulping the words breathlessly:

"Oh, I am so glad! So glad! It's quite some time since you've been to see me! Come in, come in!"

It also maddened Pyotr Petrovich that Grandfather insisted on telling all and sundry that Tonya had gone to Lunevo to stay with Olga Kirillovna. "Tonya is ill with melancholy; she's gone to spend the autumn with her aunt." What might the guests think on hearing this uncalled-for announcement? Her affair with Voitkevich was now common property, of course. Perhaps Voitkevich had really had honourable intentions, sighing at Tonya's side, playing duets with her, reading *Ludmila* to her in a hollow voice, or saying to her with a gloomy pensiveness: "The sanctity of vows betroth you to the dead..." But Tonya flared up wildly whenever he made an attempt to express his feelings, even when these attempts were of the most innocent sort, such as bringing her a flower, and, abruptly, Voitkevich left. But now that he was gone, Tonya no longer slept at night, she took to sitting in the darkness beside her open window as if waiting for a moment that she alone knew, and then suddenly bursting into loud sobs, waking up Pyotr Petrovich. He would lie awake for a long time, with clenched teeth listening to her sobs and the soft, sleepy murmur of the poplars in the dark garden which sounded like a never ending drizzle. Then he would go to comfort her. The sleepy housemaids also trailed in to comfort her, and sometimes Grandfather would hurry in anxiously as well. And Tonya would start stamping her feet and shrieking: "Leave me alone, you are my mortal enemies!"—and everything would end in an ugly brawl, almost a fight.

"Do try to understand, do try," Pyotr Petrovich hissed savagely after he had driven out the housemaids and Grandfather and, slamming the door shut, stood holding on tightly to the handle. "Try to understand, you viper, what people might think."

"Papa!" Tonya screeched in a frenzy. "Papa! He's abusing me, he says I'm pregnant!"

And, clutching his head in his hands, Pyotr Petrovich would rush out of her room.

The day of the party he was also very uneasy about Gervaska, afraid he might be insolent if they weren't careful.

Gervaska had grown terribly. Huge, awkward, but the best-looking and the most clever of all the servants, he, like the others, was dressed up in a blue coat, blue trousers and soft kidskin top-boots with flat soles. A worsted mauve neckchief was knotted round his thin dark neck. His thick, brittle black hair was parted on the side; he had refused to have it cut short and instead had it trimmed in an even bob round his head. There was nothing for him to shave, for he only had two or three coarse black hairs curling on his chin and one each at the corners of his big mouth, "a slit from ear to ear," they teased him in the servants' hall. Lanky, very broad in his flat, bony chest, with a small head and deep eye sockets, thin ash-blue lips and large bluish teeth, this ancient Aryan, a Persian from Sukhodol, had already been nicknamed "borzoi". Looking at his grin, hearing his cough, many were struck with the thought: "Borzoi, you'll soon croak, you know." And yet to his face they called this cheeky youngster Gervasy Afanasyevich, thus setting him apart from the other servants.

His masters were afraid of him too. The masters and the

serfs had this trait in common: they could either rule or cringe. To the amazement of all the servants, Gervaska received no punishment whatsoever for his insolent retort to Grandfather the day of Pyotr Petrovich's arrival. Arkady Petrovich told him curtly: "You're really a swine, brother," and the reply he received to this was as curt: "I can't stand him, sir." But to Pyotr Petrovich Gervaska came of his own free will; he stood in the door in his customary and unduly familiar pose, slumping his body backwards on his disproportionately long legs in the widest of trousers, jutting his left knee forward, and requested to be flogged.

"I'm too hot-tempered and impertinent, sir," he said nonchalantly, flashing his great black eyes.

And Pyotr Petrovich, sensing a hint in the words "hot-tempered", turned coward.

"Oh, we've plenty of time, old chap! Plenty of time!" And he shouted with feigned sternness, "Leave the room! I can't stand the sight of a bold-faced chap like you!"

Gervaska stood a moment saying nothing. Then he spoke, "It's up to you."

He stood there a little longer, twirling a coarse hair on his upper lip and baring his bluish teeth in a dog-like grin, his face empty of all feeling, and walked out. This instance convinced him firmly that the best way to act was to keep his face expressionless and to be as curt as possible in his replies. And as for Pyotr Petrovich, he not only began to avoid conversation with Gervaska, he actually avoided looking into his face.

On the day of the party Gervaska behaved with the same nonchalance and inscrutability. All the servants were run off their feet making preparations for the dinner, giving and taking orders, swearing, bickering, scrubbing floors, cleaning the dark, heavy silver of the icons with chalk, kicking the dogs back as they tried to get into the hall, worrying that the jelly wouldn't set, that there wouldn't be enough forks to go round, that the sugar cakes and the pancakes would be burnt; Gervaska alone smirked composedly and said to Kazimir, the drunkard chef, who was in a proper frenzy:

"Easy now, father deacon, your under-cassock might split."

"Mind you don't get drunk," Pyotr Petrovich said absently to Gervaska, his anxious mind on the marshal.

"Never drank in my life," Gervaska threw back as to an equal. "What's the fun?"

And afterwards, with the guests there, Pyotr Petrovich shouted for all to hear, trying to ingratiate himself with Gervaska.

"Gervasy! Don't disappear, for heaven's sake. We're lost without you."

While Gervaska called back in the most polite and dignified voice:

"Don't worry, sir. I'm at your service."

He served as never before. He fully justified the words Pyotr Petrovich said to his guests in Gervaska's presence:

"You'd never believe how impertinent that big lout is! But he is really a genius! Hands of gold!"

Could he ever have thought that he was adding the very drop that would make the cup run over? Grandfather heard his words. He started tugging at the neck of his coat and suddenly cried to the marshal at the other end of the table:

"Your Excellency! Lend me a helping hand! I appeal to you like to a father, and lodge a complaint against this servant of mine! This one here, this one–Gervasy Afanasyevich Kulikov! He flouts me at every turn! He–"

They did not let him finish, they comforted and pacified him. Grandfather's agitation reduced him to tears, but they all took to consoling him with such vigour and deference, which was a farce of course, that he succumbed and felt childishly happy again. Gervaska stood rigidly by the wall without looking up, his head turned away. Grandfather could see that the giant's head was too small, that it would have been smaller still if his hair had been cropped, that the back of his head was markedly sharp and his hair particularly thick on the nape–coarse hair, crudely trimmed, jutting out over his thin neck. Gervaska's face was peeling in spots from sunburn and from exposure to the wind when out shooting, and the spots showed pale mauve. And Grandfather darted frightened and uneasy glances at Gervaska, but he nevertheless went on shouting gleefully to the guests:

"All right, I'll forgive him, but only on one condition,

my dear friends, that you will stay with me for at least three days. I positively refuse to let you go. I beg you particularly, do not leave me now that evening is nigh! When dusk falls I'm not myself at all: it's so melancholy, so sinister! Clouds are gathering in the sky now; they say two of Bonaparte's Frenchmen were caught in Troshin Wood again... I'm sure to die at night, mark my words. Martin Zadeka, the book of dreams, says so..."

But he died early in the morning.

He had his way after all: "to please him" a number of people stayed for the night; they drank tea all evening long, there was any amount of jam of so many different kinds that they could come up and taste one sort, come up again and taste another; and then more tables were laid, great clusters of spermaceti candles were lit; they were reflected in all the mirrors and lent the golden glitter of a church to the rooms which swam in expensive, aromatic smoke, and hummed with noise and conversation. But to Grandfather the most important thing was that many of the guests were staying overnight. And therefore it did not only mean another pleasant day ahead but also a great deal of fuss and worry: why, if it had not been for him, for Pyotr Kirillich, the party would never have been such a success, the dinner so sumptuous and gay.

"Yes, yes," Grandfather was thinking excitedly that night as he stood in his bedroom with his coat off in front of the *prie-dieu* with thin wax candles burning on it, and gazed at St. Mercury's dark visage. "Yes, yes, evil shall slay the wicked. Let not the sun go down upon your wrath..."

But then he remembered it was something quite different he wanted to think about; hunching his shoulders and whispering the fiftieth psalm, he walked across the room and back, trimmed the pastille smouldering on his bedside table, picked up his psalter and, opening it, once again raised his eyes to the decapitated saint with a blissful sigh. And, suddenly, he came upon the thought that was escaping him and beamed with a smile:

"Yes, that's it, that's it: an old man's a nuisance, but he has his uses."

He hardly slept that night, worrying lest he should oversleep and fail to give the necessary orders. And early next morning, while the rooms, as yet untidied and unaired, stood hushed in the silence which is peculiar only to the morning after a party, he tiptoed cautiously in his bare feet into the drawing-room, anxiously picked up some pieces of chalk lying on the floor beside the green card-tables, and gasped weakly in delight as he saw the garden through the glass doors: the clear brilliance of the cold azure skies, the silver of the morning frost covering the terrace and the balustrade, the brown foliage in the bare shrubs beyond. He opened the door and sniffed: the shrubs still had the bitter, fermenting smell of autumnal decay, but this smell was swallowed up in the wintry crispness. And everything was motionless, stilled and almost solemn. The sun, peeping from behind the village, lit up the tops of the half-bare birches lining the picturesque walk, and those white and gold treetops, with their thin little golden leaves and transparent against the blue of the sky, had a lovely, joyous and elusively lilac tint. A dog ran past in the cold shadow of the terrace, and the grass, scorched by the frost and seemingly sprinkled with salt, crunched underfoot. This sound was reminiscent of winter, and Grandfather, twitching his shoulders in pleasurable anticipation, turned back into the drawing-room and, panting, started moving the heavy furniture, which rumbled when pushed about, and threw occasional glances at the sky reflected in the mirror. Suddenly Gervaska walked in quietly and quickly, without his coat, fuddled with sleep and "mad like hell," as he himself described it afterwards.

He came in and shouted sternly in a loud hiss:

"Quiet, you! Who's asking you to shift the furniture?"

Grandfather raised his excited face and whispered with the same kindliness he had been feeling all the previous evening and all night:

"Look what you're like, Gervasy! I forgave you last night, but instead of being grateful to your master, you—"

"I'm fed to the teeth with your snivelling," Gervaska cut him short. "Let go of that table!"

Grandfather threw a frightened look at the back of Gervaska's head that seemed to jut more than ever above the thin neck sticking out of the white shirt, but he flared up and stood between Gervaska and the card-table which he was going to drag into a corner.

"*You* let go!" he shouted after a moment's thought, but

his voice was not loud. "It's you who should give in to the master. You'll drive me too far: I'll stick a knife in your ribs."

"You will, will you?" Gervaska said angrily, flashing his teeth—and struck Grandfather hard on the chest.

Grandfather slipped on the polished oak floor, threw up his hands and, as he fell, struck his temple against the sharp corner of the table.

When Gervaska saw the blood, the senselessly slanting eyes and the gaping mouth, he tore from Grandfather's still warm neck the sacred golden medalion and the amulet on its grimy string. Looking over his shoulder, he pulled Grandfather's wedding ring off his little finger, too. Then he left the drawing-room soundlessly and swiftly, and vanished into thin air.

The only person at Sukhodol who ever saw him again was Natalia.

7

While she was at Soshki, two other major events took place at Sukhodol: Pyotr Petrovich got married and the brothers went as volunteers to fight in the Crimean War.

She only came back after two years' exile: they had forgotten about her. And when she did come back, she did not recognize Sukhodol, just as Sukhodol did not recognize her.

That summer evening, when the cart that had been sent from the manor-house to fetch her came creaking up to the cottage and Natalia appeared in the door, Yevsei Bodulya cried in surprise:

"Can it be you, Natalia?"

"Who do you think it is?" Natalia replied with a barely perceptible smile.

Yevsei shook his head:

"You've grown mighty uncomely, you know."

But she only looked different, that was all. She was no longer the crop-haired, round-faced, bright-eyed girl; she was a young woman, slender, not very tall, serene, reserved and gentle. She had on a Ukrainian checked wool skirt, and an embroidered blouse, and though her kerchief was dark, she wore it the way we do. She was somewhat sunburnt and her face was sprinkled with little freckles the colour of millet. But to Yevsei, a true Sukhodolian, the dark kerchief, the sunburn and the freckles looked ugly, of course.

On the way to Sukhodol Yevsei asked:

"Well, lass, you're old enough to marry now. I suppose you want to get married, eh?"

She only shook her head and said:

"No, Uncle Yevsei, I'll never marry."

"Why's that?" In his amazement Yevsei even took his pipe out of his mouth.

And unhurriedly she explained: marriage wasn't everyone's lot; they'd give her into Miss Tonya's keeping, probably, but since Miss Tonya had dedicated herself to God, that meant she wouldn't let Natalia marry either; and then she'd had many a dream that made it obvious enough...

"What kind of dreams?" Yevsei asked.

"It wasn't anything really," she said. "Gervaska scared me to death that time he told me the news; I began to brood on it, so I had those dreams."

"Did he really stay and eat with you, Gervaska I mean?"

Natalia thought a little.

"Yes, he did. He came and said, 'The master sent me to you on a very important matter, but let me have something to eat first.' We set out the meal on the table thinking no ill of him. When he finished eating, he walked out of the cottage and beckoned me to follow. I ran out after him, and behind the cottage he told me everything, and was off."

"But why didn't you call the people?"

"Not me. He threatened to kill me if I did. He said I wasn't to tell before nightfall. And to them he said, 'I'll go and sleep under the shed.' "

All the servants at Sukhodol were very curious to see her when she got back; her old friends the housemaids pestered her with questions. She answered them shortly, almost as though she gloried in the part she had taken upon herself to play.

"All was well," she repeated. And once she said in the tones of an old pilgrim woman, "God has many mercies. All was well."

And quietly, without delay, she took up her ordinary, humdrum duties about the house, as if she were not at all surprised that Grandfather was no more, that the young masters had gone to the war as volunteers, that Miss Tonya was "touched" and wandered through the rooms imitating Grandfather, that Sukhodol was ruled by a new and utterly strange mistress–short, fat, very lively and pregnant...

The mistress called out imperiously from the dining-hall:

"Tell her to come here ... what's her name ... Natalia."

And Natalia walked on swiftly and noiselessly, crossed herself, bowed to the icons in the corner, then to the mistress and miss, and stood still, waiting to be questioned and given orders. It was only the mistress, of course, who questioned her. Miss Tonya, who had grown very tall, thin and sharp-nosed, her unbelievably black eyes staring with a dull fixedness, did not say a word. It was the mistress who appointed her to Miss Tonya. Natalia bowed and said simply: "Yes, ma'am."

Miss Tonya, her gaze as fixedly indifferent, suddenly pounced on her that same evening and, squinting her eyes in a fury, tore at Natalia's hair with cruel delight for tugging clumsily at her stocking when she helped her to undress. Natalia burst into childish tears but said nothing. Going into the maids' room, she sat down on the window-seat, and, as she picked out her broken hairs, she actually smiled through the tears that hung on her eyelashes.

"My, she's fierce," she said. "I'm going to have a hard time."

Miss Tonya, awakening next morning, lay in bed for a long time, while Natalia stood by the door with lowered head, and cast sidelong glances at her pale face.

"Well, what did you dream about?" Miss Tonya asked with such apathy as if someone else were doing the talking for her.

Natalia replied, "Nothing, I don't think."

Whereupon Miss Tonya, as suddenly as the night before, jumped out of bed and in a savage fury hurled her cup of tea at Natalia, and then, falling across her bed, started sobbing bitterly and screaming. Natalia dodged the cup, and soon she learnt to duck with extraordinary nimbleness. When the stupid maids said, "Nothing, miss," in answer to

Miss Tonya's question about their dreams the night before, she would sometimes shout at them, "Well, make up some lie then!" But since Natalia was not good at lying, she was obliged to train herself in the art of ducking, instead.

A doctor was brought to see Miss Tonya at last. He prescribed many different pills and drops. Fearing that they wanted to poison her, Miss Tonya made Natalia try out the medicines first, and, submissively, she tasted them all, one after the other. Shortly after her return she learnt that Miss Tonya had been waiting for her "like for a ray of sunshine"; it was, in fact, Miss Tonya who had thought of her, and had been straining her eyes to see if the cart was coming from Soshki, passionately assuring everyone that she would be perfectly well the minute Natalia came back. Natalia did come back—and was met with utter indifference. Could it be that Miss Tonya's tears were caused by her disappointment in Natalia? The girl felt a pang when this occurred to her one day. She went out into the passage, sat down on a trunk and cried again.

"Well, do you feel better for the medicine?" Miss Tonya asked when Natalia came back into the room with her eyes swollen from weeping.

"Yes, miss," Natalia whispered, though her heart beat faintly and her head spun from all the medicines, and, coming up to her, she kissed her mistress's hand with feeling.

And for a long time to come she went about with downcast eyes, not daring to raise them to Miss Tonya, moved by pity for her.

"Oh, you Ukrainian snake, you!" Soloshka, one of the housemaids, once snapped at her. She, more than the others, had been striving to become Natalia's bosom friend and confidante of her thoughts and secrets, but all her advances had invariably met with curt, plain answers, which offered none of the delights of intimate friendship.

Natalia smiled sadly.

"Oh, well," she said pensively. "That's right too. You do get to be like the people you're with. Sometimes, you know, I miss my Ukrainians more than I do my own father and mother..."

Her new surroundings had been quite lost on her when she had first arrived at Soshki. They arrived there early in the morning and the only thing that seemed strange to her then was that the cottage was very long and white, seen from afar amid the plains, that the woman who was lighting the stove greeted her pleasantly and the man did not stop to listen to Yevsei's gossip. Yevsei prattled on without a pause—of his masters, of Demyan, of the hot journey, of what he ate in town, of Pyotr Petrovich and, of course, of the theft of the mirror; while the Ukrainian, Shary by name but known as Badger at Sukhodol, only shook his head and, when Yevsei had finished, glanced at him absently and with a very cheerful glint in his eye sang under his breath with a twang: "Whirl on, whirl on, snowstorm..." Little by little Natalia came back to normal and began to marvel at Soshki, finding in it more and more charm and difference from Sukhodol. The cottage alone was worth seeing, with its snow-white walls, its smooth roof evenly thatched with reeds, and the way the interior was decorated—how rich it seemed in comparison to the slovenly wretchedness of the Sukhodol huts. Look at the sumptuous tinselled icons hanging in the corner, the lovely paper flowers wreathed round them, and the bright embroidered towels framing them. And look at the flowered tablecloth. The rows of blue glazed pots and bowls on the shelves beside the stove. But the Ukrainian couple were the most amazing of all.

Natalia did not quite understand what was so amazing about them, but she was conscious of it all the time. Never before had she seen anyone as neat, unruffled and sound as Shary. He was not tall; he had a wedge-shaped head covered with cropped hair threaded thickly with silver; he did not wear a beard, and his moustache, scanty like a Tatar's, was also silver; his face and neck were burnt black by the sun and lined with deep wrinkles, which were neat, well defined and necessary for some reason. His gait was clumsy, for the top-boots he wore over his bleached linen trousers were too heavy; the shirt he tucked into the trousers was of the same material, hanging loose under the arms, its collar turned down. He slouched a bit when he walked. But neither this, nor his wrinkles and grey hair aged him; there was none of our weariness or drowsiness in his face; his somewhat small eyes had a keen look in them, with a hint of mockery. He reminded Natalia of the old

Serbian who had once come to Sukhodol with a little boy who played a fiddle.

Marina, the Ukrainian woman, had been nicknamed Pike by the Sukhodolians. This woman of fifty was tall and slender. A yellowish tan lay evenly on the fine skin—not a Sukhodolian skin—of her high-cheekboned face which, if somewhat coarse, was almost beautiful for its straight lines and the bright look in her stern eyes; these were either agate or amber-grey, changing colour like a cat's. A kerchief of black and gold with red dots was wound round her head in a tall turban; a short black skirt, against which her white blouse looked even whiter, hugged her hips. She wore hobnailed shoes on her bare feet, her calves were slim though rounded and the sunburn gave them a quality of brown polished wood. And when she sang at her work, her eyebrows drawn together, in a strong deep voice, the song about the infidels storming Pochayev,

The evening glow
Went down below
Pochayev's walls...

and of the Mother of God Herself defending the holy monastery, her voice rang with such melancholy and despair but, at the same time, with such majesty, power and menace, that Natalia could not tear her eyes away from her, looking on in awe-struck fascination.

They had no children, and Natalia was an orphan. Had she been staying with some Sukhodolian couple, they would have called her "daughter dear" at times and "dirty thief" at others, they would have fondled her one day and thrown it in her face the next. The Ukrainians, however, treated her almost coldly but fairly; they were neither inquisitive nor talkative. In the autumn a number of girls and women were brought from Kaluga, hired for the mowing and threshing, but Natalia shunned the company of these women dressed in bright, flowered sarafans: they were said to be dissolute and sick with foul diseases; they were large-breasted, brazen and insolent; they swore lustily and dirtily; they simply scattered bawdy little couplets; they sat their horses like men and galloped them madly. Natalia's sorrow would have been dispelled in familiar surroundings, in confidences, tears and songs. But who was there for her to confide in or to sing songs with? These harsh-voiced women would start one of their songs and then the rest of them would join in too readily and raucously, with whooping and whistling. Shary sang nothing but his humorous dance ditties. And as for Marina, she was stern, proud and pensively gloomy when she sang, even if it was a love song.

Willows I planted
Close to the water,
Rustling above,

she would recite in a plaintive, despondent voice, and pitching her voice low, she would add firmly and hopelessly:

Gone is my darling,
Gone now for ever
Gone is my love...

And in solitude Natalia slowly drank to the dregs her first cup of the bitter-sweet poison of unrequited love; she went through the agony of shame and jealousy, and the frightening and sweet dreams which often came to her at night, vain fancies and hopes which tormented her sorely through the silent days she lived in the steppe. Often the scorching pain in her heart would give way to tenderness, passion and despair, to submissiveness, and the desire for the most humble, insignificant existence close to *him*, for love that would for ever be hidden from the whole world, love that expected nothing and demanded nothing. News and messages coming from Sukhodol would sober her for a while. But if there was no news for a long time, she lost the sense of the humdrum side of Sukhodol life, and it began to appear so beautiful to her, her yearning for it was so strong, that she could hardly endure her loneliness and sorrow... Then suddenly Gervaska came. He hurled all the news of Sukhodol at her with hasty brusqueness, and in half an hour told what another would not have managed to tell in a day. He told everything, including the fatal "shove" he had given Grandfather. He ended resolutely:

"Good-bye for ever now."

And, with his enormous eyes burning through the dumbfounded girl, he called back as he got to the road:

"It's time you, too, had your foolishness knocked out of you. He's getting married any day now, so even as a mistress you'd be no use to him... Get some sense back."

And she did. She suffered this horrible news, pulled herself together and got her senses back.

After this her days dragged on bleakly and dully, they were like those pilgrim women who trailed on and on past the farm down the highroad and, stopping for a rest, held long conversations with her, teaching her to be patient and to rest her hopes in the Heavenly Father, whose name was pronounced with a dull plaintiveness, and above all instilling the rule: not to think at all.

"Whether we think or not, it won't be the way we want it," the women would say, stopping to re-tie their bast shoes, wrinkling their wan faces and gazing ruefully into the vastness of the steppe. "The Lord has many mercies... Pick us a few onions on the sly, there's a good girl..."

There were others, of course, who would put the fear of God into her, frightening her with her sinfulness, threatening her with hell-fire, and presaging calamities and horrors she had never known. And then she had two frightful dreams, almost one after the other. Her mind was constantly on Sukhodol—it was difficult not to think of it at first. She thought of Miss Tonya, of Grandfather, of her future, wondering whether she would get married and if so when and to whom. Her thoughts merged into a dream so imperceptibly one night that she saw with perfect clarity a sultry, dusty and alarmingly windy evening, and herself running with a couple of pails to fetch some water from the pond, when suddenly on the dry and clayey slope she saw a hideous, big-headed old dwarf in battered top-boots, hatless, with his red straggly hair tousled by the wind and a fiery-red unbelted shirt streaming behind him. "Oh dear, is there a fire?" she screamed, alarmed and frightened. And the dwarf screamed too, his voice muffled by the hot wind: "Ruin, ruin, all is lost! A storm of untold horror is nigh! It comes, it comes. Think not of marriage!" Her other dream was even more horrible. She was standing in a hot, empty cottage at midday, with someone outside jamming the door tight, and was waiting breathlessly for she knew not what–and suddenly a huge grey goat leapt out from behind the stove, reared and made straight for her, obscenely excited, with eyes burning like coals, gleefully mad and beseeching. "I am your mate!" he shouted in a human voice, trotting towards her quickly and clumsily, his small rear hoofs clop-clopping rapidly, and with all his might he brought his front ones down on her breast...

She jumped down from her bed in the hallway, jolted awake; the hammering of her heart, her terror of the darkness and the thought that she had no one to run to, almost killing her.

"Oh, Jesus! Holy Mother of God! Oh, Holy Saints!" she whispered in a quick patter.

But because all the saints she could picture were dark brown and decapitated like St. Mercury, her terror increased.

And when she started thinking these dreams over, it occurred to her that her youth was past, that her fate was already sealed (no wonder something extraordinary, the love for the master, had fallen to her lot), that more trials were awaiting her, that she should try and imitate the Ukrainians' reserve and the pilgrim women's humility and simplicity. And since the Sukhodolians are fond of playing a part, of convincing themselves in the inevitability of something which they themselves have invented, so Natalia, too, chose a part to play.

8

Her knees gave way from happiness when, running out on to the porch on the eve of St. Peter's Day, she realized that Bodulya was there to fetch her, when she saw the dusty, shabby Sukhodol cart, when she saw Bodulya, a ragged cap on his tousled head, his matted beard bleached in the sun, and his face, tired and excited, old before its time and ugly, even strange with its mean and incongruous features, when she saw the old dog, shaggy, too, looking not only like Bodulya but like all of Sukhodol, its back a dingy grey, while its chest and the thick hair on its neck so dark as though the black smoke of a chimneyless hut still clung to it. But Natalia soon took herself in hand. On the way home Bodulya rambled on in a desultory fashion about the Crimean War, happy about it one minute, complaining of it the next, while Natalia observed reasonably:

"Oh well, it seems we've got to pull them up, the French that is."

She had an uncanny feeling all the long way to Sukhodol, looking with new eyes at things old and familiar, living her former self over again as she neared her old home, noticing changes, recognizing people. A two-year-old colt was running about the fallow land overgrown with cowslips, where the road forked off to Sukhodol; a youngster, putting a bare foot into the rope bridle and clutching at the colt's neck, was trying to swing his other leg over its back, but the colt wouldn't let him—it jumped about and tried to shake him off. And Natalia felt a wave of happy excitement on recognizing the youngster as Foma Pantyukhin. Next she saw the hundred-year-old Nazarushka, who no longer drove like a man but now sat in his empty cart like a woman—with his legs stretched out straight before him, his shoulders raised high, stiffly and feebly, his pitifully sad eyes faded, and his body so emaciated it was nothing but skin and bones dressed in a long, shabby shirt that had become a dusky blue, like the ashes on the stove-bed where he was wont to lie. And her heart flinched again as she remembered how some three years before Arkady Petrovich, the most kind-hearted and carefree man of all, had wanted to flog this same Nazarushka who had been caught red-handed with a radish in the vegetable garden, and who stood weeping, more dead than alive, among the servants who surrounded him and shouted through guffaws of laughter:

"Nothing doing, no whimpering now! You'll have to take your trousers down, it seems! You can't get out of it!"

But how her heart began to throb when she saw the common, the row of cottages and the manor-house, the garden, the tall roof, the rear walls of the servants' quarters, the barns and stables. Yellow rye fields, thickly dotted with corn-flowers, came up close to the walls, to the tall grass and the thistles; someone's calf, white with brown spots, stood deep in the oats, chewing away at the tassels. Everything was peaceful, simple and ordinary—everything appeared more and more extraordinary and alarming, and her mind grew utterly dazed when the cart rolled briskly down the wide courtyard spotted with sleeping white borzois as a graveyard is spotted with tombstones, when, after two years in a cowshed, she walked into the cool house which smelt so dearly of wax candles and lime blossom, the pantry, Arkady Petrovich's Cossack saddle lying on a bench in the front hall, the now empty quail cages at the window—and glanced timidly at St. Mercury who had been brought from Grandfather's rooms to hang in the corner of the hall...

The sun, streaming in from the garden through the little windows, lit up the gloomy dining-hall as merrily as ever. A chicken, which had somehow got into the house, was clucking disconsolately as it wandered about the drawing-room. Lime blossom, drying on the hot, bright window-sills, sent up its fragrance... It seemed to her that all the old things she was seeing about her had grown younger, and this you usually feel in a house after a funeral. In everything, in everything, and particularly in the fragrance of the lime blossom, she felt a particle of her own self, her childhood, her adolescence, her first love. And she felt sorry for those who had grown up, died and changed—sorry for herself and Miss Tonya. Friends of her own age had grown up too. Many of the old men and women, whose heads used to shake with old age and who sometimes used to peep out dully at the world from behind the doors of the servants' rooms, had forever disappeared from this world. Darya Ustinovna was gone. Gone was Grandfather, who had been so childishly afraid of death, thinking that death would overpower him gradually, preparing him for the hour of doom, but which was to mow him down with its scythe so unexpectedly and swiftly. And it was hard to believe he was no more, that it was really his body that lay decaying under the mound of earth close to the church in the village of Cherkizovo. It was hard to believe that this black, gaunt, sharp-nosed woman, listless one moment, frenzied the next, nervously talkative and at times outspoken with her as with an equal, or suddenly tearing at her hair—was Miss Tonya. It was hard to understand why the house was being managed by some Klavdia Markovna, a short, shrewish little woman with a black moustache...

One day Natalia threw a timid look into her bedroom, and there she saw the fatal silver-framed mirror. A sweet pain wrung her heart and all her old terrors, joys, tenderness, anticipation of shame and bliss, and the smell of dewy burdocks at sundown, overwhelmed her... But all her feelings, all her thoughts she kept in secret and tried to suppress. Very, very ancient Sukhodol blood coursed through her veins. Too flat tasted the bread she had eaten, grown on the clayey soil that surrounded Sukhodol. Too flat tasted the water she had drunk from the pools which her forefathers had dug in the bed of the dried-up little river. She had no fear of the usual, exhausting workdays; she dreaded the unusual. She had no fear of death; but dreams, the darkness of night, storms, thunder and fire set her trembling with fright. And, she carried in her heart the vague premonition of some imminent disaster...

This premonition aged her. But then she also kept telling herself that her youth was past and she sought proof of this in everything. And before she had been back a year, that youthful feeling with which she had crossed the threshold of Sukhodol had vanished without a trace.

Klavdia Markovna was delivered of a boy. Fedosya, the poultry woman, was promoted to the post of nurse, and though a young woman, she put on the dark garb of old age, grew humble and pious. The young Khrushchov, blowing bubbles, toppling over, helplessly overbalanced by the weight of his own head, and howling angrily, could hardly focus his milky, senseless eyes although he was already being called the young master, while from the nursery came the age-old muttered admonitions: "There he comes, there he comes, the old man with the bag... Go away, old man, go away! Keep away from us, we won't let you take the young master, he won't cry, he's a good boy..."

And Natalia copied Fedosya, considering herself a nurse too, nurse and companion to the sick young lady. Olga Kirillovna died that winter, and Natalia got permission to accompany the old women, who were ending their days in the servants' rooms, to attend the funeral. She ate frumenty there which nauseated her with its insipid and sickly-sweet taste, and on returning to Sukhodol she gave a sentimental account of the old mistress "lying there in death as if she were alive", although even the old women had not ventured to look at the coffin holding that monstrous body.

And in the spring a sorcerer was brought to see Miss Tonya from the village of Chermashnoye, the famous Klim Yerokhin, a prosperous *odnodvorets,* a dignified and handsome man, with a large grey beard and curly grey hair parted in the middle, a very competent farmer, whose conversation was very reasonable and straightforward as a rule, until he transformed himself into a sorcerer at the sick-bed. The clothes he wore were exceptionally strong and neat—a *poddyovka* of steel-grey coarse woollen cloth, a red sash and top-boots. His small eyes were sly and keen; they piously sought the icons when he walked into the house, stooping his well-made body a little, and started his polite talk. To begin with he spoke of the harvest, of rains and drought, after that he took a long time over his tea, drinking it very tidily, then he crossed himself again, and only after all this did he ask about the patient, instantly changing his tone.

"Twilight ... night is falling ... the time has come," he would begin mysteriously.

Miss Tonya, shaking with fever, ready to collapse on the floor and writhe in convulsions, sat in her twilit bedroom and waited for Klim to appear at her door. Natalia, too, standing by her side, was numbed with horror from head to toe. The whole house grew still—even the mistress packed her room full of servant girls and talked to them in whispers. No one dared to light a single candle, no one dared to raise a voice. Soloshka, the gay and carefree girl who stood on guard in the corridor in case she was wanted to carry out Klim's orders, felt everything grow dim before her eyes and her heart hammering in her throat: he walked past her, unwrapping a handkerchief with some magic bones in it. And then the funereal silence was rent by his loud, weird voice coming from the bedroom:

"Arise, woman!"

Then he thrust his grey head out of the door and uttered lifelessly: "The board."

And Miss Tonya, cold as a corpse, her eyes bulging from terror, was stood on the board which lay on the floor. It was so dark by then that Natalia could hardly make out Klim's face. And suddenly he began to intone in a disembodied, uncanny sort of voice:

"Filat is coming... Windows he'll open... Doors he'll throw wide... He'll cry and say: woe, woe!"

"Woe, woe!" he cried with sudden force and stern authority. "Be gone, woe, into the dark forests below, that's where you belong, woe! Across the oceans and the seas," his muttering was rapid, gruff and ominous now, "the stormy Buyan Island rears, and on it lies a bitch obese, upon its back a thick grey fleece..."

And Natalia felt there could never be words more hideous than these, which instantly whisked her soul away to the ends of some wild, fabulous and primordially coarse world. There was no disbelieving the power of these words, just as Klim himself could not disbelieve it. With them he sometimes worked miracles over those sick in spirit—that same Klim who, his sorcery over, sat in the hall, talking so simply and modestly, wiping the sweat off his brow with his handkerchief and settling down to tea again.

"Well, two more nights left now... God willing, perhaps she'll feel a little easier... Have you sown any buckwheat this year, ma'am? The buckwheat's good this year, they say. Mighty good!"

The masters were expected back from the Crimea that summer. But Arkady Petrovich sent a registered letter demanding more money and informing them that they could not get back before the autumn on account of Pyotr Petrovich's wound which, though slight, would keep him bedridden for a long time. A messenger was sent to Danilovna, the prophetess in Cherkizovo, to find out if this illness would end safely. Danilovna began to dance and crack her fingers which meant, of course, that the outcome would be good. This reassured the mistress. As for Miss Tonya and Natalia, they had other worries to think about. Miss Tonya had been feeling a little better at first, but towards St. Peter's Day it started all over again: melancholia, and so ghastly a dread of thunderstorms, fires and of something else she kept a secret, that she could not be bothered with her brothers. Natalia had no mind for them any longer, either. She remembered Pyotr Petrovich in her prayers without fail, praying for his quick recovery, as in later years to her dying day she prayed for his immortal soul; but it was Miss Tonya who meant more than anyone else to her now. And Miss Tonya infected her more and more with her terrors, her premonitions of disasters, and that something which she kept a secret.

Summer happened to be sultry, dusty and windy that year, with thunderstorms breaking out every day. Rumours were rife, obscure and alarming, of some new war or other, of riots and fires, some said that all the serfs would be set at liberty any day now, others said that, on the contrary, in the autumn every single one of the men would be recruited into the army. And, as usual in the summer, an endless stream of vagabonds, half-wits and monks made their appearance. And Miss Tonya all but fought with the mistress over them, and went handing out bread and eggs to them. Dronya came too, tall and red-haired, in tatters that failed description. He was just a drunkard but he pretended he was a saintly natural. He walked across the yard straight to the house, so lost in reverie that he knocked his head against the wall and jumped back with a radiant face.

"Shoo, my little birdies!" he cried in a high-pitched voice, leaping and twisting his whole body, crooking his right arm to screen his eyes from the sun. "Up we go, up we fly to heaven, my birdies!"

And Natalia, in imitation of the other women, stared at him the way one was supposed to stare at the saintly naturals: dumbly and piteously. Miss Tonya darted to the window and, weeping, screamed in a pathetic voice:

"Oh, holy Dronya! Pray for me, pray for my sinful soul!"

And on hearing this scream, Natalia's eyes popped with horrible surmise.

Timosha Klichinsky from the village of Klichin was another one. This was a short, effeminately plump little man with large breasts, yellow hair and the face of a squint-eyed infant, stupefied and smothered with fat. He wore a white calico shirt and short calico trousers; he planted his plump little feet hastily and mincingly, toe first, as he tripped up to the porch, and his narrow little eyes had a look in them as if he had just been rescued from the deep or had escaped some fatal catastrophe.

"Misery!" he muttered breathlessly. "Misery..."

They comforted him, fed him and sat waiting to hear

something from him. But he remained silent, wheezing and grunting greedily over his food. When he had eaten his fill, he would once again sling his bag on his shoulder and look about him nervously for his long staff.

"When will you come again, Timosha?" Miss Tonya screamed to him.

And he called back, screaming too, in a ridiculously high contralto, for no reason at all distorting Miss Tonya's name:

"In Holy Week, Lukyanovna!"

And Miss Tonya wailed pitifully after him:

"Oh, holy man! Pray for my sinful soul, pray to Mary of Egypt!"

Every day brought news of calamities from everywhere—of thunderstorms and fires. And in Sukhodol the ancient fear of fire mounted stronger and stronger. The moment the sandy-yellow sea of ripening wheat began to dim in the shadow of a thundercloud appearing behind the manor-house, the moment the first whiff of wind whirled across the common and the first distant roll of thunder rumbled, the women would rush indoors to bring out their wooden icons and get bowls of milk ready, which, as everyone knows, is the quickest way to appease fire. And from the manor-house scissors would come flying into the nettles, and the sacred and frightening towel would be taken out; curtains would be drawn across the windows and wax candles lighted with shaking hands... Even the mistress was affected by the panic, perhaps sincerely or perhaps feigning sincerity. In the old days she used to say that a thunderstorm was a "natural phenomenon". Nowadays she, too, crossed herself, closed her eyes tight, and gasped at every flash of lightning, and in order to whet her own fear and that of the others she kept talking of some extraordinary thunderstorm that broke out in Tirol in 1771 and killed one hundred and eleven people outright. And her listeners capped her story and hastened to tell their own: of the willow tree on the highroad burned to the ground by lightning, of a woman struck down dead by a thunderbolt in Cherkizovo, of a troika hit so hard that all the three horses fell to their knees... And finally a certain Yushka, an "erring monk" as he called himself, joined them in their morbid devotions.

9

Yushka was a peasant by birth. But he had never done a stroke of work in his life, and he lived the life of a stray, paying for the temporary hospitality offered him with stories of his complete idleness and of his "misbehaviour".

"I'm a peasant, brother, but I'm smart and I look like a hunchback," he would say, "so why should I work?"

And, indeed, he did look like a hunchback. His eyes were mocking and wise, his face was hairless; he kept his shoulders raised high on account of his rickety chest; he bit his nails and kept brushing back his long copper-coloured hair with fingers that were slim and strong. He thought it "indecent and boring" to till the land, and so he went off to the Kiev Monastery, "matured" there and was eventually banished for his "misbehaviour". And then, realizing that acting the part of a holy pilgrim, a man saving his soul, was too old a trick and might prove unprofitable, he tried another ruse: without taking off his cassock, he began to flaunt and brag about his idleness and lecherousness, to smoke and to drink as much as he could hold (he never got drunk), to make a mock of the monastery and explain with the aid of obscene gestures and movements exactly why he had been banished.

"Of course," he told the men with a wink, "of course, they threw me out for that right away. And so I turned back home to Russia... I'd get along, I thought."

And get along he did. Russia gave the bawdy sinner as hearty a welcome as she gave those who were saving their immortal souls. She fed him, sheltered him at night and listened to him enraptured.

"And so you swore you'd never work, did you?" the men asked him, their eyes glinting with the expectation of thrilling confidences.

"The devil couldn't make me work now," Yushka replied. "I'm spoiled, brother. I've got more rut in me than a monastery goat. Those girls now—I have no use for married women at all—they're scared to death of me, but they love me. And why shouldn't they? I'm not bad myself—my feathers aren't pretty, but I've got what it takes."

When he arrived at Sukhodol, being a man of experience, he walked straight into the house, into the hall.

There Natalia sat on a bench, humming: "I swept and swept the floor that day, and found a piece of sugar..." When she saw him she started up, terrified.

"Who are you?" she cried.

"A man," Yushka replied, taking her in from head to toe in one rapid glance. "Tell the mistress."

"Who's that?" the mistress cried from the drawing-room.

But Yushka calmed her fears in a moment. He told her he was a monk and not an escaped soldier, as she must have supposed, and was on his way home. He asked her to search him and then to permit him to spend the night there and rest a little. He so astonished the mistress with his outspokenness that the very next day he found he could move into the servants' quarters and become quite one of the family. Thunderstorms followed one after another, but he was indefatigable in amusing his hostesses with his stories; he thought of boarding up the dormer windows to protect the roof from lightning; he would dash out to the porch at the most frightening thunderclaps to show how little danger there was in them, and he helped the maids to kindle the samovars. The maids distrusted him, conscious of his quick, lecherous looks on their bodies, but they laughed at his jokes, while Natalia, whom he had accosted in the dark corridor several times whispering rapidly: "I've fallen in love with you!" dared not raise her eyes to his. He was repulsive to her, with the smell of makhorka drenching the whole of his cassock, and frightening, so frightening...

She knew quite definitely what would happen. She slept alone in the corridor close to her mistress's bedroom door, and Yushka had already hissed at her: "I'll come. I'll come even if you kill me for it. And if you start yelling, I'll burn the place to the ground." But what sapped her strength more than anything else was the realization that something *inevitable* was happening, that the horrible dream she had at Soshki about the goat was to come true shortly, that evidently it was preordained that she should perish together with Miss Tonya. It was clear to everyone now: the devil himself dwelt in the house at night. Everyone understood what it was, apart from the thunderstorms and the fires, that was driving Miss Tonya crazy, what made her moan voluptuously and wildly in her sleep, and then jump up with screams so terrifying that they drowned out the most deafening of thunderclaps. "The snake of Eden, of Jerusalem is strangling me!" she would shriek. And who could that snake be if not the devil, the grey goat that comes into the rooms of girls and women in the night? And was there anything more frightening in the world than his coming in the darkness, on rainy nights when thunder rumbled in incessant rolls and lightning flashed across the black icons? The passion, the lust with which he whispered to Natalia was also inhuman: so how could she struggle against it? Brooding on the fatal hour that would inevitably strike, sitting on her horsecloth on the floor in the corridor, peering into the darkness with beating heart, listening to the slightest rustle or creak of a board in the slumbering house, she already felt the first attacks of that grave illness which was to possess her for a long time to come: the sole of one of her feet would suddenly begin to itch, she'd feel a sharp, piercing cramp in it twisting and turning her toes inward, this spasm would run up her legs contorting her nerves cruelly and sweetly, right up to her throat, and in a moment she would want to shriek more madly and with more ecstasy and agony than Miss Tonya ever shrieked.

And the inevitable happened. Yushka came—on that ghastly night towards the end of the summer, on the eve of St. Elijah's, the ancient flame-thrower's day. There was no thunder that night, nor was there any sleep for Natalia. She fell into a doze and suddenly she was startled awake as if she had been jolted. It was the dead hour of the night—she knew it by her madly beating heart. She jumped up, looked down one end of the corridor, down the other, and wherever she looked she saw the sky, silent and full of fire and mystery, flaring up, blazing and quivering with blinding flashes of gold and pale blue. For a moment the corridor grew light as day. She started running—and froze to the spot: the aspen logs, long since stacked in the yard, looked blindingly white in the flashes. She tried the dining-hall: one of the windows was open, she could hear the steady swish of the trees; it was darker there, but the flash of lightning outside the windows was the brighter for it, darkness would envelop everything for a moment and instantly it would be all aquiver again, lightning would flash here and there, and the garden, with all its lacy tree-tops, its ghostly pale green birches and poplars, would flicker, swell and tremble against the vast heavens of gold and pale violet.

"Across the oceans and the seas the stormy Buyan Island rears," she started whispering as she rushed back, aware that she was bringing on her ruin by repeating this eerie incantation, "and on it lies–" And just as she pronounced these primitively menacing words, she looked back and saw Yushka, his shoulders raised high, not two paces away from her. Lightning lit up his face–pale with black hollows for eyes. He pounced on her soundlessly, grasped her with his long arms and, crushing her, brought her down to her knees in a moment, then on her back, on to the cold floor...

Yushka came to her the following night too. He kept coming on many successive nights and she, faint with horror and disgust, meekly surrendered to him. It never even occurred to her to resist him or to seek protection with her mistress or the other servants, just as it never occurred to Miss Tonya to dare resist the devil who took his pleasure with her at night, or Grandmother herself, the imperious beauty who, they said, had not dared resist her serf Tkach, a desperate scoundrel and thief, eventually sent into exile in Siberia... At last Yushka grew tired of Natalia, tired of Sukhodol, and he vanished as suddenly as he had appeared.

A month later she felt she was with child. And in September, on the day following the return of the young masters from the war, the manor-house caught fire and burned long and terribly. Her second dream had come true as well. It was evening, rain was pouring down in torrents when the house was struck by lightning, by a golden ball which, according to Soloshka, leapt out of the stove in Grandfather's bedroom and sped bouncing through the rooms. And Natalia, who on seeing the smoke and the flames rushed for all she was worth from the bath-house where she had been spending her days and nights in tears, related afterwards that in the garden she came upon someone dressed in a red coat and tall gold-braided Cossack hat, that he, too, had been running for all he was worth through the dripping shrubs and burdocks... Whether she had really seen all this or had only fancied it, Natalia could not tell for certain. All she knew for a fact was that the horror of it released her from her future child.

And that autumn she began to wilt. Her life got into a humdrum groove and never stirred out of it again. They took Aunt Tonya to Voronezh to kiss the holy relics of the saint. After that the devil no longer dared to approach her and she calmed down, took up her existence like everyone else, the derangement of her mind and spirit only manifesting itself in the brilliance of her wild eyes, her extreme untidiness and a savage irritability and despondency when the weather was bad. Natalia had accompanied her on this pilgrimage and she, too, had her peace restored to her on that trip where she found a solution to all that had seemed impossible to solve. How she used to tremble at the very thought of meeting Pyotr Petrovich! No matter how she tried to prepare herself for it she could never think of it calmly. And what about Yushka, her disgrace and ruin! But the very singularity of her ruin, the extraordinary depth of her sufferings, that element of doom in her downfall (for, surely, it had not been accidentally timed with the horror of the fire!), her pilgrimage to the saint, gave her the right to look calmly and frankly into the eyes of Pyotr Petrovich, to say nothing of everyone else. The damning finger of the Lord had pointed at her and Miss Tonya—was it for them to be afraid of people now? When she returned from Voronezh and walked into the Sukhodol house, she was like a nun, a humble and simple servant to all, light and pure in heart as if she had partaken of the last Holy Sacrament on her deathbed, and she bravely came up to kiss Pyotr Petrovich's hand. And only for a moment, when her lips touched his small, dark hand with the turquoise ring, did her heart tremble youthfully, tenderly, and thrillingly...

Life grew bleak at Sukhodol. There were definite tidings of freedom for the serfs and this news actually alarmed the servants and the villagers. What would the future bring, they wondered. Would it be worse, perhaps? They were to begin living in a new way, and this was easier said than done. The masters would have to live in a new way as well, and they had never even learnt the old way. Grandfather's death, the war, the comet which had frightened the whole country, then the fire, and the tidings of freedom—all this wrought a swift change in the faces and the hearts of the masters, depriving them of youth and light-heartedness, of their former easily appeased irascibility, replacing it with malice, boredom and a rancorous fractiousness; they started having "differences", as Father put it, and ended by arming themselves with whips for dinner... Need knocked at the door, reminding them of the dire necessity of somehow straightening out their affairs, which had been completely ruined by the Crimean War, the fire and debts. But in estate management the brothers only got in each other's way. One was ridiculously greedy, hard and mistrustful, while the other was ridiculously generous, kind and trusting. They managed to come to an understanding at last and agreed upon a venture that was bound to bring in a great profit. Mortgaging their property they bought about three hundred miserable horses. A certain Gipsy, Ilya Samsonov, helped to collect them from practically all over the district. They planned to feed the horses up during the winter and sell them at a profit in the spring. But, having devoured vast quantities of flour and hay, the horses began to sicken and die for some unknown reason one after the other, and by spring almost all of them were dead.

The discord between the brothers grew stronger. Their quarrels went so far that at times they snatched up knives and guns. And no one knows how it would all have ended if another calamity had not befallen Sukhodol. One winter day, four years after his return from the Crimea, Pyotr Petrovich drove to Lunevo where he had a mistress. He spent two days there, drinking heavily all the time, and he was drunk when he started back home. Show was deep that winter; two horses were harnessed to the low, wide sledge, covered with a rug. Pyotr Petrovich ordered the off-horse, a spirited young mare, which sank belly-deep into the flaccid snow, to be unharnessed and tied to the rear of the sledge, while he lay down to sleep with his head towards it, so they said. Evening descended, misty and blue. Before he dropped off, Pyotr Petrovich shouted an order to Yevsei Bodulya, whom he was in the habit of taking along with him instead of the coachman Vaska Kazak, who, he feared, might kill him because feeling was running high against him for his maltreatment of the servants. "Get going!" he shouted, and kicked Yevsei in the back. And then, the powerful bay wheeler, already sweating, and steaming, tore off along the difficult snowbound road, towards the misty haze of the desolate fields, into the darkening, gloomy winter night... And at midnight, when everyone was sleeping the sleep of the dead at Sukhodol, someone rapped quickly and alarmingly on the window of the corridor where Natalia slept. She jumped down from her bench and ran out on to the porch in her bare feet. She saw the dim dark silhouettes of the horses and the sledge, and Yevsei standing with a whip in his hands.

"Trouble, there's trouble, lass," he started mumbling hollowly and strangely as though in sleep. "Master's been killed by the horse ... the off-horse... She ran up, stumbled and kicked him... Smashed his face right in... He's getting cold already... It wasn't me, it wasn't me, I swear to God it wasn't!"

Without a word Natalia went down the porch steps, her bare feet sinking in the snow; she came up to the sledge, fell on her knees, clutched the icy, blood-clotted head to her breast, showered kisses on it and screamed at the top of her voice with a wildly joyous scream, choking with sobs and laughter...

10

Whenever we happened to take a rest from city life in the quiet and destitute remoteness of Sukhodol, Natalia would tell us again and again the story of her wrecked life. And at times her eyes would darken and stare blankly, her voice would change to a stern, clear half-whisper. I kept recalling the crude image of the saint which had hung in the corner of the hall in our old home. Decapitated, the saint came to his people, bearing his dead head in his hands, to prove the truth of his story...

Even those few material traces of the past which we had once found at Sukhodol were no longer there. Our fathers and forefathers had left us neither their portraits, nor their letters, nor even any of their ordinary household things. And whatever there had been, had perished in the fire. There was a chest in the corridor, which had stood there for many years, covered with tatters of the stiff, hairless sealskin that had bound it almost a hundred years before. This was Grandfather's chest with drawers of speckled birch, filled with singed French dictionaries and prayer-books, hopelessly spattered with wax. And then even this chest disappeared. The heavy furniture which had stood in the drawing-room and the dining-hall had been taken out, piece by broken piece. The house was getting old, it was subsiding more and more. All those long years it had weathered since the last events related here, were years of lingering death... And its past became more and more legendary.

The Sukhodolians lived in a world that was remote and dark, yet it had been a complex world with a semblance of stability and prosperity. Judging by the stagnancy of this life and the Sukhodolians' attachment to it, one might have thought it would never come to an end. But they were compliant, weak and "weaklings when it came to punishment", those descendants of the steppe nomads. And we witnessed the nests of the Sukhodolians disappear swiftly without leaving a trace, just as the little mounds that top the underground channels and burrows of hamsters vanish one after the other when a field is ploughed. And the inhabitants of the Sukhodol nests perished or fled too, and those who somehow managed to survive ended their days somehow. So what we lived to see was not the Sukhodol world any longer, it was not life but only a memory of it, an existence that was semi-wild in its simplicity. Our visits to our home in the steppe became rarer as the years went by. And we grew more and more estranged from it; we felt less and less our connection with the world and the class from which we were descended. Many of our countrymen were, like us, descendants of an illustrious, ancient lineage. The chronicles recorded our names: our ancestors were dapifers and commanders and "eminent men", the closest associates and even relatives of tsars. And had they been called knights, had we been born in the West, how confidently we would have talked of them, how much longer we would have held on. A scion of the knights could not have said that a whole class had almost vanished off the face of the earth in as little as half a century, that so many of us had become degenerate, insane, had committed suicide, become out and out drunkards, had gone to seed, or had simply got lost somewhere. He could not have confessed as I am doing now that we have not even a slightly accurate idea of the life of our great-grandfathers, to say nothing of our earlier ancestors, that with every day we are finding it more difficult to picture things that took place a mere fifty years ago.

The spot where Lunevo had once been has been tilled and sown a long time ago, and so have the sites of many of the other estates as well. Sukhodol still held on by a miracle. But having cut down the last of the birches in the garden and sold practically all the arable land piecemeal, the owner himself, the son of Pyotr Petrovich, abandoned it—to take on the job of a railway conductor. And the old inhabitants of Sukhodol—Klavdia Markovna, Aunt Tonya and Natalia—dragged out the last years of their lives in wretchedness. Spring gave way to summer, summer waned into autumn, and then came winter... They lost count of the seasons. They lived in their memories and dreams, in wrangles and worries about their daily bread. In the summer the peasants' rye-fields rolled over the acres where once the garden spread, and the manor-house, standing amid these fields, was now visible from afar. The shrubs, which were all that remained of the garden, had become such a wild growth that you could hear the call of the quail right by the terrace. But summer was no problem. "It's as good as heaven in summer," the old women would say. It was the long rainy autumns and the snow-swept winters that were so depressing and tedious at Sukhodol. There was cold and hunger in the empty crumbling house. Blizzards drifted snow over it and icy winds pierced it through. And as for heating, they lighted the stoves very seldom. In the evenings a little tin lamp would shed its frugal light from the room of the old mistress—the only habitable room in the house. The mistress, wearing spectacles, a sheepskin coat and felt boots, would sit and knit a sock, bending close over the lamp. Natalia would doze on the cold stove ledge, while Miss Tonya, who looked like a Siberian *shaman*, sat in her cottage and smoked a pipe. When Aunt Tonya and Klavdia Markovna were not quarreling, the latter would place her lamp on the window-sill instead of the table. And then a strange faint half-light would glow from the manor-house into Aunt Tonya's icy cottage, crowded with pieces of broken furniture, cluttered with bits of smashed crockery, and obstructed by the piano which had collapsed on its side. This cottage was so cold that the chickens, to whose care Aunt Tonya gave her remaining strength, had frost-bitten feet from sleeping on these broken bits and pieces.

But there is no one left in Sukhodol at all now. All those mentioned in these annals, all their neighbours and contemporaries are dead. And sometimes you wonder if indeed they ever really lived.

You only feel that they did live in this world when you come to the graveyards, you even sense an eerie closeness to them. But even this requires an effort, you must first sit down and think awhile beside one of the family graves, that is, if you can manage to find it. This is a disgraceful admission but it has to be made: we do not know the graves of Grandfather, Grandmother or Pyotr Petrovich. All we know is that they are not far from the altar of the little old church in Cherkizovo. You could never get there in winter: snowdrifts are waistdeep there, with a few crosses and the tops of bare shrubs and branches sticking out of the snow. In the summer you walk down the hot village street, empty and quiet, tie your horse to the churchyard fence which has a dark-green wall of firs behind it, the trees languishing in the sultry heat. When you walk through the gate you see a whole grove of short spreading elms, ash and lime-trees beyond the white church with its rusty cupola, and all will be shadow and coolness. You wander for a long time between the shrubs, over mounds and down hollows, covered with thin graveyard grass, you tread on stone slabs which have become porous from rains, overgrown with black, crumbly moss and almost completely sunken into the ground... You see two or three iron monuments. But whose are they? They have become such a greenish gold that you can no longer read the inscriptions. Which of these mounds guard the bones of Grandmother, of Grandfather? God alone knows! All *you* know is that they are here somewhere close. And you sit there and think, trying to picture those Khrushchovs whom everyone has forgotten. And the world they lived in seems for a moment infinitely far, and then, suddenly, it seems so close. And then you say to yourself:

"It's not difficult to imagine, not difficult at all. All you've got to remember is that this gilded cross standing lop-sidedly against the blue summer sky was the same in their time ... that the rye ripened then as it does now in those desolate and sultry fields ... that shade, coolness and shrubs have been here always ... and a jaded mare roamed here and fed in this shrubbery just like that one over there, old and white with the thin greenish forelock and the pink battered hoofs."

Vasilyevskoye, 1911

The Last Rendezvous

1

The moonlit autumn night was damp and cold when Streshnev ordered his horse to be saddled.

Moonlight fell in a streak of blue smoke through the narrow window of the dark stable, lighting up one eye of the saddle-horse with the fire of a precious stone. The groom flung a headstall and a heavy, high Cossack saddle on the horse, pulled it out of the stable by the bridle, and tied up its tail in a knot. The horse was submissive. Only when it felt the saddle girth, did it blow out its ribs in a deep sigh. One of the girths was broken. The groom managed to buckle it and pulled the end through with his teeth.

The stumpy horse looked sprucer now that it was saddled. The groom led it up to the front porch, wound the bridle round a rotting pole and walked away. For a long time the horse stood gnawing and biting at the pole with its yellow teeth. Now and then it blew out its ribs, whinnied, and let out an abdominal neigh. In a puddle beside it was the greenish reflection of the waning moon. A hazy mist was settling on the bare garden.

Streshnev appeared on the porch, hunting-crop in hand. Hook-nosed, lean and broad-shouldered, with his small head thrown back, he looked tall and smart in his brown *poddyovka*, with a silver-chased leather belt gripping his slim waist, and a crimson topped astrakhan hat on his head. But even in the light of the moon, you could see that his face was drawn and weather-beaten, that his coarse curly beard was touched with grey, and his neck was stringy. You could also see that his tall boots were old and the skirt of his coat showed dark spots of long-dried hare's blood.

A small, dark window beside the porch was pushed open, and a timid voice asked:

"Andrei dear, where are you going?"

"I'm not a child, Mother," Streshnev replied frowning, and took up the bridle.

The window was pulled to. But now a door banged in the hall. Pavel Streshnev, shuffling his slippered feet, came out on to the porch. His face was bloated and bleary-eyed, his grey hair combed back; he was in his underwear with an old topcoat thrown over his shoulders, half-drunk and talkative as usual.

"Where are you off to, Andrei?" he asked in a husky voice. "Please give my sincere regards to Vera Alexeyevna. I've always respected her most deeply."

"Can you respect anyone?" Streshnev replied. "And why do you always meddle in other people's business?"

"Sorry, sorry," said Pavel. " 'To a secret rendezvous rides the lovelorn gallant youth...' " he recited.

Clenching his teeth, Streshnev began to mount. The moment his foot touched the stirrup, his horse came to life and started prancing clumsily. Seizing his opportunity, Streshnev mounted easily and sat back in the creaking saddle. The horse flung up its head and, smashing the moon in the puddle with a hoof, set off at a brisk amble.

2

The balks in the damp, moonlit fields were blurred white with wormwood. Owls, spreading their large wings, soared suddenly and noiselessly from the balks, and the horse snorted and shied. The road ran through a thin wood, desolate and cold with moonlight and dew. The bright, wet-looking moon flashed through the bare treetops, and the bare branches merged with its moist gleam

7—904

and vanished into it. There was a bitter smell of aspen bark, of dead leaves in the gullies... Now came the descent into the meadows which seemed bottomless, flooded with a thin white steam. The horse breathed white steam, too, as it threaded its way through bushes crystalline with dew. The snap of twigs under its hoofs was echoed on the opposite side, in the tall forest shadowing the mountain slope... Suddenly, the horse pricked up its ears. Two wolves—sturdy, thick-necked and thin-legged—stood in the meadow's pale haze. They let Streshnev come up quite close, then they jumped round and loped clumsily up the hill across the radiantly glistening grass, white with rime.

"And if she stays for one more day?" said Streshnev, throwing back his head and looking at the moon.

The moon hung to the right over the desolate, hazily silver meadows... Oh, the melancholy beauty of autumn!

The saddle creaked as the horse, straining with all its might, climbed up the side of a deep gully where the path had been washed away by streams, towards the tall, dense forest above. Suddenly, it missed its footing and almost crashed down the bank. Fury distorted Streshnev's features, he swung his crop and brought it down hard on the horse's head.

"You old dog!" his shout rang across the forest with despondent vexation.

Stark fields stretched beyond the forest. On the hillside, amid dark buckwheat stubble, lay a poor estate with a few outbuildings and a thatched manor-house. How mournful it all looked in the moonlight! Streshnev stopped. It seemed too, too late, it was so quiet here. He rode into the yard. The house was in darkness. Streshnev jumped down from the saddle. The horse remained standing with meekly drooping head. An old hunting dog lay curled up on the porch, its nose between its paws. It did not move, but just looked at Streshnev, lifting its eyebrows and rapping its tail on the floor in welcome. He walked into the entry which had a stale privy smell in it coming from the closet. The front hall was dusky, the window-panes in icy sweat gleamed golden. A small woman in a soft, light negligee ran in on soundless feet from the dark corridor. Streshnev bent down to her. She twined her bared arms round his thin neck in a quick and close embrace, and cried happily and softly, pressing her head to the coarse cloth of his coat. He could hear her heart beating like a child's, he could feel the little golden cross on her bosom, her grandmother's cross, all her remaining wealth.

"You'll stay till tomorrow?" she asked in a rapid whisper. "You will? Oh, it's too wonderful to believe!"

"I'll go and put the horse away, Vera," Streshnev said, freeing himself. "Till tomorrow, till tomorrow," he repeated, thinking the while: "Oh God, she's growing more rapturous with every day! And what a hard smoker she is, how immoderate in her caresses!"

Vera's face was sweet and velvety with powder. She rubbed her cheek against his lips, then kissed him hard upon them with her soft mouth. The cross gleamed on her uncovered breast. She had put on her sheerest night-gown, her cherished night-gown, the one she saved for the most important occasions.

"To think that fifteen years ago I knew quite definitely that I'd give fifteen years of my life, without a moment's hesitation, for just one rendezvous with her!" Streshnev thought while trying to remember her as a young girl.

3

It was almost dawn. A candle was burning on the floor beside the bed. Streshnev lay on his back, the neck of his shirt undone, his long body stretched out, his small hook-nosed face turned haughtily away into the shadow, his arms flung above his head. Vera sat beside him with her elbows propped on her knee. Her glowing eyes were red and swollen from weeping. She sat smoking and staring dully at the floor. She crossed her legs and found the sight of her small foot in its dainty, expensive shoe very pleasing. But the pain in her heart was too strong.

"I gave up everything for you," she said softly and her lips quivered.

Her voice held so much tenderness, so much childish grief! But, opening his eyes, Streshnev asked her coldly:

"What did you give up?"

"Oh, everything, everything. And above all my honour, my youth..."

"You and I are not so terribly young."

"How rude you are, you don't understand me at all!" she said tenderly.

"All the women the world over always say the same thing. 'Understand' is a favourite word of theirs, only they pronounce it differently. With delight and admiration at first: 'You are so clever, you understand me so!' And later: 'How rude you are, you don't understand me at all!' "

Weeping softly, she went on as if she was not listening:

"Granted I am a failure... But I have always loved music and I love it passionately still, and I would have achieved something, even if it wasn't much..."

"Oh, it wasn't music! And the moment Podarsky—"

"That's rude, Andrei dear... And now I'm a miserable dancing class pianist at a boarding-school, and where, of all places? In the same cursed town I've always hated so! Yet even now, I could have found a man who'd give me a home and children, who'd love and respect me. But the memory of our love—"

Streshnev lit a cigarette and answered her, letting the words drop slowly:

"Vera, we, the breed of noblemen, cannot take love simply. It's poison for us. And it's my life, not yours, that's been ruined. Fifteen or sixteen years ago I came here every day, and I was willing to spend my nights at your threshold. I was a mere youngster then, an emotional and sentimental fool..."

His cigarette went out. He flung it away, dropped his arm down beside his body, and lay staring at the ceiling.

"The love stories of our ancestors, their portraits in the oval frames with a golden rim round the blue... The images of Gury, Simon and Aviv, the patron saints of our ancient families... Who if not you and I were destined to inherit it all? I even wrote love verses then:

And loving you, I dreamed of those
who dreamed
And loved each other here a hundred
years ago.
Beneath the stars that once for them
had gleamed,
I thought of you and wandered to and
fro...

He glanced at Vera and changed to a harsher tone: "Why did you go away—and with whom! Did he belong to your race, your tribe?"

He sat up and fixed a hard, angry stare at her brittle black hair.

"I always thought of you with reverence and rapture, only as my wife to be. But when did fate bring us together? And what did you become to me? My wife? And yet there had been youth, joy, innocence, a dark blush, a fine lawn shirt... What it had meant to me to come here every day, to see your frock, also of lawn, light and youthful, your naked arms, browned by the sun and the blood of our ancestors, your flashing Tatar eyes—eyes that did not see me—the yellow rose in your black, black hair, your smile—somehow amazed and silly then, but a lovely smile—even your walking away from me down the garden path, thinking of someone else, and the way you hit your croquet ball pretending you were really in the game, and hearing your mother's insulting words to me from the balcony—to me it was..."

"She is to blame for everything, not I," Vera brought out with an effort.

"No! Remember the first time you went away to Moscow; you were packing, singing something absently, without seeing me, engrossed as you were in your dreams, your certainty that you would find happiness? I went to see you off on horseback that clear, cold evening. The bright green grass, those rosy stubble fields, and that curtain in the open window of your train... Oh, God!" he said with rancour and tears in his voice, and lay back on the pillow again. "Your hand was scented with verbena that left its fragrance on my hand, too. It got mixed up with the smell of the bridle, of my saddle, of horse sweat, but I could feel it still. I rode along the highroad in the dusk and wept... So if there's anyone who has given up everything, sacrificed his whole life, it's I, old drunkard that I am!"

And, feeling on his lips the salty warmth of tears rolling down his cheeks and moustache, Streshnev swung his legs down on the floor and walked out of the room.

The moon was setting. White, flaky fog clung to the fields below the hill, tinged with deathly blue. A purple glow of sunrise was spreading far beyond. A cock was crowing in the forester's hut in the cold, distantly darkling wood.

Streshnev sat down on the porch steps and felt the waves of dampness chilling his body through the thin shirt.

"And afterwards, of course, the roles were changed," he said quietly, with loathing. "Oh well, it doesn't matter now. It's all over..."

4

They had their morning tea served on a huge chest in the cold hall. The samovar was tarnished and covered with verdigris; the fire in it had gone out long ago. The cold sweat beading the window had receded from the top panes and now they could see the sunny brilliance of the frosty morning and a gnarled tree amid the colourless green which still survived here and there. A barefooted, red-haired servant girl, her face puffy from sleep, came in and said:

"Mitry's come."

"He can wait," said Streshnev without raising his eyes.

Vera did not raise her eyes either. Her face had become pinched overnight, brown smudges lay on her eyelids and under her eyes. Her black dress made her look younger and prettier, and her black hair enhanced the rosy tinge of her face powder. Streshnev's lean, hard face was deathly pale. His head was thrown back and his prominent Adam's apple showed through his coarse, curly grey beard.

Though still low the sun was blinding. The whole of the front porch was white with frost. Rime lay sprinkled like salt on the grass and in the bluish-green shells of cabbage leaves strewn about the yard. The man with leaden eyes who had driven up to the porch in his cart, filled with straw and also covered with frost, was now walking around pressing down the straw. He was holding a pipe between his teeth and a spiral of lilac smoke trailed back over his shoulder. Vera came out of the house wearing a fur coat that had once been expensive but was now shabby and old-fashioned; on her head was a summer hat of black straw trimmed with stiff, rusty satin flowers.

Streshnev accompanied her as far as the highroad, riding behind the cart along paths on which the frost had melted. His horse strained towards the straw. He struck the horse across the nose with his crop and it flung its head and wheezed strenuously. They went on at a crawl and did not speak. The old hunting dog had followed Streshnev from the house, and now it trotted behind him. The sun was warm, the sky gentle and clear.

When they were nearing the highroad, the driver suddenly spoke:

"I'll be sending my youngster to you again next summer, Miss. I reckon he'll help with the shepherding again."

Vera turned round with a shy smile. Streshnev took off his hat, leaned down from the saddle, took her hand and gave it a long kiss. Her lips clung to his greying temple, and she said softly:

"Take care of yourself, dearest. Don't think ill of me."

Once out on the highroad the driver changed to a trot and the cart clattered away. Streshnev turned back and rode straight across the fields without picking his way. The dog followed him at a distance, standing out clearly in the golden fields. He stopped now and again and shook his hunting-crop at it. The dog would stop too and, sitting back on its haunches, it seemed to ask, "But where am I to go?" And the moment he rode on, the dog ambled unhurriedly after him again. His thoughts were on the railway station far away, on the gleaming rails, the smoke pouring from the south-bound train...

He rode down into the desolate fields, rocky in parts, where it was almost hot. There was no sound in the dazzling autumn day beneath the clear blue skies. The stark fields, the gullies, the whole of this great Russian steppe was locked in silence. Fluff from the thistles floated slowly in the air. Finches sat on the burdocks. Thus they would remain all day, only occasionally flying on to another spot, there to continue their quiet, lovely, happy lives.

Capri, December 31, 1912

Light Breathing

Over a fresh mound of earth in the cemetery stands a new cross of oak—strong, heavy and smooth.

In April, the days are grey. Through the bare trees the tombstones in this spacious provincial cemetery are visible from afar, and the cold wind rings on and on in the porcelain wreath at the foot of the cross.

There is a rather large convex porcelain medallion set in the cross, bearing the photograph of a schoolgirl with happy and amazingly lively eyes.

This is Olya Meshcherskaya.

As a little girl she was indistinguishable from the crowd of brown-frocked schoolgirls. What could one say of her, except that she was one of those pretty, rich and fortunate girls, that she was quick to learn but was naughty and quite unimpressed by the admonitions of her form mistress? And then she began to blossom out and to develop very rapidly. By the time she was fourteen—slim-waisted and slender-legged—her breasts and all those curves whose fascination has never yet been expressed in words, were already well outlined; by fifteen, she was known as a beauty. How carefully some of her schoolmates did their hair, how meticulous they were about their persons, how they watched their every controlled movement! But she was afraid of nothing—neither inkstains on her fingers, nor a reddened face, nor tousled hair, nor a knee suddenly bared if she fell when running. Without any effort at all she gradually came to possess all that set her so far apart from the rest of the girls in the last two years—gracefulness, elegance, litheness, and a clear brilliance in her eyes. No one danced at balls as beautifully as Olya did, no one skated as well as she, no one was more popular at the dances and, for some reason, no one was adored by the junior forms more than she was. And then she was no longer a child, and imperceptibly her reputation at school has established: talk started and spread that she was frivolous, that she could not live without admirers, that a boy called Shenshin was madly in love with her, that she was thought to love him too but was so fickle in her treatment of him that he once tried to end his life...

During this last winter of hers, Olya quite lost her head

in a whirl of gaiety, so they said at school. The winter abounded in snow, sun and frost: the sun sank early beyond the tall fir-trees in the snow-swept playground, it was invariably serene and smiling, bringing promise of frost and brightness for the morrow, of strolls along Sobornaya Street, skating in the city park, a rosy glow in the evening sky, music, and the crowd of skaters gliding this way and that, among whom no one seemed more carefree and happy than Olya Meshcherskaya. And then one day, during the midday break, as she raced about the assembly hall, running away from a flock of happily squealing first-form girls, she was suddenly summoned to the headmistress. Abruptly she stopped in her flight, took just one deep breath, smoothed her hair with a quick and already typically feminine gesture, hitched up the corners of her apron on her shoulders, and with radiant eyes ran upstairs. The headmistress, young-looking but grey-haired, sat knitting serenely at her desk beneath the tsar's portrait.

"Good morning, Mademoiselle Meshcherskaya," she said in French, without raising her eyes from her knitting. "I'm sorry to say it's not the first time that I have been obliged to call you here in order to talk to you about your conduct."

"Yes, madame, I am listening," Olya replied, coming closer to the desk. She looked at the headmistress with bright and lively eyes but with no expression whatsoever on her face, and dropped a curtsey as lightly and gracefully as she alone could do.

"You will not listen well, I'm certain of it, unfortunately," the headmistress said and, with a tug at the wool which made the ball spin on the polished floor, drawing Olya's curious glance to it, she looked up and said: "I shall not repeat myself, nor shall I speak at great length."

Olya liked this large and scrupulously clean room very much, with the gleaming tiles of the stove breathing warmth on a frosty day, and the bunch of lilies of the valley on the desk sending up a cool fragrance. She looked up at the young tsar, painted full height in some brilliant hall or other, then at the even parting in the headmistress' neatly marcelled hair and remained expectantly silent.

"You are no longer a child," the headmistress said ponderously, her irritation growing.

"No, madame," Olya replied simply and almost merrily.

"But you are not a woman either," the headmistress said even more ponderously, and the lustreless skin on her face crimsoned slightly. "To begin with, how dare you do your hair like that? It is the style of a grown-up woman!"

"It's not my fault that I have nice hair, madame," replied Olya and raised both hands to touch her beautifully dressed hair.

"Oh, so it's not your fault!" the headmistress said. "Your hair style is not your fault, the expensive combs are not your fault, it's not your fault that you're ruining your parents with those twenty-ruble shoes you're wearing! But I repeat, you are quite losing sight of the fact that you are a mere schoolgirl still..."

At this, Olya Meshcherskaya, retaining all her simplicity and composure, suddenly interrupted her politely:

"Excuse me, madame, but you are wrong. I am a woman. And do you know whose fault it is? It was Alexei Mikhailovich Malyutin, my father's friend and neighbour and your brother. It happened last summer in the country..."

And a month after this conversation, a Cossack officer, unattractive and plebeian-looking, who had no connection at all with the society to which she belonged, shot Olya Meshcherskaya on the station platform in full view of a great crowd of people who had got off the train. Olya's unbelievable confession, which had dumbfounded the headmistress, was confirmed. The officer made a statement to the court officer that Meshcherskaya had lured him on, had been intimate with him, had promised to marry him and then, on the day of the murder, had suddenly told him at the railway station, where she had come to see him off to Novocherkassk, that she had never loved him, that she was only making sport of him with all this talk of marriage, and showed him a page of her diary where she had written about Malyutin.

"I read those lines while she strolled up and down the platform, waiting for me to finish reading them, and there and then I shot her," the officer said. "Here is the diary, see what she wrote in it on July 10 last year..."

This is what they read:

"It's almost two in the morning... I fell into a sound

sleep but instantly I awoke... I have become a woman! Daddy, Mummy and Tolya, all went away to town and I was left alone. I was so happy to be alone! In the morning I walked in the garden and the meadow, I went into the woods, and I fancied I was alone in the whole world, and never in my life did I have such fine thoughts as I had then. I had dinner alone, too, and then I played the piano for a whole hour, and the music made me feel that I would live for ever and be happier than anyone in the world. After that I fell asleep in Daddy's study, and at four Katya woke me up and said that Alexei Mikhailovich had come to call. I was very glad to see him, I so enjoyed receiving and entertaining him. He arrived in a carriage drawn by a pair of very handsome horses, and they remained in front of the porch all the time; he did not go at once because it had been raining and he hoped the road would dry a little towards evening. He was sorry he did not find Daddy at home; he was very jolly and acted the gallant with me, joking and pretending he had been in love with me for a long time. When we were walking in the garden before tea, the weather turned lovely again, the whole of the dripping garden was pierced with sunlight, though it had turned quite cold, and he held my arm and said that we were Faust and Margarete. He's fifty-six, but he's still very good-looking and he's always well turned out. The only thing I didn't like about him was that he came wearing a cape. He smelled of English toilet water, and his eyes were quite young and black, though his beard, elegantly parted in two long strands, was perfectly silver. We had tea on the verandah; I felt a sort of faintness and lay down on the sofa, while he sat and smoked in his chair, and then he came and sat beside me; he spoke pleasantries to me again, then he started examining my hand and kissing it. I covered my face with my silk handkerchief, and he kissed me on the lips through the silk, again and again... I can't understand how it could have happened; I must have gone out of my mind; I never thought I was like that! There's only one way out for me now... I feel such loathing for him, I can't endure it..."

The town becomes so clean and dry in these April days and the cobble-stones so white, that it is easy and pleasant to walk along them. Every Sunday, after church, a little woman dressed in mourning, with black kid gloves and an ebony-handled umbrella, starts down Sobornaya Street on her way out of town. She follows the paved road across the dirty square, surrounded by a great many smoke-blackened smithies and swept by the crisp wind blowing in from the fields; farther on, between the monastery and the prison, there shows a white line of clouds in the sky and a grey patch of fields; after that the way lies through the puddles, close to the monastery wall, a turn to the left and then there is a big, low garden, fenced in with a white wall, with the icon of the Dormition of the Holy Virgin over the gate. The little woman crosses herself discreetly and rapidly and walks down the main alley with sure steps. When she reaches the bench facing the oaken cross, she sits down and stays there for an hour, or perhaps two, in the wind and the coolness of spring, until her feet in their light shoes and her hands in their thin gloves become completely chilled. Sometimes, listening to the spring birds singing sweetly even in the cool, and to the wind ringing in the porcelain wreath, she thinks she would give anything in the world, half a lifetime, so this dead wreath before her need never have been. The wreath, the mound, the oaken cross! Could it really be that beneath the cross lay the girl whose eyes shone so immortally from the porcelain medallion on the cross? How could one reconcile the purity in those eyes with the horror now associated with Olya Meshcherskaya's name? But at heart the little woman is happy, like everyone who has some terrible dream to cherish.

This woman is Olya Meshcherskaya's form mistress, a spinster no longer young, who has long been living in one dream or another that took the place of real life for her. Her brother was the first of these fanciful dreams—a poor and in no way remarkable junior officer—and she put all her hopes in him, in his future which for some reason she thought would be brilliant. After he was killed in action at Mukden, she tried to convince herself that she was working for an idea. The death of Olya Meshcherskaya carried her away on a new dream. And now the girl has become the object of her persistent thoughts and feelings. She visits her grave every holiday, she sits gazing for hours at the oaken cross, she calls up Olya's pale little face as she lay in the coffin among the flowers, and she remembers the words she had once overheard. Walking in the playground during the midday break, Olya Meshcherskaya had been speaking very, very quickly to her best friend, the tall and plump Subbotina.

"I read in one of Daddy's books–he has lots of funny old books–I read what a woman should possess in order to be beautiful... You know, the things it said, I simply can't remember them all! Well, naturally, she had to have black eyes, eyes like boiling pitch–word of honour, that's exactly the way it was put: like boiling pitch! Eyelashes, black as night, a gentle blush caressing the cheeks, a slender body, arms longer than ordinary–can you believe it, longer than ordinary?–small feet, a moderately large bosom, calves with just the proper curve, knees the colour of seashells, sloping shoulders–I learnt a lot of it by heart it's all so true!–but the main thing, d'you know what the most important thing is?–light breathing! And I've got that, you know–listen how I can sigh! I do it lightly, don't I?"

And now this light breathing has been dispelled in vapour over the world, in the clouded sky, in the cold spring wind.

1916

Chang's Dreams

What difference does it make about whom a story is told? Everyone who has ever lived on earth deserves it.

Once upon a time Chang came to know the world and the Captain, his master, with whom his earthly existence became united. A whole six years had passed since then, they flowed away like sand in the ship's sandglass.

Here it was night again–dream or reality?–and again morning was coming–reality or dream? Chang was old, Chang was a drunkard, he dozed all the time.

It was winter in the town of Odessa. The weather was mean and glum, even worse than that Chinese weather had been when Chang and the Captain met for the first time. A fine, stinging snow was falling; the wind drove it at a slant along the slippery ice-clad asphalt of the deserted esplanade and spitefully whipped the face of every Jew who, hunching and thrusting his hands into his pockets, ran to the right or to the left with inept mincing steps. Beyond the harbour, also deserted, beyond the gulf misted with snow, the bare shores were only faintly visible. The mole seemed to be completely enveloped in thick grey smoke; from morning to night the sea rolled its frothing waves over the mole. And the wind whistled shrilly in the telephone wires...

On days such as this life in town begins late. Chang and the Captain do not wake up early either. Six years—is it much or little? In those six years Chang and the Captain have grown old, although the Captain is not yet forty, and their life has changed drastically. They no longer sail the seas, they have been bilged, as the sailors say, and they live not where they once lived, but in a narrow and rather gloomy street, in the attic of a five-storey house smelling of coal and inhabited by Jews of the type who come home only in the evening and eat supper with their hats on, pushed to the back of the head. The room in which Chang and the Captain live is large and cold, the ceiling is low. For another thing, it is always dusky in this room: the two windows in the slanting roof are small and round, much like portholes. Between the windows stands a chest of drawers of sorts, and along the wall—an old iron bedstead. That is all there is in their bleak dwelling, if you do not count the fireplace from which a fresh wind is always blowing.

Chang sleeps in the corner behind the fireplace. The Captain sleeps on the bed. Anyone who has ever lived in attics will easily picture this bed, with the springs sagging down almost to the floor, and the state of the mattress on it; as for the grimy pillow, it is so thin that the Captain has to stuff his pea jacket under it. However, even on this bed the Captain sleeps very soundly, lying on his back with his eyes closed and his face grey—as motionless as a corpse. Oh, what a wonderful bed he used to have! A trim, tall bed with pull-out drawers, a deep, cosy bed, with fine, slippery sheets, and cool snow-white pillows. But even then, even in a swell, the Captain did not sleep so soundly as he does now; he grows very tired in the course of the day, and then he need not worry now if he oversleeps. And, what glad news can a new day bring him? Once, there were two truths in life, perpetually changing places—the first truth was that life was inexpressibly beautiful, and the second that life was only possible for madmen. Nowadays the Captain declares that there is, always was, and shall be forevermore only one truth, the ultimate truth of the Jew Job, a wise man from an unknown tribe, from Ecclesiastes. Very often, sitting in the beer hall, the Captain says: "Remember now thy Creator in the days of thy youth, while the evil days come not, nor the years draw high, when thou shalt say, I have no pleasure in them." Just the same the days and nights still exist, and here it is night again with morning coming again. And the Captain and Chang wake up.

But the Captain, though he is awake, does not open his eyes. What he is thinking about at that moment is not known even to Chang, lying on the floor before the never heated fireplace from which a cool smell of the sea comes all night long. Chang knows only one thing, that the Captain will remain lying thus for no less than an hour. After glancing at the Captain out of the corner of his eye, Chang closes his eyes again and falls into a doze. Chang is also a drunkard, in the morning he is also queasy, weak, and feeling that languid aversion for the world which everyone who sails the seas and suffers from sea-sickness is so familiar with. And so, falling into a doze in that early morning hour, Chang sees a tedious, dreary dream.

This is what he sees.

An old, slant-eyed Chinaman came up on deck, squatted on his haunches, and started whining, begging everyone who walked past him to buy the basket of rotten little fishes which he had brought to sell. The day was dusty and cold on that wide Chinese river. In the Chinaman's boat with a reed sail sat a puppy—a ginger-coloured pup with something of both the fox and the wolf about him, and a collar of thick, coarse fur round his neck. He swept his black eyes sternly and intelligently over the tall metal side of the ship, and held his ears pricked up.

"Better sell me your dog," the ship's young captain, standing on his bridge with nothing to do, shouted in a loud, merry voice to the Chinaman as if he were deaf.

The Chinaman, Chang's first master, glanced up and, astounded by the shout and his stroke of luck, began to bow and lisp: "Velly good dog, velly good dog!" And the pup was bought—for only a dollar—and named Chang, and that very same day he sailed off with his new master to Russia, and at first, for three whole weeks, he was so terribly seasick, so dazed, that he did not see anything—not the ocean, not Singapore, not Colombo...

It was the beginning of autumn in China, the season of bad weather. And Chang began to feel sick as soon as they came out into the mouth of the river. Rain and murk came sweeping straight at them, white caps flickered and flashed, the greyish-green water hurried somewhere nervously and senselessly, swaying and splashing, the flat banks moved farther and farther apart, vanishing in the fog, and there was more and more water around the ship. Chang, his coat glistening with silver raindrops, and the Captain, in his raincoat with the hood raised, stood on the bridge, which felt higher than ever. The Captain gave the orders, while Chang shivered and flinched away from the wind. The water grew ever wider, it spread over the grey horizon and became one with the foggy sky. The wind ripped the spray off the large, roaring waves, hurled itself at the ship blindly, whistling in the yards and noisily slapping the canvas tents down below, as the sailors in their hobnailed boots and wet capes untied them and rolled them up. The wind was on the lookout for a chance to hit the ship a really telling blow, and the moment the ship, which had been bowing slowly to the wind, turned rather sharply to the right, the wind lifted her on to a wave so tall and seething that she teetered on the crest, crashed down, burying her nose in the foam, and in the charterhouse a coffee cup the waiter had forgotten to remove fell off the table to break into clinking smithereens. And after that all hell broke loose!

All kinds of days followed: now the sun scorched them with fire from the sparkling blue skies, now sinister clouds massed together and discharged bolt upon bolt of terrifying thunder and torrents of rain fell on the ship and the sea; and the ship rolled incessantly, even when in port. Chang, utterly exhausted by his sufferings, did not once in those three weeks leave his corner in the hot, darkish passage between the vacant second-class cabins on the quarter-deck, and lay near the high threshold of the door which opened only once a day when the Captain's servant brought him his food. And of the whole long voyage to the Red Sea Chang remembered only the laboured creaking of the timbers, his nausea and the sinking of his heart which went plummeting into the abyss together with the vibrating stern or else was sent flying upward, and that prickly sensation of mortal fear when into the upended stern, which had suddenly toppled sideways, with the screw propellor rattling in the air, smashed a veritable mountain of water with the roar of a firing gun and, blocking out the daylight, poured down the thick glass of the portholes in turbid streams. Chang, lying ill, heard the Captain shouting commands in the distance, he heard the rattling whistles of the bosun, the clatter of the sailors' boots somewhere overhead, the splashing and the slapping of the water, through his half-closed eyes he made out the darkish passage cluttered with straw bales of tea, and became befuddled, dizzy from the heat, from nausea and the strong smell of the tea...

Here Chang's dream breaks off.

He starts and opens his eyes: no, this is not a wave hitting the stern, it is the door downstairs slammed shut by someone. And the next thing, the Captain clears his throat noisily and slowly gets up from his sagging bed. He pulls on and laces his down-at-heel boots, takes his black pea jacket with the brass buttons from under his pillow, puts it on and walks to the chest of drawers, while Chang, shivering in his threadbare ginger coat, rises from the floor, and yawns with a resentful squeal. An almost full bottle of vodka is standing on the chest of drawers. The Captain takes a drink straight from the bottle, his breath catches a bit, and puffing and blowing into his whiskers he goes to the fireplace and pours some vodka for Chang into the saucer that stands near it. Chang starts lapping up the vodka thirstily. The Captain lights a cigarette and goes back to bed, to wait until it grows quite light. They can already hear the distant hum of the tramcar, the clatter of hoofs is already continuous down in the street below, but it is still too early to go out. The Captain lies in bed, smoking. Now that Chang has lapped up all the vodka he wants to lie down too. He jumps on to the Captain's bed, curls up at his feet, and slowly enters that blissful state which vodka invariably produces in him. His half-closed eyes become misted, he gazes weakly at his master and, feeling a mounting tenderness for him, thinks what in human language may be expressed thus: "Ah, you stupid, stupid dear! There's only one truth in the world, and if you only knew how wonderful it is." And once again Chang either dreams or remembers that long-ago morning when after that awful, restless ocean the ship, sailing from China with the Captain and Chang, entered the Red Sea.

And Chang dreams or remembers this:

As the ship passed Perim, she slowed down her flinging and tossing to a lulling swing, and Chang fell into a sweet, deep sleep. Suddenly he was awake. And when he awoke he could not have been more surprised: everything was so quiet, the ship vibrated gently and did not go up or down, the water running somewhere beyond the walls made a quiet, swishing sound, and the kitchen smell coming from under the door was lovely... Chang sat up and looked into the empty mess room: there, in the dusk, something lilac-and-gold was glowing softly, something that eluded the eye but gladdened the heart amazingly; there, the back port-holes had been opened wide into the sunny blue emptiness, into freedom, space and fresh air, and along the low ceiling flowed undulating mirror-clear streams, they flowed and flowed and did not flow away. And the same thing that often happened in those days to the Captain then happened to Chang: all at once he knew that there was not one but two truths in life—one, that living in the world and sailing was awful, and the other... But before he could put this second truth into words, the door was suddenly flung wide and he saw the ladder going up to the spar-deck, he saw the huge black shiny funnel, the clear summery sky, and the Captain coming quickly from the engine room, freshly washed and shaved, a radiant look in his keen light eyes, the tips of his moustache turned up in the German fashion, smelling of toilet water, and dressed in everything snow-white and stiffly starched. And when Chang saw all this he sprang forward so joyfully that the Captain caught him in flight, kissed him on the head and, turning back, leapt on to the spar-deck in three jumps with

Chang in his arms, and from there even higher up to that same bridge where it had been so frightening to be when they were in the mouth of the great Chinese river.

Once there, the Captain went into the chart-house while Chang, who had been dropped on the floor, sat there with his fox's tail fluffed out on the smooth boards. Behind Chang it was hot and light from the sun that had not yet risen very high in the sky. It was probably as hot in Arabia which was moving past very close on their right with its golden beaches, black-and-brown ranges, the peaks like mountains on a dead planet and also heaped with dry gold, and the whole of its mountainous sandy desert seen so clearly that it looked near enough for a jump across. Here, high up on the bridge, it was still early morning with a light, fresh freeze blowing, and there was the First Officer briskly walking up and down—the same officer who so often drove Chang insane with fury by blowing into his nose—a man wearing a white uniform, a white topee, and horrible black glasses through which he kept glancing at the sky-high tip of the front mast above which curled the flimsiest of clouds, like an ostrich feather... And then the Captain shouted from the chart-house: "Chang, breakfast!" And Chang jumped up at once and smartly leapt over the brass threshold into the chart-house. It was even nicer here than on the bridge. There was a wide leather sofa, secured to the wall on which hung some strange round things under gleaming glass with dials and hands like wall clocks, and on the floor stood a finger bowl with a swill of bread and sweet condensed milk. Chang began to lap it greedily, and the Captain got down to work: he unrolled a large sea chart on a counter that ran under the window across from the sofa, and placing a ruler on it drew a long line with red ink. Chang, who had finished eating and still had milk on his whiskers, jumped on to the counter and sat close to the window from which he saw the wide navy blue blouse of a sailor who, with his back to the window, stood behind a wheel with horns on it. And here the Captain, who, it later transpired, was very fond of talking when alone with Chang, said:

"See, laddie, this here is the Red Sea. We must navigate it very cleverly, see how speckled it is with all those little islands and reefs, and I've got to deliver you to Odessa safe and sound because they already know of your existence. I've already blabbed out the secret about you to one very, very spoiled little girl, I bragged to her about you over that long cable which clever people have laid along the floor of all the oceans and seas. You know, Chang, I really am terribly happy, I'm so happy that you can't even imagine how I'd hate to run into one of those reefs and cover myself with disgrace from head to toe on my very first long voyage..." Saying this, the Captain suddenly glared at Chang and slapped him: "Paws off the chart!" he shouted peremptorily. "Keep off the ship's property!" Chang tossed his head, growled and screwed up his eyes. This was the first time in his life that he was slapped on the face; he felt injured, and once again believed that living in this world and sailing was rotten. He turned away, contracting his transparently bright eyes, and, snarling softly, bared his wolfish teeth. But the Captain paid no attention to Chang's hurt feelings. He lit a cigarette, sat down on the sofa, took his gold watch out of his breast pocket, and using a hard finger nail to open the lids gazed at the shiny, strangely alive and hurrying something that ran inside the watch with a merry, tinkling sound, and again spoke to Chang in a friendly tone. He told him once again that he was taking him to Odessa, to Elizavetinskaya Street, that in this Elizavetinskaya Street he had, first, a flat, second—a beautiful wife, and third—a lovely daughter, and that he was really a very fortunate man.

"I am fortunate, Chang, no matter what," the Captain said, and after a moment continued: "This daughter of mine is a very lively, inquisitive and stubborn little girl, it's going to be rough for you at times, for your tail especially. But if you only knew, Chang, what a charming creature she is! I love her so much that it even frightens me: you see, she is my whole world, or perhaps I should say almost she alone, and is that how it should be? And anyway should one love anyone so terribly? Surely all those Buddahs of yours were no stupider than you and I, and just listen to what they say about this love of the world and everything corporeal in general—from sunlight, from a sea wave, from air, down to a woman, a child, and the smell of white acacia. Or again, d'you know what Tao is, also invented by you Chinese? Frankly, I don't know it any too well myself, mate, nor does anyone else, but from what I can understand of it what does it mean? The Mother of All Things produces all things and absorbs them, and in absorbing them again produces all living things in the world, or in other words it's the Way of All Living Things which nothing living should go against. And yet we are always going against it, we always want to change everything our way, not just the heart of the woman we love, but even the whole world! Living in the world is frightening, Chang, it's very good but frightening at the same time, especially for people like me. I'm much too greedy for happiness, and I stray far too often: is this Way dark and malicious, or the very, very opposite?"

After a silence he added:

"Where's the main rub? *When you love someone no power on earth will make you believe that the person you love can possibly not love you.* And that's where the crux is, Chang. But life is marvellous, Lord, it's marvellous!"

The ship, heated by the sun, that had now risen high in the sky, and trembling slightly on the run, was tirelessly cleaving the Red Sea, becalmed in the abyss of sultry air. The radiant void of the tropical sky showed through the open door. It was nearing midday, and the brass threshold blazed in the sun. The glassy waves, flaring up with a dazzling sparkle that lit up the chart-house, were rolling more and more slowly. Chang was sitting on the sofa, listening to the Captain. The Captain, who had been stroking Chang's head as he spoke, suddenly pushed him off to the floor, saying: "It's too hot, mate, get off," but this time Chang did not mind, for life was too good on this wonderful day. And then...

Once again Chang's dream breaks off.

"Come on, Chang, let's go," says the Captain, swinging his legs over the side of the bed. And again Chang sees to his amazement that he is not on the ship in the Red Sea, but in an attic in Odessa, and that it is indeed high noon outside, only the day is not wonderful at all, it's overcast, bleak and unfriendly. And Chang growls softly at the Captain for disturbing his sleep. But the Captain, taking no notice of Chang, puts on his old navy cap and overcoat and walks to the door, hunching his shoulders and stuffing his hands in his pockets. So Chang has to jump down from the bed, whether he likes it or not. The Captain walks down the stairs with a heavy, reluctant tread, as if he were performing a necessary but tiresome task. Chang rolls down the stairs rather quickly, buoyed up by the still tingling irritation which always follows upon the blissful state produced by the vodka...

Yes, it's two years now that all Chang and the Captain have been doing, day in day out, is going from one restaurant to the other. There they drink, eat, and look at the other drunks, eating and drinking at the other tables amid the noise, the tobacco smoke and all kinds of stench. Chang lies on the floor at the Captain's feet, and the Captain sits and smokes with his elbows firmly planted on the table, from force of a seaman's habit, waiting for the hour when, in obedience to some rule he himself has invented, it will be time to shift to another restaurant or café. They have breakfast at one place, drink coffee at another café, have dinner somewhere else, and supper at a different restaurant again. As a rule, the Captain sits locked in silence. But sometimes, when he meets one of his old friends, he will talk all day, with never a pause, about the worthlessness of life, treating himself and his friend to more and more wine all the time, and not forgetting Chang who always has a saucer or something set beside him on the floor. This is exactly how they will spend today too. They have arranged to have breakfast with the Captain's old friend, an artist in a top hat. And this means that they will first sit in a smelly beer hall among ruddy-faced Germans—dull, matter-of-fact people who work from morning to night in order to eat, drink, work again and produce their like,—then they'll go to a coffee house packed with Greeks and Jews, whose whole existence is as senseless but very anxious, engrossed in constant anticipation of stock market rumours, and from the coffee house they will go to the restaurant where all the dregs of humanity forgather, and there they will stay till late at night...

A winter day is short, and it is even shorter when you sit chatting with a friend over a bottle of wine. Chang, the Captain and the artist have already been to the beer hall and the coffee house, and they have been sitting and drinking for hours in the restaurant. And again the Captain, his elbows planted on the table, is passionately asserting to his friend that there is only one truth in life, a malicious and vile truth. Take a look about you, he is saying, just think of all those people you and I see every day in the beer hall, in a coffee house, in the street. My friend, I've seen the whole planet, life is the same everywhere. It's all a pack of lies that people supposedly live by some higher feelings: they have no god, no conscience, no sensible aim in life, no love, no friendship, no honesty—not even simple compassion. Life is a bleak winter day in a filthy pub, that's all it is...

And Chang, lying under the table, listens to all this talk in a drunken haze from which the excitement has now evaporated. Does he agree or disagree with the Captain? He can't answer definitely, and since he can't he must be in a bad way. Chang does not know, he cannot understand whether the Captain is right or wrong, but then, of course, it's only in sorrow that we all say: "I don't know, I can't understand." In gladness, every living creature is certain that it knows everything, understands everything... But suddenly a ray of sunlight seems to pierce this fog: the band leader raps his baton sharply on the music stand, a violin begins to play, then a second one, a third one... They sing more and more passionately, more and more tunefully, and now Chang's soul overflows with quite another sadness, quite another anguish. His soul trembles from some inexplicable rapture, from some dulcet pain, from a yearning for something and Chang no longer knows if he's asleep or awake. He surrenders to the music with his entire being, he follows it meekly into some other world, and again he seems himself on the threshold of that beautiful world as a foolish, trusting puppy on the ship in the Red Sea...

"Now, how was it really?" he is either thinking or dreaming. "Ah yes, I remember: it was good to be alive on that hot day in the Red Sea." Chang and the Captain sat in the chart-house and then stood on the bridge... Oh, how gloriously bright was the sun, the sparkle, the infinite blue! How wonderfully colourful against the blue of the sky were all those sailors' blouses—white, red and yellow—hung up with the sleeves spread out to dry on the poop. And then Chang, together with the Captain and the other seamen, all of whom had brick-red faces, oily eyes and white, sweating foreheads, had lunch in the hot first-class mess room where the electric fan hummed and blew air from a corner, and after lunch he took a nap, after tea he had dinner, and then sat upstairs again outside the chart-house where a servant had placed a canvas armchair for the Captain, and stared beyond the sea at the variously coloured and variously shaped little clouds tinted with the palest of greens, and at the wine-red sun which was shorn of rays and which, on touching the hazy horizon, suddenly stretched out to look like a dark, flame-coloured mitre... The ship ran after the sun so quickly that the smooth humps of water with a sheen like bluish-purple leather seemed to race past, but the sun was hurrying, the sea seemed to be sucking it in, and it grew smaller and smaller until it became a long red-hot coal, then it shuddered and went out, and the moment it went out a shadow of sorrow fell upon the whole world, and the wind that had been blowing harder as night approached became more agitated. Gazing at the dark flame of the sunset, the Captain sat with uncovered head, his hair ruffled by the wind, a pensive, proud and sad look on his face, but *even so* he appeared happy and not just this whole ship, hurrying in obedience to his will, but the whole world was in his power, because in that moment the whole world was in his soul–and also because already then there was the smell of wine on his breath...

But when night came, it was frightening and magnificent. It was pitch-black and alarming, with the erratic wind and the waves, full of a light of their own, smashing against the ship so noisily that at moments Chang, running after the Captain who paced the deck quickly with never a pause, jumped back from the railing with a terrified squeal. And again the Captain picked Chang up and putting his cheek to Chang's excitedly beating heart–it was beating just as excitedly as the Captain's–walked with him to the very end of the deck, to the end point, and stood there in the darkness for a long time, fascinating Chang with a wondrous yet terrible spectacle: from under the tall and enormous stern, from under the gruffly churning screw, myriads of white-hot needles burst forth with a crisp rustle and instantly flew away into the snowily glittering wake, left by a brilliant flash inside the seething humps of water, and as the flash waned they went on smoking mysteriously with a pale green phosphorescence. The wind whipped at Chang's face from this side and that, now painfully, now softly, and chilled the thick fur on his chest as it blew the hairs apart. Clinging hard and familiarly to the Captain, Chang smelt something like cold sulphur, he breathed of the ploughed-up bowels of the sea, and the stern trembled, lifted and lowered by some great and unutterably free force, while he himself rocked and rocked, excitedly watching the blind and dark but prodigiously alive and gruffly mutinous Deep. Now and again, a particularly wayward and heavy wave, noisily racing past the stern, shed an eerie light on the Captain's hand and silvered his clothes...

That night the Captain took Chang to his cabin, a large and cosy cabin softly lit by a desk lamp with a red silk shade. On the desk, which was fitted tightly into the space next to the Captain's bed, stood two framed photographs in the light and the shadow thrown by the lamp. One was a photograph of a pretty and cross-looking girl, her hair done in tight sausage curls, who sprawled in a deep armchair with a petulant air. The other showed a young woman, standing with a white lace parasol on her shoulder and wearing a wide-brimmed lace hat and a lovely spring frock. She was slender, delicate, charming and wistful like a Georgian princess. And with the black waves roaring outside the open window, the Captain said:

"No, Chang, that woman is not going to love you and me. *There are women, you see, who are always pining with a melancholy sort of longing for love and who, for this reason, never love anyone*. There are such women, and how can you blame them for their heartlessness, deceitfulness, their dreams of the stage, of an automobile of their own, of picnics on private yachts, of some sportsman who unsticks his greasily pomaded hair into a central parting? Who can solve the riddle of such women? To each his own, Chang, and do they not, perhaps, obey those most mysterious biddings of Tao as obeyed by some marine creature, freely moving about in these black waves covered with a lurid carapace?"

"Phew," the Captain said, sitting down on a chair and shaking his head as he unlaced his white shoes. "If you only knew what hell it was when I felt for the first time that she was already not wholly mine, the night she went to a ball at the yacht-club by herself for the first time and returned in the early hours looking like a wilted rose, pale because she was tired and because her excitement had not yet subsided, with eyes that were all black pupils and so remote from me! If you only knew what a priceless fool she wanted to make of me, with what innocent amazement she asked me: 'Poor dear, still up?' At that, the words stuck in my throat, she understood me at once, said no more, she only darted a look at me and silently began to undress. I wanted to kill her, but she said to me dryly and calmly: 'Help me undo my dress at the back,' and meekly I went to her and with shaking hands started undoing all those hooks and snaps, and no sooner did I see her body in the opened dress, the hollow between her shoulder blades, her chemise which was tucked into her corsets, and no sooner did I catch the smell of her black hair and glanced into the lighted mirror which reflected her breasts, pushed up by her corset, than I..." And, with a hopeless gesture, the Captain let the sentence trail.

He undressed, lay down and put out the light, and Chang, twisting and turning before he settled down to sleep on the leather armchair beside the desk, saw the black pall of the sea furrowed by intermittent streaks of a white flame, he saw some lights flickering ominously on the black horizon, he saw a frightening, live wave starting from back there and coming at them with an angry hissing and growling to rear higher than the side of the ship and peeping into the cabin—a fairy-tale dragon with glowing eyes of transparent emeralds and sapphires, the whole of it translucent from the glow—he saw how the ship pushed the dragon away and ran on at an even speed amid the heavy, heaving masses of this antemundane natural element, which had become alien and hostile to us, called the ocean...

In the night the Captain suddenly shouted something and himself startled by his shout, which rang out with a humiliating pitiful passion, woke up instantly. He lay still for a minute, then he sighed and said with a bitter chuckle:

" 'As a jewel of gold in a swine's snout, so is a fair woman without discretion!' You never said a truer word, Solomon the Wise!"

Groping in the dark, he found his cigarette case, lit a cigarette, drew on it once or twice, then dropped his hand

and fell asleep with the tip of the cigarette glowing between his fingers. All became silent again, and only the waves glittered, swayed and noisily raced past the ship. The Southern Cross emerged from behind the black clouds...

Suddenly, there is a deafening, thunderous crush. Chang jumps up in fright. What's happened? Has the ship struck some underwater reef again as it did three years ago because the Captain was drunk? Or has he fired his pistol again at his lovely, melancholy wife? No, it's not night, there is no sea, nor is it a sunny winter day in Elizavetinskaya Street. This is a very brightly lit, noisy and smoke-filled restaurant, and it was the drunken Captain who crashed his fist down on the table as he shouted to the artist:

"Rot, rot! A jewel of gold in a swine's snout, that's what your woman is. 'I have decked my bed with coverings of tapestry, with carved works, with fine linen of Egypt: come, let us take our fill of love ... the goodman is not at home... Ah, woman! her house is the way to hell, going down to the chamber of death...' But enough, enough, my friend. It's late, they're locking up, let's go."

In another minute the Captain, Chang and the artist are already out in the dark street where the snow-laden wind blows out the lamps. The Captain kisses the artist and they go their different ways. Chang, half-asleep and sour-tempered trots along the pavement behind the quickly striding and swaying Captain. Another day has passed—dream or reality? And again there's darkness, cold and weariness in the world...

And that is how monotonously pass Chang's days and nights. And then, all of a sudden one morning the world, like their ship, runs head-on into an underwater reef, hidden from inattentive eyes. Awakening that winter morning Chang is amazed by the great silence reigning in the room. He jumps up quickly, runs to the Captain's bed and sees him lying with his head thrown back, his face pale and frozen, and his half-closed eyes motionless. At the sight of those eyes Chang lets out such a heart-rending howl that one might think an automobile speeding along the esplanade had knocked him down and cut him in two.

Later, when the door never stands still because of all those people coming and going, coming and going, and talking in loud voices—janitors, policemen, the artist, and all the other gentlemen with whom the Captain used to sit and drink in the restaurants, Chang turns to stone. Oh, what terrible words the Captain once spoke: "In the day when the keepers of the house shall tremble ... and those that look out of the windows be darkened ... and also when they shall be afraid of that which is high, and fears shall be in the way ... because man goeth to his long home, and the mourners go about the streets ... for the pitcher be broken at the fountain, or the wheel broken at the cistern..." But even horror Chang does not feel now. He is lying on the floor, with his muzzle turned to the corner and his eyes shut tight so as not to see the world, to forget it. And the world hums above him, hollowly and remotely, like the sea over someone who is sinking deeper and deeper into its infiniteness.

It is only on the porch of the church that he recovers his senses. He sits there with drooping head, feeling half-dead and dull, and shivering all over. Suddenly the door of the church is thrown wide open, and a beautiful picture, woven of sound and song, smites at Chang's eyes and heart: he sees before him a darkish Gothic hall, lights like red stars, a whole forest of tropical plants, an oakwood coffin raised high on a black platform, a black crowd of people, two women—divine in their marble beauty and deep mourning, who may have been the elder and the younger sister,—and above all that a hubbub, bursts of thunder, the priests and deacons crying out in ringing voices about some sorrowful rejoicing of the angels, jubilation, confusions, grandeur, and heavenly singing covering everything. And at this sonorous spectacle Chang feels such heartache and rapture that all his hair stands up on end. The artist, emerging from the church in that very moment with eyes red from weeping, stops in amazement.

"Chang, Chang, what's the matter with you?" he asks anxiously, bending down to Chang.

Touching Chang's head with a trembling hand, he bends lower still, and their eyes, filled with tears, hold so much love for each other when they meet that Chang's whole being shouts soundlessly to the whole world: "No, no, there is some other truth on earth, a third truth, unknown to me!"

That same day, on returning from the cemetery, Chang moves over to the house of his third master, once again to the top floor, into an attic, but a warm one smelling beautifully of cigars, softly carpeted, comfortable with old-world furniture, hung with huge pictures and samite draperies... Darkness descends, the fireplace is heaped full of somberly crimson heat, Chang's new master sits in an armchair. He has not even taken off his overcoat and silk hat; he sits in this deep armchair smoking a cigar and gazes into the dimness of his studio. Chang is lying on the hearthrug, his eyes closed and his nose resting on his paws.

Someone else is also lying down now, there, outside the darkening town, behind the cemetery wall in something that is called a tomb or a grave. But that someone is not the Captain, no. If Chang loves and senses the Captain, if he sees him with the vision of memory, that deity which is something no one understands, it means that the Captain is still with him in that world without beginning or end to which Death has no access. In that world there must be only one truth—the third—and what that truth is is known to his Master to whom very soon now Chang must return.

Vasilyevskoye, 1916

Mitya's Love

1

Mitya's last happy day in Moscow was on March 9th. At least that's how it seemed to him.

That morning, some time after eleven, he and Katya were walking along Tverskoy Boulevard. The winter had suddenly given way to spring, and it was almost hot in the sun. It was as if the larks* had really come and brought

*Buns shaped like birds were baked for Forty Martyrs' Day, March 9th (Old Style), and people greeted each other with the words: "The larks have come!"—*Tr.*

warmth and joy with them. Everything was wet and thawing, melted snow dripped from the houses, the yard-keepers were breaking up the ice on the pavements and sweeping the sticky snow from the roofs, and there was an air of animation in the crowded streets. The high-sailing clouds were dissolving into fine white smoke and merging with the moistly blue sky. There, in the distance, they could see Pushkin standing on his tall pedestal in an attitude of benevolent meditation, and the Passions Monastery, bathed in radiance. But the nicest thing of all was that Katya, looking especially pretty that day, seemed so close in her artless mood, often taking Mitya's arm with such childlike trustfulness and glancing up into his face, while he, feeling happy almost to the point of arrogance, walked with such a free stride that she could hardly keep up with him.

When they came to Pushkin's monument she said unexpectedly:

"You have such a funny, such a boyishly sweet, self-conscious way of stretching your big mouth when you laugh. Please don't mind, because it's this smile I love you for. And also for your Byzantine eyes..."

Trying not to smile and not to show that he felt both flattered and slightly hurt, Mitya replied in a friendly tone, looking at the monument that now towered over them:

"As for boyishness, it seems to me that there is not much difference between us in this respect. And a Byzantine I resemble as much as you a Chinese empress. You've simply gone crazy over all these Byzantiums and Renaissances... I just cannot understand your mother!"

"If you were Mother I suppose you'd lock me up in the *terem,** wouldn't you?" Katya asked.

"Not in the *terem*, but I'd simply lock the door against all that Bohemian crowd, all those future celebrities from the studios and conservatories and theatrical schools," Mitya replied, still trying to keep calm and speak in a casually friendly tone. "You told me yourself, didn't you, that Bukovetsky had already asked you to the Strelna for midnight supper, and Yegorov wanted to sculpt you naked as a sort of dying sea wave or something, and

**Terem*—in ancient Russia the women's quarters where no male outsiders were allowed.—*Tr.*

you were terribly flattered by the honour, of course."

"I won't give up art even for you," Katya said. "Perhaps I am wicked, as you often tell me," she said this although Mitya had never told her she was wicked, "perhaps I am bad, but just take me the way I am. And let's not quarrel, do stop being jealous just for once, it's such a glorious day! Can't you understand, that for me you're anyway the best, the only one?" she asked quietly and insistently, now looking into his eyes with conscious seductiveness, and recited slowly and dreamily:

Our souls have pledged a troth,
In secret, and unvoiced...

This was the last drop, this verse, and Mitya felt really badly hurt. By and large, even that morning there had been much that was unpleasant and hurtful. There was that joke of hers about his boyish self-consciousness, he had heard similar jokes from Katya before, and she meant what she said. She often showed, in one way or another, that she was more grownup than he, frequently (involuntarily, that is, quite naturally) demonstrating her superiority, and it pained him to recognise it as a sign of her being secretly and corruptly experienced. Then there was her *anyway*. "You're *anyway* the best", and her saying it in a voice suddenly lowered for no reason that he could see. But what had been most unpleasant were those two lines of verse, and her affected manner. However, even the verse and the affectation, which more than anything else reminded him of the set which was taking Katya away from him and which incited his hatred and jealousy, Mitya bore relatively well on that happy March 9th, his last happy day in Moscow, as he often thought of it afterwards.

That day, as they walked back from Zimmermann's on Kuznetsky Most, where Katya bought several pieces by Scriabine, she alluded in passing to Mitya's mother, and with a laugh, said:

"You can't imagine how frightened I am of her already now!"

For some reason they had never spoken of the future in all the time of their love, or what their love would end in. And now Katya suddenly spoke of his mother as if she were taking it for granted that Mitya's mother was her future mother-in-law.

2

After that day everything seemed to go on as usual. Mitya escorted Katya to the drama classes of the Art Theatre, to concerts, literary evenings, or spent the evening with her in her house in Kislovka, staying till two o'clock in the morning, enjoying the strange freedom given Katya by her mother, a lady with raspberry-pink hair who always had her face rouged and was always smoking a cigarette, a nice, kind woman (she had long been living apart from her husband who had another family now). Katya sometimes came to Mitya's room at the students' rooming-house in Molchanovka, and as before their rendezvous, almost from beginning to end, were heavily drugged with kissing. Still, Mitya could not help thinking that something frightening had begun, that something had changed, that Katya was becoming different.

How quickly that unforgettable, light-hearted time had flown past, when at the very beginning of their acquaintance they suddenly felt that they enjoyed nothing so much as talking *tête-à-tête* (from morning till night, if they could), and when Mitya so unexpectedly found himself in that fabulous world of love, which he had been secretly anticipating since childhood, since boyhood. This light-hearted time was December—a frosty, fair December that adorned Moscow with thick rime every day and with the opaquely red ball of the low-hanging sun. January and February swept Mitya's love into a whirl of continuous happiness already attained or, at any rate, on the point of being attained. But already then something began (more and more often) to disturb, to poison this happiness. Already then he often fancied that there were two Katyas: one was the Katya whom Mitya had desired and demanded from the moment they met, and the second was the authentic, ordinary girl, and the two failed dismally to correspond. Even so, what he felt then was incomparable to what he was going through now.

Everything could be explained away. Spring had

brought its seasonal feminine worries, purchases had to be made, new clothes had to be ordered, alterations made to one thing or another, and Katya really had to go to the dressmaker's very often with her mother. Besides, she was to have her exams soon at the private theatrical school where she was studying. And so her preoccupation, her absent-mindedness might be quite natural. And Mitya drew on this thought for comfort every minute of the day. But it did not help, for that which his mistrustful heart told him to the contrary was stronger, and was confirmed more and more clearly: Katya's inner inattentiveness to him increased, and with it grew his mistrustfulness and jealousy. The praise lavished on Katya by the director of her theatrical school turned her head, and she could not deny herself the pleasure of telling Mitya about it. "You are the pride of my school," the director had said to her. During Lent, in addition to class studies, he undertook to give her private instruction so as to show off his pupil at the forthcoming exams with especial brilliance. It was known that he depraved his pupils, and every summer took one of them along with him to the Caucasus, to Finland, or abroad. And now it occurred to Mitya that the director had his eye on Katya for this summer, and although it wasn't her fault, she probably felt and understood everything and this, to Mitya's mind, already made her relationship with the director both dirty and sinful. This thought tormented him all the more as Katya's attention drifted too obviously away from him.

Something seemed to be distracting her from him. He could not think calmly of her director. And not just the director. Some other interests seemed to prevail over Katya's love. Interest in whom, in what? Mitya did not know, and he was jealous of everyone and everything, mainly of that imagined life which she had already begun to live in secret from him. She was being irresistibly drawn away from him to something that might be too appalling to even contemplate.

Once Katya said to him, perhaps more in earnest than in jest, in the presence of her mother:

"Yours is a *Domostroi** attitude to women in general,

**Domostroi*—an old Russian book of rules on strict family behaviour.—*Tr.*

Mitya. You'll develop into a perfect Othello. Falling in love with you and marrying you is the last thing I'd ever do!"

"And I cannot imagine love without jealousy," her mother said. "If there's no jealousy there's no love, I always think."

"No, Mummy," Katya said, as usual parroting someone else's words, "jealousy means a lack of respect for the person you love. If I am not trusted, it means I am not loved," she said, avoiding Mitya's eyes.

"And I still say that jealousy is, in fact, love," her mother insisted. "I've even read this somewhere. It was very well proved, with examples from the Bible, too, where God Himself is called jealous and revengeful..."

As for Mitya's love, it expressed itself almost exclusively in jealousy these days. It was not a simple jealousy either, but a special kind, he imagined. He and Katya had not yet overstepped the last line of intimacy, but they did permit themselves too much in those hours when they remained alone. Katya was even more passionate than before. But even this seemed suspect to him now, and at times roused a terrible thought in him. All the thoughts and feelings which comprised his jealousy were terrible, but there was one among them which was more terrible than the rest and which Mitya could neither define nor really understand. Those manifestations of passion, that which was so wonderful, sweet, sublime and most beautiful in the world when shared by him and Katya, seemed unspeakably revolting and even perverse when he thought of Katya with another man. He hated her violently then. Everything that *he* did with her when they were alone was heavenly and chaste, but the moment he pictured another man in his place the shamelessness of it made him want to strangle Katya, and not his imagined rival but Katya in the first place.

3

On the day of Katya's exam, which at last took place (in the sixth week of Lent), the torment which Mitya had been suffering seemed to be fully justified.

Katya simply did not see him, she did not notice him, she belonged wholly to the public, she was entirely estranged from him.

She was a great success. She was dressed all in white like a bride, and her nervous excitement made her lovely. Everyone applauded her warmly, and the director—a self-opinionated actor with dispassionate, sad eyes—who sat in the front row, corrected her now and again from sheer conceit, speaking in a low voice which was yet projected for all to hear and which sounded unbearable.

"A bit less reciting," he told her calmly, confidently, and so imperiously as if Katya were his private property. "Do not act. Live the part," he articulated impressively.

And it was unbearable. As unbearable as the reading itself which earned her applause. Katya's cheeks burnt from embarrassment, her voice broke at moments, she ran out of breath, and it was touching and sweet. But she read her part with that cheap melodiousness, sham emotion and silliness in every sound which was considered the height of artistic rendering in that hateful set where Katya already belonged heart and soul. She did not speak, she ejaculated all the time with a sort of sickeningly languid passion, an immoderate, unreasonably insistent entreaty, and Mitya suffered such shame for her that he did not know where to look. The most terrible thing of all was that mixture of angelic purity and depravity in her, in her flushed face, in her white dress which seemed shorter than it ought to be because everyone looked at her from below as she stood on the stage, in her white slippers and white silk stockings. "The girl sang in a church choir," Katya was reciting with affected, immoderate naiveté about some girl or other who was supposed to be innocent as an angel. Mitya felt both a sharpened closeness to Katya, as one always does feel in a crowd to someone one loves, and a spiteful animosity while being proud of her and aware that after all it was to him that she belonged, at the same time realising with a heart-rending pain: no, no more!

After the exam, there were days of happiness again. But Mitya could not believe in them as light-heartedly as before. Katya, recalling the exam, told him:

"You silly goose! Didn't you feel that it was for you alone that I read the poem so well?"

He could not forget what he felt at the exam, nor could he admit that he still felt the same. Katya sensed his hidden feelings and once, during a quarrel, she cried:

"I can't understand how you can love me if you think there's only bad in me! And what do you want of me anyway?"

He himself could not understand what he loved her for, although he was aware that his love, far from diminishing, grew all the stronger as he waged his jealous struggle against someone or something because of her, because of this love, because of its mounting strength and its increasing demands.

"You love only my body, and not my soul," Katya once told him bitterly.

These were again someone else's, theatrical words, but for all their silliness and banality they touched upon a tormentingly insolvable problem... He did not know what he loved her for, he could not tell exactly what he wanted. To love–just what did it mean? It was impossible to answer this question because the word "love" had never been given an exact definition in anything he had ever heard or read about it. Both in books and in life there seemed to be a tacit agreement made for all time to speak only of a sort of incorporeal love, or only of passion, as it was called, of sensuality. His love was not like either. What did he feel for her then? That which was called love, or that which was called passion? Was it Katya's soul or her body that drove him to the point of fainting, of dying in an agony of bliss, when he unbuttoned her blouse and kissed her breasts, heavenly, lovely and virginal, exposed with a soul-shattering submissiveness and the shamelessness of the purest innocence?

4

She was changing more and more.

The success of her exam meant a great deal. But still, there were some other reasons besides.

With the coming of spring Katya suddenly turned into a young society lady, all dressed up and always hurrying somewhere. Mitya now felt frankly ashamed of his dark corridor when she came to his rooming-house—she always came in a cab now, she never came on foot—and walked swiftly down this corridor with her silk skirts rustling and the short veil pulled down over her face. She was invariably tender with him now, but as invariably she came late and cut short their rendezvous, saying that she had to go to the dressmaker's with her mother.

"We're cutting a swath for all we're worth!" she said, looking at him gaily with wide, shining eyes, knowing perfectly well that Mitya did not believe her and still saying this, as there was nothing left to talk about any more. She hardly ever took her hat off now or let go of her umbrella as she sat away from him on his bed, driving him crazy with her silk-stockinged legs. And before she left, telling him that she would not be at home again that evening as she had to go somewhere with her mother of course, she invariably repeated the little trick that was clearly intended to dupe him and reward him for all his "silly torments" as she put it: with a histrionically thievish glance at the door, she would slip down from the bed, wiggling her hips along his legs, and say in an urgent whisper: "Kiss me, quickly!"

5

At the end of April Mitya at last decided to give himself a rest and go to the country.

He had tormented himself and Katya into a state of utter exhaustion, and his suffering was all the more unbearable because it appeared to be so groundless. Indeed, what had happened, what had Katya done? And Katya said to him once with the firmness of despair:

"Go away, yes, go away, I can't stand any more! We have to part for a time to clear up things between us. You've grown so terribly thin that Mother is convinced you have consumption. I can't go on!"

And so Mitya's departure was decided. To his great surprise, although he was beside himself with grief, he was almost happy to be going away. Once the matter was settled, the happiness he knew before was unexpectedly restored to him. After all, he terribly wanted not to believe in that horror which haunted him day and night, and the slightest change in Katya was enough to reassure him. Katya became tender again and passionate without any play-acting now–he felt it with the unerring sensitiveness of jealous natures–and as before he stayed with her in her house until two in the morning, and again they had something to talk about, and the nearer came the day of his departure the more ridiculous seemed their separation and the need to "clear up things between them". Once Katya even cried, and since she never cried her tears made her terribly dear to him, he felt a stab of acute pity for her and something like guilt.

Katya's mother was leaving at the beginning of June to spend the whole summer in the Crimea, and she was taking Katya with her. They arranged that Mitya would come to Miskhor and they would meet there.

As he made his preparations for departure, he walked about Moscow in that state of strange intoxication which a person who is already gravely ill but is still bravely keeping his feet may feel sometimes. He was morbidly, drunkenly unhappy, and at the same time he was morbidly happy and touched by Katya's returned closeness and the fuss she made over him–she actually went with him to buy the leather belts for his bags as if she were his fiancée or his wife–and by the return of almost everything that reminded him of the beginning of their love. He perceived everything about him in the same spirit–the houses, the streets, the people driving or walking along, the weather threatening rain as it always did in spring, the smell of dust and rain, and the church-like smell of the poplars breaking into leaf behind the garden walls in the side streets. Everything spoke of the bitterness of separation and the sweetness of the prospective rendezvous in the Crimea where nothing would stand in their way any more and everything would come true (what he meant by everything, Mitya did not really know).

On the day of his departure his friend Protasov dropped in. Among school seniors and university students one encounters quite a number of youths whose cultivated style of behaviour is to regard everything with a good-naturedly sullen mockery, and assume an air of someone older and more experienced than everyone else in the world. Such was Protasov, one of Mitya's closest friends, his only real friend for that matter, who knew all the secrets of Mitya's love in spite of his secretiveness and reticence. He watched Mitya tightening the belts on his suitcase, he saw how his hands shook, and with a sadly wise smile said:

"What innocents you are, heavens above! But when all's said and done, it's time you realised, my dear Werther from Tambov, that Katya is, first and foremost, a most typical female being, and no one can do anything about it, not even the chief of police himself. You, a male being, are climbing up a wall, setting the highest demands on her, prompted by the procreative instinct, which is, of course, perfectly legitimate and even sacred in a sense. Your body is the supreme reason, as Herr Nietzsche has so rightly observed. But it is as legitimate that you might break your neck upon this sacred course. After all, you know, there are males in the animal world who have to pay with their lives for their first and last love act. But since this doesn't quite apply to you, take care of yourself and hold your horse! What I mean is, don't do anything hasty. Remember? 'Cadet Schmidt, I promise you, summer will come back!' Katya is not the only pebble on the beach. I see that you don't agree, judging by your efforts to strangle the suitcase, and that this pebble is a pebble after your own heart. Come, forgive me for offering you advice you didn't ask for, and may St. Nicholas keep you safe!"

Protasov squeezed Mitya's hand hard and left. As Mitya tightened the belts on the hold-all with his pillow and blanket, he heard through the open window the trial blasts emitted by the student who lived across the yard, took singing lessons and practised from morning till night. Now he began to sing "The Asra". Mitya hurried with his packing, buckled the belts carelessly, grabbed his cap, and went to Kislovka to say good-bye to Katya's mother. The tune and the words of the song sounded so obstinately and repetitiously in his head that he saw neither the streets nor the passers-by, and walked more drunkenly than he had done these last few days. It really did seem that Katya was the only pebble on the beach and that "Cadet Schmidt wanted to shoot himself". Ah well, there was nothing for it if she was the only pebble on the beach, and his mind turned back to the song and the part where the Sultan's daughter, walking in the garden, saw a black slave who stood beside the fountain "paler than death"; she asked him who he was and where he came from, and he answered her, beginning grimly, yet meekly, with morose simplicity:

My name is Mohammed...

and ending in an exultantly tragic shriek:

I come from those poor Asra,
*Once we have loved, we die!**

Katya was getting dressed to go to the railway station to see him off, and called to him affectionately from her room—the room where he had spent so many unforgettable hours!—that she would be there before the first bell went. Her dear, kind mother with the raspberry-pink hair was sitting alone in the drawing-room, smoking, and gave Mitya a very sad look—she must have understood everything long ago, and guessed what was going on. Mitya, blushing furiously and trembling inwardly, kissed her soft, flabby hand, inclining his head filially, and she kissed him on the temple several times with a mother's gentleness, and made the sign of the cross over him.

"Ah, my dear," she said with a shy smile, and quoted Griboyedov: " 'Live laughing!' Well, God bless you, go now, go..."

6

Having done the last thing that had to be done in the rooming-house, he packed his luggage with the help of the servant into the lopsided cab, squeezed himself in beside his things, started off and instantly had that peculiar feeling that grips one upon leaving a place—a stretch of life is finished (and forever)!—and together with it comes a sudden lightness, a hopeful expectation of something new

**"My name is Mohammed... Once we have loved we die!"* These lines are from a lied by Anton Rubinstein (1829-1894) to a poem by Heinrich Heine. V. Muromtseva-Bunina says that her husband was haunted by these lines for twenty-two years, and finally put them into "Mitya's Love".

about to begin. He was calmer now, and took a new, brighter look about him. It was the end. Good-bye to Moscow and to everything he had gone through here. A thin rain was falling, the sky was overcast, the side streets were desolate, the cobblestones gleamed darkly like iron, and the houses looked dirty and wretched. The cabman went at a pace so leisurely that it was sheer agony for Mitya who, what was more, had to turn away every other minute and try to hold his breath in from the man's hangovery stench. They passed the Kremlin, then Pokrovka, and again turned down side streets where in the front gardens crows cawed huskily, presaging rain and night, but it was spring anyway, and the air smelt of spring. They arrived at long last, and Mitya dashed after a porter, ran through the crowded waiting rooms, out to the platform, and on to the third tracks where the long and heavy Kursk train stood ready and waiting. In this huge and ugly crowd of passengers that were assaulting the train, and over the heads of all the porters, pushing the clattering luggage trundles and yelling warnings, he instantly saw her standing all by herself in the distance as a creature apart not just in this crowd but in the whole wide world. The first bell had already gone—this time it was Mitya who was late, not Katya. It was touching of her to come earlier, she had been there waiting for him, and now she rushed to him, once again full of wifely concern, saying:

"Dearest, hurry and take your seat! The second bell will go in a moment!"

After the second bell, she gazed at him more touchingly still as he stood in the doors of the third class coach, already packed full and stinking. Everything about her was lovely—her dear, pretty face, her small, trim figure, her freshness, her youth in which womanliness was still mixed with childishness, her raised, shining eyes, her modest blue hat which had a certain elegant jauntiness in the curve of the brim, and her dark-grey suit. Mitya could actually and adoringly feel the very cloth from which it was made and the silk of the lining. He stood there, lean and clumsy, wearing tall, coarse boots for the journey, and an old jacket with tarnished copper buttons. But all this notwithstanding, Katya was gazing at him with a sincerely loving and sad look. The third bell smote his heart so unexpectedly and harshly, that he jumped down madly to the platform, Katya rushed to him as madly and as stricken with horror, he pressed his lips to her gloved hand, leapt back into the coach, and waved his cap to her in frenzied rapture. Through his tears he saw her gather up her skirts with a hand, and sail backwards together with the platform, still keeping her eyes on him. She sailed faster and faster, the wind tousled Mitya's hair more and more angrily as he poked his head out of the window, the locomotive gathered speed, demanding the right of way with an ever more relentless, brazen and menacing roar, and all at once she seemed to be swept off, together with the end of the platform...

7

The long, spring twilight, darkened by the rainclouds, had begun some time ago, the heavy train rumbled across the bare, cool field—it was still early spring in the open country—the conductors came down the corridor checking tickets and putting candles into the lanterns, and Mitya still stood beside the rattling window cherishing the smell of Katya's glove on his lips, his entire being still aflame with the piercing fire of that last moment of parting. And the whole of that long Moscow winter, a happy and painful winter that had transformed his whole life, passed before his mind's eye, and he saw it in a new, different light. And Katya, too, appeared before him in a new light, again in a new light... Who was she, what was she? Love, passion, soul, body, what did they mean? No, there was something different, quite different, and not this at all! The smell of Katya's glove—was it not also Katya, was it not love, soul, body? And the peasants, the workmen in his coach, the woman taking her ugly child to the toilet, the dim candlelight in the rattling lanterns, the twilight in the bare fields—all of this was love, soul, anguish, and ineffable joy.

In the morning they arrived at Orel, and Mitya changed into the local train that stood at the farthest platform. What a simple, serene and familiar world this was compared with the Moscow world which had already receded into the fabulous past, and whose centre had been Katya, who seemed so lonely now, so pathetic, and loved with tenderness only! Even the sky, touched here and there with the pale blue of rainclouds, even the wind here was simpler and calmer... The train started from Orel at an unhurried pace, and Mitya, sitting in an almost empty coach, was unhurriedly eating a honey cake. Little by little the train gathered speed and rocked Mitya to sleep.

He only woke up at Verkhovye. The train had stopped. The station had a back of beyond look, for all that it was a busy, bustling place. A pleasant smell of cooking came from the kitchen. Mitya had a plate of cabbage soup and a bottle of beer, enjoying both, and then fell into a doze again, feeling terribly tired. The train was racing through a birch forest when he awakened; this was familiar country, and he was to get off at the next station. The spring twilight was gathering again, and a smell of rain and, perhaps, mushrooms poured in through the open window. The forest was still quite bare, but the rumble of the train resounded more clearly here than it did in the open country. The tiny station lights twinkled with a springtime wistfulness in the distance. Here was the tall semaphore, the green light looking especially charming in a bare birch forest in twilight like this, and now the train, clattering and knocking, changed to another track... O Lord, how rustically shabby and dear was the labourer waiting for his young master on the platform!

The twilight and the clouds darkened as they drove from the station across a large village which was still muddy as in early spring. Everything was submerged in this incredibly gentle twilight, in the profound silence of the earth, the warm night, merging with the darkness of the indistinct, low-hanging rainclouds, and Mitya marvelled happily again: how serene, simple and plain was the village with its smelly chimneyless cottages, long locked in sleep—good people don't waste any kindling for light after Annunciation—and how nice it was in this dark and warm steppeland world! The tarantas jolted over the ruts in the muddy road past the homestead of a wealthy peasant behind which rose tall oak trees, still bare and grim-looking with dark rooks' nests stuck in the branches. A peasant stood at the cottage door peering into the dusk—a strange figure of a man who might have come from ancient times: bare-footed, wearing a ragged cloth coat and a sheepskin hat on his long, straight hair. It began to rain. A warm, dulcet, fragrant rain... Mitya thought about the girls and young women sleeping in these cottages, about the intimately feminine which he had come close to in that winter with Katya, and everything merged into one whole–Katya, the village girls, the night, the spring, the smell of rain, the smell of earth, ploughed up and waiting to be fecundated, the smell of horse sweat, and the remembered smell of Katya's kid glove.

8

Life in the country began for him with peaceful, enchanting days.

That night, as he drove from the station, Katya's image seemed to fade and become dissolved in his surroundings, but it didn't really, he only imagined it and went on imagining it for a few days longer while he caught up on his sleep, found his bearings, and adjusted himself to the newness of the impressions, familiar to him since childhood, of his home, the village, springtime in the country, and the vernal nudity and emptiness of the world, chaste and young again in its readiness to blossom out anew.

The estate was not a large one, the house was old and plain, and the simple farm work did not call for a large staff. A quiet time began for Mitya. His sister Anya was in the second form of grammar school, and his brother Kostia was in the cadet corps, and they were not expected home from Orel until the beginning of June when their summer holidays started. Mitya's mother, Olga Petrovna, was always busy, as she managed the estate herself with only the steward to help her, and because she often had to go out into the fields to see to the work she went to bed as soon as it turned dark.

When the day after his arrival Mitya, having slept for twelve hours, having bathed and changed into clean clothes, came out of his sunny room which faced the garden and had an eastern exposure, and walked through all the other rooms, he was keenly aware of their homeliness and their comforting, peaceful simplicity. All the furniture stood where it had stood for many years, and there was the same familiar and pleasant smell everywhere. The rooms had been given a spring cleaning for his homecoming, and the floors had been scrubbed everywhere except for the dining-room which adjoined the front hall. A freckled village wench, hired for the spring cleaning, stood on the window-sill near the door opening on to the veranda, straining upward to reach the topmost pane which she polished with a swishing sound, and her reflection in the bottom panes was bluishly remote. Parasha, the housemaid, carrying the large washrag she had rinsed in a pail of hot water, walked barefoot across the flooded floor, stepping on her small heels, and, pausing to wipe the sweat off her flushed face with the crook of her bare arm, said to Mitya with friendly familiarity in a quick patter of words:

"Go and have your breakfast, your Mama left for the station with the steward before it was light, and you didn't even hear them leave, I shouldn't wonder..."

And instantly Katya reminded him of herself compellingly. Mitya caught himself lusting after that bare, feminine arm, after the feminine curve of that body straining upward to the top window pane, after her skirt and the sturdy bare legs it covered, and elatedly welcomed Katya's power over him, his belonging to her, and her unseen presence in all his impressions of that morning.

He felt this presence more and more keenly with every day, and it became more and more beautiful as he recovered his balance, and began to forget that other, ordinary Katya who, in Moscow, had so frequently and so hurtfully failed to become one with the Katya of his dreams.

9

This was the first time that he was living at home as a grownup treated even by Mother in a new way, but the most important thing of all was that he was living with the first real love in his heart, already living the love which his entire being had secretly yearned for since childhood, since boyhood.

He was only a child when something inexpressible in the language of humans stirred in him both wondrously and mysteriously. Some time and somewhere, it must have also been in spring, in the garden near the lilac shrubs—he remembered the pungent smell of the blister beetles—he, a very young child, had been standing with some young woman, probably his nanny, and suddenly a heavenly light fell on something before him, perhaps his nanny's face or else the sarafan on her ample bosom, and some emotion passed through him in a hot wave, stirring to life inside him, indeed as a baby stirs in its mother's womb... But he remembered it as in a dream. And everything that happened afterwards—in his childhood, boyhood and school years, also had that dreamlike quality. He went into raptures of a special kind, that were not like anything else he knew, over one or another of the girls who came to his parties with their mothers, and with a secret, devouring curiosity followed every movement of these small, enchanting creatures, who were also unlike anything else he knew, wearing their pretty party dresses, slippers, and silk bows in their hair. He was enraptured (this was later, when he went to school in town) much more consciously too, and for the duration of almost the whole autumn, with a schoolgirl who often appeared in the evening in the garden next door to sit in her favourite tree; he was enraptured with her sportiveness, her mocking air, her brown dress, the round comb in her hair, her dirty hands, her laughter, and her shrill shouting—it all held such magic that Mitya thought about her from morning till night, moping and sometimes even crying, wanting something from her with a gnawing longing. Then this infatuation also passed and was forgotten, there were new ones, longer or shorter ones, but always as deeply secreted, then there were the joys and sorrows of momentous infatuations at school dances ... there was a sort of languor in his body, and a vague premonition of something, an anticipation in his heart...

He was born and bred in the country, but when he started going to school he always had to spend the spring in town except for one year, the year before last, when coming home for Butter Week he fell ill and stayed behind the whole of March and half of April to recuperate. It was a time he would never forget. He was in bed the first two weeks, and it was only through the window that he could see how the sky, the snow, the garden, the tree trunks and branches changed with every day as warmth and light increased in the world. One morning it was so warm and sunny in his room that flies were awakening and crawling over the window panes; and in the afternoon of the following day, when the sun was behind the house shining into the windows on the other side, the snow seen through his window had already taken on its springtime, bluish pallor, and the big clouds–white against the blue of the sky–seemed to rest on the crowns of the trees; and then, a day later, the sky turned such a bright blue in the gaps between the clouds, the bark of the trees glistened so wetly, and the melting snow dripped so busily from the roof that he looked and looked and could not look his fill! After this came warm mists and rain, the snow melted and was nibbled away in a matter of days, the ice on the river broke, and the ground in the garden and the yard eagerly shed the last of the snow and showed dark once more. Mitya was long to remember that day at the end of March when he went for his first ride. The sky was not a vivid blue, but it glowed with youthful vigour through the pale and colourless trees in the park. Out in the open the wind was still rather fresh, the stubble had a wild, rusty look, and where the field was being ploughed–it was already being ploughed for oats–there was something primordially virile in the black, unguent earth that lay upturned in clods. He rode across the stubble and these clods to the forest, and in the clear air he saw it from afar–bare and small, visible all through–then he descended into the dells, his horse's hoofs rustled through the deep layer of last year's leaves, dry and pale in places, wet and brown in others, and crossed the gullies filled in with the leaves but still streaming with melted snow, where sultry-golden woodcocks, tearing out of the bushes with a crashing noise, started up from right under his horse's hoofs. What did that spring mean to him, and especially that day out in the country when the wind blew so freshly into his face, when his horse, after the hard going across the sodden stubble and the upturned black earth, breathed so noisily through its inflated nostrils, snorting and emitting a growl from its depths with such magnificent, savage strength? That spring, it seemed to him then, was his first real love, when he was in love with someone or something all day and every day, when he loved all the schoolgirls and all the village wenches in the world. How remote that time seemed to him now! What a child he was then, an innocent, simple-hearted boy whose modest sorrows, joys and daydreams were so poor, really! His objectless, incorporeal love was but a dream or, rather, a remembrance of some beautiful dream. Now, there was Katya, there was someone who embodied the entire world and triumphed over this world.

10

In his first week at home, Katya reminded him of her existence ominously, just once.

Late one evening, Mitya went out to the back porch. It was very dark, quiet, and smelt of damp earth. The tiny stars, peeping from behind the clouds above the vaguely darkling park, seemed to be blinking away their tears. Suddenly, the quiet was rent by a wild, fearful hooting that rose to a yelp, a screech. Mitya froze with fear, then he cautiously descended the porch steps, stepped into the darkness of the garden that seemed to be watching him hostilely from all round, and stood still, listening alertly: what was it, where was it, the creature that had screamed so startlingly and so horribly? It was probably a screech owl performing his love act, that's all, Mitya told himself, and yet his whole being cringed as if the devil himself were invisibly present in this darkness. And suddenly a soul-shattering wail sounded somewhere quite close, there was a crackling and rustling in the tops of the trees, and the devil flew soundlessly into some other part of the garden. There, he first began to yelp, then whimper piteously, imploringly like a child, sob, flap his wings and gurgle in agonising ecstasy; he uttered little squeals, and then went off into peals of such perverted laughter as if he were being tickled or tortured. Trembling all over, Mitya peered into the darkness, straining his hearing to catch every sound. Suddenly, the devil's voice broke on a sob, and piercing the dark garden with a shriek of mortal ecstasy, died away. There was no sight or sound of him. After waiting a few minutes longer for a repetition of these mating horrors, Mitya quietly returned home, and all night long he was tormented in his sleep by all those morbid and revolting thoughts and feelings which his love had come to in Moscow that March.

However, his torments were soon dissipated in the morning's sunlight. He remembered how Katya cried when they decided that he really had to leave Moscow for a time, he remembered how gladly she clutched at the thought that he, too, would come to the Crimea at the beginning of June, how touchingly she helped him in his preparations for departure, and how she saw him off... He took out her photograph, and for a long, long time peered at her face, at the beautifully dressed hair on her small head, and marvelled at the innocence and clearness of her direct, open (and a bit wide-eyed) glance... He wrote her an especially long and especially warm letter that was full of faith in their love, and after this he again felt her constant, loving and radiant presence in everything he lived by and delighted in.

He remembered what he felt when his father died nine years ago. It also happened in spring. The day after his father died, Mitya feeling dismayed and terrified walked timidly across the dining-room where his father, decked out in his nobleman's full-dress coat, lay on the table with his large, pale hands folded on his raised chest, his sparse beard looking very black, and his nose white. Mitya came out on the front porch, glanced at the huge coffin lid, covered with gold brocade, that stood beside the front door, and suddenly felt death in the world. It was everywhere: in the sunlight, in the new grass there in the yard, in the sky, in the garden... He went into the garden, to the lime walk dappled with sunlight, to the side paths that were even sunnier, gazed at the trees and the first white butterflies, listened to the first, sweetly trilling birds, and did not recognise anything. In everything there was death, the frightening table in the dining-room and the long brocaded lid on the porch! The sun did not shine quite as before, the sprouting grass was not the same green, the butterflies did not hover as before over the grass that was as yet only hot on the surface—everything was different from the day before, everything had changed because the end of the world seemed so near, and even the loveliness of spring and its eternal youth seemed pitiful and sad. This lasted for a long time, it lasted all spring, the feeling was as tenacious as the fearsome, nauseating, sweetish smell that lingered, or was fancied to linger, for such a long time in the scrubbed and many times aired house...

Mitya was under a similar spell now, only it was a spell of quite another order: this spring, the spring of his first love, was unlike any spring he had known before. Once again the world seemed changed, it was filled with something extraneous, as it were, but this something was by no means hostile or horrible and, on the contrary, it blended beautifully with the joy and youthfulness of spring. This extraneous something was Katya, or rather that sweetest thing in the world which Mitya wanted and demanded of her. As the spring days passed he demanded more and more of her. And now that she was not there herself and there was only her image, a non-existent and merely desired image, she did not in any way upset the immaculateness and beauty of that which was demanded of her, and with every day Mitya became more and more keenly aware of her in anything he glanced at.

11

He was delighted to know this was so before he had been home a week. That was only the eve of spring. He sat at the open window in the drawing-room with a book and looked through the spaces between the silver firs and pines growing in the front garden at the muddy little river meandering across the meadow and at the village on the hillside beyond. In the bare branches of the ancient birches in the neighbouring garden, the rooks were still cawing incessantly from morning till night, exhausted by their blissful fussiness, as they cawed only in early spring; the village on the hillside still had its drab, wintry look, and only the willows were turning a yellowish green. He went into the garden: the garden had not gained stature yet, it was bare and transparent—only the lawns were green and dotted with little blue flowers, and acacias along the walks had opened up, and one solitary cherry-tree in the depression in the southern part of the garden had blossomed out in pale little flowers... He went out into the country: the fields were still desolate and grey, the stubble still bristled, and the mud on the roads across the fields had dried in mauve-coloured humps. All this was the nakedness of youth, of expectation, and all of it was Katya. And it only seemed that he was diverted by the village girls, hired to do this or that job in the house, by the labourers in the servants' hall, by books, walks, visits to the peasants he knew in the village, conversations with his mother, and drives to the distant fields in a droshky with the steward (a big, rough-spoken retired soldier).

Then another week passed. It had been raining hard in the night, and the very next day the hot sun seemed to come into its own, the spring was no longer timid and pale, and the world began to change in leaps and bounds. The stubble fields were ploughed up and changed into black velvet, the balks sprouted grass, the sward everywhere looked more succulent, the sky became a deeper and brighter blue, the garden quickly donned its new, green finery that looked soft to the touch, the grey clusters of lilac turned mauve and fragrant, and a multitude of large, black flies, glinting with the blue of metal, appeared on the dark-green lacquered leaves and on the hot sunspots on the paths. The branches of the apple and pear trees still stood out starkly, their small, greyish and childishly soft leaves barely showing, but these apples and pears, stretching their crooked boughs under the other trees, were already bursting into curly, milky-white blossom, and with every day the flowers became all the whiter, thicker and more strongly scented. Mitya watched all the springtime changes taking place about him with a glad keenness. Katya's image did not retreat or get lost among these changes, and on the contrary she participated in them, lending them herself, and her beauty that blossomed out together with the efflorescence of spring, with the garden growing ever more luxuriantly white, and the deepening blue of the sky.

12

One day, coming for tea to the dining-room, flooded with the late afternoon sun, Mitya was startled to see the mail which he had been vainly awaiting all morning, lying beside the samovar. He walked to the table quickly—Katya should have answered at least one of his many letters by now—and was dazzled and frightened by the sight of a small, exquisite envelope, addressed in her familiar, pathetic writing. Clutching the envelope, he marched out of the house into the garden and down the main walk. He went to the farthest part of the garden where the gully ran across it, stopped, took a look about him, and quickly ripped open the envelope.

It was a short letter, just a few lines, but Mitya had to read it five times to understand what it said. "My beloved, my only one!" he read again and again, and his head spun from these exclamations. He looked up from the letter: the sky above the garden was gloriously and radiantly clear, all round him the garden was a glory of snowy whiteness, a nightingale, sensing the cool breath of approaching night, was trilling clearly and strongly, with delicious and utter abandon in the fresh, new leafage of the distant bushes—and the blood receded from his face as a chill ran over his scalp.

He walked home slowly—the cup of his love was full to the brim. And the following days he carried it as carefully and gently, happily awaiting her next letter.

13

The garden was decking itself out variously.

The huge old maple which towered over the whole southern part of the garden and was visible from everywhere, looked even taller and more conspicuous in its new green garb.

The main walk at which Mitya was always looking from the windows of his room also appeared more imposing now. The crowns of the old limes which had also burst into leaf had risen higher and were spreading their pale-green lace over the garden.

And under the maple and under the limes were the dense, curly, fragrant and cream coloured blossoms.

All of this: the huge, luxuriant crown of the maple, the pale-green range of limes, the bridal whiteness of the apple, pear and bird-cherry blossoms, the sunlight, the blue of the sky, the lilac bushes, the acacias, the currant shrubs, the nettles, the burdocks, the wormwood, and whatever else grew and spread at the farther end of the garden, in the gully, along the side paths, and at the foot of the house's southern wall–all of it was astonishingly lusty, new and fresh.

The verdure advancing on all sides upon the clean, green courtyard made it seem less spacious, and the house–smaller and prettier. It looked as if it were expecting guests, for all the doors and windows stood open all day long: in the white dining-room, the old-fashioned blue drawing-room, the small sitting-room, also blue and hung with oval miniatures, in the sunny library, and the large and empty corner room with old icons in the corner facing the door and low ashen bookcases along the walls. The trees, now that they had come nearer, looked into the windows everywhere, and with their various greens and the bright blue bits of sky between the branches enhanced the holiday look of the house.

But there was no letter. Mitya knew that Katya had no flair for letter-writing, he knew what an effort it always cost her to get down to it, to seat herself at her writing table, find a pen, note-paper and an envelope, and buy a stamp... But sensible reasoning was once again of little help to him. The happy, even proud confidence with which he had for several days looked forward to her next letter vanished, and he worried more and more. After all, a letter like her first one had to be immediately followed by something even more promisingly wonderful. But Katya did not write.

He did not go to the village as often or for rides in the country. He sat in the library leafing through journals that had been lying for years in the bookcases, yellowing and drying up. In these journals there were many beautiful poems by poets of old, wonderful lines which almost always spoke of the same thing, of that which since the beginning of the world has filled all poems and songs, which lived in Mitya's soul now and could always in one way or another be applied to himself, to his love, to Katya. For hours on end he sat in the armchair beside the open bookcase and with self-inflicted torture read over and over again:

Come to the garden, dearest heart, our tryst to keep,
There's none but stars to see us, all the world's asleep.

All these magic words, all these appeals seemed to be his own and addressed only to her, to the one Mitya saw in everything and everywhere all the time. At moments, the appeal sounded almost wrathful:

O'er the water slowly moving
Sail the swans so smoothly, smoothly,
And the river runs its course.
Come! The clouds are fast assembling,
And the leaves are trembling, trembling.
Come, while shine the stars on us!

Closing his eyes he repeated this plea again and again, the call that came from a heart brimming with potent love, yearning for its moment of triumph, for the bliss of consummation. Then, he just sat there for a long time staring into space and listening to the deep rural silence surrounding the house, and shook his head sorrowfully. No, she did not respond to his call, she was silent, sparkling somewhere far away, in the alien and remote Moscow world! And once again tenderness ebbed from his heart, and he repeated as a grim, wrathful incantation:

Come! The clouds are fast assembling,
And the leaves are trembling, trembling,
Come, while shine the stars on us!

14

One day, he took a nap after lunch—they had lunch at noon—and then left the house, going with unhurried step into the garden. Village girls worked there most days digging round the apple trees, and they were there now. It was already becoming a habit of his to go and sit beside them in the afternoon, and chat.

It was a hot, still day. He walked in the lacy shadow of the limes and saw the snow-white curliness of the blossoms all round him. The blossoms were especially dense and vigorous on the pear trees, and their whiteness, combined with the bright blue of the sky, produced a sort of mauve impression. The pears and the apples were flowering and shedding their blossoms at the same time, and the dug-up ground under them was strewn with the pale petals. The warm air was filled with their sweetish, delicate scent mixed with the smell of manure, heated by the sun, in the barnyard. When an occasional white cloud diluted the deep blue of the sky, the warm air and the smell of decay became even more delicate and sweet. The fragrant warmth of this paradise of spring hummed contentedly with the buzzing of the honey-bees and bumble-bees immersed in the melliferous curly snow. And all the time, a nightingale here or another one there gave voice to relieve its complacent daytime boredom.

The walk ended at the gate to the threshing floor. There was a fir grove in the far corner of the garden to the left, and two girls wearing something colourful were working among the apple trees close to it. Mitya, as usual, turned off the main walk and, bending low, made his way through the spreading branches that brushed his face with a feminine touch and smelt of honey and, perhaps, lemon. And, also as usual, one of the girls—the red-haired, skinny Sonka—gave a burst of wild laughter on catching sight of him and screamed in mock alarm:

"Help, the master is coming!"

.She jumped down from the thick branch of the pear tree on which she was resting, and rushed to her spade.

Glashka, the second girl, pretended not to notice Mitya at all. With no sign of flurry, she put her foot down firmly on the iron spade—she wore short boots made from soft black felt and the tops were full of white blossoms—pushed it in hard, turned over the slice of earth she had cut off, and sang in a loud, strong and pleasant voice: "Ah, my garden, my garden, who are you flowering for?" Glashka was a tall, strong wench who always kept a serious mien.

Mitya went and sat on the old pear branch lying in the fork of the tree where Sonka had been sitting. The girl flashed a look at him and asked with a forced gay familiarity in her loud voice:

"Just out of bed, are you? Mind you don't sleep through everything!"

She was in love with Mitya and tried hard to hide it from him, but her efforts failed her and she was self-conscious in his presence, said things without thinking yet always hinting at something, instinctively knowing that there was something behind the absent-minded mood in which he always came and went. She suspected him of sleeping with Parasha, or at any rate trying to get her to sleep with him; she was jealous, and betrayed her feelings by speaking to him now tenderly, now sharply, and looking at him with amorously dreamy or else coldly hostile eyes. And Mitya derived a strange pleasure from all this. There was no letter from Katya, and he did not really live now—he existed day after day in constant waiting, the tedium of waiting becoming as hard to bear as the impossibility of confiding the secret of his love and his torments to anyone, of speaking about Katya and the hopes he pinned on the Crimea, and so Sonka's hints at his being in love with someone were pleasing to him, for in a way they did touch upon the secret anguish in his heart. Nor was he unmoved by her infatuation with him, which meant that her feelings were more or less close to his, making her a sort of secret participant in the love life that went on in his soul, and giving him a strange hope at moments that in Sonka he might find a confidante, or even a substitute in something for Katya.

And here Sonka, without knowing it, had again touched upon his secret by saying: "Mind you don't sleep through everything!" He looked about him. The dense, dark-green fir grove looked almost black in the brilliant light of the day, and the sky showing through the peaked crowns of the trees appeared extravagantly blue. The new foliage of the limes, maples and elms, pale-green from the sunlight seeping through it everywhere, formed a light and jolly canopy for the garden, and all the lawns and paths were dappled with bright sunspots. The hot, fragrant blossoms seemed to be made of porcelain, glowing and gleaming where the sun pierced this canopy. Smiling in spite of himself, Mitya asked Sonka:

"Just what can I sleep through? That's the whole trouble that I haven't anything to do."

"Go on with you! I'll believe you!" Sonka shouted back with gay impudence, once again giving him the pleasure of being disbelieved that he had no love affair on, and suddenly she screamed at the top of her voice at the small red calf with a curly white fringe that had slowly emerged from the fir grove and, stealing up to her from behind, started chewing the flounce of her cotton dress: "The plague take you! Here's one that wants mothering!"

"Is it true what people say about your turning down that suitor?" Mitya asked, not knowing what to say yet wanting to keep the conversation going. "It's a rich home, they say, and he's a good-looking fellow, so why did you refuse him and go against your father's wishes?"

"He's rich, but a bit of a fool, his wits don't last him a full day," Sonka replied saucily, feeling somewhat flattered. "I maybe have someone else on my mind..."

The silent and serious Glashka shook her head in disapproval and without pausing in her work said:

"The way you talk, letting your tongue run like that! It'll get you talked about in the village."

"Oh, shut up, don't croak!" Sonka snapped. "I'm no sheep, I hope, I can stand up for myself."

"And who is that someone else you're thinking about?" asked Mitya.

"As if I'd tell you!" Sonka replied. "I've fallen in love with our old shepherd, every time I see him I go hot all over! I ride old horses too, no worse than you," she said with a challenge, obviously hinting at Parasha who at twenty was already considered an old maid.

Suddenly she threw down her spade with an audacity to which by virtue of her secret infatuation with the young master she felt she had a sort of right, flopped on the ground, stretched out her legs, shod in coarse old boots worn over motley woollen stockings, and dropped her hands helplessly.

"Oh dear me, I've done no work and I'm so tired," she said, laughing, and suddenly burst into a shrill song: "There's a hole in my old boots with the patent-leather toes..."

Screaming with laughter, she said: "Come with me to the hut to take a rest, I'm game for anything!"

Infected by her laughter, Mitya smiled a wide, awkward smile, jumped down from the branch, lay down beside Sonka and pillowed his head in her lap. She pushed his head off, and he put it back again, repeating in his mind one of the many poems he had been feeding on lately:

Here's a rose, it's happiness
That its petals has unfolded
And has moistened them with dew...
And a world of love, immense,
Fragrant, beautiful, untold,
Lies before me, me and you...

"Don't touch me," Sonka shouted with genuine alarm now, as she tried to lift his head and push it away. "I'll give such a yell that all the wolves in the woods will start howling! I have nothing for you, it's all burnt out!"

Mitya closed his eyes and lay without speaking. The sun, percolating through the branches, leaves and blossoms, dappled his face hotly and tickled it. With both tenderness and spite Sonka gave his coarse black hair a tug, saying: "It's like horsehair, honestly!" and pulled his cap down over his face. With the back of his head he felt her legs—women's legs are the most fearsome thing in the world!—and touched her stomach; he could smell her cotton skirt and blouse, and all of it became mixed with the flowering garden and with Katya. The amorous calls of the nightingales far away and close to, the incessant voluptuously drowsy buzzing of the countless bees, the warm mellifluous air, and the very feel of the ground under his back filled him with a yearning for a superhuman happiness. And suddenly, in the fir grove, something rustled, chortled with malicious humour, and then called out: "Coo-coo! Coo-coo!" so startlingly close, so eloquently and distinctly, that he could actually hear the sharp little tongue rasping and trembling, and his wanting Katya, his imperative desire that she should immediately give him this superhuman happiness gripped Mitya so furiously that, to Sonka's astonishment, he sprang to his feet and strode off with resolute step.

Together with this mad desire, this urgent demand of happiness and that resonant voice, sounding with such terrible clarity in the fir grove directly above him and cleaving this entire vernal world down to its very bowels, came a thought that there was not going to be a letter, there could not be one, that something had happened in Moscow or was about to happen, and that he was done for, finished!

15

In the house, he stopped before a mirror for a brief moment. "She is right," he thought. "If not Byzantine, my eyes are anyway those of a madman. And look at this scragginess, this crude, bony clumsiness, the sombre black eyebrows, the coarse blackness of the hair, horsehair really as Sonka said!"

He heard the patter of bare feet behind him, and turned round in embarrassment.

"You must be lovesick to stare in the mirror like that," Parasha said in a fondly teasing tone as she ran past to the veranda with a steaming samovar in her hands.

"Your Mama has been looking for you," she added, plunking the samovar down on the table set for tea, and turning round to give Mitya a quick, keen glance.

"Everybody knows, everyone has guessed," Mitya said to himself, and forced himself to ask:

"Where is she?"

"In her room."

The sun, having travelled round the house, now peeped from the western sky under the branches of the pines and silver firs surrounding the veranda. The spindle bushes below also shone with a summery glassiness. Hot spots of sunlight lay on the faintly shadowed table, covered with a gleaming tablecloth. Wasps hovered over the pretty bread-basket, the cut-glass jam bowl, and the teacups. It was a picture of summer bliss in the country where one could be happy and carefree. To forestall his mother who, of course, guessed as much as everybody else, and to show her that he had no secrets at all, Mitya left the dining-room and went down the corridor into which opened the door of his own room, his mother's and two spare rooms where Anya and Kostia lived in the summer. It was dusky in the corridor, and his mother's room was shadowed with blue. The room was cosily crowded with the most old-world furniture there was in the house: chiffoniers and chests of drawers, a large bed, and an icon stand with an icon-lamp usually burning before it, although Olga Petrovna was never known to be particularly devout. The open windows faced the deeply shadowed and neglected flower garden where the main walk began, and beyond the shadow stretched the cheerfully green and white garden on which the sun shone straight down. Olga Petrovna, a tall, lean, black-haired, serious woman of forty, was sitting in an armchair near the window with her spectacles on and her eyes on her knitting as she quickly dug in and out with her crochet hook, and never a glance at the long familiar view.

"Is there something you wanted, Mother?" Mitya asked, entering the room and stopping in the door.

"Oh no, I simply wanted to see you. I hardly ever see you nowadays, except at dinner," Olga Petrovna replied somehow too casually, without pausing in her work.

Mitya remembered Katya telling him on March 9th that she was afraid of his mother, and he remembered the secret, lovely implication there certainly had been in her words...

"Perhaps you wanted to say something to me?" he mumbled.

"Nothing really, except that it seems to me that you've had the doldrums these last few days," his mother said. "Perhaps you should go for a drive ... to the Meshcherskys, for instance... They have a houseful of girls," she added, smiling. "They're a very nice and hospitable family altogether, I think."

"I'll go with pleasure one of these days," Mitya replied with an effort. "Come, let's have tea, it's so lovely on the veranda. We'll talk over tea," Mitya said, knowing perfectly well that his mother was too perspicacious and reserved to return to this useless conversation.

They stayed on the veranda until almost sunset. After tea, Olga Petrovna took up her knitting again and talked about the neighbours, household affairs, Anya and Kostia—Anya, imagine, had failed in one of her exams again and would have to take it in August! Mitya listened and replied now and then, but all the time he felt he was going through something similar to what he went through just before leaving Moscow—his mind was befuddled again as though he were gravely ill.

That evening, he paced the house for two solid hours, walking across the dining-room, drawing-room, sitting-room and library, and starting back from its southern window that stood open into the garden. From the windows of the dining-room and the drawing-room he saw the soft, crimson glow of the setting sun through the branches of the pines and silver firs, and heard the labourers talking and laughing as they gathered outside the servants' hall for supper. The even, nondescript blue of the evening sky with a motionless pink star high above showed through the library window and the other windows he passed; the green crown of the ancient maple and the wintry whiteness of everything that was blossoming in the garden looked beautifully picturesque against this blue background. And he paced on and on, no longer worrying how this pacing would be interpreted in the house. He clenched his teeth so hard that a pain shot through his head.

16

After that day he stopped following all those changes round him which the approaching summer was bringing about. He saw and even felt these changes, but they had lost their individual meaning for him and the enjoyment he derived from them was only morbid now: the better it was the more agonising it was for him. Katya had become a real obsession; he sensed Katya's presence in everything and behind everything to the point of absurdity, and as each new day confirmed more and more frighteningly that she no longer existed for him, that she was already in someone else's power, that she was giving herself and her love to someone else, her love that had to belong wholly to him, everything in the world appeared unnecessary and tormenting, and the more beautiful it was the more unnecessary and tormenting it was to him.

He hardly slept at night. The magic of these moonlit nights was inimitable. It was very, very quiet in the milky garden. The nightingales, exhausted with yearning, sang their song with care, vying with one another in the sweetness and refinement of the melodies as well as in the purity and sonority of the perfectly rendered notes. The tender and very pale moon hung low over the garden, and it was invariably accompanied by an ineffably charming ripple of pale, bluish clouds. Mitya slept with the curtains drawn back, and all night long the garden and the moon looked into his windows. And every time he opened his eyes and glanced at the moon, he mentally pronounced, as one obsessed, "Katya!" with such rapture, such pain, that he himself thought it mad. Really, how could the moon remind him of Katya, and yet it did, it did bring something to mind and, most amazing of all, he could actually see it! And sometimes he was simply blind to everything: his desire and the memory of what there had been between them in Moscow, overwhelmed him so powerfully that, trembling all over as in a fever, he prayed God—and, alas, always in vain!—that he might see her here, in this bed with him, if only in a dream. Once, that winter, he had gone with her to the Bolshoi Theatre to hear Sobinov and Chaliapine sing in *Faust*. That night everything seemed especially wonderful to him: the brilliantly lit already hotly and fragrantly crowded abyss yawning below them, the tiers of red-velvet and gold boxes overflowing with gorgeous finery, the pearly radiance of the gigantic chandelier over the abyss, and the strains of the overture, now thunderous and demoniac, now infinitely tender and sad, puring far down below where the conductor could be seen waving his baton. "There lived a King in Thule..." Afterwards, he took Katya home, walking with her to Kislovka in the frosty, moonlit night, and stayed longer than usual with her; their kissing left him more drained than ever, and he took away with him the silk ribbon with which Katya tied her hair for the night. He had come to such a state these sleepless May nights that he could not think without a shudder even of this ribbon which he kept in his writing desk.

In the daytime he slept, and then rode to the village where there was a railway station and a post office. The weather continued fair. Sometimes it rained, there were brief thunderstorms and downpours, and then again the sun shone hotly, doing its urgent, incessant work in the gardens, fields and forests. The garden was shedding its blossoms, but it was vigorously growing more dense and dark. The woods were already submerged in tall grasses and countless flowers, and the nightingales and cuckoos ceaselessly called one into the green, resonant depths. The fields were no longer bare, they were now richly and variously carpeted with different sprouting crops. And Mitya spent whole days in these woods and fields.

He had become ashamed of sticking on the veranda or in the middle of the yard every morning, waiting for the return of whoever had gone to the post office—the steward or a labourer. Nor could the steward or the labourers always spare the time for the eight-verst drive for a trifling thing like letters. And so he took to going there himself. To be sure, he too invariably returned with only the day's Orel paper or a letter from Anya or Kostia. He was coming to the limit of what he could suffer. The woods and fields he rode through oppressed him so unbearably with their beauty and their happiness that he began to feel a physical pain somewhere in his breast.

Late one afternoon, he was riding back from the post office through the uninhabited neighbouring estate, surrounded by an old park that merged with the birch woods around it. He rode down the estate's main avenue, bordered by huge, black firs. The broad, magnificently sombre avenue, thickly covered with slippery, rusty needles, led to the ancient house at the far end. The red, dry and serene light of the sun, setting behind the park and the forest on the left and slanting through the trunks of the firs, caught golden glints in the carpeting of needles. A silence so enchanted reigned here, with only the nightingales singing lustily everywhere at once, the smell of the firs and the jasmine shrubs, thronging round the house, was so sweet, the happiness—someone else's and long ago—that Mitya sensed in all this was so great, and the clarity with which he suddenly pictured Katya, as his young wife, standing on this huge, dilapidated veranda among the jasmine shrubs, was so frightening that actually feeling the deathly pallor spreading over his face he said in a loud, firm voice:

"If no letter comes this week I'll shoot myself."

17

The next day he got up very late. After lunch he sat on the veranda with a book on his knees, and looking at the pages covered with print asked himself dully: should he go to the post office or not?

It was hot, white butterflies in pairs hovered over the

hot grass and the glassily glinting spindle bushes. He watched the butterflies, and again asked himself: should he go, or put an end to these shameful trips once and for all?

The steward appeared on horseback in the gates, rising into view from under the slope. He glanced at the veranda and rode straight to it. Reining in his stallion, he said:

"Good morning! Reading again?" Grinning, he looked about him and lowered his voice to ask: "Is your mama asleep?"

"I think so. Why?" Mitya replied.

The steward did not speak for a minute, and then said with sudden earnestness:

"A book's all very well, young master, but there's a time for everything. Now, why do you live like a monk? Aren't there enough wives and wenches here?"

Mitya dropped his eyes and stared at the page before him.

"Where have you come from?" he asked, without looking up.

"From the village. I went to the post office and, of course, there are no letters, nothing but the one newspaper."

"Why 'of course'?"

"Because they're still writing, they haven't finished writing yet," the steward replied rudely and mockingly, offended by Mitya's refusal to continue the conversation he had started. "Here you are then," he said, handing the newspaper to Mitya and giving his horse a touch, rode off.

"I'll shoot myself," Mitya thought resolutely, looking at his book and seeing nothing.

18

Mitya could not fail to understand that nothing crazier than this could even be imagined: shooting himself, shattering his skull, abruptly stopping the beating of his healthy young heart, stopping thought and feeling, going deaf and blind, vanishing from the ineffably beautiful world which had only now revealed itself completely to him for the first time, instantly and forever denying himself any part in this very life where there was Katya and the approaching summer, the sky, the clouds, the sun, the warm wind, the corn in the fields, the villages, the girls, mother, the estate, Anya, Kostia, the poems in the old magazines, and somewhere over there–Sevastopol, the Baidar Pass, mauve sultry mountains clad in pine and beech forests, a dazzlingly white hot highway, the gardens at Livadia and Alupka, burning sand and radiant sea, sunburnt children, sunburnt women, and Katya again, in a white dress, with a white parasol sitting on the pebbles which were gently licked by the waves, blindingly sparkling and inviting an involuntary smile of sheer happiness...

He did understand this, but what was he to do? How could he break free from this vicious circle where the better it was, the more tormenting and unbearable? The most unbearable thing was, in fact, this happiness which the world overwhelmed him with and which lacked that most essential something.

Here he woke up in the morning, and the first thing he saw was the cheerful sunlight, beating straight down on him, and the first thing he heard was the cheerful ringing of the village churchbells, familiar since childhood, over there, beyond the dewy garden, full of shade and brilliance, birds and flowers; the very wallpaper was a cheerful yellow, the same, sweet wallpaper that had been there ever since he could remember. And, in the next instant, the thought: Katya! stabbed his very soul with rapture and horror. The morning sun was shining with her youth, the freshness of the garden was her freshness, the merry, lilting peal of the churchbells rang with the prettiness and grace of her image, and the old-fashioned wallpaper demanded that she should share with Mitya the dearness of this old country world, the life which his ancestors had lived on this estate, and this home where they had lived and died. And Mitya flung away his blanket, jumped out of bed in his nightshirt with the collar unbuttoned, long-legged, lanky, but anyway strong, young, and warm from sleep, quickly pulled out his desk drawer, snatched up the treasured photograph and, falling into a stupor, peered at it anxiously. All the loveliness, grace, all that inexpressible, radiant and appealing charm of maidenhood and womanhood were there, in that small, graceful head, and the slightly defiant innocent glance! But this glance was enigmatic and its gay unresponsiveness could not be broken down, and where was he to find the srength to endure it when it was so close and yet so far, perhaps alienated forever now, when it had allowed him to discover what happiness it was to live and had then deceived him so shamelessly and terribly?

That evening, as he rode from the post office through Shakhovskoye, that ancient, uninhabited estate with the dark fir-lined avenue, he expressed most accurately in that impulsive exclamation the state of extreme exhaustion which he had reached. Stopping at the window of the post office and looking down from his saddle at the clerk rummaging hopelessly in the pile of newspapers and letters, he heard a train approaching the station, and the sound and smell of it smote him with the happiness of that remembered farewell at Kursk Railway Station and of Moscow in general. Riding back through the village, he was so unnerved that he caught something of Katya in every short girl he met, in the movement of her hips. Out in the open, he met a troika coming from the opposite direction at a great pace; he saw two hats in the tarantas as it flashed past him, one of them was a girl's hat, and he almost shouted: "Katya!" The white flowers growing on the balks were instantly associated in his mind with her white gloves, and the blue mullein with the colour of her veil... And when, at sunset, he rode into Shakhovskoye the dry, sweet smell of the firs and the gorgeous fragrance of the jasmine gave him such a poignant awareness of summer and someone's summer life once lived in this rich and beautiful country place that, glancing down the avenue filled with the reddish gold light of the setting sun and at the house at the end of it, he suddenly saw Katya at her loveliest walking down the veranda steps into the garden, almost as clearly as he saw the house and the jasmine shrubs. He had long lost his realistic picture of her, she appeared before him more extraordinary and more and more transformed with every day, and that evening her transformed image was so overpowering, so jubilantly triumphant that Mitya felt more terrified than he had felt that day when the cuckoo startled him with its sudden cries.

19

He stopped going to the post office, compelling himself to stop by a desperate, extreme effort of will power. He also stopped writing to her. After all, he had already tried everything: he wrote her frenzied love letters, telling her he loved her as no one had yet loved on this earth, he pleaded humbly for her love or at least her friendship, he lied shamelessly that he was ill and was writing in bed, hoping to make her feel sorry for him and show some concern, if only that. He even resorted to veiled threats: all that was left to him, he wrote, was to spare Katya and his "luckier rivals" his continued presence in this world. And now that he had stopped writing and begging for an answer, compelling himself with all his might not to expect one (but still hoping at heart that a letter would come just when he had succeeded in hoodwinking fate, feigning indifference, or really achieving indifference), when he tried not to think about Katya and sought ways to escape from her, and again started reading anything he could lay his hands on, again accompanied the steward on business to the neighbouring villages, and repeated tirelessly to himself: "What will be, will be."

One day they were returning from a homestead not far away, in their droshky and going fast, as usual. Both of them sat astride the long bench—the steward in front, as he was driving, and Mitya behind, both of them all but jolted out of their seats, especially Mitya who had to hold on to the seat for all he was worth, seeing nothing but the back of the steward's red neck and the fields jumping before his eyes. When they were almost home, the steward dropped the reins, letting the horse go at a walk, rolled a cigarette and, grinning into his open pouch, said:

"You were vexed by what I said the other day, young master, but you shouldn't have been. Isn't it true what I said? A book's all very well, why not read a bit when you've nothing better to do, but it won't run away from you, you know, and there's time for everything."

Mitya turned red, and then, to his own surprise, replied with simulated casualness and an awkward smile:

"There's no one I have an eye for somehow..."

"How come? With all those wives and wenches about!"

"The wenches only lead you on," Mitya said, trying to speak in the same key as the steward. "You can't hope for much from the wenches."

"It's just that you don't know the right approach," the steward said, speaking instructively now. "And you're close-fisted besides. An empty hand is no lure for a hawk."

"I wouldn't be close-fisted if it was something worthwhile and sure," Mitya said suddenly losing shame.

"Well, since you say so, everything will be fine," the steward said, lighting his cigarette, and then continuing in the tone of a man who has been misunderstood: "It's not a ruble tip I want or a gift from you, what I want is to give you some pleasure. Every time I look I see that the young master is moping. And so I say to myself: no, you can't leave it like that. I always take my masters into account. It's over a year now that I've been in your service and I've never heard a cross word either from you or from the mistress, heaven knows. Some others, now, what do they care for the masters' cows? They've eaten their fill—good, they haven't—to hell with it. That's not my way, no. With me the masters' cows come first. That's what I'm always telling the fellows too, I shall have the cows well fed, I tell them, and that's that!"

Mitya was beginning to think that the steward had been drinking, but suddenly the man dropped his confiding, injured tone and glancing at Mitya over his shoulder asked:

"Now, what could be better than Alyonka? She's a tasty little woman, young too, and her husband's at the coal mines... Only, of course, she too will have to be given some trifle. Well, you'll spend, say, five rubles all told. A ruble, say, to bring her a treat, and two you just hand to her. Well, and me you'll give something for a pinch of tobacco..."

"That will be quite all right," Mitya said, again against his will. "Only what Alyonka are you talking about?"

"Why, the forest guard's Alyonka, naturally," said the steward. "Can it be that you don't know her? She's the daughter-in-law of the new forest guard. It seems to me you saw her in church last Sunday. That's when it struck me that she'd be just right for our young master. She's only been married a year, she keeps herself neat..."

"Oh well, why not," Mitya replied, smiling. "Go ahead and arrange it."

"I'll do my best then," the steward said, picking up his reins. "I'll ask her then, soon as I see her. And don't miss any chances either. Tomorrow, she's coming to fix the bank in the garden with the other girls, so why don't you come there too? As for that book of yours, it won't run away, you'll do all the reading you want when you go back to Moscow, I should think..."

He gave the reins a slight tug, and they drove homewards, jolting and bouncing again. Mitya kept a tight hold on the seat and, trying not to look at the back of the steward's thick, red neck, gazed into the distance over the trees in his garden and the village, sprawling on the slope and running down to the riverside meadows. Something unexpected, ridiculous and yet so thrilling that a feverish eagerness ran through his whole body was already half settled. And there was already something different about the belfry he had known since childhood, thrusting up behind the tops of the trees in the garden and twinkling with its cross in the late afternoon sun.

20

The village girls called Mitya a borzoi for his lankiness. He belonged to that breed of men whose black eyes seemed to be permanently dilated, and who could hardly grow a proper moustache or a beard even in adulthood, because all that ever sprouted was a curly, sparse, bristly growth. Still, the morning after his conversation with the steward, Mitya shaved and put on his new yellow silk shirt which gave an unusual, becoming colour to his gaunt, inspired-looking face.

Some time after ten, he went slowly into the garden trying to put on the slightly bored air of someone going for a stroll for lack of anything better to do.

He started from the front porch that faced north. A slate-black murkiness hung over the roofs of the coach-house, the barnyard, and that part of the garden behind which the belfry usually showed. It was a bleak day altogether, there was a sultriness in the air, and a smell came from the kitchen chimney. Mitya turned the corner of the house and started down the lime walk, gazing at the crowns of the trees and the sky. A hot, feeble wind came from the south-east where some indeterminate clouds were suspended behind the garden. The birds did not sing, and even the nightingales were silent. The bees flew in soundless multitudes across the garden with their loot.

The girls were again working near the fir grove fixing up the earthen bank, filling in the grooves worn through by the trespassing cows and calves with earth and steaming, pleasantly smelly manure which the labourers kept bringing in carts from the barnyard by way of the main walk, and as a result it was spattered all the way down with shiny, moist dollops. There were about six girls there. Sonka was not among them any more—she had, after all, become engaged to the man of her father's choice, and now stayed at home working on her trousseau. There were several quite immature girls, there was the fat, comely Anyutka, there was Glashka, looking sterner and manlier than ever, and there was Alyonka. She caught his eye at once, he knew at once that she was Alyonka, although he had never seen her before, and what struck him at once, startling him with the unexpectancy of it, was that she had something in common with Katya, or perhaps he only fancied she had. It was so amazing that he stopped short for a stunned moment. Then he walked resolutely straight at her, never taking his eyes off her for a second.

Like Katya, she was small and lively. Although the work she had come to do was dirty, she had put on a pretty blouse, a white one with red dots and a black patent-leather belt, a skirt of the same stuff, a pink kerchief, red woollen stockings, and black felt low boots in which (or rather in her small, graceful feet) there was something of Katya again, that is, something womanly and childish mixed together. Her head was also smallish, and her dark eyes were set and shone almost like Katya's. She was the only one who wasn't working, feeling her exclusiveness perhaps, and stood with her right foot on the pitchfork, speaking with the steward. The steward lay under an apple tree on his coat with a torn lining, and smoked, propping himself up on an elbow. When Mitya came up he politely moved over to the grass, leaving room for him on the coat.

"Sit down, Mitry Palych, have a smoke," he said in a comradely, off-hand manner.

Mitya stole a quick look at Alyonka—the pink of the kerchief tinged her face nicely—sat down and, dropping his eyes, lit a cigarette (that winter and spring he had made several attempts to give it up, and now he was smoking regularly again). Alyonka did not so much as nod to him in greeting, and ignored him completely. The steward continued with what he had been saying to her, and as Mitya had not heard the beginning of their conversation he did not understand a word. She was laughing, but somehow it seemed that neither her mind nor her heart was in it. The steward put an obscene insinuation into each of the sentences he dropped in a slighting, mocking tone. Her quick replies were also mocking, and implied that in his designs upon someone he had behaved stupidly, too brashly, and cowardly at the same time, because he was afraid of his wife.

"Ah well, there's no outtalking you," the steward said at last, cutting short the argument as if its pointlessness had bored him. "You'd better go and sit with us awhile. The master wants to say a word to you."

Alyonka rolled her eyes, not looking at Mitya, tucked some escaping dark ringlets under her kerchief, and made no move.

"Come, you fool, I'm telling you," the steward told her.

Making a momentary decision, Alyonka jumped down lightly from the bank, ran to Mitya and squatted not two paces away from where he lay on the steward's coat, and looked at him gaily and curiously with her wide dark eyes. Then she burst out laughing, and asked:

"Is it true, young master, that you don't sleep with women? Like a monk or something?"

"And how do you know he doesn't?" the steward asked her.

"I just do," Alyonka said. "I've heard so. And the master can't anyway. The master's got someone in Moscow," she finished with a mischievous sparkle in her eyes.

"There's no one suitable, that's why he doesn't sleep with anyone," the steward explained. "A lot you understand in the masters' business!"

"How d'you mean, no one suitable?" Alyonka objected, laughing. "There are so many married women and girls here! Take Anyutka, could anyone wish for a better? Hey,

Anyutka, come here a moment, I want to tell you something," she called out in a ringing voice.

Anyutka, the girl with the broad, fleshy back and somewhat short arms, turned round with a nice, kind smile on her pretty face, answered something in a melodious voice, and went on working harder than ever.

"Come, I'm telling you!" Alyonka shouted the louder.

"Not me, I have no truck with that business," Anyutka sang out gleefully.

"We don't want Anyutka, we want someone neater, made of finer stuff," the steward said knowledgeably. "We know without you telling us whom we want."

The look he gave Alyonka was very expressive. She was a bit discomfited, and blushed slightly.

"No, no, no, you won't find anyone better than Anyutka," she said, smiling to hide her embarrassment. "And if you don't want Anyutka, there's Nastya, she too is always neat, she lived in town..."

"Enough of that, shut up now," the steward said with unexpected rudeness. "Get back to your job, you've jabbered enough. As it is I get trouble from the mistress, she says I let you get too cheeky..."

Alyonka sprang to her feet—with extraordinary lightness again—and picked up her pitchfork. Just then, the labourer who had dumped the last lot of manure on the ground, shouted: "Lunchtime!" and, tugging at the reins, drove off at a brisk pace, the now empty cart rattling and clattering.

"Lunchtime, lunchtime!" the girls shouted in a discordant chorus, threw down their spades and pitchforks, jumped over the bank with a flicker of bare legs above the varicoloured woollen stockings, and ran to the fir grove where they had left their bundles.

The steward looked at Mitya out of the corner of his eye, gave him a wink to say that matters were going well, and rising to his feet pronounced:

"Well, if it's lunchtime, it's lunchtime."

The girls, making a gay splash of colour against the wall of dark firs, flopped down on the ground, undid their bundles, took out the flat cakes they had brought for lunch, laid them out on the skirts over their outstretched legs, and started chewing the bread, washing it down with milk or kvas drunk straight from the bottle, and talking loudly and excitedly all the time, laughing at anything anyone said and darting curious, provocative glances at Mitya. Leaning close to Anyutka, Alyonka whispered something in her ear. Smiling her charming smile in spite of herself, Anyutka gave her a hard shove (Alyonka, doubled over with laughter, fell forward) and with mock indignation shouted for all to hear in her melodious voice:

"Fool! What's there to giggle about? What's the joke?"

"Come on, Mitry Palych, let's go where it's safer," the steward said. "Look at them raising merry hell!"

21

The next day it was Sunday, and so no work was done in the garden.

There had been a downpour in the night, the rain swished wetly over the roof, and the garden was lit up again and again with a pale but sweeping and fantastically beautiful light. Towards morning, however, the sky had cleared, everything became plain and safe again, and Mitya awakened to the merry, sunny ringing of the churchbells.

He washed and dressed without haste, drank a glass of tea, and went to church. "Your Mama has already gone," Parasha told him with gentle reproach, "and you're as bad as a Tatar or someone..."

One could go to the church either across the common pasture, through the main gate and then turning right, or else through the garden down the main walk and then, turning left, along the road between the garden and the threshing floor. Mitya chose to walk through the garden.

Everything looked and felt just as if it were already summer. Mitya walked straight at the sun, shining down on the threshing floor and the field. This sunshine and the pealing of the churchbells, blending so nicely and peacefully with the whole of this pastoral morning, and his having just washed, combed his wet, glossy black hair, and put on his student cap, felt so nice that Mitya, who again had not slept all night and had again gone through a multitude of the most diverse thoughts and feelings, was suddenly filled with hope that his torments would be happily resolved, and he'd be delivered, liberated from them. The churchbells rang invitingly, the threshing floor ahead of him glittered hotly, a woodpecker paused for a moment, lifting its tufted head, and then hurried up the gnarled trunk of the lime tree into the pale-green, sunlit crown; bumble-bees busily dug the whole of their black-and-red velvet bodies into the flowers in the glades where the sun was hottest, and birds sang everywhere with sweet and carefree abandon... Everything was as it had been so many, many times in his childhood, his boyhood, and he remembered those lovely, carefree days so vividly that all at once he felt certain that God would take mercy on him and he'd discover that it was possible to live in this world even without Katya.

"I'll really go and visit the Meshcherskys," he told himself, and in that very moment saw Alyonka walking past the gate not twenty paces away. She was wearing her pink silk kerchief again, a pretty blue dress with flounces, and new steel-tipped boots. She walked quickly, wiggling her rump, and he leapt aside, darting behind the trees before she could see him.

Once she was out of sight, he turned back and, with beating heart, hurried home. He knew now that he had been going to church with the secret aim of seeing her, and realised that he must not go there, that church was not the place to see her.

22

During lunch, a messenger brought a telegram from the station. Anya and Kostia were to be expected home on the following evening. The news left Mitya absolutely cold.

After lunch he lay on the wickerwork settee on the veranda with his eyes closed, feeling the hot sun almost reaching him, and listening to the summerlike buzzing of the flies. His heart fluttered, and questions to which he had no answers harassed his mind: what about that arrangement with Alyonka? When would the matter be settled at last? Why hadn't the steward asked her in so many words if she was willing, and if she was, then when and where? Something else worried him at the same time:

should he or should he not go back on his firm resolve not to ride to the post office ever again? What if he went that afternoon, just once more, for the last time? What for? To senselessly lacerate his own pride with this new humiliation? To senselessly torment himself with this new, futile hope? But, on the other hand, what could his going to the post office (actually, an ordinary ride) add to the torments he was suffering already? Was it not perfectly obvious now that everything there, in Moscow, was finished forever for him? What was there for him to lose?

"Young master," someone standing near the veranda called him in a voice kept low. "Young master, are you asleep?"

Mitya quickly opened his eyes. Before him stood the steward wearing a new cotton shirt and a new cap. His face showed that this was a holiday: it was smug, a bit sleepy, and not quite sober.

"Let's go to the forest quickly, young master," he whispered. "I told the mistress that I've got to see Trifon about the bees. Let's go quickly while the mistress is taking her nap, or she may change her mind when she wakes up... We'll take a bottle along for Trifon, he'll get fuddled, you keep talking to him, and I'll take my chance to whisper a word to Alyonka. Hurry up, I've already harnessed the horse..."

Mitya ran across the front hall where he picked up his cap, and hurried to the coach-house where a mettlesome, young stallion stood harnessed into the droshky.

23

The stallion took off eagerly and flew like the wind through the gate. The steward brought him to a stop outside the village store opposite the church, went in to buy a pound of bacon and a bottle of vodka, and off they flew again.

Mitya had a fleeting vision of Anyutka, all dressed up and, with nowhere to go, standing at her gate at the edge of the village. The steward shouted something to her that was meant in fun for all its coarseness, and cutting a drunken, senseless and angry dash, gathered in the reins and with them hit the stallion sharply on the croup. The stallion ran the faster.

Mitya held on for dear life as he bounced on his seat. He liked the feel of the hot sun on the back of his neck, and the hot air that blew into his face from the fields, smelling of the already flowering rye, road dust, and wheel grease. The rye rippling in the breeze was shot with silvery-grey like some beautiful fur; skylarks took wing from it one after the other, they sang, streaked over the field at a slant and dropped; and in the distance far ahead the forest stood cloaked in soft blues...

It took them about a quarter of an hour to reach the forest, and they flew on as briskly, bumping into tree stumps and roots, along the shady road, gay with sun spots and the masses of flowers growing in the thick, tall grass on either side of it. Alyonka, wearing her pretty blue dress and holding her feet in the new boots carefully straight before her, sat among the young oaks beside the cottage, doing some embroidery. The steward drove past her, shaking his whip at her, and reined in smartly at the door. Mitya was struck by the bitter, fresh smell of the forest and the opening oak leaves, and deafened by the shrill barking of the dogs that had surrounded the droshky and were making the whole forest resound with their yelps. They stood barking furiously at every conceivable pitch, but their shaggy faces had a kind look, and they were wagging their tails.

The steward and Mitya climbed down from the droshky, tied the stallion to a dry tree that must have been struck by lightning and walked into the dark closed porch.

Inside the cottage it was very clean, very cosy and very cramped; it was hot from the sun which shone from behind the forest into its two windows, and also from the stove in which bread had been baked that morning. Fedosya, Alyonka's mother-in-law, a neat, pleasant-looking little old woman, sat at the table with her back to the small sunny window, specked all over with tiny flies. When she saw that it was the young master who had come in, she stood up and gave him a low bow. Mitya and the steward said how-d'you-do to her, sat down and lit cigarettes.

"And where might Trifon be?" asked the steward.

"He's gone to lie down for a bit in the shed," Fedosya

said. "I'll go and call him."

"Matters are moving!" the steward whispered to Mitya, winking with both eyes, as soon as Fedosya left them.

Mitya didn't see that anything was moving so far. So far it was unbearably embarrassing, that's all. Mitya suspected that Fedosya understood the purpose of their visit perfectly. The thought which had been frightening him for three days now flashed through his mind again: "I am going mad. What am I doing?" He felt like a sleepwalker who, dominated by someone's will, was walking faster and faster towards a fatal, but irresistibly luring abyss. Still, he went on sitting there, smoking, looking about the room, and trying to appear casual and composed. He felt especially ashamed at the thought of facing Trifon: he was said to be a mean-tempered, clever man, and so he'd understand everything at once even better than Fedosya. And at the same time he was thinking: "Where does she sleep, I wonder? On that plank-bed, or in the shed?" In the shed, of course. A summer night in the forest, the windows in the shed had no frames or panes, the forest whispering sleepily all night long, and she, lying there asleep...

24

Upon entering, Trifon gave Mitya a low bow, but did not look into his eyes or say anything. Then he sat on a bench at the table, and spoke to the steward in a dry, unfriendly tone: what was the matter, what had he come for? The steward hastened to reply that the mistress had sent him to ask Trifon to come and take a look at her bee-garden, because her bee-keeper was an old, deaf fool, while he, Trifon, was probably the cleverest and most knowing bee-master in the whole gubernia—whereupon he pulled the bottle of vodka from one of his trouser pockets, and the bacon, wrapped in rough grey paper which had by then become greased through, from the other. Trifon cast a cold, mocking look on the bottle, but still he got up and took a teacup down from the shelf. The steward poured some vodka for Mitya first, then for Trifon, then for Fedosya, who drank up all there was with pleasure, and finally for himself. He started pouring the second round at once, masticating the bread and flaring his nostrils.

Trifon became drunk rather quickly, but the vodka did not soften his dryness or his mocking unfriendliness. The steward had a stonily stupid look after the second round. Their conversation took on the appearance of friendliness, but there was distrust and malice in the eyes of both men. Fedosya sat there without speaking, and though she looked on politely she was obviously cross. Alyonka did not put in an appearance at all. Losing all hope that she'd ever come, and seeing too clearly that only an utter fool could count on the steward in his present state to "whisper a word" to her even if she did come, Mitya rose to his feet and told the man sternly that it was time to go.

"All right, all right, there's plenty of time," the steward replied with sullen insolence. "I still have to say something to you in confidence."

"Good, you'll say it to me on the way back," Mitya's tone was controlled but sterner still. "Let us go."

The steward slapped the table with his hand and said with drunken mysteriousness:

"And I'm telling you that this can't be said on the road! Come out with me a minute..."

Heaving himself up with an effort, he pushed open the door into the covered porch. Mitya followed him out.

"Well, what is it?"

"Keep quiet," the steward whispered dramatically, closing the door behind Mitya and swaying on his feet.

"Keep quiet about what?"

"Keep quiet!"

"I don't understand you."

"Keep quiet! She'll be ours! For sure!"

Mitya pushed him aside, went outside and stopped, wondering what he should do: should he wait a little longer, drive off alone, or simply go home on foot?

There, before him, ten paces away stood the dense green forest, it was already touched with the shadows of evening, and this made it all the fresher, cleaner and lovelier. A clear, serene sun was setting behind the treetops, and the pure gold of its rays was generously sifted through the branches. And suddenly a woman's melodious voice rang out in the heart of the forest somewhere far away, beyond the ravines it seemed, and the sound reverberating through the forest was so alluring, so enchanting, as a voice can sound only in the forest on a summer evening.

"Yoo-hoo!" the owner of this voice called out, evidently amusing herself with the forest echoes.

"Yoo-hoo!"

Mitya sprang forward and ran over the grasses and flowers to the forest. The forest dipped sharply into a stony gully. Mitya ran to the edge and stopped. Down below in the gully stood Alyonka eating cowslips. She glanced up, and there was amazement in her eyes.

"What are you doing here?" Mitya asked in a low voice.

"Looking for our Marussya and the cow. Why d'you ask?" Alyonka also kept her voice low.

"Will you come or not?"

"Why should I come for nothing?"

"Who told you it's for nothing?" Mitya's voice had dropped to almost a whisper. "You needn't worry about that."

"When?" she asked.

"Tomorrow... When can you come?"

Alyonka thought for a minute.

"I'm going to my mother's tomorrow to shear her sheep," she said, peering warily into the forest behind Mitya. "I'll come in the evening, as soon as it's dark. Only where? We can't go to the threshing floor because someone might come in... Would you like to come to the hut in your garden, in the gully? Only mind you don't cheat me, I don't agree if it's for nothing... This isn't Moscow for you," she glanced up at him with laughing eyes. "The women there, they say, pay for it themselves..."

25

The return trip was awful. Trifon had set out a bottle in his turn, and the steward got so drunk that he could not get on to the droshky at the first attempt and fell across it, frightening the young stallion into all but tearing off by himself. Mitya did not say anything, he watched the steward unemotionally, and patiently waited for him to settle down in the driver's seat. Once again the steward whipped on the horse with senseless vehemence. Mitya did not say anything, he held on fast, and looked at the evening sky and the fields, trembling and jumping before him. The skylarks were singing the last of their brief songs for the day, and summer lightning flared up in the eastern sky, already turning a dark blue for the night, they were distant, peaceful flashes that held no threat and only promise of good weather. Mitya was aware of the enchantment of the evening, but at the moment it meant nothing to him. There was only one thing in his mind, in his entire being: tomorrow evening!

News awaited him at home: a letter had come confirming the arrival of Anya and Kostia on the evening train on the morrow. Mitya was aghast: as soon as they arrived they'd run into the garden, they might run to the hut in the gully... But instantly he realised with relief that it would be after nine by the time they were brought home from the railway station, and then they'd be fed, and there'd be tea...

"Are you going to meet them?" his mother asked.

Mitya felt the blood receding from his face.

"No, I don't think I will... I don't feel like it... And then there'll be nowhere to sit..."

"Ah well, you might go on horseback..."

"No, I don't know... And actually, what for? At the moment anyway I don't feel like going..."

Olga Petrovna gave him a keen look.

"Are you well?" she asked.

"Perfectly well," Mitya said almost rudely. "I'm terribly sleepy, that's all..."

He went to his room at once, lay down on the sofa in the dark, and fell asleep in his clothes.

In the night he heard the remote sounds of slow music and saw himself hanging over a huge, faintly lit abyss. The abyss grew lighter and lighter, more bottomless, more golden, brighter, and more crowded, and then, quite distinctly now, something rang and sang in it with infinite sadness and tenderness: "There lived a King in Thule..." The stirring sound made him quiver with emotion, then he turned on his other side and went back to sleep.

26

The day seemed to drag on forever.

Mitya emerged from his room for tea and dinner, he sat at the table woodenly, then went back to his room, lay down again, took the volume of Pisemsky that had long been lying about on his writing table and read, without understanding a word, or just stared at the ceiling and listened to the soothing, silky rustle of the sunlit garden outside his window... He got up once and went to the library to take another book. But this room, so charmingly old-world and serene, with the ancient maple seen from one window and the clear western sky from the other, reminded him so acutely of those spring days (now infinitely distant) when he had sat here reading poems in old journals, and it was so poignantly Katya's, that he turned on his heel and quickly walked back to his own room, thinking with annoyance: "To hell with it! To hell with all this poetic tragicalness of love!"

He angrily remembered his intention to shoot himself if there was no letter from Katya, lay down again and picked up the volume of Pisemsky once more. But he still could not understand a word he read, and at moments, staring at the page before him and thinking about Alyonka, began to tremble all over from the trembling which started in the pit of his stomach and grew worse and worse. And as the evening drew nearer these trembling fits seized him at shorter and shorter intervals. The voices and footsteps in the house, the voices in the yard—horses were already being harnessed into the tarantas to go to the station—everything jarred on him as such sounds do when you are ill, lying alone in your room, while ordinary, everyday life goes on about you, indifferent to you and therefore alien and even hostile. At last he heard Parasha calling to his mother: "The horses are ready, ma'am!" There came the crisp prattle of the bells, the thudding of hoofs, and then the swish of wheels as the tarantas rolled up to the front porch. "O Lord, won't this ever end!" Mitya mumbled, beside himself with impatience, making no move yet straining to hear his mother giving her last-minute orders in the front hall. Suddenly the bells began to jingle, the sound swelling in volume as the tarantas rolled downhill, and then growing muffled and fading away...

Quickly getting up, Mitya went into the dining-room. It was empty and light from the clear and yellowish setting sun. The whole house was empty, somehow strangely and frighteningly empty. With a strange feeling that was like a farewell, Mitya walked down the length of the silent, wide-open rooms—the drawing-room, the small sitting-room, the library where in the window he saw the southern sky turning the deep blue of evening, the picturesque green crown of the maple tree and above it Antares, a pink dot... He looked into the front hall, wondering if Parasha was there. Having made sure that the coast was clear, he grabbed his cap off the hall-tree, ran back to his room, and jumped out of the window, throwing his long legs far out on to the flower bed. For a moment he stood still on the flower bed, and then crouching low, dashed across the open space into the garden, slipping at once into a dark side-path, thickly overgrown with acacia and lilac shrubs.

27

There was no dew, and so the smells of the late-evening garden could not be particularly strong. But to Mitya it seemed, for all the unconsciousness of his actions that evening, that he had never known these smells to be so strong and so various, except, perhaps, in early childhood. Everything had its overpowering fragrance—the acacia shrubs, the leaves of the lilac and the currant bushes, the burdocks, the wormwood, the flowers, the grass, the earth...

He walked on quickly with the chilling thought: "What if she doesn't come?" for it seemed to him now that his whole life depended on whether Alyonka came or not. He caught the smell of chimney smoke, wafted from the village to mingle with the garden fragrances, and, stopping, looked quickly behind him. A beetle sailed past slowly, humming close to his ear, as though it were sowing quiet, peace and twilight, but it was still light from the even, long undimming sunset glow of early summer that spread across half the sky where high-up in the transparent blue void glittered a silver of the nascent moon right above the roof of the house showing here and there behind the trees. Mitya glanced at the crescent, made a quick, small sign of the cross over the pit of his stomach, and stepped into the acacia shrubs. The path led to the gully, but not to the hut which was off to the left. Mitya strode through the shrubs, then broke into a run, bending low or pushing out of the way the low, far-spreading branches. Within the minute he was at the hut.

With his heart in his mouth he stepped into the hut, into its darkness smelling of dry rotting straw, peered about him and saw, almost with relief, that Alyonka was not there yet. But the fatal moment was drawing nigh and, standing beside the hut, he strained all his senses to the utmost. An extraordinary physical excitement had not left him for a minute all that day. And now it had reached its peak. But, strange thing, now, just as all that day, it did not penetrate his whole being, the excitement seized only his body and left his soul alone. True, his heart was beating terribly. And all around it was so amazingly quiet that he heard only the beating of his heart. Soft, colourless moths fluttered soundlessly and indefatigably about the grey leaves of the apple trees, etched fancifully and variously against the evening sky, and the quiet seemed to be enhanced by these moths, tracing their magic circles and casting a spell. Suddenly something snapped behind him, and he was thunderstruck by the sound. He swung round, looked between the trees in the direction of the earthen bank, and saw something black rolling at him from under the branches of the apple trees. Before he could collect his wits, this dark something was upon him, it made a sweeping sort of movement—and turned out to be Alyonka.

She pushed back the hem of her black homespun-wool skirt with which she had hooded her head, and he saw her frightened, happily smiling face. She was barefoot, and wore only a plain unbleached linen blouse, tucked into her skirt. Her girlish, pointed breasts were taut under the blouse. The wide neckline revealed her neck and part of her shoulders, and the sleeves, rolled up above the elbows, left her rounded arms bare. Everything in her, from her dainty head under the yellow kerchief to her small bare feet—a woman's and yet a child's—was so lovely, so neat and so charming that Mitya, who had until then only seen her dressed-up and was seeing her for the first time in all the loveliness of this simplicity, gasped inwardly.

"Come, let's hurry, shall we," she whispered gaily and thievishly as, with a quick look round, she ducked into the strong-smelling darkness of the hut.

Once inside she paused and Mitya, clenching his teeth to control their chattering, hurriedly thrust his hand into his pocket—his legs were tensed and as hard as iron—and pushed a crumpled five-rouble note into her hand. She quickly slipped it down the neck of her blouse, and sat down on the ground. Mitya sat down beside her and put his arm round her neck, not knowing what to do—must he kiss her or not? The smell of her kerchief, her hair, the spring-onion smell of her whole body, mixed with the smell of a peasant cottage and chimney smoke, was so good that it made his head spin, and he appreciated its wholesomeness with both his mind and his senses. Even so, he felt what he had felt earlier: an overpowering physical desire that did not grow into a desire of the heart, into bliss, into rapture, into a longing of his whole being. She pulled away and lay down on her back. He lay beside her, pressed to her, and stretched out his hand. Laughing softly and nervously, she caught his hand and pulled it down.

"Not allowed," she said, and Mitya could not tell if she meant it or had said it in fun.

She drew his hand away, holding it fast in her own small hand, and gazed through the triangular window frame at the apple branches, at the already dark-blue sky behind these branches, and at Antares, a motionless red dot that was still all alone up there. What did her eyes express? What was he expected to do? Kiss her on the neck, on the mouth? Suddenly, she took hold of the hem of her black skirt and said quickly:

"Come on, hurry up, why don't you..."

When they got up from the floor—Mitya in a daze of disappointment—Alyonka, re-tying her kerchief and fixing her hair, asked in an eager whisper with already the intimate familiarity of a mistress:

"People say you went to Subbotino the other day. The priest there is said to be selling his suckling pigs cheap. Is it true or not? Have you heard?"

28

That Saturday, the rain which had been going since Wednesday, became a proper downpour.

It would slacken for a while, only to start up again all the more angrily and somberly.

All that day Mitya walked about the garden, and all that day he cried so terribly that at moments he himself marvelled at the strength and copiousness of his tears.

Parasha had been sent to look for him, calling from the yard and from the lime walk that dinner and, later, tea was served, but he made no response.

It was cold, piercingly raw, and dark from the rain-clouds; against their blackness the dense foliage of the wet garden looked all the denser, fresher and brighter. The wind, blowing in gusts, shook down the raindrops from the trees, causing a second rain of its own. But Mitya saw none of this, he did not notice anything. His white student cap was soddenly shapeless and dark-grey, his university jacket had turned black, and his legs were spattered with mud up to the knees. Soaking wet, his face bloodless, his eyes insane and swollen from tears, he was terrible to see.

He smoked one cigarette after another, splashed through the mud on the walks, or turned at random and walked through the tall, wet grass among the apple and pear trees, bumping into their crooked, gnarled branches, patchy with greyish-green soggy lichens. He sat on benches, dark and swollen with moisture, he went down into the gully and lay on the damp straw in the hut, on the very spot where he had lain with Alyonka. His large hands turned blue from the cold and the icy dampness of the air, his lips were purple, and his gaunt, deathly pale face was tinged with mauve. He lay on his back with his legs crossed and his arms behind his head, and stared wild-eyed at the black straw roof dripping large, rusty raindrops. Suddenly his jaws would clench and his eyebrows twitch, he would spring to his feet, take from his trouser pocket the soiled, crumpled letter which the land surveyor arriving on business for a few days had brought from the post office the night before, and read it for the hundredth time with devouring attention:

"Dear Mitya, don't think ill of me, and forget, forget

everything that has been! I am bad, I am hateful and wicked, I am not worthy of you, but I madly love art! I have made up my mind, the die has been cast, I am going away—you know with whom... You are sensitive, you are clever, you'll understand me, I implore you, don't torture yourself and me! Don't write me anything, it's no use!"

When Mitya reached this place he crumpled the letter into a ball and sobbed, burying his face in the wet straw and madly clenching his teeth. That intimate *tu* she had let slip into the sentence "I implore you" instead of the formal *vous* was such a frightening reminder of their intimacy, actually seeming to reinstate it, that his heart overflowed with a tenderness which was more than human strength could stand! And next to this intimate *tu* was that hard statement that even writing her was no use now! Oh yes, yes, yes, he knew it was no use! Everything was finished, finished forever!

As evening approached, the rain, crashing down on the garden with ten times its earlier force and accompanied by unexpected thunderbolts, drove him indoors at last. Soaked from head to toe, his teeth chattering from the chilling shivers that had taken hold of his whole body, he peeped out from under the trees and, reassured that there was no one there to see him, ran to the window of his room, raised the frame from outside—luckily it was an old-fashioned window frame, half of which could be lifted—climbed in, locked the door, and collapsed on his bed.

It was quickly growing dark. There was the sound of rain everywhere—on the roof, around the house, in the garden. The rain had two different sounds: one in the garden, and another near the house where it was augmented by the water pouring and splashing into the puddles from the drain pipes. For Mitya, who had instantly fallen into a torpor, this duality of sound held something inexplicably alarming and, together with the heat with which his nostrils, his breathing and his head were burning, it immersed him in a narcosis, as it were, creating another world for him, another kind of evening in some other, strange house where there was a terrible presentiment of something.

He knew, he felt that he was in his own room, almost quite dark now from the rain and the approaching dusk, he heard the voices of his mother, Anya, Kostia and the land surveyor having tea in the dining-room, but at the same time he was walking through a strange house after a young nanny who was going away from him, and he was gripped by a mounting, inexplicable terror, mixed strangely with lust, with a presentiment of intimacy between some two people, an intimacy in which there was something unnaturally revolting, but in which he also participated in some way. He felt all this through the medium of the baby with a large white face whom the young nanny, leaning back a little, was carrying in her arms and rocking; Mitya made haste to overtake her, and he did overtake her and was already going to look into her face to see if it was Alyonka, perhaps, when suddenly he found himself in a gloomy classroom where the windows were smeared with chalk. The woman who stood there in front of the chest of drawers, before the looking glass, could not see him, for he had suddenly become invisible. She wore a silk yellow petticoat clinging to her rounded hips, high-heeled slippers, and sheer black stockings which her flesh showed through, and she, tremulous and ashamed, knew what was going to happen now. She had already hidden the baby in one of the drawers. She was quickly braiding her hair and, watching the door out of the corner of her eye, looked into the mirror which reflected her powdered face, bare shoulders and small milky-blue breasts with pink nipples. The door was flung open and a gentleman in evening dress, with a bloodless clean-shaven face and short, curly black hair, walked in, glancing about him with a buoyant and horrible look. He took out a flat gold cigarette case and proceeded to light a cigarette rather unceremoniously. She looked at him shyly as she finished braiding her hair, knowing the purpose of his visit, then she flung her braid over her shoulder, and raised her bare arms... He embraced her condescendingly, and she threw her arms round his neck, showing her dark armpits, clung to him, and hid her face on his chest...

29

Mitya awakened in a sweat with a shatteringly clear awareness that he was finished, that everything was so monstrously hopeless and gloomy in the world as it could not be even in hell beyond the grave. The room was dark, the rain poured noisily and splashed outside his window, and this noise and this splashing were unbearable (even just the sound alone) for a body shaking all over with fever. But the most unbearable and horrible thing was the monstrous unnaturalness of human copulation which he seemed to have just shared in with the clean-shaven gentleman. The sound of voices and laughter reached him from the dining-room. They, too, were horrible and unnatural in their estrangement from him, in the rudeness of life that was indifferent, merciless to him...

"Katya!" he said, sitting up in bed and swinging his legs over the side. "Katya, what's happening, what?" he said out loud, perfectly certain that she could hear him, that she was there and was keeping silent and not answering him simply because she, too, was crushed, she, too, understood the irreparable horror of what she had done. "Oh, it doesn't matter, Katya," he whispered bitterly and tenderly, wanting to tell her that he would forgive her everything if only she'd rush to him as before so that together they could be saved, they could save their beautiful love in that most beautiful of spring worlds which had been like paradise itself such a little while ago! But the instant he had whispered: "Oh, it doesn't matter, Katya!" he realised that it did matter, that there was no salvation, no return to that divine vision he was once granted to see in Shakhovskoye, on the terrace thronged by jasmine shrubs, there could be no return, and feebly he cried from his heart-rending pain.

This pain was so severe, so unbearable, that instinctively, without giving thought to the outcome, and with just one driving desire to get rid of it if only for a minute and not find himself once more in that horrible world where he had spent all that day and where he had just been involved in the most horrible and hideous of nightmares there could be on earth, he groped for the drawer of his bedside table, pulled it out, gripped his cold, heavy revolver and, drawing a deep, glad breath, opened wide his mouth and pressed the trigger hard, with relish.

Maritime Alps, September 14, 1924

Sunstroke

After dinner they came up on deck and stood close by the rail, leaving the bright, hot lights of the dining-room behind them. She closed her eyes, pressed the back of her hand to her cheek, laughed a frank, charming laugh—everything was charming about that small woman—and said: "I'm quite drunk... Where did you come from? Three hours ago I didn't even know you existed. I don't even know when you came on board. Was it in Samara? But it does not matter. Am I dizzy or are we turning round somewhere?"

Ahead lay darkness and lights. A soft steady breeze blew into their faces from the darkness, and the lights rushed away from them in an arc. With the dash of a Volga craft, the boat swung in a wide curve as it ran up to a small pier.

The lieutenant took her hand and raised it to his lips. The hand, small and strong, smelt of sunburn. And his heart came to a blissful and frightening standstill when he thought how strong and tanned her whole body must be under that light linen dress, after lying on the hot sand beneath a southern sky for a whole month (she told him she was on her way from Anapa).

"Let's get off..." he muttered.

"Where?" she asked surprised.

"At this stop."

"What for?"

He said nothing. She pressed the back of her hand to her hot cheek again.

"It's madness..."

"Let's get off," he repeated dully. "I beg you."

"Oh, have it your own way then," she said turning away.

Coming on at full speed, the ship thudded softly against a dimly lit pier, and they almost fell on top of one another. A cable flew over their heads, the ship was driven back, water churned noisily and gang-planks rumbled... The lieutenant rushed for their luggage.

A minute later they passed the sleepy little office, came out on the beach, sinking ankle-deep in the sand, and silently climbed into a dusty carriage. They drove up a long slope, soft with dust and marked by infrequent crooked lamp-posts and seemingly endless. But now they topped the rise and the wheels clatterd on the cobble-stones: there was a market square or something, office building, a fire-tower, and the warmth and scents of a provincial town on a summer night. The driver stopped before a lighted doorway beyond which they could see a steep old wooden staircase and an old, unshaven porter in a pink shirt and a frock-coat, who took their suitcases with a disagreeable air and led the way upstairs on his shambling feet. He brought them to a large but terribly stuffy room, heated by the day's sun, with white curtains at the windows and a couple of new candles on the dressing-table. And the minute the porter left them, closing the door behind him, the lieutenant turned to her so impetuously, and a desire so frenzied swept over them both when they kissed, that this moment was to remain in their memories for many years to come: neither he nor she had ever experienced anything like it in all their lives.

At ten o'clock in the morning—a sunny, hot and joyous morning with churchbells pealing, with the noise and bustle of the market in front of the hotel, with the smell of hay, tar and again all those strong mixed scents of a Russian provincial town—she, that small nameless woman who had not told him her name after all, but, laughing, had called herself a fair stranger, went away. They had not had much sleep, but in the morning, when she left the bed and came round the screen, washed and put on her clothes in five minutes, she looked as fresh as a girl of seventeen. Was she feeling embarrassed? Only very slightly. She was as simple and cheerful as ever, and her common sense was already asserting itself.

"No, no, dearest," she said in answer to his plea that they continue their voyage together. "No, you must stay behind until the next boat. If we go on together everything will be spoilt. It will be very unpleasant for me. I give you my word of honour that I'm not at all what you might have thought me to be. Nothing even remotely like this has ever happened to me before, nor will it ever happen again. I must have lost my senses... Or, rather, we both had something like a sunstroke..."

And the lieutenant agreed with her with a certain light-heartedness. He took her as far as the pier with a light and happy heart, arriving there just as the pink *Samolyot* was ready to cast off, he kissed her in front of everyone on deck and barely managed to jump down the gang-plank before it was hauled up.

He returned to the hotel feeling as light-hearted and carefree as before. However, he found that some change had already occurred there. Without her the room looked quite different. It was still filled with her presence, but empty! That was odd! The room still smelt of her good English toilet water, her unfinished cup of tea was still standing on the tray, and yet she was no longer there... And the lieutenant's heart was suddenly wrung with such tenderness that he hastened to light a cigarette and take a brisk walk up and down the room.

"What a strange adventure!" he said aloud with a laugh, conscious of the tears welling up in his eyes. " 'I give you my word of honour I'm not at all what you might have thought me to be...' And now she's gone..."

The screen had been moved back, the bed not yet made. And he felt he simply could not bear to look at that bed now. He put the screen back to hide it, closed the windows to shut out the noise of the market crowd and the squealing of wheels, he let down the white, puffed-up curtains, and sat down on the sofa. Well, that was the end of his "shipboard adventure"! She was gone and by now she was far away, probably sitting in the white glass lounge or lying back in a deck chair, gazing at the vast river gleaming in the sun, at the timber rafts moving downstream, at the yellow shoals, at the bright vista of water and sky, at all this infinite expanse of the Volga... And good-bye now, for ever and ever... For where could they ever meet again? "After all," he thought, "how could I, for no reason at all, suddenly appear in the town where she lives with her husband, her three-year-old daughter, all the rest of her family and her whole everyday world!" And this town seemed to him different somehow, a sacred town, and the thought that she would just go on living her lonely life there, perhaps thinking of him often, remembering their chance meeting and those fleeting hours, while he would never see her again—this thought shocked and stupefied him. No, that could not be! It would be too mad, too unnatural and incredible! And he felt a pain so poignant, such futility in all the life that stretched before him without her that terror and despair gripped him.

"What the hell!" he thought, getting up and starting to pace the room again, trying not to look at the bed behind the screen. "What's come over me? And what's so wonderful about her? What did happen? It really is like a sunstroke! But the main thing is how on earth am I going to get through the rest of the day without her in this miserable town?"

He still remembered everything about her, all the slightest details that belonged to her alone; he remembered the smell of her sunburn and her linen dress, her strong body, and the lilting, frank and cheerful sound of her voice. He still felt with extraordinary vividness the ecstasy he had experienced from all her feminine charms, and yet this other, this quite novel feeling was the more important now, this peculiar, strange feeling which he did not have at all when they were together, of which he had never suspected himself capable when he started the affair the night before, thinking it would be an amusing experience, this feeling which he could tell to no one, no one now! "And the worst of it is, I'll never be able to tell her!" he thought. "What am I to do? How can I live through this endless day with these memories, this agony that cannot be appeased, in this god-forsaken little town on the same gleaming Volga that has carried her away in that pink ship?"

He had to find some escape, do something to distract his mind, go somewhere. He resolutely put on his cap, picked up his cane, briskly walked down the empty corridor and with a jungle of spurs ran down the steep staircase to the front door. Yes, but where was he to go? A cab stood by the entrance, and the driver, a young chap, smartly dressed, sat calmly smoking a cigarette. The lieutenant threw a perplexed and amazed look at him: how could he sit on his coach-box so calmly, smoke a cigarette and, altogether, be so ordinary, carefree and indifferent? "I expect I'm the only one in this whole town who's so dreadfully unhappy," he thought as he started out towards the market place.

The market crowd was already thinning. He walked aimlessly between carts loaded with cucumbers, stepping on the fresh manure, and strolled among new pots and bowls, while the women sitting on the ground vied with one another offering him their wares. They picked up their pots and tapped them with their fingers making them ring to show their quality, while the men deafened him with their shouts: "Here, the best cucumbers ever, Your Honour!" It was all so stupid and preposterous that he fled from the market. He dropped into the cathedral towards the end of the service, where the singing of the choir was already loud, joyful and deliberate, with the consciousness of duty done; and after that he walked for a long time, round and round the little neglected garden perched on the cliff above the boundless, steel-grey expanse of the river... The shoulder-straps and buttons on his tunic were too hot to touch. The band inside his cap was sticky with sweat, his face was flaming. When he got back to the hotel he was delighted and relieved to walk into the large, empty, cool dining-room on the ground floor, to take off his cap and sit down at a table close to an open window which let in hot air, but it was air anyway, and to order iced beetroot soup.

Everything was fine, everything held immeasurable happiness and great joy; even in this very heat, in the market smells, in all of the strange, wretched little town and in this old provincial hotel, there was joy, and yet his heart was breaking. He drank several glasses of vodka and while he ate his dill pickles he was thinking he would be willing to die on the morrow, without a moment's hesitation, if only she could be brought back by some miracle, if only he could spend one more day with her—spend it with her just so that he could tell her, convince her, prove to her somehow that he loved her desperately and rapturously... But why prove it? Why convince her? He did not know why, but it was more essential than living.

"My nerves are all shot to blazes!" he muttered, pouring out his fifth glass of vodka.

He pushed his soup away, ordered some black coffee and sat smoking and thinking hard: what was he to do now, how to shake off this sudden and unexpected love? But to shake it off was impossible. All at once he got up, took his cap and cane, asked the way to the post-office and hurried off towards it, already framing the wording of his telegram in his mind: "From now and for ever my life is in your power until death." But when he came to the old, thick-walled building of the post-office and telegraph, he stopped, horrified: he knew the town where she lived, he knew that she had a husband and a three-year-old daughter, but he did not know her name! He had kept asking her to tell him at dinner the night before and afterwards at the hotel, but every time she merely laughed and said:

"But why do you want to know my name?"

There was a photographer's window on the corner, next to the post-office. He stood staring for a long time at a large photograph of an officer with thickly fringed epaulets, protuberant eyes, a low forehead, amazingly sumptuous sideburns and the broadest of chests completely covered with decorations... How mad, how absurd and horrible was all that was ordinary and trivial when your heart was smitten—yes, it was smitten, he knew it now—with that frightening "sunstroke", with a love that is too strong, with happiness that is too great! He looked at a wedding group—the young bridegroom in a long frock-coat and white tie, with cropped hair, standing rigidly to attention, arm in arm with a girl in a bridal veil—he brought his eyes to rest on a picture of a pretty and saucy-looking girl wearing a student's cap at a rakish angle... And then, tormented by agonising envy for all these people he did not know, people who were not suffering, he looked with strained attention down the street.

"Where shall I go? What shall I do?"

The street was quite empty. The houses were all alike, white, two-storeyed, middle class homes with large gardens, and there did not seem to be a soul in any of them; the street was carpeted with thick white dust, and all of it blinded one, all of it was flooded with sunlight, passionate and joyous, but somehow purposeless. In the distance the street humped uphill and butted into the cloudless, greyish and shimmering sky. There was a hint of the south in this, reminding him of Sevastopol, Kerch, Anapa. This was particularly unbearable. And with drooping head, squinting in the glare, staring fixedly at the ground before him, staggering and stumbling, getting tangled in his spurs, the lieutenant made his way back.

He felt so shattered with weariness when he reached the hotel that he might have traversed great spaces somewhere in the Sahara Desert or in Turkestan. Mustering his remaining strength he entered his large and empty room. It had already been tidied, deprived of all trace of her, and only a hairpin she had dropped lay on the bedside table. He took off his tunic and looked at himself in the mirror: his face—an ordinary officer's face, dark-grey with sunburn, with a colourless moustache bleached in the sun and bluish eyeballs which looked whiter still against his tan—now held an agitated, insane expression, and there was something youthful and profoundly unhappy in his thin white shirt with its starched upstanding collar. He went to the bed and lay down on his back, putting his feet in their dusty top-boots on the rail at its foot. The windows were open, the curtains down, and a gentle breeze puffed them out now and again, bringing into the room the heat of the sweltering iron roofs and all that brilliant and now utterly desolate, soundless Volga world. He lay with his hands behind his head, staring fixedly before him. Then he clenched his teeth and closed his eyes, feeling the tears crawling down his cheeks, and at last he fell asleep. When he opened his eyes, the reddish-yellow sunset was already aglow behind the curtains. The breeze had died down, the room was stuffy and as hot as an oven. And he recalled the previous day and that morning as if they had been ten years ago.

Unhurriedly he got up, unhurriedly he washed, drew the curtains, rang, asked for a samovar and his bill, and then leisurely drank his lemon tea. After this he ordered a cab, had his suitcases taken down, and as he got into the carriage and settled on its seat of faded, rusty brown, he tipped the porter a whole five-ruble note.

"Looks to me, Your Honour, it was I who brought you here last night," the driver said cheerfully as he picked up his reins.

When they came down to the pier, the blue summer night had already spread over the Volga, and many little lights of different colours were already scattered down the river, and lanterns hung suspended from the masts of the ship as it swung up to the pier.

"Got you here on time!" the driver said ingratiatingly.

The lieutenant tipped him with a five-ruble note too, bought his ticket and went down to the pier. Just like the night before, there was the soft thud against the mooring-block, a slight dizziness because of the heaving floor, and then a flying cable, the noise of water churning and rushing forward beneath the wheels of the boat which was driven back somewhat. And this crowded ship, already fully lighted and smelling of the kitchen, gave him a feeling of extraordinary friendliness and contentment.

A minute later they were on their way, up river, the same way that she had gone off earlier that morning.

The dark glow of the summer sunset died away far ahead, casting its sombre, drowsy and varicoloured reflection upon the water that still quivered and glimmered here and there with ripples far below the glow, and the lights, scattered in the darkness about them, floated far, far away...

The lieutenant sat in a deck chair under an awning, feeling as though ten years had been added to his age.

Maritime Alps, 1925

Ivan Bunin's mother

Ivan Bunin's father

The house in which Ivan Bunin was born in Voronezh

Yelets. The school Ivan Bunin went to

Ivan Bunin in 1889. Written in his hand on the photograph: "Yes, this one. I. A. Bunin at the start of his literary career."

Ivan Bunin and his first love Varvara Paschenko. Poltava. 1892

The writer's son Nikolai. He was born in Odessa on August 30, 1900 and died on January 16, 1905

Anna Tsakni. On the back of the photograph Bunin has written: "23 September, 1898. Odessa." It was the day they were married

Vera Muromtseva, Bunin's future wife, in her school days. "Without you I would not have written anything. I'd have perished. I. Bunin."

Anton Chekhov. "To dear Ivan Alexeyevich Bunin from his colleague. Anton Chekhov. 1901. 11. 19."

Anton Chekhov's house in Yalta

Anton Chekhov and Ivan Bunin. Written by Bunin on the back of the photograph: "Chekhov and I in his study, in the house in Autka, on the outskirts of Yalta. As usual I am telling some story and acting a drunk."

Sofia Lavrova, Maria Chekhova, Ivan Bunin. Yalta. 1900-1902

Ivan Bunin. 23 December, 1902. On the photograph Bunin wrote to Chekhov's sister, Maria: "Handsome, eh? I kiss your hands and send my regards to dear Anton Pavlovich and Yevgenia Yakovlevna, and please write to me. I'm off to Odessa with Naidenov: 5 Sofievskaya. 29 December, 1902, Yours, I. Bunin."

Fyodor Chaliapine. 30 October, 1902. He gave the photograph to Bunin with this inscription: "Dear Vanya! My God is free from censorship and I rejoice! Your loving Chaliapine."

The house where Yuly Bunin lived and where the writer often stayed.
32 Starokonyushenny St., Moscow

Ivan Bunin, Sergei Naidenov, Alexander Fyodorov

Ivan Bunin and his wife Vera. Written in Bunin's hand on the back of the photograph: "Spring 1907. Our first trip to Syria, Palestine." On April 23, 1936, he wrote in his diary: "On that day—10 April, 1907—I went with Vera to Palestine, and we married."

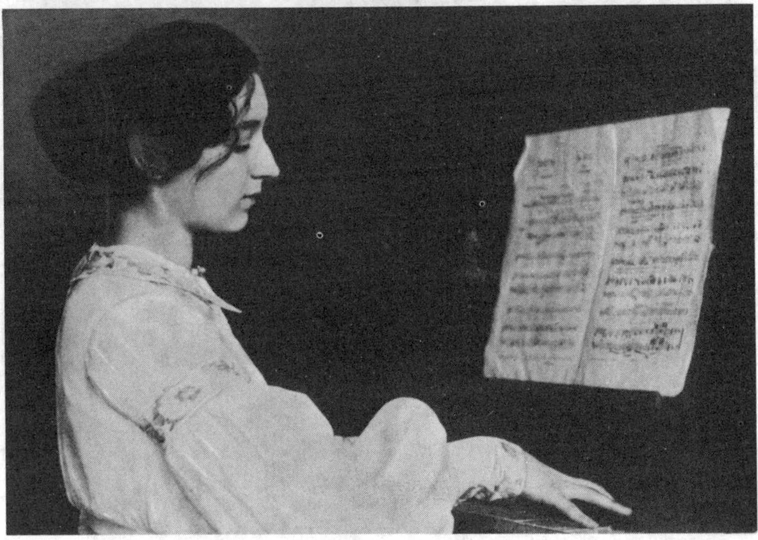

Vera Bunina. 1907

Ivan Bunin's brothers Yuly (left) and Yevgeny with his wife (standing), and their sister Maria. 1900 or thereabouts

Ivan Bunin, N. Pusheshnikov, 1906

Bunin's inscription on the photograph says: "Capri. Spring 1910. On the balcony of Gorky's villa. Ivan Bunin, Gorky, his adopted son Zinovy, Vera Muromtseva (my wife), M. Andreyeva, O. Kamenskaya."

Nikolai Teleshov's inscription on the back of this photograph says: "Gorky's study. Capri. 1913. Taken after Bunin's reading of his story. Sitting: Gorky, Chaliapine, Gorky's son Maxim; Ivan Bunin; in front of Bunin—Yevgeny Lyatsky; next to Bunin—his wife Vera Nikolayevna; Chaliapine's wife Maria Valentinovna; Yekaterina Pavlovna Peshkova; Novikov-Priboy. Standing: Tikhonov's wife Varvara Vasilyevna, Leonid Nikolayevich Stark, Alexei Tikhonov, Sergei Gusev, Maria Sikorskaya and her husband Lorenz."

The house of the painter Yevgeny Bukovetsky in Odessa where Bunin lived between 1918 and January 1920. In 1980, on the 110th anniversary of Bunin's birth, a memorial plaque was unveiled here

Bunin wrote across the top corner of this photograph: "Summer 1923, *Montfleuri* (the first villa where we lived in Grasse). Iv. B." "Shmeleva, Bunina, J. Bounine, Shmelev."

Bunin's inscription on the back: "S. V. Rachmaninov and I. A. Bunin. Summer 1926. Cannes. A. M."

Ivan Bunin and the photographer. Grasse. 1932

Vera Bunina. On the back Bunin wrote: "V. N. Bunina. 1927, Paris."

Bunin and his wife Vera (in the window of his study) at Villa Belvédère. Grasse. 1926

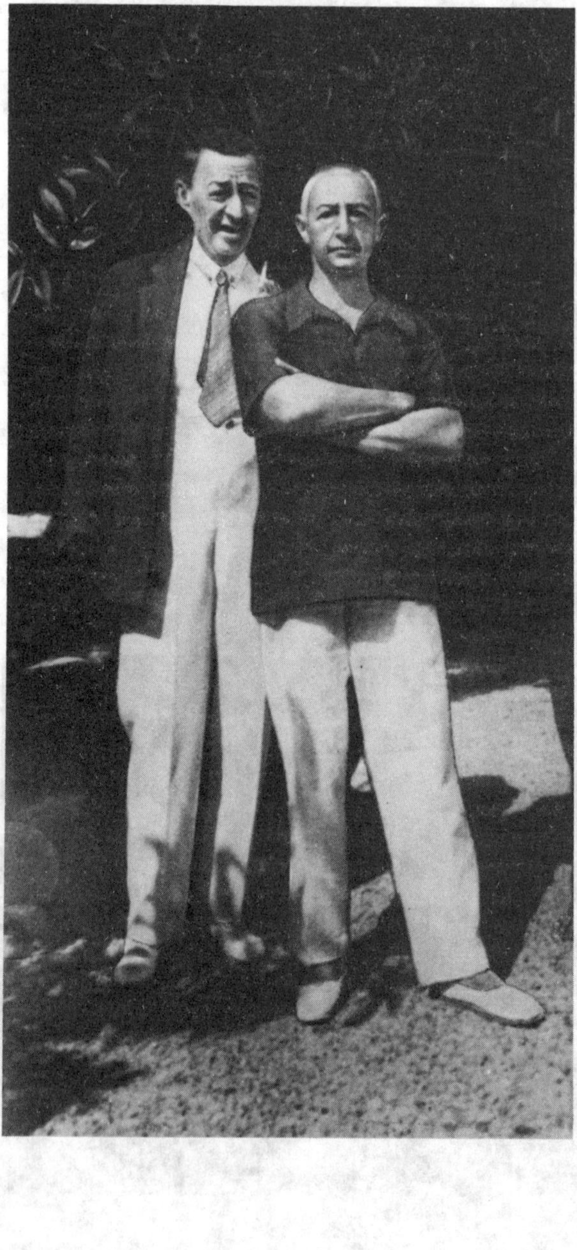

Sergei Rachmaninov, Ivan Bunin. In the 1930's

Ivan Bunin. Grasse. In the 1930's

The Bunins'
Paris flat

Ivan Bunin. 7 January, 1930. His inscription on the back says: "Grasse. A. M. –1933. At the window of "Belvédère". (Bunin made a mistake in the date)

Ivan Bunin. Grasse. In the 1930's
Ivan Bunin. Grasse. 10 November, 1933

Ivan Bunin. Paris. 5 July, 1948

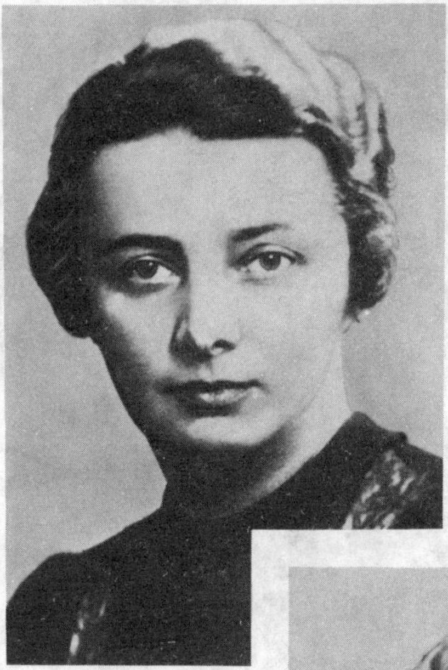

Vera Bunina. Stockholm. December 1933

Galina Kuznetsova. Paris. 1934

27 November, 1973. The unveiling of the memorial plaque on the rock at the entrance to Villa Jeannette, and the stele on the road to Villa Belvédère, to mark the day, fifty years earlier, when Bunin first came to live in Grasse and also twenty years since his death. Left to right: Vladimir Nemtsov, the Soviet Consul in Marseilles, the Mayor of Grasse Henri de Fonmichel and Sergei Lifar, famous dancer, owner of a big Pushkin collection. The inscription on the stele says: "Ce chemin mène à la Villa Belvédère où demeura pendant seize ans Ivan Bounine écrivain russe 1870-1953, Prix Nobel."

FROM THE BOOK *Shadowed Paths*

Shadowed Paths

One cold rainy day in autumn a mud-spattered coach with the hood half up, drawn by three rather ordinary horses abreast, their tails tied up out of the mud, came rolling along one of the Tula highways that was awash with rain and cut with numerous deep black ruts. The troika stopped in front of a long timber building, one section of which was occupied by the post-station, and the other by a private-owned inn, where travellers could rest or spend the night, have dinner or order a samovar. On the box sat a large, sturdy man, tightly belted into his peasant's overcoat, with a dark, grave face and a thin pitch-black beard which made him look like an outlaw of old. And in the coach was a lean old man in a large cap and a grey officer's cloak with an upstanding beaver collar, with eyebrows still black but the moustache already grey, its tips touching his sideburns of the same grey; his chin was clean-shaven, and all in all his appearance was not unlike that of Alexander II, a style that was very much in vogue among the officers during his reign. His eyes, too, had the same look—questioning, stern and yet weary.

When the coach came to a stop, he threw out a leg encased in a closely fitting military boot, and, holding his cloak together with chamois-gloved hands, ran up the porch steps.

"To your left, Your Excellency," the driver called huskily from his box, and the man, stooping a little in the doorway because of his great height, walked into the entry and then into the room on his left.

The place was warm, dry and neat; a new icon glistened goldenly in the left-hand corner, under it stood a table covered with a clean table-cloth of unbleached linen, and well-scrubbed benches were ranged around it; the stove, which took up the right-hand corner of the room, was freshly whitewashed; nearer the door stood a kind of couch draped in horse-cloths and pushed up against the side of the stove; a delicious smell of soup—well-cooked cabbage, beef and bay leaf—came from behind the oven door.

The newcomer threw his cloak down on the bench—appearing even more erect and slender in his tunic and top-boots—then he took off his gloves and cap and with a weary gesture passed his pale thin hand over his hair—his grey hair, brushed forward from the temples towards the corners of his eyes, had a soft curl in it, and his handsome, long, dark-eyed face showed tiny pockmarks here and there. There was no one in the room and, pushing the door slightly ajar, he shouted querulously:

"I say, is anyone there?"

Whereupon a dark-haired woman came into the room. Her eyebrows were black like the man's and, like him, she still retained a beauty that was not in keeping with her years. She resembled a middle-aged Gipsy woman in that her upper lip and the sides of her face were shadowed with a soft down; she was light on her feet though her body was heavy, with large breasts under her red blouse, and a stomach, triangular like a goose's, outlined by her black woolen skirt.

"Welcome, Your Excellency," she said. "May I offer you something to eat or would you rather have a samovar?"

The newcomer threw a cursory glance at her rounded shoulders and her slim feet in their shabby red Tatar slippers, and answered carelessly and brusquely:

"A samovar. Are you the inn-keeper or the servant?"

"The inn-keeper, Your Excellency."

"You mean you run the place yourself?"

"I do, sir."

"How's that? Are you a widow that you're all alone in business?"

"I'm not a widow, Your Excellency, but I have to make a living somehow. And I like to be in business."

"I see, I see. That's good. And your room is so clean and pleasant."

The woman kept her slightly narrowed eyes fastened on him with a searching look.

"I like cleanliness too," she said. "After all, I was brought up in the gentry's service, I ought to know how to keep my place decent, Nikolai Alexeyevich."

He drew himself up at once, opened his eyes wide and blushed.

"You can't be Nadezhda?" he asked quickly.

"Yes, Nikolai Alexeyevich," she replied.

"Good God! Good God!" he said, sitting down on the bench and staring hard at her. "Who would have ever thought it! How many years is it since we last saw each other? About thirty-five, I should imagine?"

"It's thirty, Nikolai Alexeyevich. I'm forty-eight now and you're close on sixty, I think?"

"Something like that... Good God, how strange!"

"What's strange, sir?"

"Why, everything, everything... Surely you must understand!"

His weariness and his indifference vanished, he got up and started pacing the room with resolute strides, his eyes upon the floor. Then he stopped and, with a blush creeping through his grey sideburns, began to speak:

"Since then I have heard nothing about you at all. How do you come to be here? Why didn't you stay on with your masters?"

"They gave me my freedom soon after you left."

"And where did you go then?"

"It's a long story, sir."

"And you say you were never married?"

"No, never."

"But why? A girl as beautiful as you were then?"

"I couldn't do it."

"Why not? What are you trying to say?"

"What is there to say? I expect you remember how much I loved you."

He blushed so hard that tears welled up in his eyes, and with a scowl he resumed his pacing.

"Everything passes, my friend," he muttered. "Love, youth, everything, everything. It's an ordinary, trivial story. Everything passes with time. What does it say in the Book of Job? 'As the waters fail from the sea and the flood decayeth and drieth up.' "

"It's all God's will, Nikolai Alexeyevich. Youth does pass for all of us, but love—that's a different thing."

He raised his head and, stopping in front of her, asked with a strained smile:

"But surely you couldn't have loved me all your life?"

"I did, you see. I lived by that alone and the passing years made it no different. I knew that you had changed long ago, that it meant as little to you as if it had never been, but still... It's too late for reproaches now, but it's true you abandoned me very heartlessly then. At times I wanted to lay hands upon myself from the hurt of it alone, to say nothing of the rest. You know there was a time, Nikolai Alexeyevich, when I used to call you Nikolenka, and you called me—remember? And you were always reciting poetry to me about all sorts of 'shadowed paths', remember?" she added with a grim smile.

"Ah, how lovely you were then!" he said, nodding in reminiscence. "How passionate! How beautiful! What a body, what eyes! Remember the way everyone gazed at you?"

"I remember, sir. You were exceptionally handsome too. And it was to you that I gave my beauty and my passion, you know. That's something that can never be forgotten."

"Ah! Everything passes. One forgets everything."

"Everything passes, but one does not forget everything."

"Go," he said, turning away and walking to the window. "Please go."

And pulling out a handkerchief, he pressed it to his eyes and added in a quick patter:

"I only hope God forgives me. You have, I see."

She went towards the door and paused there:

"No, Nikolai Alexeyevich, I have not forgiven you. Since we have begun to talk about our feelings, I'll be frank with you. I have never been able to forgive you. I never had anything more precious in this world than you—either then or afterwards. And that is why I cannot forgive you. Oh well, what's the use of remembering, you don't bring the dead back from the graveyard."

"Yes, yes, there's no sense in it, tell them to get the horses ready," he replied walking away from the window, and now his face was stern. "I'll only say this to you: I have never been happy in my life, please don't think I have. Forgive me, I may be wounding your pride, but I'll tell you frankly–I loved my wife to distraction. Yet she deceived me, she abandoned me much more hurtfully than I abandoned you. I adored my son while he was a child–what hope I placed in him! But he grew up to be a scoundrel, a rake and a cad without a heart, without honour or conscience... However, that too is the most ordinary and trivial of stories. I wish you luck, my dear. I think that in you I, too, lost the most precious thing I ever had in my life."

She came up to him and kissed his hand, and he kissed hers.

"Tell them I'm ready to go..."

As he drove away he was thinking glumly: "How sweet she used to be! How bewitchingly lovely!" He remembered with shame his parting words to her and his kissing her hand, and, instantly, he felt ashamed of his shame. "Isn't it true that she gave me the best moments of my life?"

A pale sun appeared low in the western sky. The driver kept his horses at a trot, changing from one black track to another, choosing those that were less muddy, and he also seemed to be engrossed in thought. At last he said with grave brusqueness:

"She kept looking from the window, Your Excellency, when we were driving away. You've known her long, I suppose?"

"Yes, Klim."

"That's a very wise woman. And she's getting richer all the time, they say. She lends money out to folks."

"That doesn't mean a thing."

"Oh, doesn't it! Don't we all want to better our lot? And if you're decent about the interest, there's little harm done. And they say she's fair on that score. But she's hard too! If you don't pay back on time–you've only yourself to blame."

"Yes, yes, you've only yourself to blame... Hurry, please, I'm afraid we'll miss the train..."

The sun, sinking low, cast a yellow light over the desolate fields, the horses splashed steadily through the puddles.

He drew his black eyebrows together and mused, absently following the flickering horseshoes before him.

"Yes, you've only yourself to blame. Yes, of course, the best moments of my life. And not only the best, the truly magic ones! 'Around us bloomed sweet brier red, and paths with lime trees tall were shadowed...' But, good heavens, what would have happened then? Supposing I hadn't left her, what then? Heavens, what rubbish! This Nadezhda woman—not the owner of a wayside inn, but my wife, the mistress of my house in Petersburg, the mother of my children?"

And, closing his eyes, he shook his head.

October 20, 1938

The Caucasus

When I came to Moscow I thievishly put up at an inconspicuous rooming house in a side-street off Arbat Street and lived the dreary life of a recluse—from one rendezvous with her to the next. She only came to my room three times, and each time came in hastily, with the words: "I can only stay a minute."

Her face was pale with the beautiful pallor of a stirred up, loving woman, her voice broke, and the way she threw her parasol just anywhere and fumbled with her nose veil to kiss me overwhelmed me with a feeling of tenderness and adoration.

"I think he suspects something," she said. "Or even knows something. Maybe he has read a letter of yours or fitted a key to my writing table, I believe that with his cruelty and vanity he's capable of anything. Once he told me very directly: 'I shall stop at nothing to defend my honour, the honour of a husband and an officer!' I don't know why, but he's taken to watching my every step, and if our plan is to succeed I've got to be terribly careful. He has consented to let me go because I've convinced him that I shall simply die if I don't see the mountains and the sea, so please, please be patient."

Our plan was very bold: to go by the same train to the Caucasian seacoast and for three or four weeks live together in the wildest of wilds there. I knew the coast well, I once lived near Sochi for a time when I was young and unattached, and all my life I would remember those autumn evenings amid the black cypresses, with the cold, grey waves below... And she paled when I said: "And now I'll be there with you in those mountain wilds, on the shore of the tropical sea..." Until the very last minute we did not believe that our plan would be accomplished, for the happiness it promised seemed too enormous to us.

Cold rain persisted in Moscow, it seemed that summer was quite over and would not come back, it was muddy and sullen, the streets gleamed wetly and blackly with the open umbrellas of the pedestrians and the raised tops of the cabs quivering from the motion. It was a dark, horrible evening when I drove to the railway station, and my whole being was numbed by anxiety and cold. I went at a run down the platform to my coach, keeping my hat pulled down over my eyes and my chin tucked in the upraised collar of my overcoat.

In the small first-class compartment which I had booked in advance, I could hear the rain noisily drumming on the roof. I quickly drew the window curtain, and as soon as the porter had taken my tip, first wiping his wet hand on his white apron, and gone, I locked the door. Then I pulled back the curtain a chink and froze, peering into the motley crowd that scurried up and down the train with bags and bundles in the dim light of the station lamps. We agreed that I'd come to the station as early as possible and she'd come at the last minute, so that we should not bump into each other on the platform. It was now time for her and her husband to be there. I watched more and more tensely—still no sight of them. The second bell rang, and I turned cold from fear. Were they late, or had he suddenly changed his mind at the last moment? But in the next breath I gasped at the sight of his tall figure, his officer's cap, his long, narrow greatcoat, and his chamois-gloved hand holding her arm as he strode freely down the platform. I shrank back from the window and collapsed into the corner of my berth. The coach next to mine was a second-class one, and in my mind's eye I saw him entering with a proprietory air, looking about him to make sure that the porter had arranged her luggage properly, then pulling off a glove and his cap, kissing her goodbye and making the sign of the cross over her. The third bell deafened me, and the starting train petrified me. It took off, swaying and rocking at first, then the pace evened out and the train flew at full speed... With ice-cold fingers I thrust a ten-ruble note into the hand of the train attendant who brought her and her luggage over to my compartment...

When she came in she did not even kiss me, she only gave me a piteous little smile as she sat down to take off her hat, unpinning it from her hair.

"I couldn't eat a thing at dinner," she told me. "I thought I'd never play out that awful role to the end. I'm terribly thirsty. Give me some mineral water, will you. I gave him two addresses, one in Gelendzhik and the other in Gagra. You'll see, he'll be in Gelendzhik in three or four days' time... Oh, let him, better death than this torture..."

In the morning, when I came out into the corridor I found it sunlit and stuffy, with the scent of soap and eau de cologne coming from the toilets, and smelling of everything a full passenger car smells of in the morning. Outside the dusty, sun-baked windows stretched a level, scorched steppe, I could see the wide, dusty roads, carts drawn by bullocks, trackmen's cabins flashing past with canary-yellow sunflowers and hollyhocks in the front gardens... And now all round us were bare, boundless plains with their tumuli and burial mounds under an unbearably dry sun and a sky like a dust cloud, and then the faint outlines of the mountains appeared on the horizon...

She sent him a postcard from Gelendzhik and another one from Gagra, telling him that she did not yet know where she was going to stay.

And now the train rolled along the shore, heading south.

We found a truly pristine spot, overrun by plane trees, flowering shrubs, mahoganies, magnolias and pomegranates, among which towered great frondiferous palms and dark cypresses.

I woke up early, and while she slept until breakfast which we had at seven, walked up the rises and down the dips to the forest thickets. The hot sun would already be shining strongly, clearly and joyfully. A fragrant mist would be dissolving in the forest in a blue radiance, and behind the distant wooded mountain range sparkled the everlasting whiteness of the snow-capped peaks... I came back by way of the market-place in our village; it was hot here, and a smell of burning manure briquettes rose from the chimneys; business was in full swing and the place was thronged with people, saddle horses and donkeys. Every morning a motley crowd of mountain dwellers assembled at the market-place. Circassian women seemed to glide along rather than walk in their red leather hose, black floor-length robes, and with some black stuff wound round their heads; now and then they darted swift glances from this mourning wrappage of theirs.

After breakfast we went down to the beach, which was always completely deserted, and we bathed and lay about in the sun until lunch. After lunch, which was invariably fried fish, white wine, nuts and fruit, we closed the window shutters, and jolly streaks of light stole into the sultry duskiness of our little tile-roofed cabin through the slats.

We opened the windows when the heat lessened, and the bit of sea visible between the cypresses growing on the slope below us was the colour of violets and was so still and tranquil that it seemed there would never come an end to this peace, this beauty.

At sundown, amazing clouds often piled up beyond the sea; they blazed so magnificently that the sheer beauty of the sight made her cry, and she would lie down on the couch, and cover her face with her gauze scarf and weep—just two more, three more weeks, and then Moscow again!

The nights were warm and impenetrable, fire-flies sailed in the blackness with their shimmering topaz light, and tree-frogs tinkled like little crystal bells. When our eyes became accustomed to the darkness, we saw the stars above and the mountain ranges, and also trees, higher up than the village, which we had not noticed in the daytime. And all night from the village came the hollow beating of the drum and the guttural, monotonously, and hopelessly elated wailing of what seemed to be always the same, endless song.

Not far from our cabin, a clear, shallow little river leapt swiftly along its stony bed at the bottom of a gully running down from the forest to the sea. How beautifully the seething sparkle of the water was fragmented in that magic hour of the night when the late moon, like some wondrous being, looked down watchfully from behind the mountains and forests!

Sometimes, at night, ominous clouds crept down from the mountains, heralding an angry rainstorm, and then fantastic green abysses yawned open in the sky above the noisy blackness of the forest, and antemundane thunder crashed up high. And then, in the forests, baby eagles awoke and miawed, the snow leopard roared, young jackals barked... Once a whole pack of young jackals came running to our lighted window—they always run to human habitation on such nights—we opened the window and looked down at them as they stood under the downpour and yelped, begging to be let in... Watching them, she wept tears of pure joy.

He tried to find her in Gelendzhik, Gagra and Sochi. His second day in Sochi, he bathed in the sea in the morning, had a shave, put on a fresh shirt and a snow-white tunic, had lunch on the terrace of his hotel, drank a bottle of champagne, had coffee with Chartreuse, and smoked a leisurely cigar. When he returned to his room, he lay down on the couch and with a revolver in each hand fired at his temples.

12 November, 1937

Ballad

From Christmas, through to the New Year, the country house was always heated to a steambath temperature, and presented a strange picture with the doors between all the spacious, low-ceilinged rooms standing wide open, all the way from the entrance hall to the sitting-room at the farthest end of the house, and all the rooms aglow with the light of wax candles and little oil lamps burning before the icons.

Just before Christmas, the smooth oakwood floors were scrubbed throughout the house, they dried quickly in the heat and were then covered with clean horsecloths; the furniture which had been moved out of the way while the scrubbing went on was carefully put back in place, and the little oil lamps and candles were lit before the icons with gilded or silver covers, and all other lights were put out. By this hour the night sky outside the windows would already be a dark blue, and the household would retire to their bedrooms. Perfect quiet would then descend on the house, that reverential and expectant silence, most befitting to the holy look of the icons in their mournful and stirring illumination.

Mashenka, a small, wizened and grey-haired pilgrim, sometimes spent the winter at the house. And of the whole household she was the only person who stayed awake on nights such as these. After supper in the servants' hall she came into the front hall and, taking off her felt boots, went about the hot, mysteriously illuminated rooms, her small feet in their wool socks stepping soundlessly on the horsecloths. She stopped in every room, knelt before the icons and crossed herself, and then returned to the front hall, sat down on the black chest that had been there since the beginning of time, and recited psalms or prayers in a whisper, or simply talked to herself. That was how I happened to learn about that "God's beast, the wolf" for I heard Mashenka praying to him.

I could not fall asleep and so, late at night, I went to the sitting-room by way of the ballroom to find something to read in the book-cases there. Mashenka did not hear me. She was muttering something, sitting in the dark front hall. I stopped and listened. She was reciting some psalms by heart.

"Hear my prayer, O Lord, and let my cry come unto thee," she muttered in a tone utterly devoid of expression. "Let Thine ears be attentive to the voice of my supplications ... for I am a wanderer of Thine and a stranger on earth like all my fathers before me... Say unto God: how terrible are thou in thy works... He that dwelleth in the secret place of the most High shall abide under the shadow of the Almighty... Thou shalt tread upon the lion and adder; the young lion and the dragon shalt thou trample underfoot..."

These last words she uttered with conviction, raising her voice gently yet firmly: "the young lion and the dragon shalt thou trample underfoot." After a thoughtful moment, she drew a slow sigh and said as if she were speaking to someone:

"For every beast of the forest is His upon a thousand hills..."

I looked into the front hall: she was sitting on the black chest, her small feet in their wool socks dangling primly, and her hands folded on her breast. She was looking straight ahead and did not see me. Then she raised her eyes ceillingward and pronounced distinctly:

"And thee too, God's beast, the Lord's wolf, pray the Mother of God for us."

I approached her and said softly:

"Mashenka, don't be afraid, it's I."

She dropped her hands, stood up and bowed low. "Good evening, sir. No, I'm not afraid, sir. What have I to fear now? It's when I was young and foolish that I feared everything. The dark-orbed One disturbed my spirit..."

"Sit down, please do," I said.

"No, sir. I'll stand," she replied.

I placed a hand on her bony shoulder with a too large collar bone, made her sit down, and perched on the chest beside her.

"Sit down, or I'll go away. Tell me, who were you praying to? Is there such a saint as the Lord's wolf?"

She tried to stand up again. Once again I held her down.

"Oh, come now! And you're telling me you're not afraid of anyone! I'm asking you: is there really such a saint?"

She thought for a moment, and then replied gravely:

"That there is, sir. After all, there is the Tiger-Ephrates beast, isn't there. And since it's painted in church it means there is such a saint. I saw him with my own eyes, sir."

"What d'you mean? Where? When?"

"A long time ago, sir, time out of mind. As for where? I cannot name the place now. All I remember is that we drove there for three days and three nights. There was a village there called Steep Hills. Myself I hail from far away, from Ryazan, maybe you've heard of it, and that place was even farther away, beyond the Don it was, and such rough country too, no words could describe it. It's there that our prince's forsaken estate was, the one that their grandfather loved best–mud houses scattered over the bare hills, maybe a whole thousand of them, and there, on the top of the highest hill, on the ridge above the Kamennaya river, stood the manor house, as bare as the hills, a three-storey house and a yellow church with columns, and in that there church was the God's beast himself. In the middle of the church, you see, was the grave of the prince who was killed by the wolf, there was an iron slab on the grave and on the column to the right of it was painted the wolf, in full size and might.* He sits there on his thick tail, his front legs hard on the ground, and the whole of him straining forward, and his eyes glaring straight into your face. His coat is grey, his collar's grey, thick and rough, his head's big, sharp-eared with bared fangs, his eyes are wild, and around his head there's a golden halo like saints and

***There are, in fact, paintings of the wolf in Russian churches. For instance, the Church of the Saviour (built in 1198) on the bank of the Volkhov near Novgorod has a fresco on which the Beast (a wolf) is carrying the Harlot to hell.**

angels have. Such a wonder of wonders, frightening just to remember. He looked so terribly alive, sitting there, you thought he'd pounce on you next thing!"

"Hold on, Mashenka, I don't understand a thing," I said. "Who could have painted that frightening wolf in the church, and what for? You say he killed the prince, then why is he a saint and why should he be painted there next to the prince's grave? And how did you happen to go there, to that awful village? Tell me everything properly."

And this is what Mashenka told me:

"I happened to go there, sir, because I was a serf girl then and a servant in the house of our princes. An orphan I was, my father, so people said, was a stranger, a fugitive most likely, he seduced my mother and disappeared heaven knows where, and my mother died soon after I was born. Well, the master and mistress were sorry for me, they took me into the house soon as I turned thirteen, and placed me in the service of the young mistress to run errands for her, and she grew so fond of me that she would not let me leave her side for a minute. It was she who took me along on that journey when the young prince decided to go with his lady to his grandfather's heritage, to that very same forsaken village, to Steep Hills, that is. That estate had long been neglected and deserted, the manor house boarded up and forsaken since the grandfather's death, and, well, our young master and mistress wanted to go and see what it was like. And as for his grandfather dying a horrible death, that was known to all of us from legend."

Something crackled in the ballroom and fell on the floor with a small thud. Mashenka slid down from the chest and ran to the ballroom whence came the smell of burning from that fallen candle. She pinched out the still smoking wick, stamped out the smouldering nap on the horsecloth, climbed on to a chair, re-lit the candle from the others burning in the silver stand before the icon and stuck it into the groove from which it had fallen: she held the candle upside down, let some wax drip into the groove like hot honey, stuck it in, quickly snuffed the other candles with her thin fingers, and jumped down from the chair.

"See how prettily they're burning again," she said, crossing herself and admiring the revived golden flames of the candles. "And what a churchy smell too!"

There was, indeed, a smell of sweet smoke, the candle-flames trembled and lit up the holy face in the little circle cut out in the silver icon cover. Black was the night seen in the top, clear panes of the windows where the bottom ones were thickly encrusted with grey hoarfrost, and white and near were the snow-laden branches of the trees in the front garden. Mashenka glanced at them, crossed herself once again, and went back to the front hall.

"It's time you went to bed, sir," she said, sitting down on the chest and swallowing a yawn, covering her mouth with a small bony hand. "The night's already creepy..."

"Why creepy?"

"Because it's secret time now when only the alectryon, a cock we call him, and the nocturnal raven, the owl that is, can stay awake. The Lord God Himself now listens to the earth, the most important stars begin to dance, and ice-holes freeze over on the seas and the rivers."

"What about yourself, why don't you sleep?"

"I do, sir, I sleep all I need. Old people don't need much. No more than a bird on a branch."

"Lie down then, only first finish telling me about that wolf."

"But it's an old, dark business, you know, sir, and maybe just a ballad."

"A what?"

"A ballad, sir. That's what all our masters used to say, they loved reading those ballads. I'd listen and a chill would run through my head.

Howls the forest 'yond the mountain,
Snow drifts over the fields,
Blizzards blow all day and night long,
Roads all disappear...

O Lord, how lovely!"

"But what's lovely about it, Mashenka?"

"It just is and you don't know why! It's creepy, sort of."

"In the old days everything was creepy, Mashenka."

"Was it, sir? Maybe it was at that, but it all seems wonderful now. Because when did it happen? Such a long time ago—all the kingdoms have been and gone, all the oak trees have crumbled from old age, all the graves have been levelled. Now this business too, it was repeated word for word among the servants, but had it ever really happened? They say it happened far back in the reign of the great Empress, and they say the prince lived in Steep Hills because she got angry with him for something, banished him from her sight and presence, and he grew very fierce, turning his fierceness mostly to abusing his serfs and lusting after women. He still had all his strength, and as for looks, he was a fine, handsome man, and they say there wasn't a girl among his domestics or in his village who wasn't ordered to come to his bedroom on her wedding night. Well then, he now fell into the most terrible of sins: he lusted after the bride of his own son. The son was an officer in the tzar's army in Petersburg, and when he met the young lady after his own heart, he asked for his father's blessing, married, and came with his young bride to do homage to his father at Steep Hills, the estate, that is. And he, the father, went and fell in love with her. No wonder, sir, the song about love says:

Love burns hot in every kingdom,
All the world makes love...

And surely it's no sin for a man, even if he's an old man, to dream of his beloved and pine for her? But this was something else, you see, she was sort of his own daughter, and he lusted after her with dishonourable intentions."

"And so what happened?"

"What happened was this. When the young prince guessed what his father was up to, he decided to run away with his wife on the quiet. He got the coachmen to help, lavishing gifts of money on them, and ordered them to have the most mettlesome troika ready and waiting at midnight. And as soon as his father, the old prince, went to sleep, he stole out of the house with his young wife, and off they went in the troika. But the old prince never intended to sleep: he had learnt everything from his informers, and immediately started in pursuit. It was night, the cold was so fierce that rings lay round the moon, the snowdrifts in the open were taller than a man, but he didn't care, and galloped on, hung all over with sabres and pistols, and with his beloved huntsman beside him. And there, ahead of them, they sighted the troika. He cried like an eagle: stop or I'll shoot! But they, in the sleigh, paid no heed to him and whipped and whipped on the horses. Then the old prince fired at the horses and killed first the right trace-horse and then the left one at full gallop, and was taking aim at the wheelhorse when he glanced to the right and saw, in the light of the moon, a huge wonder-wolf loping towards him over the snow with burning red eyes and a halo round his head. The prince started firing at the wolf, but the wolf never blinked an eye, he came charging at the prince, pounced on his chest and tore his throat open with his fangs."

"Heavens, what horrors, Mashenka! A ballad, indeed," I said.

"It's a sin to laugh, sir," she told me. "The Lord has a lot that's wondrous."

"Of course, Mashenka, only it does seem strange that this wolf was painted beside the grave of the prince he had killed."

"It was painted at the prince's own request, sir. He was still alive when they brought him home, and he confessed, and took Holy Communion, and with his last dying breath ordered that wolf to be painted in church beside his grave, that is to say, for the edification of all his descendants. Whoever could disobey him in those days? Besides, the church was his own family church, he owned it."

3 February, 1938

Stesha

Evening was nigh when Krasilnikov, a young merchant driving to Chern, was caught in a rainstorm.

Turning up the collar of his coat and pulling low the cap from which the rain poured in streams, he drove fast on his brake, straddling the boards right up front, his legs in tall boots set against the front axle, tugging at the wet, slippery leather reins with his wet, frozen hands, and urging on his naturally mettlesome horse. His brown pointer, with his long tongue lolling, was running at an even pace to the left of him, beside the front wheel which revolved in a veritable fountain of thin mud.

At first, Krasilnikov drove along a furrow in the black soil that ran parallel to the highway, but when it turned into a grey stream with bubbles on the muddy water, he swung on to the highway and clattered over the road metal. The surrounding fields and the sky were hidden behind the curtain of rain smelling of cucumber freshness and phosphorus; every other minute a jagged, branchy lightning, flashing with a blinding ruby fire as if it were the sign of the end of the world, streaked down the great wall of clouds before him, while overhead flew a hissing, crackling tail which exploded with blasts of an extraordinary all-destroying might. At every blast the horse jerked forward, laying back its ears, and the dog started to go in leaps...

Krasilnikov grew up and went to school in Moscow, he finished the university there, but when he came for the summer to his Tula estate, which was more like a sumptuous summer residence, he lived to feel himself a merchant-landowner with a peasant background, and as such he drank Lafite, carried a gold cigarette case, wore blacked boots, a peasant blouse and a *poddyovka*, prided in his Russian physique, and even now, in the downpour and crashing thunder, with the cold water pouring on to his nose from the peak of his cap, he was energetically enjoying his country life. This summer he often remembered the summer before when because of the affair he was having with a well-known actress he had been martyred in Moscow until as late as July, that is, until she went to Kislovodsk. The idleness, the heat, the hot stench and green smoke rising from the asphalt boiling in iron bins in the quitted streets, the lunches in the Troitsky cafe with the Maly Theatre actors and actresses who were also going off to the Caucasus, sitting for hours afterwards in Trambler's coffee shop, and then the evenings when he sat waiting for her to come to his flat with the furniture in dust covers, the chandeliers and paintings shrouded in cheesecloth, and the whole place smelling of mothballs... In Moscow, the summer evenings are endless, it does not grow dark until eleven, and he'd be there waiting and waiting and thinking she'd never come. And then at last the doorbell would ring and there she'd be in all her summer finery, saying in her gasping voice: "Do forgive me, I was prostrate with headache all day, your tea rose has quite wilted, I was in such a hurry that I took a cab, and I'm terribly hungry..."

When the downpour and the shattering rolls of thunder began to abate and recede, and the sky started clearing up in front, he saw to the left of the highway the inn he knew well which was owned by Pronin, an old widower. It was still about twenty versts to the town, and Krasilnikov thought he'd better take a rest, the horse was covered with lather and, for another thing, the sky was so black where he was heading with lightning still flashing there that there was no knowing if the rain would not start all over again... At the crossing to the inn, he turned sharply and drew up in front of the small wooden porch.

"Hullo there!" he called out in a loud voice. "Open up, a guest has come!"

But the windows in the timber house with a rusty iron roof remained dark, and no one answered his call. Krasilnikov wound the reins round the front-board of his brake, mounted the porch steps after his wet and filthy dog had jumped there, pushed back the cap from his perspiring brow, took off his sodden coat, threw it over the porch railing, and standing there in his *poddyovka* girded with a silver-encrusted leather belt, wiped his mud-spattered face and scraped the mud off the legs of his tall boots with the handle of his whip. The outer door was open, but the house felt empty. Old Pronin and his help were probably tending to their cow, he thought, and straightening up looked at the fields about him, wondering if perhaps he should drive on. The evening air was motionless and humid; here, there and everywhere quail were calling cheerfully in the rye, weighted down with rain, the rain had stopped, but night was approaching, the sky and the ground were somberly dark, a cloud hung darker and gloomier than ever behind the low, inky wall of forest beyond the highway, and a red glow kept flaring up broadly and ominously, and so Krasilnikov stepped into the covered porch, groped for the door handle in the darkness, and entered the house proper. It was dark and silent except for the ticking of a cheap clock on the wall. He slammed the front door shut, turned left, groped and found another door, but here, in this room, there was no one again, just the flies buzzing sleepily and resentfully in the hot darkness on the ceiling.

"Have they all croaked or what?" he said aloud, and instantly heard the quick, melodious, still childish voice of Stesha, the owner's daughter, who had climbed down from the plank bed in the darkness.

"Is it you, Vasily Alexeyich? And I'm all alone here, the cook quarrelled with father and went home, and father took our labourer and went off to town on business and I don't think they'll come back tonight... I was frightened to death by the thunderstorm, and suddenly I heard someone driving up, and got more frightened still... Good-evening then, forgive me, please..."

Krasilnikov struck a match and the tiny flame illumined the girl's dark eyes and swarthy face.

"Hullo, silly child. I'm also on my way to town, but you see what's going on, and so I decided to stop here and wait a bit... And you thought some robbers had driven up?"

The match was burning down but he could still see her blushing, smiling face, the coral string round her throat, her small breasts under the sarafan... She was almost half his size, and looked little more than a child.

"I'll light the lamp in a minute," she said hastily, growing even more embarrassed under Krasilnikov's keen glance, and dashed to the lamp hanging over the table. "Providence itself sent you, what would I do here all by myself," she said in a songful voice, standing on tiptoe and awkwardly pulling the glass chimney out of the toothed rack round the burner.

Krasilnikov struck another match and gazed at her figure as she stretched up and leaned backwards.

"Leave it for the moment," he said, dropping the match and putting his hands round her waist. "Turn round to me, will you."

She gave him a frightened look over her shoulder, dropped her arms and turned round. He drew her close, she did not struggle, she only looked at him wild-eyed and tossed back her head in amazement. Towering over her, he looked hard and straight into her eyes through the dusk, and laughed:

"More frightened than ever?"

"Vasily Alexeyich..." she mumbled pleadingly, and tried to draw away.

"Wait. Don't you like me? I know you're always glad

when I come here."

"There's no one better than you in the world," she said quietly and fervently.

"Well, there you are then..."

He kissed her lingeringly on the lips, and his hands slipped down her body.

"Vasily Alexeyich... for the love of God... You've forgotten about your horse, you've left it beside the porch... father might return... Oh, don't, don't!"

Half an hour later he came out of the house, took his horse into the backyard, put it under the shed there, removed the bridle, gave it an armful of wet, freshly mown grass from the cart standing in the middle of the yard, and walked back to the house, glancing up at the serene stars in the cleared sky. Lightning still flashed here and there in the distance, and the glow faintly lit up the hot darkness of the silent room. She lay on the plank bed, curled up, having cried her fill from the horror, rapture, and suddenness of what had happened to her. He planted a kiss on her cheek, wet and salty from tears, lay down on his back, and placed her head on his shoulder while holding a cigarette in his right hand. She lay meekly and quietly, and as he smoked his cigarette he gently and absently stroked her hair, which tickled his chin. She fell asleep. He lay staring into the darkness and grinning complacently. "Father's gone to town..." He was gone, that's true. But the rotten thing was that he'd understand everything at once, that dried-up, quick little old man with a snow-white beard and still black bushy eyebrows and an extraordinarily sharp eye. He talked his head off when in his cups, but he saw right through everyone.

Krasilnikov lay without sleep until the darkness in the room began to thin out between the ceiling and the floor. Turning his head to the window he saw the greenishly pale eastern sky and in this half-light he could already make out the large icon in the corner with the saint on it in church vestments, his hand raised in blessing and his eyes implacably wrathful. He looked at her, she still lay huddled, her knees drawn up, everything forgotten in sleep. A sweet and pitiful slip of a girl...

When it grew quite light in the room and outside a cock started crowing in different voices, he made a movement to rise. She started up and sitting sideways with her blouse unbuttoned and her hair tousled stared at him with utterly bewildered, unseeing eyes.

"Stesha, I've got to go," he said quietly.

"Going already?" she whispered senselessly.

And suddenly she came to, and striking herself on the chest with her crossed hands cried:

"But how can you go? What about me? What am I to do now?"

"Stesha, I'll come again soon..."

"But father will be at home then, how will I see you alone? I'd come to meet you in the forest behind the highway, but how am I to slip out of the house?"

Clenching his teeth, he pushed her down on her back. She flung out her arms and cried out: "Ah!" in an agony of blissful despair.

Afterwards, he stood facing the plank bed already wearing his *poddyovka* and cap, holding his whip in his hand, with his back to the window and the glare of the sun which had just risen, while she knelt on the plank bed and, childishly and unbeautifully opening her mouth, spoke jerkily through her sobs:

"Vasily Alexeyich ... for the love of Christ ... for the love of the Heavenly Father himself, marry me! I'll be your humblest slave, only please marry me! I'll sleep at your threshold... I'd go with you anyway, without marriage, but who'll let me? Oh, Vasily Alexeyich..."

"Shut up," Krasilnikov told her sternly. "In a day or two I'll come to your father and tell him I'm going to marry you. Do you hear?"

She sat back on her heels, choked down her sobs, and opened her wet, radiant eyes wide in disbelief.

"Really and truly?"

"Of course."

"I turned fifteen on Twelfth Night, you know," she hastened to inform him.

"Oh well, that means we can be married in six months' time."

As soon as he returned home he started packing at once, and that same evening was driven in his troika to the railway station. Two days later he was in Kislovodsk.

5 October, 1938

Muse

Although I was already past my first youth, I decided to learn the art of painting—I have always had a passion for it—and so, abandoning my estate in Tambov Gubernia I went for the winter to Moscow. I took lessons from one giftless but rather well-known artist, an untidy fat man who had perfectly mastered the required artifices: long hair thrown back in large greasy curls, a pipe clenched in his teeth, a velvet garnet-coloured blouse, dirty-grey spats worn over his shoes—I hated these particularly—a careless manner with everyone, a condescending glance at a pupil's work with narrowed eyes, and a comment as if spoken to himself:

"Amusing ... very amusing ... Unquestionable progress..."

I lived at the Stolitsa Hotel, next door to the Prague Restaurant in the Arbat. In the daytime I worked either at my teacher's or in my room and my evenings I mostly spent in cheap restaurants with my various new friends from the artistic brotherhood, some young, some the worse for wear, but all of them equally devoted to billiards and to beer and crayfish. The life I lived was unpleasant and boring. That effeminate, slovenly painter with his "artistically" untidy studio, cluttered with all sorts of dusty props, and that gloomy Stolitsa Hotel... I shall always remember the snow falling and falling outside the windows, the horse-drawn trams rumbling and jangling down Arbat Street, the sour smell of beer and gas in the dimly lit restaurant... I cannot understand why I led such a wretched existence, for, after all, I was far from poor then.

And then one day in March when I was making pencil drawings in my room, when the air coming in through the small opened frame in the double window no longer smelt of the chilly dampness of wet snow and rain, when the horseshoes clacked on the asphalt not as they did in winter, and the jangle of the horse-drawn trams sounded more musical, someone knocked on my door. I called out: "Who is it?" But no answer came. I waited a bit, then called out again, and again there was no responses, only another knock. I got up and opened the door: there stood a tall girl in a grey fur hat, a straight grey coat and grey felt overshoes, staring straight at me with acorn-coloured eyes framed in long eyelashes, drops of rain and snow glistening on her hair and face. Staring at me, she said:

"I'm a conservatoire student, Muse Graf. I heard that you were an interesting person, and so I came to make your acquaintance. D'you mind?"

Rather surprised, I replied cordially, of course:

"I'm very flattered, come in please. Only I must warn you that what you heard about me is hardly true: I'm sure there's nothing interesting about me..."

"At least let me come in, don't keep me in the doorway," she said, still looking me straight in the face. "If you're flattered, show me in."

She came into the room and, as if she were at home, stopped in front of my silvery-grey and in places tarnished mirror to take off her hat and pat her rust-coloured hair in place, then she took off her coat, threw it on a chair, sat down on the sofa and, sniffling with her snow-and-rain wet nose, ordered me:

"Pull off my overshoes, and get me a hankie from my coat pocket."

I handed her the handkerchief, she wiped her nose and stretched her legs out to me.

"I saw you last night at Shor's concert," she told me casually.

Trying not to grin asininely with pleasure and bewilderment—what a strange visitor!—I obediently pulled off her overshoes, one after the other. She still smelt of the freshness outside and that smell excited me: I was also excited by the combination of courage with everything that was so femininely young in her face, in her straight look, her large beautiful hands, with everything that I glimpsed and felt as I pulled off her overshoes from under her plaid flannel dress and saw her shapely legs in sheer grey stockings and her long, narrow feet in patent leather court shoes.

She settled herself comfortably on the sofa, obviously with no intention of leaving soon. Since I did not know what to say, I asked from whom and what she had heard about me, and if she lived with her family, and where in Moscow.

"Never mind what I heard about you and from whom," she replied. "I came more because I saw you at that concert. You're rather good-looking. And I'm the daughter of a doctor, and we live not far from here in Prechistensky Boulevard."

Her manner of speaking was curt and somehow unexpected. Again, not knowing what to say, I asked:

"Would you like some tea?"

"Yes," she said. "And if you have the money send a servant out to buy some apples at Belov's, here in Arbat Street. Only do tell him to look sharp, I'm impatient."

"But you appear so composed."

"Appearances are deceptive."

When the servant brought the samovar and a paper bag of apples, she made the tea and wiped the cups and spoons. After eating an apple and drinking a cup of tea, she shifted fartherback on the sofa and, patting the place beside her, told me:

"And now come and sit with me."

I sat down, she put her arms round me, unhurriedly kissed me on the lips, drew away, looked, and as if finding me deserving, closed her eyes and kissed me again–assiduously and lengthily...

"Well then," she said with something like relief. "Can't do more now. The day after tomorrow."

The room was already quite dark save for the melancholy light coming in from the street-lamps. It's easy to imagine what I was feeling. What a stroke of luck! She was young, strong, and the shape of her lips was out of this world... As in a dream I heard the monotonous jangling of the horse-drawn trams and the clacking of the horseshoes...

"I want to have dinner with you at the Prague after tomorrow," she said. "I've never been there, and altogether I'm very inexperienced. I can imagine what you're thinking of me... Actually, you're my first love."

"Love?"

"But what else is it called?"

Needless to say, I soon dropped my painting lessons while she continued her studies half-heartedly. We were together all the time, we lived like newlyweds, went to picture galleries, exhibitions, concerts, and even public lectures, I don't know why. In May, at her wish, I rented and moved into a small cottage, one of many built in the grounds of an ancient country estate near Moscow, and she came to me every day, going back to town at one in the morning. A country house in the environs of Moscow was another thing I never expected; I had never lived as a vacationer in complete idleness on a country estate, so different from our steppeland estates, and in such a different climate.

It rained all the time, and all around were pine forests. Again and again white clouds gathered in the blue sky above them, thunder rolled, and then a sparkling thin rain started falling through the sunbeams quickly changing the heat into a fragrant pine steamness. Everything was wet, unguent and crystal-clear... The trees in the park were so tall that the cottages built here and there seemed as small as the under-tree dwellings in tropical lands. The pond lay like a huge black mirror, a good half of it covered with green duckweed. I lived on the edge of the park, in the forest. My cottage had not been quite finished when I moved in—the log walls had not been caulked, the floors not planed, the stoves had practically no dampers, and there was hardly any furniture. My boots, left lying under the bed, were covered with a velvety mold from the perpetual dampness.

Night did not fall until midnight. The half-light from the west seemed to hang forever over the motionless, silent forests. When the moon was out, this half-light blended strangely with the moonlight which was as motionless and spellbound. And everything—the calm reigning everywhere, the clear air and sky—seemed to promise that there would be no more rain. But at night, when I went to bed after taking her to the station, I heard thunder and a downpour descending on my roof again, all was plunged in darkness, and lightning streaked across the sky. In the morning, the purple ground on the damp walks would be speckled with shadows and dazzling sun spots, flycatchers were chirping and thrushes were chattering huskily. By noon it would grow sultry again, clouds gathered and a drizzle started. Just before sunset the sky cleared up, and the waning light falling through the foliage into my window made a tremulous, glassily golden net on my log walls. It was time for me to go to the station to meet her. The arriving train disgorged countless passengers on to the platform, there was a mixed smell of coal from the locomotive and of the forest's damp freshness, and I saw her in the crowd carrying a shopping net heavily weighted down with packages of food, fruit, and a bottle of Madeira. We had dinner, just the two of us. Before her departure we walked in the park. She became somnambulistic and walked with her head drooping on my shoulder. The pond lay black and still, the ancient trees were silently reaching for the starlit sky... Ah, that pale, spellbound night, infinitely mute, with infinitely long shadows of the trees on the silver glades that were like lakes.

In June she came with me to my Tambov estate—we did not wed, she lived with me as my wife, and managed my household. She spent a long autumn without getting bored, she had her daily cares and her reading. Of our neighbours our most frequent visitor was a certain Mister Zavistovsky, a poor landowner whose estate was about two versts away from ours. He was a bachelor, skinny, reddish-haired, timid and not too bright, but not a bad musician for all that. In the winter he came over almost every evening. I had known him since childhood, and had become so used to him now that an evening without him seemed strange. He and I played draughts, or else he played piano duets with her.

Just before Christmas I made a trip to town. The moon was already out when I returned. I could not find her anywhere in the house, and sat down to tea all by myself.

"And where's the mistress?" I asked the maid. "Gone out for a walk?"

"I don't know, sir. The mistress has been gone since breakfast."

"She got dressed and went," my old nanny said glumly, without raising her head, as she passed through the dining-room.

"I suppose she walked across to Zavistovsky's place, and will probably come back with him soon, it's already seven," I was thinking. I went to my study and lay down, and before I knew it I was asleep—after all, I'd been freezing on the road all day. And as suddenly I came wide awake an hour later with the crazy and perfectly clear thought: "She has left me. She hired someone in the village to drive her to the station in time for the Moscow train—it's quite like her! But maybe she has come back?" I went through the house—no, she was not back. It was embarrassing because of the servants...

At about ten o'clock, not knowing what to do, I put on a sheepskin coat, took my gun for no reason, and set off along the highroad to Zavistovsky's place, thinking: "He didn't come over this evening either, worse luck, and I have a whole ghastly night ahead of me. Has she really left me and gone away? Oh no, it can't be!"

The packed snow on the much travelled road creaked under my feet, to the left of me the snow-clad fields glistened under the low, pale moon... I turned off the road, went along the avenue of bare-branched trees running across the field to Zavistovsky's estate, and entered the front yard where, on the left, stood his old, wretchedly poor house. There were no lights in the windows. I went up the ice-covered porch steps, with some difficulty pushed open the heavy front door with tatters of cloth and stuffing on it, and entered the warmth and darkness of the front hall where the open door in the corner stove glowed redly. It was as dark in the parlour.

"Vikenty Vikentich, hullo!" I called.

Soundlessly, for he was wearing felt boots, he appeared in the door of his study, also dark and illumined only by the moonlight falling into the triple window.

"Oh, it's you... Come in, come in please. And I, as you can see, am woolgathering in the dusk, without lights..."

I went and sat down on the bumpy sofa.

"Can you imagine, Muse has disappeared somewhere..."

He said nothing to this, and then all but whispered: "Yes, yes, I can understand how you feel..."

"What do you mean? What do you understand?"

And in that very moment Muse came out of the bedroom as soundlessly, for she, too, was wearing felt boots.

"You brought a gun," she said. "If you want to shoot, shoot me, not him."

And she sat down on the other sofa, facing me.

I looked at her felt boots, at her knees under the grey skirt—I could see her very well in the golden light from the window—and I wanted to shout: "I can't live without you, I'd gladly give my life just for those knees, that skirt, those felt boots!"

"It's all over and done with. Scenes would be useless," she said.

"You are monstrously cruel," I spoke with difficulty.

"Give me a cigarette, dear," she told Zavistovsky. With cowardly haste he held out his cigarette case to her and started searching through his pockets for matches.

Gasping, I said: "In my presence, at least, you don't have to speak to him in that intimate manner."

"Why not?" she asked, raising her eyebrows and holding her cigarette in a carelessly outflung hand.

My heart was hammering in my throat, and blood was pounding in my temples. I rose and, staggering, went out.

17 October, 1938

The Hour Was Late

Ah, it's such a long time since I've been there, I said to myself. Since I was 19. I once lived in Russia, I felt that it belonged to me, I was perfectly free to go about where I wished, and it was not much trouble to travel those three hundred versts or so. But still I did not go, I still kept putting it off. And years passed, decades passed. But now I could put it off no longer: now or never. I had to take this only and last chance, all the more so because the hour was late and no one was likely to see me.

And so I started across the bridge, seeing everything about me for many versts around in the light of the new moon on that July night.

The bridge was so familiar, so unchanged, that I might have seen it only yesterday. It was a crudely ancient, humped bridge, and it seemed not made of stone but turned to stone with time to a state of everlasting indestructibility—as a schoolboy I believed that it had already been there in the days of the Tatar invasion. However, the only other thing that evidenced the antiquity of the town was the remains of what had once been the town wall on the edge of the drop at the foot of the cathedral. All the rest was merely old and provincial. One thing was odd though, one thing said that something had changed here since my boyhood, my youth: the river which in those days was not navigable must have been dredged and deepened. The new moon was on my left, quite far beyond the river, and in its wavering light and the shimmering sparkle of the water I saw a white paddle-ship which was so silent that it seemed deserted, although lights were on in all the portholes that looked like motionless golden eyes, reflected in the water as streaming golden pillars that seemed to keep the steamer afloat. I have seen that in Yaroslavl, in the Suez Canal and on the Nile. In Paris the nights are damp and dark with a hazy pink glow in the pitch-black sky, and the Seine flows under the bridges like black tar, but there, too, there are streaming pillars reflected on the water from the lamp posts on the bridges, only there they are tricoloured like the Russian national flag: white, blue, and red. Here there are no lamp posts on the bridge, and it is dry and dusty. And ahead, on the rise, are the darkling gardens of the town, and sticking up from these gardens is the fire tower. Oh my God, what ineffable happiness it had been for me! It was during a fire that broke out in the night that I first kissed your hand and you pressed mine in response—I shall never forget your secret consent. In that uncanny, sinister light the whole street was flooded with the black shapes of people. I was at your party when the alarm bell went and everyone first rushed to the windows and then poured outside, into the street. The fire was far away, beyond the river, but it was burning with terribly hot, greedy haste. Smoke poured in thick black-and-red fleecy clouds from which sheets of bright-red flames shot high up and were reflected in trembling coppery lights in the dome of the Church of Archangel Michael, not far from us. And in the crush, in that crowd, amid the talk, now frightened, now pitying, now gleefully excited, of the common folk who had come running from everywhere, I caught the smell of your hair, your neck, and your linen dress, and suddenly I found the courage to kiss your hand...

The bridge now behind me, I walked up the rise and headed for the town along the paved road.

In the town not a single light was burning, not a soul was about. Everything was mute and spacious, serene and melancholy, with the melancholy of night in the Russian steppe or in a sleeping steppeland town. Only the gardens were awake, rustling their leaves very faintly and cautiously in the steady stream of the gentle July breeze coming from the fields somewhere and blowing gently in my face. I walked on, and the large moon also moved on, rolling like a round mirror, glimpsed through the blackness of the branches. The wide street lay in shadow, and only the houses on my right which the shadow could not reach caught the moonlight with their white walls and their window panes shining with a black funereal gloss. I walked in the shadow, stepping on the pavement patterned in black and white or though covered with black silk lace. She had an evening dress like that, long and slender. It suited her slim body and dark young eyes wonderfully. In that dress she had an air of mystery about her, and she took insultingly little notice of me. Where was it? At whose party?

My destination was Staraya Street. I could take a short cut, but I turned into these wide garden streets because I wanted to take a look at my old school. When I reached it, I marvelled yet again: everything was the same as half a century ago—the stone wall, the stone-paved yard, the large stone building in that yard—everything was as featurelessly institutional and dreary as it was in my day. I paused at the gate, wanting to evoke some nostalgic memories in my heart, but I simply could not. To be sure, I used to pass through this gate—first as a boy of ten with cropped hair and wearing a brand new blue uniform cap with tiny silver palm fronds on the band and a brand new uniform overcoat with metal buttons, and later as a skinny youth in a grey jacket and modish trousers with footstraps, but was that I?

Staraya Street looked only a little narrower to me than before. Everything else was the same. The thoroughfare in pits and bumps, not a tree planted along it, dusty merchant-class houses on either side, and the pavements so bumpy too that it was safer walking in the middle of the street where the moonlight was brightest. And even the night itself was almost exactly like *that* night. Only *that* night had been at the end of August, when the whole town was fragrant with apples, heaped in veritable mountains at the market-place, and so warm that it felt lovely wearing just a Russian shirt girded with a slender Caucasian leather belt. Why did I remember that night as if it had been somewhere remote, in the sky, in heaven?

Still, I did not venture to go as far as your house. Probably it had not changed either, and therefore I was all the more afraid to see it. Some strangers, some new people were living in it now. Your father, your mother, your brother, they had all outlived you, a young girl, but they, too, died in their time. And all my people have also died; not just my relatives, but many, very many of my friends with whom I began my life. How short a time ago they too began their lives, convinced that there'd be no end, but then everything began, ran its course and ended before my very eyes, so quickly and before my own eyes! I sat down on a low post in front of some merchant's house, secure behind its barn locks and gates, and thought about her as she looked in those long ago days of ours: dark hair simply dressed, clear eyes, a touch of sunburn on her young face, a thin summer dress, and under it the chastity, firmness and freedom of a young body. That was the beginning of our love, a time of as yet unclouded happiness, intimacy, trustfulness, rapturous tenderness, joy...

There is something quite special in the warm, clear, late summer nights in Russian provincial towns. What peace, what a sense of security! At night, an old watchman with a clapper wanders about the streets, but only for his own pleasure, for there is nothing to guard. Sleep soundly, good people, you are guarded by God's good grace and by this lofty, radiant sky which the old man gives a carefree glance now and again as he shuffles along the pavement, still warm from the day's sun, and at rare intervals plays a dance trill on his clapper just for fun.

And it was on a night like that, at that late hour when the watchman alone in that whole town was up and about, that you waited for me in your already autumnally wilting garden, and I slipped in quietly; quietly I opened the gate you had unlocked beforehand, quietly and swiftly I ran across the yard to the far end, past the shed, and stepped into the grey-and-black dust of the garden where your dress made a faint white blur on the bench under the apple trees, and quickly coming to you I saw with a thrill of fright the sparkle of your expectant eyes.

And we sat there, we just sat there in a sort of bewilderment of happiness. I embraced you with one arm and felt the beating of your heart, and with my other hand I held your hand, and through it felt the whole of you. It was so late that even the clapper was heard no more—the old watchman must have lain down on a bench, basking in the moonlight, and dozed off, pipe clenched in his teeth. When I glanced to the right I saw how high and how innocently shone the new moon above the yard and how the roof of your house glittered as if made of fish scales. When I glanced to the left I saw a path overrun with dry grasses disappearing under the other apple trees, and behind them a solitary green star peeping out from behind some other garden, hanging low in the sky, burning dispassionately yet expectantly, and soundlessly saying something. But I gave the star and the yard only a passing glance, because the dusk and the radiant glimmer of your eyes in that dusk comprised the whole world for me then.

Afterwards, you walked me to the gate, and I said:

"If there is life hereafter and if we meet in that life, I shall go down on my knees before you and kiss your feet for everything you had given me in this world!"

I came out into the middle of the moonlit street and started homewards. When I looked back the blur of your white dress was still there, at the gate...

And now, I rose and walked back the way I had come. Besides Staraya Street there was one other place I wanted to go to, I dreaded admitting this wish even to myself, and yet I knew that fulfilling it was inevitable. And so I went there, to take one look and go away, this time forever.

The way there was familiar again. Straight on, then turn left, cross the market-place, then along Monastyrskaya Street to the end of town.

The market-place was like a different town within the town. The rows of stalls gave out a very strong smell. A gloom hung over the long tables and benches under canopies in Cooked Food Row. An icon of a big-eyed Christ with a rusty metal cover hung from a chain over the entrance to Hardware Row. In Flour Row whole flocks of pigeons were always running about the stone floor and pecking—we saw them on our way to school in the morning and always marvelled at the number. All of them were fat, with rainbow coloured crops, they pecked and ran about, wiggling and mincing effeminately, dipping their heads monotonously, and taking no notice of you, and only when you almost stepped on one of them did they take flight with their wings whistling. And in the night, horrible, huge dark rats darted about the floor, swiftly and busily.

Monastyrskaya Street was the passage into open country and the road for those who were returning to town, for others leaving town, and for people going to the city of the dead. In Paris, a house—number so-and-so in such-and-such a street—is set apart from the others for two days by having the entrance draped with black crepe and silver ribbons, like a stage setting for a house of plague, and having a small table placed in front of it with a sheet of paper in a mourning surround on which, in the course of those two days, well-bred acquaintances can pen their signatures as a mark of condolence. And then, at a certain ultimate hour, a huge chariot with a black canopy stops at the door. The wood of the chariot is black and pitchy like a plague victim's coffin, the rounded ends of the canopy are adorned with large white stars to impersonate the heavens above, while the corners of the roof are crowned with curly black plumes—the feathers of an ostrich from hell. Harnessed into this chariot are great monsters wearing coal-black, sharp-cornered horsecloths with white-edged holes for the eyes. On the enormously high box sits an old drunkard, also dressed the part in a theatrically funereal coat and tricorn, waiting for the coffin to be borne out and perhaps always chuckling silently at these solemn words: *"Requiem aeternam dona eis, Domine, et lux perpetua luceat eis."**

Here it is all done differently. The wind from the fields blows down Monastyrskaya Street, and against this wind is borne an open coffin, swaying gently on linen towels, and in that coffin is a face the colour of rice with a printed paper band on the forehead above the closed, convex eyelids. That's how she was borne too.

As you leave the town, to the left of the highroad is a monastery dating back to the reign of Tsar Alexei surrounded by fortress walls with a permanently locked gate, behind which tower the gilded onion-shaped domes of the cathedral. Further on, right in the field, there is another large, walled-in rectangle, the walls much lower here, and

*Latin: Grant them eternal peace, Oh Lord, and may perpetual light illumine them.

they surround a grove criss-crossed with long avenues, the ground under the old elms, maples and birches, almost entirely covered with tombstones, slabs and crosses. The gate stood wide open, and I saw the main avenue, endless and smooth. I took off my hat hesitantly and went in. How late it was and how mute! The moon already hung low behind the trees, but everything around, as far as the eye could see, was still clearly visible. The entire grove of the dead, with the crosses and tombstones, made a fanciful pattern of light and shadow. The wind had died down in this pre-dawn hour and all the light and dark blurs under the trees were sleeping. And suddenly something appeared from behind the church at the far end of the grove and rushed at me in a dark ball with terrific speed. Beside myself with fear, I dashed aside, my head froze and tensed, my heart gave a jerk and stood still... What was it? It tore past me and vanished. But my heart remained standing still. And carrying my stilled heart like a heavy vessel in my body, I moved on. I knew where to go, I kept straight along the main avenue and at the very end, with only a few steps to go to the rear wall, I stopped: before me, on a level plot among dry grasses, lay a solitary gravestone, elongated and rather narrow, with the head to the wall. From behind the wall a green star glowed like a wondrous emerald, it hung low and was as radiant as the one before, but it was mute and motionless.

19 October, 1938

Rusya

The Moscow-Sevastopol passenger train stopped at a small station just past Podolsk, where it was not supposed to stop at all, and stood waiting for something on the second track. It was after ten in the evening. A lady and gentleman came to the lowered window of their first-class compartment, and the lady called out to a railwayman carrying a red lantern in his hand, who was then crossing the first track.

"Conductor, why have we stopped?"

The conductor replied that it was because the express from Sevastopol was late, and they had to let it pass.

The station was a dark, dismal place. Dusk had long fallen, but in the west behind the station, beyond the darkling wooded country, the sunset glow that lingers for hours in Moscow's summer skies still shone with a deathly pallor. A damp, swampy smell poured into the open window. Even the far-away monotonous screech of a landrail somehow sounded damp too.

He leaned on the window edge, and she leaned on his shoulder.

"Once I lived hereabouts during my summer holidays," he told her. "I tutored a boy in the family's summer place about five versts from here. Bleak country. Thinly wooded, magpies, mosquitoes and dragonflies. No scenery anywhere. It was only from the attic window that one could enjoy some sort of view. The house, of course, was built in the Russian summer residence style, and was in a state of sad neglect—the owners were impoverished landowners, you see. There was a semblance of a park behind the house, and beyond the park there was a lake or I should better say a stagnant pool, choked with lilies and rushes, and with the inevitable flat-bottomed boat at the slimy bank."

"And, needless to say, a damsel bored with country life whom you took for boat rides on this pool," said his wife.

"Yes, all true to form, only the damsel was not the bored sort at all. I mostly took her for boat rides at night, and it was actually quite poetic. The western sky remained transparent and greenish the whole night long, and something on the horizon seemed to be smouldering all the time, like it is now... There was only one oar to be found, it was more like a shovel too, and so I paddled like a savage—on my right, then on my left. The opposite, wooded shore was dark, but that strange half-light stayed behind it all night. The stillness everywhere was incredible—just the dragonflies and the whining mosquitoes. I never knew that dragonflies flew about at night, but apparently they do for some reason of their own. Quite frightening, that."

At last the approaching express was heard. It tore into

the station roaring and raising a wind, and flew past as one long golden streak of lighted windows. The passenger train started off at once. The attendant came into their compartment, lit the lamps and made up the beds.

"Well, and what happened between you and that damsel? A proper love affair? I wonder why you never told me about her. What was she like?" asked his wife.

"Thin and tall. She wore a yellow cotton sarafan and a peasant woman's sandals, woven from coloured wool or something, on her bare feet."

"*A la Russe*, you mean."

"I think the style was dictated by poverty more than anything else. She had no fine clothes to wear, so she wore a sarafan. She was a painter besides, and studied at the Stroganov School in Moscow. She herself was like a painting, even like an icon painting, I'd say. A long black braid hung down her back, her face was swarthy and had tiny black birthmarks here and there, her nose was straight and narrow, the eyes dark, and the eyebrows black... Her hair was dry and coarse, slightly curly. All this, plus the yellow sarafan and the white muslin sleeves, looked very beautiful. Her ankles and her feet in those woollen sandals were quite fleshless, and her ankle bones stood out under the fine, swarthy skin."

"I know the type," said his wife. "I had a friend like that at school. Given to hysterics, I shouldn't wonder."

"Possibly. And all the more probably because she looked like her mother, a woman with Oriental blood, who suffered from melancholia or something. The mother only appeared for dinner. She'd come to the dining-room, sit down, and never saying a word or raising her eyes would keep shifting her knife and fork, and sort of coughing dryly. And if she did suddenly say something, she did it so unexpectedly and loudly that you actually jumped."

"And what of the father?"

"He, too, was taciturn, a tall, dry stick of a man, a retired officer. The little boy I tutored was the only simple and nice person in that family."

The attendant, saying the beds were ready, wished them a good night and left the compartment.

"And what was her name?"

"Rusya."

"What fancy name is that?"

"It's very simple–Maria, Marusya, Rusya."

"And were you very much in love with her?"

"Of course I thought I was, terribly."

"And she?"

He replied dryly after a pause:

"She thought so too, probably. Let's go to sleep, shall we? I had a very tiring day."

"Aren't you nice? After rousing my curiosity! Tell me, at least, how the romance ended."

"In nothing. I left, and that was that."

"But why didn't you marry her?"

"Obviously because something told me that I'd meet you."

"No, seriously, why?"

"Well, because I shot myself, and she stabbed herself with a dagger."

After making their toilet for the night, they locked themselves into their compartment, undressed in the cramped space, and with relief lay down on the fresh, gleaming linen sheets and matching pillows which kept sliding down the raised headrests.

The small purple eye above the door glowed softly in the darkness. She fell asleep at once, and he lay smoking and remembering that summer.

She had many little black birthmarks on her body as well–a charming peculiarity. And because she wore soft, flat sandals, her whole body moved under the sarafan when she walked. The sarafan was loose and light, and her long, girlish body felt beautifully free in it. One day she got her feet wet in the rain; she came running into the sitting-room from the garden, and he rushed to her to take off her wet sandals and kissed her wet, narrow feet. He had never known such happiness in his life. The fresh and fragrant rain poured harder and faster outside the open french windows, everyone in the house was taking an after-dinner nap, and oh! What a fright they had when suddenly a black cockerel with metallically gleaming feathers and a large fiery-red comb dashed in from the garden, his claws tapping on the floor, and in that hottest moment, too, when they utterly forgot caution! They jumped up from the sofa when they saw the cockerel, and the cockerel, with tactful haste it seemed, ran back into the rain, with bent head and gleaming tail hanging...

At first, she seemed to be taking his measure all the time; when he spoke to her she blushed a dark red and replied with a mocking mumble; at table she often taunted him, addressing her father in a loud voice:

"Don't press food on him, Daddy, it's no use. He doesn't like cherry dumplings. And he doesn't like kvas soup either, he doesn't like noodles, he detests yoghurt and hates cottage cheese."

In the mornings he tutored the boy and she was kept busy by her household cares–it was she who ran the house. They had dinner at one o'clock, and after dinner she either went up to her attic room or, if it was not raining, to the garden where, setting up her easel under a birch tree, she painted from nature, waving off the mosquitoes all the time. Later, she started coming out to the balcony where he sat reading after dinner in a lop-sided armchair, and would stand there, her hands behind her back, watching him with an enigmatic little smile.

"Might I enquire what wisdoms you are studying?"

"The history of the French Revolution."

"Good Lord, I didn't know we had a revolutionary in the house!"

"Why are you neglecting your painting?"

"I'm about to give it up altogether. I know for certain now that I'm hopeless."

"Will you show me something you've done?"

"Do you think you're any judge of painting?"

"You're terribly vain."

"I do have that failing."

Once she suddenly suggested a boat ride, saying in a resolute tone:

"I believe the rainy season in our tropics is over. Let's have some fun. Our boat is wretchedly old, of course, the bottom has rotted through, but Petya and I have stuffed up all the holes with rushes."

It was a hot, sultry day; the grasses along the shore, thickly speckled with small yellow buttercups, were steaming with a heady, humid warmth, and countless pale green butterflies hovered low over them.

He had now assimilated her perpetually mocking tone

and, going down to the boat, said:

"You have condescended to me at long last."

"And you have, at long last, collected your wits to respond in kind," she said saucily and jumped into the boat, frightening the frogs that went plopping into the water from everywhere, and suddenly gave a wild screech and, picking up her skirt knee-high, started stamping her feet and screaming:

"There's a snake, a snake!"

He grabbed the oar, catching a glimpse of her bare legs' swarthy sheen as he did so, and hit the snake, writhing on the bottom of the boat, then picked it up and flung it far away into the pool.

She was pale with a sort of Indian pallor, the birth-marks on her face standing out all the darker for it, and her hair and eyes seeming all the blacker. She heaved a sigh of relief and said:

"Oh, what horrid creatures! Snakes in the grass they really are. This place simply crawls with them, they're everywhere, in the garden and under the house... And Petya, just imagine, takes them in his hands!"

It was the first time she spoke to him simply, and the first time they looked straight into each other's eyes.

"How quick you were! And that was some hit!"

She had quite recovered from her fright and, smiling, tripped to the stern of the boat and sat down. In her fright she had looked amazingly beautiful, but looking at her now he thought with tenderness: why, she's still a child at heart! Putting on an indifferent mien, he stepped into the boat and, sticking the oar into the jelly-like bottom, pushed off over the tangled mass of underwater weeds, on to the rushes and the water lilies whose thick, round leaves completely covered the water, and when he had finally brought the boat into the clear he sat down on the middle seat and started paddling, first right, then left, in turn.

"Lovely, isn't it?" she cried.

"Very," he replied and, taking off his cap, turned to her: "Be a dear, keep this beside you or I'll sweep it off into this tub which does leak, I'm sorry to say, and is full of leeches."

She placed the cap on her knees.

"Oh, just throw it somewhere!"

Pressing the cap to her breast, she said:

"No, I'll keep it safe."

His heart was stirred with tenderness again, but again he turned away and pushed the oar deep into the pond where the water sparkled amid the rushes and the lilies.

Mosquitoes plastered his hands and face, everything was blindingly and hotly silver: the steaming air, the wavering sunlight, and the curly white clouds in the sky reflected on the water between the isles of rushes and lilies; it was so shallow everywhere that he could see the bottom of the pool with its underwater grasses, but somehow this shallowness did not spoil the impression of fathomless depths which swallowed up the reflection of the sky and the clouds. Suddenly the boat keeled over and she shrieked again. She had dipped her hand in the water, caught the stem of a water lily and given it such a hard tug that she almost went overboard and overturned the boat. He leapt to his feet and caught her under the arms just in time. She burst out laughing, collapsed on her back and flipped her wet hand right into his face. Then he gathered her up and impulsively kissed her laughing mouth. She quickly put her arms round his neck and kissed him awkwardly on the cheek.

After that, they went boat-riding at night.

The next day after dinner she called him into the garden and asked:

"Do you love me?"

"Since the first day we met!" he replied ardently, remembering their kissing in the boat the day before.

"Me too," she said. "No, I hated you at first, I thought you did not notice me at all. But thank goodness that's all in the past now. Come down there again tonight as soon as everyone goes to bed and wait for me. Only be very quiet leaving the house, my mother watches my every step, she's insanely jealous."

That night she came to the boat carrying a rug over her arm. He was incoherent from happiness and only asked:

"What's the rug for?"

"Aren't you a goose! We'll be cold there. Hurry up, get in and row to the opposite shore."

All the way there neither spoke. When they reached the opposite wooded shore, she said:

17—904

"Here we are. Now come to me. Where's the rug? Oh, I'm sitting on it. Cover me, I'm cold, and sit down. Like this... No, wait. Yesterday we kissed sort of fumblingly, so now I'll kiss you myself first, very, very gently. Put your arms round me ... everywhere..."

She wore only a slip under the sarafan. She kissed the corners of his lips very, very gently, barely touching them. In a daze, he threw her on the floor of the boat, and she hugged him frenziedly...

She lay still in exhaustion for a little while, then rose on an elbow and with a smile of happy weariness and still lingering pain said:

"We are man and wife now. Mummy says she'll die if I marry, but I don't want to think about that just now. You know what, I want to take a swim, I adore bathing at night."

She pulled off her sarafan and slip over her head, her long white body making a pale blur in the dusk, and started pinning up her braid round her head, raising her arms, showing her dark armpits and uplifted breasts, quite unashamed of her nakedness and the dark triangle below her stomach. Her hair fixed, she gave him a quick kiss, fell flat on her stomach in the water, and started thrashing it noisily with her feet.

Afterwards, he helped her to dress and wrap herself in the rug. In the dusk, her dark eyes and black hair, pinned up like a diadem, belonged to a fairy-tale princess. He did not dare touch her now, he only kissed her hands, too unbearably happy to speak. They thought there was someone standing and listening in the darkness of the silent woods, lit up by glowworms here and there. At moments they heard a cautious rustle there.

"Listen, what was that?" she asked, lifting her head.

"Don't be afraid, it was probably a frog climbing out, or a hedgehog in the woods..."

"And what if it's a capricorn?"

"What capricorn?"

"I don't know, but just imagine: a capricorn comes out of the forest, he stands and watches... I feel so wonderful, I want to talk the silliest nonsense..."

Again he pressed his lips to her hands, and now and then kissed her cold breasts as something sacred. What an entirely new creature she had become for him! The green half-light, faintly reflected in the flat, pale water in the distance still hung undimming behind the blackness of the low forest, the dewey grasses along the edge of the pond smelt strongly of celery, the invisible mosquitoes whined plaintively and mysteriously, and the weird, sleepless dragonflies went on flying and flying with a small crackling sound over the boat and farther away, over the nocturnally glowing water... And all the time something was rustling, creeping and drawling somewhere...

A week later he was thrown out of the house ignominiously after an ugly scene. The horror of their utterly unexpected separation left him stunned.

After dinner that day they had been in the sitting-room looking at the pictures in the back numbers of *Niva*, their heads touching over the pages.

"D'you still love me?" he whispered, staring hard at the pictures.

"Silly you. Awfully silly," she whispered back.

Suddenly they heard soft running steps and in the door appeared her crazy mother in her shabby black silk dressing-gown and down-at-heel morocco slippers. Her black eyes blazed tragically. She ran into the room, as if making a stage entrance, and shrieked:

"I know everything! I felt it, I was watching. Yours she is not to be, blackguard!"

Flinging up her arm she fired deafeningly from the ancient pistol with which Petya sometimes frightened off the sparrows, loading it only with gunpowder. In the smoke he darted to her and gripped her claw-like hand. She pulled her hand free, hit him on the forehead with the pistol, cutting open his eyebrow, threw the weapon at him and, hearing people running, alarmed by the shouting and the smoke, she started screaming more histrionically still, foaming at her blue lips:

"Only over my dead body, she'll have to step over my dead body! If she elopes with you I'll hang myself the same day or jump from the roof. Out of my house, blackguard! Maria, choose: your mother or he!"

"You, mama, you..." she whispered.

He started and opened his eyes. The purple little eye over the door still looked at him as steadily, enigmatically and mournfully from the pitch darkness, and the train, rocking and swaying, flew on with the same steady speed. That melancholy station was left far, far behind them. And those woods, magpies, swamps, water lilies, grass snakes, cranes, had been a whole twenty years ago... Ah yes, there had been cranes too–how could he have forgotten them? Everything had been strange that remarkable summer: the couple of cranes that came now and again to the edge of the pool strangely let her alone come close to them and, curving their long, thin necks, stared up at her with stern yet gracious curiosity when she came running to them lightly and soundlessly in her woven sandals, squatted quickly before them, spreading out her yellow sarafan on the damp, warm grass, and with childish audacity looked into their stern and beautiful black pupils, narrowly surrounded by the dark-grey iris. He watched her and the cranes from afar through his binoculars, and clearly saw the birds' small, shiny heads, even their bony nostrils, and their big, powerful bills with which they killed grass snakes at a single stab. Their squat bodies with fluffy tufty tails were tightly covered with steely feathers, their scaly sticks of legs were disproportionally thin and long–the legs of one of the cranes were quite black, and the other's were greenish. Sometimes both of them stood for hours on end on one leg in inexplicable immobility, sometimes, for no reason at all, they'd start hopping and spreading wide their enormous wings; or else they would strut about with an air of importance, stepping slowly, raising a leg, the three toes bunched together, and putting it down with the toes spread like talons, and all the time nodding and nodding their small heads... However, when she went running to them, he no longer thought about anything else or saw anything, only her sarafan spread out on the ground about her, and shuddered in an agony of longing at the thought of her body under that sarafan, and her tiny black birthmarks. And on that last day of theirs, that last time they sat together on the sofa looking at the old *Niva*, she held his cap in her hands, pressing it to her breast, as that first time in the boat, and whispered, her happy crystal-black eyes shining into his:

"I love you so much now that even this smell inside the cap, the smell of your head and your nasty eau de cologne seems sweeter than anything in the world."

In the restaurant, when they had passed Kursk, and he was having coffee and cognac after lunch, his wife asked:

"Why do you drink so much? It's your fifth glass, I believe. Still feeling sad, remembering your damsel with the bony feet?"

"I am feeling sad, very sad," he replied with an unpleasant smirk. "My damsel with the bony feet... *Amata nobis quantum amabitur nulla.**"

"Latin, is it? What does it mean?"

"No need for you to know."

"How rude you are," she said with a careless sigh, and turned to gaze out of the sunlit window.

27 September, 1940

The Beauty

A middle-aged official, a widower, married a very young and beautiful girl, a colonel's daughter. He was quiet and modest, while she was well aware of all her qualities. He was tall and lean, with the physique of a consumptive, he wore iodine-coloured spectacles, had a rather husky voice and when he wanted to raise it, if only a little, he produced a thin, shrill squeak. She was a smallish woman with an excellent and well-knit figure, she was always well-dressed, very housewifely, and had a sharp eye. He seemed to be as unattractive in every respect as countless other provincial officials, and yet his first wife had also been a beauty,

*Beloved by us as no other beloved shall be.

and people could only wonder: why did such beautiful girls marry him?

And now this second beauty took a calm dislike to his seven-year-old boy, the son of that first beauty, and completely ignored him. Then the boy's father, for fear of displeasing his young wife, also pretended that he had never had a son. And the boy, lively and affectionate by nature, was now afraid to utter a word in their presence, and little by little effaced himself altogether, becoming non-existent, as it were, in the house.

Immediately after the wedding he was moved from his father's bedroom to the small sitting-room next to the dining-room where he was to sleep on the sofa which was part of a suite upholstered in blue plush. But he was a restless sleeper, and every night he kicked off his bedclothes. And very soon the beauty told the chambermaid:

"I won't have it, he'll rub the plush into holes with his kicking. From now on, Nastya, make him a bed on the floor on that small mattress which I told you to put away in the late mistress's large chest in the corridor."

And the boy, feeling utterly alone in the world, began to live a life of his own, quite apart from that of the household, a mouse-like existence, monotonous, inaudible and unnoticeable. Day in day out he sat meekly in the corner of the sitting-room drawing houses on his small slate; sometimes, in a small whisper, he tried to make out the words in the only picture-book he had, bought when his mummy was living, or just gazed through the window. He slept on the floor between the sofa and a tubbed palm. He made his bed himself in the evenings, and in the mornings diligently rolled up his bedding and put it away in his mummy's chest in the corridor. All his few other belongings were kept there also.

28 September, 1940

Antigone

In June, the student went from his mother's country estate to visit his uncle and aunt, a courtesy visit to enquire after the health of his uncle, a general, who had lost the use of his legs. Visiting them was a duty which the student faithfully performed every summer, and now he was travelling there with resigned composure sprawling in his second-class compartment, his young, sturdy leg flung over the arm of the sofa, indolently reading a new book by Averchenko and absently gazing through the window at the telegraph poles, their white porcelain caps shaped like lilies of the valley, which seemed to bob up and down as the train rolled past. He looked like a very young officer—only his white cap with the blue band was a student's cap, while everything else was made on a military pattern: the white uniform jacket, the greenish trousers, the topboots with patent-leather legs, and the cigarette case with an orange fuse.

His uncle and aunt were wealthy people. When he came home from Moscow for the holidays, the conveyance sent out by his mother to meet him at the railway station was a heavy springless carriage with a pair of draught horses harnessed into it and driven not by a coachman but by a labourer. But when he arrived at his uncle's station he always stepped into a quite different world for a time, the pleasant world of great wealth, and this made him feel handsome, smart and snobbish. And it was like that now. With an involuntarily foppish air he stepped into the light, rubber-wheeled carriage with a mettlesome dark-bay troika harnessed into it and a young coachman wearing a blue sleeveless coat over a yellow silk shirt sitting on the box.

A quarter of an hour later, the troika flew into the circular front court of a great estate, the little bells jingling prettily and the rubber wheels hissing on the sand around the central flower bed, and drew up before the porch of a large, new two-storey house. A tall manservant with sideburns and wearing a red-and-black striped vest and boots, came out of the house to take the young gentleman's luggage. The student performed an incredibly nimble leap from the carriage to the porch as his aunt came waddling to the front door with a smile on her large face with loose hanging jowls, a nose like an anchor, yellow bags under her brown eyes, and her big, flabby body wrapped in a wide raw-silk robe. She kissed him on both cheeks and he, with simulated joy, pressed his lips to her soft, blotchy hand, thinking: how can I keep up this pretence for three whole days with nothing to do in my spare time! Insincerely and hastily answering her insincerely anxious enquiries after his mother, he followed her into the large vestibule, glanced with cheerful hatred at the stuffed brown full-sized bear with shiny glass eyes standing somewhat hunched and pigeon-toed at the foot of the wide staircase and obligingly holding in its sharp-clawed front paws a bronze salver for visiting cards, and suddenly stopped in glad surprise: a tall, statuesque beauty in a grey linen dress, white apron and white head scarf, a beauty with big grey eyes, a vision of youth, health and cleanliness, with well-kept hands and an opaquely white skin, was smoothly pushing the wheelchair with the plump, pale, blue-eyed General. As he kissed his uncle's hand he noticed the extraordinary elegance of her dress and her legs. The General said, chuckling:

"And this is my Antigone, my kind guide, although I am not blind like Oedipus, to pretty women especially. Well then, young people, I've made the introductions."

She gave a slight smile and merely inclined her head in response to the student's bow.

The tall manservant with the sideburns and the striped red-and-black vest took him past the bear up the stairs of polished dark-yellow wood with a red runner in the middle, and then along a similarly carpeted corridor to a large bedroom with an adjoining marble toilet room. It was a different bedroom this time, facing the park and not the yard. But he was blind to all this as he walked behind the manservant. The jolly nonsense, beginning with the opening lines of *Yevgeny Onegin*—"My uncle, proper to a fault"—which he was thinking as he drove into the estate, still stuck in his head, but another thought was already uppermost: "What a woman!"

Humming a tune, he began to shave, wash and change, saying to himself as he pulled on his trousers with the fashionable foot-straps:

"To think that there are such women in the world! What would not one give for the love of a woman like that! And how come that with a beauty like hers she has to push old men and women about in their wheelchairs?"

And crazy thoughts came into his head: he'd stay here for a month or two, make friends with her in secret from everyone, become intimate with her, win her love and then say: be my wife, I am yours forever! He pictured the astonishment of his mother, uncle and aunt when he told them that they loved each other and had decided to marry; he pictured their indignation, their attempts to talk him out of it, their screams, tears, curses, threats of disinheriting him... For your sake I'll bear anything!

As he ran down the stairs to his aunt and uncle, whose rooms were on the gound floor, he thought:

"Honestly, the rubbish that comes into one's head sometimes! Of course I could stay here on some pretext or other, and I could flirt with her on the quiet, pretending that I was madly in love with her... But would it get me anywhere? And if it did, what then? How extricate myself afterwards? Or maybe really marry her?"

For an hour or so he sat with his aunt and uncle in his uncle's enormous study with its enormous writing table, an enormous ottoman covered with rugs woven in Turkestan, a carpet nailed on the wall behind it and hung with criss-crossed Eastern weapons, inlaid smoking tables here and there, and on the mantlepiece a large photographic portrait in a rosewood frame with a small gold crown at the top and "Alexander" written across the corner of the portrait in the Tzar's own sweeping hand.

"I'm so happy to be with you again, Uncle and Auntie," he said towards the end of the hour, thinking of the nurse. "And it's so wonderful here! I'll be terribly sorry to leave."

"But who asks you to leave?" replied his uncle. "What's the hurry? Stay here until you get bored with us."

"Yes, do," said his aunt absently.

Sitting and chatting thus, he kept waiting for her to come in—the maid would announce that tea was served in the dining-room and she would come to push his uncle's wheelchair there. But tea was served right there in the study—a table was rolled in with a spirit lamp and a silver kettle on it, and his aunt poured it out herself. Then he waited for the beautiful nurse to bring his uncle his medicine or something. But she never came.

"And to hell with her," he thought, going from the study to the dining-room, where the servant was drawing the curtains on the tall sunlit windows, glanced for no reason into the ballroom to his right where the glass cylinders on the legs of the grand piano made a glittering reflection on the parquet floor, then turned to the left into the drawing-room, beyond which was the sitting-room, and from there he went out on the balcony, then down to the bright and colourful flower garden, skirted it and trudged along a shady walk. It was too hot in the sun, and dinner was more than two hours away...

The dinner gong in the vestibule sounded at half past seven. He was the first to come into the dining-room, festively illumined by the great, sparkling chandelier, where already stationed beside a small serving table placed against the wall were the fat, cleanly shaven chèf all in starched white, a skinny footman wearing a frock coat and white knitted gloves, and a parlourmaid, small and shapely like a Frenchwoman. A minute later his aunt sailed in like a queen with milky-grey hair, in a pale yellow gown trimmed with cream-coloured lace, and with her swollen ankles overhanging her too tight silk slippers, and at long last—*she*! But once she had rolled up his uncle's wheelchair to the table, she turned and glided out without a backward glance, and the student had only time to notice a curious thing about her eyes—they did not blink at all. His uncle made several small crosses over the breast of his pale-grey uniform coat, his aunt and himself fervently crossed themselves standing, then they sat down pompously, and unfolded their gleaming napkins. His uncle, freshly bathed and pale, his thin wet hair dressed with care, evidenced his hopeless illness with especial apparency at dinner, although he talked a great deal and ate a lot with relish, shrugging his shoulders as he spoke about the war—the Russo-Japanese war was on at the time—saying: "What the devil for did we ever start it?" The footman served with disdainful nonchalance, the parlourmaid, helping him, trotted about on her pretty little feet, and the chèf handed them the dishes to carry to the table with the solemnity of a graven image. They had scalding burbot soup, and very rare roast beef with new potatoes, sprinkled with dill. They drank the white and red wine of Prince Golitsin, the General's old friend. The student talked, answered when questions were asked him, nodded in affirmation with gay smiles but with as little concern as a parrot because his mind was busy with the same silly nonsense he had been thinking while changing: where did she have her meals, surely not with the servants? And again waited for the moment when she would come in for his uncle, and then afterwards he'd happen upon her somewhere and exchange a few words with her. But she came, rolled the wheelchair away, and disappeared once more.

That night, the nightingales sang gently and eloquently in the park, the freshness of the air, the dew, and of the watered flowers in their beds poured into the open windows of his bedroom, and the Dutch linen sheets were pleasantly cool. The student lay for a while in the darkness and had already decided to turn to the wall and go to sleep, when he was startled by a sound into raising his head and sitting up. It must be said that as he was undressing he noticed a small door near the head of his bed, and out of curiosity he opened it, found a second door behind it, tried the handle, but it was locked from the other side. And now there was someone walking about softly behind that door and doing something quietly. Holding his breath, he slipped down from his bed, opened the first door and listened: something fell with a tinkle on the floor of the room beyond. He froze. Could it be *her* room? He peeped into the keyhole—fortunately there was no key in it—saw lamplight, the corner of a woman's dressing table, then something white which rose suddenly and blocked the view. Undoubtedly it was her room, who else's? A parlourmaid would not be given a room here, and Maria Ilyinishna, his aunt's old personal maid, slept on the ground floor next to her mistress's bedroom. And at once he became morbidly aware of her nighttime nearness right there, on the other side of the door, and her inaccessibility. He did not go to sleep for a long time, he woke up late the next morning, and immediately pictured her transparent nightgown and her bare feet in bedroom slippers.

"It's getting so bad, perhaps I'd better leave this very day," he thought and lit a cigarette.

In the morning everyone had coffee in his or her room. He drank his, wearing his uncle's wide night-shirt and his uncle's dressing gown, and throwing wide the dressing gown he examined his body with regret for its uselessness.

Lunch in the dining-room was gloomy and tedious. He had it alone with his aunt. The weather was bad, he could see the trees tossing in the wind and the dark clouds gathering above them.

"Well, my dear, I have to leave you," his aunt said, rising and crossing herself. "Amuse yourself as best you can, and do forgive your uncle and me our infirmities. Till teatime we keep to our rooms always. It looks like rain, otherwise you could go riding..."

"Don't worry about me, Auntie, I'll do some reading," he replied brightly, and went to the sitting-room where the walls were lined with bookshelves.

As he crossed the drawing-room he wondered if he shouldn't order a horse to be saddled for him after all. But in the windows he saw a mass of rainclouds and an unpleasant metallic blue between the lilac clouds above the swaying tree tops. He entered the cosy sitting-room, with a smell of cigar smoke hanging in the air and leather sofas set along three of the walls under the bookshelves, looked at some of the spines of the beautifully bound books, and sat down helplessly, sinking into the deep sofa. What killing boredom! If he could just see her, chat a bit, find out what sort of voice she had, what kind of disposition, if she were stupid or, on the contrary, a clever schemer modestly playing this role until some opportune moment. Most probably she was an ambitious bitch who played safe and knew her own worth. And stupid too, most likely. But what a beauty! And he'd have to sleep next door to her again. He got up, opened the french window leading to the stone steps into the park, heard the trilling of nightingales through the noise made by the trees, but a sudden gust of cold wind rushing through some young trees made him jump back into the room. The room grew dark, the wind tore through those trees, bending their young, green branches, and the windows and balcony doors sparkled with sharply pattering raindrops.

"And they don't turn a hair," he said aloud, thinking of the nightingales whose singing reached him from everywhere through the wind—now close to, now far away. And in that same moment he heard a level voice:

"Good afternoon."

He looked round and froze: it was she.

"I've come to change my book," she said with amiable detachment. "Books are all the joy there is here," she added with a faint smile and went to one of the shelves.

"Good afternoon," he mumbled. "I did not hear you come in."

"The carpets are very thick," she said and, turning round, gave him a long, unblinking look.

"And what do you like to read?" he asked, meeting her eyes a bit more bravely now.

"Just now I'm reading Maupassant, Octave Mirbeau..."

"Ah well, that's natural. All women like Maupassant. All his stories are about love."

"But what could be better than love?"

Her voice was modest, her eyes smiled softly.

"Oh love, love," he sighed. "Amazing encounters happen, don't they, but... Your name and patronymic, nurse?"

"Katerina Nikolayevna. And yours?"

"Call me simply Pavlik," he replied, growing ever bolder.

"D'you think I, too, am old enough to be your aunt?"

"I'd give a lot to have such an aunt. In the meantime I'm merely your unfortunate neighbour."

"Is it a misfortune?"

"I heard you last night. Your room, it appears, is next to mine."

She laughed cooly.

"I heard you too. It's bad to eavesdrop and peep."

"You're so impermissibly beautiful!" he said, frankly examining the speckled grey of her eyes, the opaque whiteness of her skin, and the sheen of her dark hair under the white nurse's scarf.

"You think so? And you wouldn't permit me to be like that?"

"I wouldn't. Your hands alone can drive anyone crazy..."

And with gay impudence he caught her right hand. Standing with her back to the bookshelves, she glanced over his shoulder into the room and without pulling free her hand looked at him with a strange little smile as though waiting to see what he would do next. And he, without releasing her hand, pulled it downward, squeezing it hard, and with his other arm embraced her. She glanced over his shoulder again and tilted her head slightly as if to evade his kiss, but at the same time pressed her body to his. Panting for breath, he strained to reach her half-open lips and pushed her towards the sofa. She frowned and shook her head, whispering: "No, no, we mustn't, because lying down we won't hear or see anything," and with dimming eyes slowly spread out her legs... In another minute he dropped his face on her shoulder. She stood thus for a few moments with her teeth clenched, then freed herself gently and walked steadily and primly out of the room, saying in a loud, matter of fact voice to the accompaniment of the pattering rain:

"It's raining so hard, and all the windows upstairs are open..."

Next morning he awakened in her bed. She lay on her back on the tumbled bedsheet that had become heated during the night, one bare arm flung behind her head. He opened his eyes, joyfully met her unblinking glance, and with his dizzied senses caught the pungent smell of her armpit. There was a nervous knock on the door.

"Who is it?" she asked calmly, without pushing him away. "Is it you, Maria Ilyinishna?"

"It's me, Katerina Nikolayevna."

"What's up?"

"Let me in, I'm afraid someone will hear me and run to the mistress, frightening her..."

When he had fled into his own room, she unlocked the door.

"His Excellency the General is feeling poorly, an injection perhaps," Maria Ilyinishna whispered, looking into the room. "The mistress is asleep, thank God, so do come quickly..."

As she spoke her eyes popped out: there was a pair of men's shoes beside the nurse's bed. The student had fled in his bare feet. Katerina Nikolayevna also saw the shoes and the look in Maria Ilyinishna's eyes.

Before lunch she went to her mistress and told her that she had to leave suddenly; she very calmly lied that she had received a letter from her father saying that her brother had been seriously wounded in Manchuria, and naturally she could not leave her father, a widower, all alone at such a time of sorrow...

"Ah, how well I understand you," said her mistress who had already learnt everything from Maria Ilyinishna. "There's no helping it, you must go, of course. Only please send a telegram to Doctor Krivtsov from the station asking him to come at once and remain with us until we find another nurse."

After this interview she knocked on the student's door and thrust a note into his hand. "All is lost, I'm leaving. The old witch saw your shoes beside my bed. Remember me kindly."

At lunch his aunt seemed a little saddened, but she talked with him as if nothing was wrong.

"Have you heard? The nurse is going away to be with her father, he's all alone, and her brother has been wounded terribly."

"I've heard, Auntie. What a wretched thing war is, there's so much grief everywhere... Oh, tell me, what was wrong with uncle?"

"Oh, nothing serious, the Lord be thanked. He's so nervous about his health. He thought it was his heart, but it was just gastric trouble..."

At three o'clock the troika took Antigone to the railway station. He said goodbye to her on the front porch without looking into her eyes and pretending that he had come out merely to order a riding horse to be saddled for him. He could scream from despair. She waved her glove to him from the carriage; she was already wearing a very pretty hat and not a nurse's white scarf.

2 October, 1940

Smaragd

Clouds, white everywhere and pale blue near the high moon, sailed slowly across the blue blackness of the sky. Watching them, you could see that it was not the clouds but the moon that was floating and, moving together with it, close to it, was a star shedding golden tears; the moon was drifting away into the infinite heights, taking the star with it, always higher and higher.

She was sitting sideways on the sill of the open window and, craning her neck a little, gazed at the sky, feeling slightly dizzy from its movement. He was standing close to her knees.

"What colour is it? I can't tell. And you, Tolia, can you?"
"The colour of what, Kissa?"
"Don't call me Kissa, I've told you a hundred times."
"Very well, Xenia Andreyevna."
"I'm talking about the sky between the clouds. What a lovely colour! It's both awesome and lovely. A heavenly colour indeed, there's none like it on earth. A true smaragd colour."
"Since it's in heaven it's obviously heavenly. Only why smaragd? I've never seen a smaragd in my life. You like the sound of the word, that's all."
"I do. Well, I don't know, perhaps it's not a smaragd but a hyacinth. Anyway it's a colour you'll only see in paradise. And when you're looking at all this you can't help believing that there is paradise, angels, the throne of the Heavenly King..."
"And golden pears growing on a willow."
"What a cynic you are, Tolia! It's true what Maria Sergeyevna says that the worst of bad girls is still more virtuous than any boy there is."
"Verily, out of the mouth of infants, Kissa dear."
She wore a dress of speckled print and cheap shoes; her legs and knees were plump and girlish, her head with her braid pinned once round it was thrown back so prettily... He put a hand on her knee, placed his other arm round her shoulders and half-jokingly kissed her slightly opened lips. She freed herself gently and pushed his hand from her knee.
"What's the matter? Angry?"
She pressed the back of her head to the window frame and he could see that she was biting her lips to hold back her tears.
"Why, what's wrong?"
"Oh, do leave me alone..."
"But really, what did happen?"
"Nothing," she whispered, jumped down from the window sill and ran away.
"She's stupid to the point of saintliness," he said, shrugging his shoulders.

3 October, 1940

Wolves

The warm August night was dark, so dark that the dim stars, shimmering here and there in the overcast sky were hardly visible. Along the road, soft with deep dust that muffled sound, rolled a trap with two young passengers in it—the daughter of a small landowner and a senior-form schoolboy. Flashes of summer lightning touched the pair of nicely running work horses with tangled manes and a plain harness, the cap and shoulders of the lad in a homespun shirt sitting on the box, and for a moment revealed the field ahead, desolate after harvest time, and also a sad little wood in the distance. The night before there had been a great rumpus in the village with much shouting and the cowardly barking and squealing of dogs: when people were already all indoors having supper, a wolf had with extraordinary audacity savaged a sheep in one of the yards and would have carried it off had not the menfolk, hearing the dogs, rushed out with clubs and beaten off the wolf, rescuing the already dead sheep with a ripped side. And now the young Miss was laughing nervously, flinging lighted matches into the darkness and screaming gaily: "I'm afraid of wolves!"

The lighted matches showed up the boy's longish and somewhat coarse face, and the girl's excited, pretty face with high cheekbones. She had a red kerchief tied round her head in the Ukrainian manner, and wore a red cotton dress with a wide neck from which rose her strong, rounded throat. Swaying with the trap, she kept striking matches and flicking them into the darkness, pretending not to notice that the boy was hugging her, kissing her on her neck, on her cheek, and seeking her lips. She pushed him off with an elbow, and he told her in a purposely loud and casual voice for the benefit of the driver:

"Here, give me the matches. If you use them all up I'll have nothing to light a cigarette with."

"Just one more, one more!" she screamed. The match flared up, then came a flash of summer lightning, and after this the warm darkness became even more blindingly dense and black, so confusing that the trap seemed to be rolling backwards. At long last she surrendered her lips to him, and in that very moment the lad reined in the horses so abruptly that the trap jolted them and stopped, as if it had run into some obstruction.

"Wolves!" the lad shouted, aghast.

A great fire had broken out far away to their right. The trap had stopped exactly opposite the small wood which had been revealed in the flashes of summer lightning. With the light of the fire behind it now, the wood looked quite black, it seemed to be shivering all over, just as the whole field in front of it was shivering in the somberly-red tremulous light of the fire spreading hungrily across the sky and, though far away, blazing with shadows of smoke hurrying through it as if no more than a verst away from the trap, burning ever more hotly and angrily, ravenously spreading higher and wider over the horizon, the heat reaching to lick their faces and hands, and they could already see the red rafters of some burnt-down cottage. And under the wall of trees, in the dark red glow, stood three large wolves, their eyes now burning green, now red—a red as transparent and bright as hot red-currant syrup. The horses, snorting noisily, suddenly dashed to the left in a mad gallop across the fields, the lad on the box fell over backwards, and the trap went bumping and clattering over the balks.

Somewhere, on the edge of a gully, the horses swerved crazily again, but here she jumped to her feet and in the nick of time tore the reins out of the hands of the panic-stricken lad. In doing this she fell across the box and cut her face against something sharp. A small scar remained for life in a corner of her mouth and, when asked how she came by it, she replied gladly, with a smile: "It's a memento of long past days," remembering that summer, the rainless August days and dark nights, the threshing floor, the heaps of new fragrant straw, and the boy who did not shave yet with whom she used to lie in that straw at night, gazing at the falling stars as they described a momentarily brilliant arc in the sky. "There were wolves, the terrified horses bolted, and I was hot-headed and reckless then, so I tried to stop them..."

The men she was to love in her life, all of them said that there was nothing sweeter than this scar which gave her mouth its delicate, constant smile.

7 October, 1940

Visiting Cards

It was the beginning of autumn, and the ship *Goncharov* was hurrying down the Volga which was already empty of river traffic. The cold had set in early that year, and a taut, fast, icy wind blew over the Volga's grey Asiatic expanses, sweeping down from its eastern and already rust-coloured banks, tearing at the ship's flag, assaulting the hats, caps and clothes of the passengers strolling on deck, crinkling their faces and whipping the sleeves and skirts of their coats. And there was only one solitary seagull accompanying the ship, flying aimlessly and joylessly, now heeling over on its pointed wings almost within reach, now taking off at a sharp slant into the distance, apparently not knowing what to do at all in the desolate vastness of the river and the grey autumnal sky.

The ship was almost empty too: there was a gang of workmen on the lower deck, and only three passengers walking up and down the upper deck. Two of the gentlemen, travelling second-class, were going to the same place and were inseparable, always pacing the deck together, talking earnestly about something all the time, and looking alike in their inconspicuousness. The third gentleman, travelling first-class, a man of thirty or so, was a writer of recent fame, and was conspicuous for his sad or perhaps angry seriousness, and partly for his looks: he was tall, strongly built–he even bent his body a little like some strong men do–well dressed and handsome after a fashion. He was dark, and his face was of that Oriental cast one sometimes encounters in Moscow among its trading folk of ancient tradition. As a matter of fact, he did hail from them, but he had nothing in common with these people any more.

In his expensive, sturdy shoes, black serge coat and an English checked cap, he paced the deck lonesomely in a firm stride, walking there and back, now in the face of the wind, now with the wind behind him, breathing deeply of the strong autumn air and of the Volga. He stood for a while in the stern, looking at the wake spreading and running in grey ripples behind the ship, then swung about sharply and walked to the bow, straight into the wind, bending his head in the wind-inflated cap and listening to the rhythmical knocking of the wheel paddles from which the water ran down noisily in a continuous length of glass-spun linen. Now he paused in his pacing and smiled wryly, for in the hatchway there appeared a cheap little black hat and then the sweet, wan face of the woman he became acquainted with the night before. He went to her with wide strides. Emerging on the deck, she also went towards him self-consciously and also with a smile, chased along by the wind, cringing from it in her flimsy coat which, clinging, outlined her thin legs, and holding on to her hat with a thin hand.

"Good morning, and did you sleep well?" he asked in a loud, manly voice, as he came towards her.

"Marvellously!" she replied with immoderate gaiety. "I always sleep like a marmot."

He held her hand in his large palm and looked into her eyes. She met his glance eagerly.

"How you do sleep, angel mine," he said with familiarity. "Good folks are already lunching, you know."

"I lay in bed daydreaming," she replied with an audacity that clashed with her whole appearance.

"About what?"

"Ha, that would be telling!"

"Watch your step, 'there's a Chechen prowling 'yond the river', remember that verse?"

"But it's that Chechen I am waiting for!" she said with the same gay flippancy.

"Let's better go and drink vodka and eat fish soup," he said, thinking: she had no money even for lunch I shouldn't wonder.

"Yes, yes, vodka, vodka! It's so damned cold," she cried, stamping her feet coquetishly.

They walked quickly to the first-class dining-room, she walking ahead and he coming behind her and already looking her up and down with a certain measure of lust. He had remembered her in the night. The evening before, when the ship was approaching some town or other, looming black in the dusk and with a scattering of lights at the foot of the tall bank, he addressed some chance remark to her as they stood at the rail, and then he sat with her on deck, on a long bench that ran the length of the first-class cabins, but did not stay long and later regretted it. To his amazement he realised in the middle of the night that he desired her already. Why? From force of habit perhaps, because strange women who chanced to be his fellow-travellers always attracted him?

And now, sitting with her in the dining-room, touching glasses and eating cold caviar with hot rolls, he already knew why she appealed to him so strongly and could not wait to bring matters to a head. And because all this—the vodka drinking and her free-and-easy manner—was so amazingly ill-suited to her, he became more and more impatient.

"Well, let's have one more and call it a day," he said.

"Oh yes, let's," she answered. "It's marvellous vodka, you know."

What had touched him, of course, was her confusion the evening before when he told her his name, and her astonishment that she had so unexpectedly made the acquaintance of a famous author. It was always pleasant to feel and see this confusion, it always disposed him towards the woman if she wasn't too ugly and stupid, and instantly created a sort of intimacy between them, entitling him to a certain boldness in his treatment of her and already giving him some right to her. But it was not this alone that stirred him this time; obviously, he had impressed her not only as a famous author, and he found her poverty and simple-heartedness very touching. He had, since his rise to popularity, quite adopted that special off-hand manner with his women admirers, that swift and easy transition from the first minutes of introduction to an "artistic" familiarity, and that rehearsed simplicity of asking: who are you? where are you from? are you married? That's what he asked her the evening before, as he gazed through the dusk at the varicoloured lights on the buoys that threw long reflections into the water darkling around the ship and at the brightly burning wood fires on the rafts, and catching the smell of smoke, thought: "I must remember this—one fancies a smell of fish soup in that smoke."

"May I ask your name?"

She readily told him her name and patronymic.

"Are you on your way home from somewhere?"

"Yes, I have been staying with my sister in Sviyazhsk.

Her husband died suddenly, and this left her in an awful situation, you see..."

She was so shy at first that when she answered him she looked away, but little by little she grew braver.

"Are you married?"

She smiled a strange smile.

"I am married. Have been for a long time, alas..."

"Why alas?"

"I was silly enough to get married too young. Before I know it, life will be over."

"Come, come, not for a long time yet."

"That isn't so, alas. And I haven't experienced anything, not anything at all yet!"

"It's not too late now."

She tossed her head and said with a chuckle:

"And I am going to!"

"What is your husband? A government official?"

She waved a hand as a sort of dismissal.

"Oh, he's a very good, kind person, but not interesting at all, I'm sorry to say. He's the secretary of our Zemstvo uyezd board."

She's so nice and so unhappy, he thought, taking out his cigarette case.

"Would you like a cigarette?"

"Very much!"

She took the cigarette bravely, and started smoking it ineptly, taking quick puffs like all women do. And again he felt the stirrings of pity for her, for her bravado, and together with the pity—a tenderness and a lustful desire to take advantage of her naivete and inexperience which, he already suspected, was certain to go with extreme daring. And now, sitting in the dining-room, he looked impatiently at her thin hands, at her withered and all the more touching face, at her thick and carelessly dressed dark hair which she kept tossing all the time, now that she had taken off her little black hat and shrugged the flimsy grey overcoat off the shoulders of her cotton-flannel dress. He was touched and excited by the frankness with which she told him the evening before about her marriage, about being past her youth, and also by the sudden audacity with which she was now doing and saying things that were so amazingly ill-suited to her. She was slightly flushed from the vodka, even her pale lips were rosy, and a sleepily mocking gleam shone in her eyes.

"You know, we've been talking about daydreaming," she said. "D'you know what I dreamed most of when I was a schoolgirl? To order some visiting cards for myself. We had become quite impoverished, we had sold what remained of our estate and moved to town, and I had absolutely no one to call on and leave a visiting card, but oh! how I dreamed of them! Terribly silly, of course..."

He clenched his teeth and took her hand firmly in his, feeling all her bones under the fine skin, but she, quite misunderstanding him, raised her hand to his lips and looked at him languidly like an experienced vamp.

"Come to my cabin," he said.

"Yes, let us go. It really is stuffy here, with everyone smoking..."

Tossing her hair, she picked up her hat.

Once in the corridor, he put his arms about her. She glanced at him over her shoulder, proudly and blissfully. He nearly bit her on the cheek with the hatred of passion and love. And she, over her shoulder, offered him her lips like a bacchante.

In the half-light of the cabin with the slatted window blind lowered, anxious to please him and boldly drink to the full the unexpected happiness of making love with this handsome, strong, famous man, she immediately undid her dress, pulling and stamping it down as it fell on the floor, and remained—as slim as a boy—in her thin chemise and white bloomers, the innocence of the sight stabbing him painfully.

"Shall I take off everything?" she whispered, quite like a little girl.

"Everything, of course," he replied, growing more and more morose.

Humbly and quickly she stepped over her discarded underclothes and stood before him stark naked, her skin that peculiar greyish lavender colour which a woman's body turns when it shivers nervously, becomes tense, cold, and covered with goose pimples. She stood there in only her cheap grey stockings with plain garters and her cheap black slippers, and gave him a triumphantly drunken look as she started taking out her hairpins. He watched her, numbly. Her body was better and younger than one might have thought. Her prominent collarbones and ribs could be expected, of course, seeing her thin face and legs. But her hips were even too full. Her stomach with the small deep navel was flat, and beneath it the prominent triangle of beautiful dark hair corresponded to the abundance of dark hair on her head. She took out the last of the hairpins, and her hair tumbled thickly down her skinny back with knobby vertebrae. She bent down to pull up her stockings, and her small breasts with the frozen and wrinkled brown nipples hung down like dry little pears, charming in their poverty. And he made her experience that ultimate shamelessness that was so unbecoming to her and therefore so excited his pity, tenderness and passion... No one could see into the cabin through the slats sticking up at a crazy angle, but she kept glancing at the blind with rapturous horror, she could hear the carefree talk and footsteps of people walking past the window, and that increased much more terribly her delight in her wantonness. Oh, how near they passed, chatting and strolling, and no one could imagine or suspect what was going on in this white cabin at arm's length from them!

Afterwards, he laid her out like a corpse on the berth. She lay with clenched teeth, closed eyes, and a look of grave quietude on her pale and now quite young face.

Late in the afternoon, when the ship berthed at the place where she had to get off, she stood on the deck beside him with modestly lowered eyes. He kissed her cold hand with that love which remains for life somewhere deep in one's heart and she, without a backward glance, ran down the gangplank into the rough crowd on the pier.

5 October, 1940

Tania

She was a maid in the house of his kinswoman, Mme Kozakova, a small landowner. She had just turned sixteen, and was a short girl which was especially noticeable when she went about in her bare feet in summer or else in felt boots in winter, swinging her skirts softly, her small breasts slightly upthrust under her blouse. Her plain face was sweet, no more, and her grey peasant eyes owed their beauty to youth alone. In those long ago days, he squandered himself mindlessly, he lived the life of a wanderer, had many incidental love affairs and entanglements, and looked upon his affair with her as one of those chance things...

She soon became reconciled with that fateful, amazing thing which happened to her so unexpectedly that autumn night. She cried for several days afterwards, but with every day she became more and more convinced that what happened was not a disaster, it was her good fortune, and felt that he was becoming ever more precious to her and dear. In moments of intimacy, which soon became more and more frequent, she already called him Petrusha love, and talked of that night as of their shared and treasured past.

At first he both believed and disbelieved her, asking:

"Do you honestly mean that you were not feigning sleep then?"

"But didn't you feel that I was fast asleep?" she asked in wide-eyed wonder. "Don't you know that boys and girls sleep like logs?"

"If I'd known that you were really asleep I'd never have touched you."

"You know, I didn't feel anything, anything at all almost to the very last! Only what made you come to my bed? When you arrived here you didn't even glance at me, and only late in the evening you asked: "I believe you're a new girl, and I think your name is Tania, is it?' And you took no notice of me all this time. Were you pretending?"

He replied that, of course, he was pretending, but it was not true because it all happened on the spur of the moment.

After spending the beginning of autumn in the Crimea, he had stopped for a visit with Mme Kozakova on his way back to Moscow, and at the end of a fortnight of living in the tranquilizing simplicity of her country estate, made ready to leave. That day, before parting with the countryside, he rode about all day with a gun and a hound over the harvested fields and denuded copses, bagged nothing at all, returned to the house feeling tired and hungry, at supper ate a whole pan of meat balls in cream sauce, drank a decanter of vodka and several cups of tea while Mme Kozakova talked as usual about her late husband and her two sons who were officers in Orel. At about ten o'clock, when all the lights were put out in the house, he saw candlelight in the study beyond the drawing-room where he was always put up when he came for a stay. He walked into the study and saw the girl kneeling on the couch where his bed had been made up and passing a burning candle back and forth along the log wall. On seeing him, she quickly put the candle on his bedside table, jumped down from the couch and dashed to the door.

"What's all this about?" he asked, amazed. "Wait a minute, what were you doing here?"

"Burning bed bugs," she replied in a quick whisper. "I was making up your bed and saw a bed bug on the wall."

Laughing, she ran away.

He followed her with his eyes, and then without undressing and only pulling off his tall boots lay down on the quilt, meaning to smoke and think–after all, he was not used to going to sleep at ten o'clock–and instantly dozed off. He awoke for a moment, bothered in his sleep by the trembling light of the candle, blew it out and fell asleep again. The next time he opened his eyes he saw a moonlit autumn night, devoid of life and beautifully wistful, looking into the room through the two windows facing the yard and the one facing the garden, which was flooded with light. He found his slippers beside his couch, went into the passage next to the study leading to the back porch to relieve himself, because the servants had forgotten to leave him a chamberpot. But he found the back-porch door secured with a bar from the outside, and so he made his way through the mysteriously lighted house to the front porch. There was a partition in the hall opposite the tall window under which stood a big old chest, and behind that partition was a windowless room where the maids slept. The door in the partition stood ajar, and the room beyond was dark. He struck a match and saw her sleeping. She lay on her back on the wooden bed in a shift and a short flannel skirt, under the shift her small breasts were roundly outlined, her legs were bare, the skirt barely reached to her knees, her right arm was flung out to the wall, and her face on the pillow looked dead... The match burnt down. He stood there for a moment, and then cautiously walked to her bed.

On his way to the front porch across the dark hall he thought feverishly:

"How strange and how unexpected! Was she really asleep?"

He stood for a minute on the porch, and then started across the yard... The night, too, was strange. The wide, empty yard was light under the high moon. Facing him were the stables, the coach house, and the barnyard buildings roofed with old straw that had hardened into stone. In the northern sky behind these roofs the mysterious night clouds, like dead snow mountains, were dissolving slowly. Overhead there were only some whispy white clouds and the high moon, dropping diamond tears into them, and as it emerged from the clouds into the dark-blue gaps of clear sky, into the fathomless stellar depths, it seemed to shed an even brighter light on the roofs and the yard. And everything around him appeared uncanny in its nocturnal existence, estranged from all that was human, and shining aimlessly. Another strange thing was that he may have been seeing this moonlit autumn world for the first time in his life.

He sat down on the step of the mud-spattered tarantas that stood outside the coach-house. The night was autumnally warm and smelled of the autumnal garden, it was solemn, passionless, beatific, and blended amazingly with those feelings which he brought away from that unexpected intimacy with that female creature who was little more than a child.

She had sobbed quietly when she quite woke up, as if only then realizing what had happened. But maybe it was not "as if", but really so? Her whole body had surrendered to him inertly. At first he tried to waken her, whispering: "Don't be afraid..." She did not hear, or pretended not to hear. Cautiously he kissed her hot cheek—no response whatever came, and so he took it for her tacit consent to anything that might follow. He spread out her legs with their sweet, hot warmth, and she only sighed in sleep, stretched weakly and threw her arms behind her head.

"And what if she wasn't pretending?" he asked himself, getting up and staring worriedly into the night.

When she burst out crying with such abandon and grief, he started kissing her neck, her breasts, and all her body smelling so deliciously of something rustic and maidenly, not just with animal gratitude for the unexpected happiness she had unconsciously given him, but also with rapture, with love. And she, still sobbing, suddenly responded to him with an instinctive womanly impulse, hugging him hard and also gratefully perhaps, and pressing his head to her breast. She was still half asleep and did not yet understand who he was, but no matter, this was the man with whom she was fated to become united for the first time in the most secret and blissful intimacy. This mutual intimacy had taken place, and nothing in the world could annul it, it would remain part of his inner self forever, and here was this extraordinary night admitting him to its incredibly radiant kingdom together with that intimacy...

How could he, when he left, remember her only incidentally and forget her dear, sincere voice, her eyes sometimes happy, sometimes sad, but always loving and devoted, how could he love other women and ascribe to some of them far more importance than he did to her!

On the following day, she served at table without raising her eyes.

"Why so careworn, Tania?" asked her mistress.

And she replied meekly:

"I've cares enough, you know, madam."

When Tania left the dining-room, his hostess told him:

"Yes, of course, the poor thing has no mother, and her father's a ne'er-do-well, a feckless character..."

That evening, when she was lighting the samovar on the back porch, he said, as he walked past her:

"Believe me, I've loved you for a long time. Stop crying and breaking your heart, what's done can't be undone..."

As she blinked away her tears and went on thrusting burning splinters into the samovar chimney, she answered quietly:

"If you really loved me, it would be easier to bear..."

After this she sometimes glanced at him as though asking timidly if it was true.

One night, when she was making up his bed, he came up behind her and put his arms round her shoulders. Startled and blushing terribly, she whispered:

"Don't, for the love of God. The old woman might come in any minute."

"What old woman?"

"Why, the mistress's maid, as if you don't know."

"I'll come to your room tonight."

"Oh heavens, no, no! I'll go out of my mind from fright!"

She jumped as though scalded. In the beginning she really went in terror of the old woman.

"Oh, well, don't be afraid, I won't come," he told her.

She now went about her duties as before, performing them with care and alacrity, flying across the yard to the kitchen, and, when no one was about, darting quick looks at him, but they were shyly happy looks now. And then, early one morning when he was still asleep, she was despatched to town to do some shopping for her mistress. At dinner, his hostess said to him:

"I don't know what to do, I've sent the steward with a labourer to the mill, and there's no one to go and fetch Tania from the railway station. Perhaps you wouldn't mind going?"

Controlling his eagerness, he replied carelessly:

"Very well, I'll gladly go for a drive."

The old chambermaid who was serving at table frowned and said:

"Why d'you want to disgrace that wench for life, Madam? She'll be the talk of the whole village after this."

"Well, go yourself then. Must she walk from the station or what?"

He set out at about four in the afternoon in the cabriolet drawn by a tall, black old mare, and once out of the village he drove her hard, afraid of being late for the train, jolting over the bumps on the dirt road which froze in the night and melted in the daytime. The last few days had been damp and misty, and on this particular day the mist was especially dense. When he was driving through the village it looked as if night was falling, smoky-red lights were already seen in the windows—eerie lights behind the veil of grey-blue mist. And out in the open it was almost quite dark, impenetrably dark because of the mist. A cold wind laden with dampness blew into his face, but the wind did not dispel the mist and, on the contrary, seemed to condense it so much so that it smothered him with its cold, pungent dampness, and he fancied that there was nothing behind this impenetrable murk—the end of the world and all living things. His cap, coat, eyelashes and moustache were beaded with tiny drops of water. The old black mare flew on with great strides, the cabriolet jumped on the slippery clots of earth, and he was jolted painfully. He managed to light a cigarette in the wind, and the sweet, fragrant and warmly human smoke mingled with the primordial smell of the mist, late autumn, and wet, desolate fields. And all around him, above and below, the darkness gathered all the more thickly and glumly, and now he could hardly see the mare's long neck and her pricked-up ears. And all the stronger in him grew the feeling of closeness with the horse, the only living creature in that desert, amid the deadly animosity of all the unknown that was so ominously lurking to the right, to the left, ahead and behind him, in that thickening smoky darkness closing in on him from all sides.

When at last he drove into the village where the railway station was he rejoiced in this habitation, in the dim lights flickering in the wretched little windows, in their sweet cosiness, while the railway station itself struck him as quite a different world—busy, wide-awake and urban. Barely had he tethered his horse when the train came roaring into the station with a glitter of its lighted windows and a sharp sulphury smell of coal. He ran into the station building with the eagerness of a husband meeting his young wife, and saw her the moment she came in through the opposite door following the station watchman who was carrying her two shopping bags. The place was filthy and stinking of the kerosene lamps that dimly lit it, but she—dressed in town clothes—was radiant, her eyes shone from the excitement of that unusual trip, and the watchman addressing her as "Miss". Suddenly she saw him and stopped short in confusion: why was he here, had something happened?

"Tania, hello, I've come to fetch you, there was no one else to send," he hastened to set her mind at ease.

Was there ever an evening as glorious in her life? "He has come for me himself, I've arrived from town, I'm all dressed up and prettier than he ever imagined I could look, always seeing me in my old skirt and cheap print blouse, and now my face is like a modiste's under this white silk scarf, and under my smart jacket I'm wearing a new woollen brown dress, I've new white cotton stockings and new ankle boots with brass cleats!" Inwardly trembling with excitement, she spoke to him in the tone of a young lady visitor and, holding up her skirt, followed him with mincing ladylike steps, saying in a shocked but condescending voice: "Oh, heavens, how slippery, how those peasants have muddied the floor here with their boots!" Tingling all over with delicious fear, she got into the cabriolet, lifting her dress high so as not to crumple it and sit on her calico underskirt, and settled beside him like an equal, awkwardly drawing her legs away from the bundles at her feet.

He started off without speaking and drove the horse into the icy darkness of the night and the mist, past the cottages with little lights twinkling here and there in the windows, jolting over the ruts of the village road at its November worst, and she did not dare utter a word, frightened by his grim silence: had she angered him in some way? He guessed what she must be feeling and kept silent on purpose. And suddenly, once they were past the village, he brought the horse to a walk, took the reins in his left hand and with his right drew her close, muttering and laughing happily: Tania, Tania darling...

She strained towards him with her whole body, and he felt her white silk scarf, her sweetly flaming face and her eyelashes, wet with hot tears, pressed to his cheek. He found her lips, reined in the horse, and kissed her long and deeply. And then blindly, unable to see a thing in the mist and dark, he climbed down from the cabriolet, threw his coat down on the ground and pulled her by the hands. Readily compliant, she jumped down to him quickly and, tucking up her precious finery, the new dress and calico underskirt, with swift care, lay down on the coat, surrendering to him forever not just her whole body, but now also her whole soul.

Again he put off his departure.

She knew he did it for her, he was so affectionate with her, he talked with her now as with his closest, most secret friend in the house, and she no longer trembled with fear, as she had trembled in the beginning, when he approached her. His love-making was simpler, less frenzied now, and she quickly adapted herself to him. She changed completely with a swiftness which the young are capable of, she became happily carefree and now easily called him Petrusha, and sometimes even pretended that she was fed up with his everlasting kisses. "O Lord, he won't let me be! The moment he catches me alone he must grab me!" And this gave her a peculiar gratification: if I can talk to him like that it means he loves me, it means he's really mine! Showing him that she was jealous, that she had a right to him, was another gratifying privilege.

"Thank God there's no threshing done now, or else there'd be a crowd of village wenches, and if you went after them, I'd show you!" And she would add with diffidence and a touching attempt at humour: "Maybe I alone am not enough for you?"

The winter set in early. After the mists came an icy wind that froze the muddy ruts in the roads, turned the ground to stone, and scorched the grass remaining in the garden and the yard. Leaden whitish clouds gathered, the utterly denuded trees thrashed restlessly and anxiously as though they were trying to escape, and at night one could see the white moon diving in and out of the banks of white clouds. The estate and the village looked hopelessly shabby and ugly. Dry snow fell, sprinkling the frozen mud with castor sugar, and the state grounds, and the fields beyond, now a uniform greyish-white, appeared more spacious somehow. The last jobs were being finished in the village: potatoes were sorted out, the rotten ones thrown away and the good ones stored in the cellars for the winter. One day, putting on his fur-lined coat and pulling his fur hat well down on his ears, he went for a stroll in the village. The northern wind tousled his moustache and stung his cheeks. The sky was low and sullen, and the greyish-blue fields rolling down to the river seemed very near. Mountains of potatoes were heaped at the doors of the cottages and sitting on top of them and sorting them out were village wives and young girls, wrapped in hempen shawls, wearing ragged jackets and old felt boots, their faces and hands quite blue from the cold and he thought, appalled, that their legs under the skirts were bare!

When he came back from his walk, he found Tania in the hall wiping a boiling samovar with a cloth before carrying it into the dining-room, and the moment she saw him she said in a low voice:

"I expect you've been to the village where the wenches are sorting out the potatoes... Oh well, go wenching all you want, pick the comeliest one for your pleasure..."

And, choking down her tears, she ran away.

Towards evening there was a heavy snowfall and as she ran past him into the drawing-room she gave him a glance of irrepressible childish glee and whispered with teasing spite:

"Much gallivanting you'll do now! That's nothing yet, the dogs are rolling all over the yard, it means there'll be such blizzards that you won't poke your nose out of doors."

And he thought: O Lord, how am I to tell her that I'm leaving soon?

He passionately wanted to be back in Moscow. The frost, the snowstorm in the square opposite the Church of Our Lady of Iviron, the sleighs pulled by a pair with muttering jinglebells, and on Tverskaya the light of electric streetlamps in swirls of snow... And at the Grand Restaurant, the chandeliers would be sparkling, lovely music pouring forth, and he, shrugging off his fur-lined overcoat into the waiting arms of the doorman, mopping the snow on his moustache with a handkerchief, would be walking briskly along the red carpet into the warmth of the packed restaurant, into the hubbub of voices, the smell of food and cigarette smoke, the bustle of the waiters, and the waves of string music now languidly sensual, now boisterously vivacious and drowning all other sounds...

Throughout supper that night he was unable to look at her carefree bustling and her as yet untroubled face.

Later, he put on the felt boots and old raccoon coat that had belonged to the late Mr. Kozakov, pulled on his fur hat, and went out through the back door into the cold for a breath of air and a look at the snowstorm. The steps of the back porch were already buried under snow, he tripped and got his sleeves full of snow. Further away it was a veritable hell, a white whirling chaos. Sinking deep in the snow, he waded through it round the house, reached the front porch at last, leapt up the steps into the dark entry, resounding with the groaning storm, stamped his feet to shake off the snow, and then entered the front hall where a candle was burning, set on the chest. She came running in her bare feet from behind the partition and cried in dismay:

"Good heavens above! Where have you been?"

He threw his coat and hat on the chest, and in a mad rapture of tenderness picked her up in his arms. She pulled free, grabbed a besom, whisked the snow off his felt boots and then pulled them off, her exaltation as madly rapturous as his.

"Mercy, they're full of snow! You'll catch your death!"

Through his sleep that night he sometimes heard the storm howling monotonously and monotonously straining against the house, then attacking it furiously, hurling crackling snow at the window shutters, rattling them angrily, and then abating, retreating and humming him to sleep. The night seemed endless and delicious, here in the warmth of his bed, in the warmth of the old house, standing solid in the white obscurity of the sweeping snow sea...

In the morning he fancied that the night's wind was

throwing open the window shutters and slamming them back against the wall, but when he opened his eyes he saw that it was already broad daylight, that a white, white whiteness stared from everywhere into the snow-encrusted windows, drifted up to the very sills, and its white reflection lay on the ceiling. The wind was still blowing and sweeping the snow, but it was quieter now, already displaying only a daytime bluster. From his bed he could see on the opposite wall the two windows with time-darkened double frames and small panes, and to the left of him the third window, the whitest and brightest of all. The snow was reflected whitely on the ceiling, the stove hummed in the corner, the furnace door knocking as the fire was drawn in... He had slept so well, he hadn't heard a thing, while Tania, darling Tania, so true and beloved, must have opened the window shutters, come in quietly in her felt boots, cold as an icicle with snow on her shoulders and her head wrapped in a hempen shawl, and going down on her knees lit the stove. And no sooner had he thought this than in she came with tea on a tray and already without the shawl. As she put the tray on his bedside table she glanced with a little smile into his eyes, clear after a good night's sleep and with a look of dreamy wonder in them.

"You're sleeping late, aren't you," she said.

"What is the time?"

She looked at the clock on the bedside table and did not answer at once, for she still could not tell the time at a glance.

"Ten o'clock... No, ten minutes to nine."

He glanced at the door, and caught at her skirt. She drew back, pushing away his hand.

"No, no, we musn't, everyone is up..."

"Oh come on, just for one minute!"

"The old woman might come in..."

"No one will come in. For just one minute!"

"My, aren't you a pest!"

Quickly pulling her legs out of her felt boots, she lay down in her woollen socks, keeping a wary eye on the door. Ah, that peasant smell of her head and breath, that apple-skin coolness of her cheek! He whispered crossly:

"Again you're kissing with your lips compressed. When will you learn!"

"Teach your ladies... Wait a sec, I'll shift a bit lower down. Now, make it quick, I'm scared stiff..."

They stared into each other's eyes intently, senselessly and expectantly.

"Petrusha..."

"Shut up. Must you always talk at this time?"

"But when else can I talk to you? Alright, I won't keep my lips compressed any more... Swear to me that you don't have anyone in Moscow..."

"Don't paw my neck like that."

"No one in your whole life will love you like I do. When you fell in love with me I sort of fell in love with myself, and I'm so glad for my sake... But if you leave me..."

Afterwards, with a burning face she rushed out through the back-porch door into the snowstorm, squatted for a moment, and then, braving the swirling snow and sinking deeper than her bare knees made a dash round the house to the front door.

There was a samovar smell in the hall. The old chambermaid was sitting on the chest under the tall window sipping tea from her saucer, and between sips she glanced askance at Tania and asked:

"And where have you been? Tumbling in the snow?"

"I've been serving tea to Pyotr Nikolayevich."

"In the backyard, or where? We know your kind of tea serving!"

"Well, if you do you do. Is the mistress up?"

"Never too late to ask. Long before you were."

"You're always so cross, honestly!"

She sighed happily, went behind the partition to fetch her tea cup, and sang under her breath:

Into the garden I shall go,
Into the garden green,
To meet my sweetheart I shall go
In that garden green...

After breakfast, he sat in the study reading and listening to the howling of the wind, now weakening, now swelling ominously round the house that was sinking deeper and deeper in the snow amid the milky whiteness madly rushing at it from all sides. He was thinking that as soon as the snowstorm abated he would leave.

In the evening he contrived to whisper to her that she must come to his room when the household went to sleep and stay with him the whole night until morning. She shook her head, thought a moment, and said: "Very well." The thought was very frightening but all the more thrilling for it.

The thought thrilled him too, and also he felt a twinge of pity for her—she did not know that it was to be their last night.

When he went to bed he kept falling asleep and starting up in alarm: would she have the courage to come? The house was plunged in darkness, the snowstorm raged around this dark house, the window shutters rattled, a wail went up in the chimney with every gust of wind... Suddenly he sat up in fright: he hadn't heard her, he could not have heard her stealing with a criminal's caution through the dark house, he had not heard her but he felt that she was there, standing beside his couch. He held out his arms and without a word she slipped into bed, under his quilt. He heard the beating of her heart, he touched her frozen feet, and whispered the most ardent words he could find and utter.

They lay for a long time, pressed close together, and kissed so hard that their teeth hurt. She remembered his telling her not to compress her lips and, trying to please him, she opened her mouth wide like a young jackdaw.

"I suppose you haven't slept at all?"

"Not for a moment," she replied in a happy whisper. "I just waited."

He groped for the matchbox on the bedside table and lighted the candle. She gasped.

"Petrusha, what have you done! What if the old woman wakes up and sees the light?"

"To hell with her," he said, looking at her flushed face. "To hell with her, I want to see you."

And as he made love to her he watched her intently.

"I'm scared," she whispered. "Why do you look at me like that?"

"Because there's no one better than you in the world. This head with the small braid pinned round it is like that of a very young Venus..."

Her eyes sparkled with laughter and happiness.

"And who may she be, this very young Venus?"

"Just Venus... And this poor chemise..."

"Buy me a good one then... Seems like you really love me very much..."

"I don't love you at all. And again you're smelling of either a quail or of dry hemp..."

"But why do you like it? You told me I was always talking at the wrong time, and now you yourself are talking!"

She held him tighter and tighter, she wanted to say something more, but now she was past speech...

Afterwards, he blew out the candle and for a long time lay without speaking, just smoking and thinking: "I've got to tell her, it's awful, but tell her I must."

"Tania darling," he began in a barely audible voice.

"Yes?" she whispered back.

"I've got to leave, you know."

She sat up.

"When?"

"Quite soon ... very soon... I have some urgent matters to attend to."

She fell back on the pillow.

"O Lord!"

Those unknown matters of his, somewhere far away in some unknown Moscow, filled her with awe. But even so, how could they part for the sake of those matters? Quickly and helplessly she searched her mind for some way out of this hopeless horror. There was no way out. She wanted to cry: "Take me with you!" but she did not dare. He couldn't take her with him, could he?

"After all, I can't stay here forever, you know," he said.

She listened and murmured: of course, of course...

"And, after all, I can't take you with me, can I?"

"Why not?" she suddenly asked in despair.

He quickly thought: Really, why not? And answered hastily: "I have no home, Tania, all my life I've been going from place to place. In Moscow I live in a rooming house.*

***This is an autobiographical detail. Bunin had no home of his own, he usually lived at a hotel, in a rooming house, or else stayed with relatives or friends.**

And I shall never marry anyone."

"Why not?"

"Because I was born that kind of person."

"And you'll never marry anyone?"

"Never, not anyone! I give you my word of honour that those matters that are calling me away are very important and urgent, and I honestly have to go. I'll come back for Christmas for certain."

She clung to him, her warm tears falling on his hands, and whispered: "I'll go now, it'll be light soon."

She got up and made the sign of the cross over him in the darkness.

"Keep him safe, Mother of God, keep him safe!"

Once behind her partition, she sat down on her bed and, pressing her hands to her breast and licking the tears off her lips, whispered, listening to the droning of the snowstorm in the entry:

"O Lord, our Heavenly Father! O Mother of God! Let it blow if only for two more days!"

Two days later he left. The snowstorm was abating, though swirls of snow still went sweeping across the yard, but he could not endure his secret agony any longer and did not succumb to the pleas of his hostess to stay if only till the morrow.

To Tania the house and the whole estate seemed desolate and dead after he left. She could not picture Moscow, she could not picture him in Moscow, his life there, and those urgent matters he had to attend to.

He did not come for Christmas. Oh, what those days were like for her! From morning till night she lived in an agony of waiting, in a misery of self-deception, pretending she wasn't waiting at all, and how the hours dragged! Throughout the holidays she went about in her best clothes—the brown wool dress and ankle boots she had worn that unforgettable evening when he came to fetch her from the train.

On Twelfthnight she believed without reason but with hungry eagerness that at any moment now she would sight the peasant's sleigh he had hired at the railway station as he had not written asking for horses to be sent out, and all that day she sat on the chest in the hall, staring her eyes out of the window until they began to smart and hurt. There was no one in the house. The mistress had gone to visit her neighbours, and the old chambermaid had remained in the servants' hall after dinner to gossip with the cook.

And Tania, Tania did not even leave her post for dinner on the pretext that she had a stomach ache.

Dusk began to gather. She took one more look at the empty yard under a sparkling snow crust, got down to the floor and told herself firmly: it's all over, I need not wait any more, I don't want to wait for anything any more! And, dressed in her best, she strolled with leisurely step across the ballroom and the drawing-room illumined by the wintry yellow sunset, and sang in a loud, carefree voice, relieved that life was finished.

Into the garden I shall go,
Into the garden green,
To meet my sweetheart...

At the word "sweetheart" she entered the study, saw his empty couch, his empty armchair at the writing table where he once sat reading, fell into that armchair, and dropped her head on the table, sobbing and screaming: "O Mother of God, let me die!"

He came in February when she had given up all hope of ever seeing him again, if only once more in her life.

And all that had been seemed to come back.

He was shocked when he saw her, for she was so thin and wan, and the look in her eyes was so timid and sad. She, too, was dismayed at first: he seemed different somehow and older, he was someone she did not know or even like—his moustache had grown thicker, his voice harsher, and his laughter and talk as he took off his coat in the hall sounded too loud and unnatural, and she shrank from looking into his eyes. But both tried to hide their feelings from each other, and very soon they picked up where they had left.

And again there approached the frightening hour of his departure. He swore to her on the icon that he would come for Easter and this time stay the whole summer. She believed him, but asked herself: "And what's going to happen in the summer, the same thing as now?" It was not enough for her any longer, she wanted not a repetition of the past, but everything to be exactly as before, or else to live with him inseparably, without partings, without more torments, without the shame of waiting and waiting in vain. Still, she tried to drive away this thought and instead picture the coming summer happiness, when they would have all the freedom they wanted, days and nights in the garden, in the fields, and he'd be with her for such a long, long time.

On the eve of his departure the night was clear and windy, already with spring in the air. The trees were swishing worriedly in the garden, and from there the wind carried the spiteful, helpless yelping of the dogs at the hole in the fir grove where crouched the fox which the forester had caught in a snare and brought to his mistress.

He lay on the couch on his back, with closed eyes. She lay close to him on her side, her woebegone face propped up on a hand. Neither spoke. At last she whispered:

"Petrusha, are you asleep?"

He opened his eyes and said, glancing into the dusky room with a golden glow coming through the side window:

"No, why?"

"You don't love me any more, you know, you ruined me for nothing."

"Don't talk rubbish."

"It'll be a sin on your soul. What's to become of me now?"

"Why should anything become of you?"

"Here you're going away, going away to that Moscow of yours, and what am I to do here with you gone?"

"Why, whatever you did before. And then I told you, didn't I, that I'll come for Easter and stay the whole summer."

"Yes, maybe you really will come. Only you never said such things to me before, like 'why should anything happen to you'. You did love me and told me you'd never seen anyone sweeter. But, of course, I wasn't like this before."

"No, you were not," he was thinking. "You have changed terribly, in every way."

"My time's past," she went on. "Before, I'd jump out of bed and run here to you, scared to death I was but glad too that the old woman had gone to sleep at last. And now, even of her I'm not afraid..."

He shrugged, and said:

"I don't understand you. Here, reach for my cigarettes on the table, will you."

She handed him the cigarettes and he lit one.

"I don't understand what the matter is with you. You're simply unwell, that's all."

"And that's why, I suppose, you stopped loving me. And what I am ill with, I'd like to know?"

"You didn't understand, I meant that you were unwell emotionally. Stop to think for a moment: has anything happened to make you imagine that I no longer love you? And why must you repeat one and the same thing over and over again—before, before..."

She made no response. The window glowed with the sunset, the garden fretted in the wind, from far away came the dogs' spiteful, hopeless, sobbing barks. She quietly slipped down from the couch and pressing a sleeve to her eyes and jerking her head, padded to the door in her woollen socks. He called her in a low, stern voice:

"Tania!"

She turned round and whispered:

"What d'you want?"

"Come here."

"What for?"

"Come here, I tell you."

She came obediently, dropping her head so he should not see the tears pouring down her face.

"Yes, what do you want?"

"Sit down, and don't cry. Kiss me, there's a good girl."

She sat down and, sobbing quietly, hugged him.

"Good God, what am I to do?" he thought in despair. "Again those warm, childish tears on her hot childish face... She doesn't even suspect how terribly I love her. But what can I do? Take her away? Where? Into what kind of life? And what can come of it? Am I to tie myself hand and foot, and wreck my life forever?"

And he began to whisper rapidly, her tears tickling his nose and lips:

"Tania, my darling, don't cry, listen. I'll come in the spring for the whole summer, and we really will go with you into the green garden I've heard you singing about and never will forget. We'll go for a drive to the forest, remember that drive back from the railway station?"

"No one will let me go driving with you," she whispered bitterly, shaking her head against his chest. "And you won't go anywhere with me."

But in her tone he already detected a note of hope, of timid joy.

"I will, Tania darling. And don't you dare cry any more."

He picked her up, a small, light thing, and sat her on his knee.

"And now say: Petrusha, I love you very much!"

She repeated it dumbly, hiccoughing from her sobs: "I love you very much."

This was in February of the frightening year 1917. And never in his life was he to come back again.

22 October, 1940

In Paris

When he was wearing a hat, walking down the street or standing in the car of the metro, and you could not see the silver threads in his cropped reddish hair, you would say he was not more than forty, judging by the freshness of his lean, clean-shaven face and his tall, lean figure in the long mackintosh. But the look in his light grey eyes was austerely sad, and he acted and spoke like a man who has gone through many trials and tribulations in his life. At one time he rented a farm in Provence, heard more than an earful of biting Provencal jokes, and when in Paris liked to insert them, with a little smile, in his always concise speech. Many knew that his wife left him at the Constantinople stage of their flight from Soviet Russia, and that since then he lived with a constantly bleeding wound in his heart. He never confided his secret pain to anyone, and only sometimes, when the conversation turned to women, hinted at it, joking sourly:

"*Rien n'est plus difficile que de reconnaître un bon melon et une femme de bien.*"*

One late, damp autumn evening he dropped into a small Russian restaurant in one of the dark side-streets in the vicinity of Passy. The restaurant also maintained a delicatessen of sorts, and he paused absently before the wide show-window displayed in which were tapering pink bottles of ashberry vodka and squat yellow bottles of Zubrovka, a dish with some stale fried meat pies on it, a dish with meatballs that had turned grey with age, a box of halva, and a tin of sprats; beyond, was a counter with assorted *zakouskas*** set out on it, and behind it the proprietress with an unfriendly Russian face. It was light in the delicatessen, and he felt drawn to this light from the dark side-street with its cold and greasy-looking paving. He walked in, said good-evening to the proprietress, and proceeded into the dimly lit adjacent room where none of the small tables, covered with white paper, was as yet occupied. Unhurriedly, he took off his hat and long mackintosh, hung them on the hall tree, sat down at a table in the farthest corner and, rubbing his reddishly-hairy hands, started reading the menu, which listed an endless choice of dishes, partly typed and partly written in running purple ink on a greasy sheet of paper. Suddenly, the lights were

*Nothing is more difficult than telling at a look if a watermelon is ripe or a women is virtuous.

***Zakouskas*—assorted small cold dishes served before dinner: fish, meat, pickles, caviar, etc.—*Tr.*

turned on in his corner and he saw a woman of thirty or so, with black hair parted in the centre and dark eyes, wearing a white pinafore trimmed with lace over a black dress, coming to take his order with an indifferently polite expression on her face.

"*Bonsoir, monsieur*," she said in a pleasant voice. She seemed so beautiful to him that he was confused and responded lamely:

"*Bonsoir*... But you are Russian, aren't you?"

"Yes, I'm Russian. I got into the habit of speaking French with our customers, you see."

"Why, do many Frenchmen come here?"

"Quite many, and all of them always want Zubrovka, pancakes and even borsch. Have you chosen anything?"

"No. There's such a huge choice. Do suggest something yourself."

She started enumerating the dishes in a studied, impersonal voice:

"Tonight we have sailors' *schi*, meatballs *a la* Cossack, you can also have a veal chop or, if you wish, a shashlyck..."

"Fine. I'll have some *schi* and meatballs, please."

She picked up the little pad hanging from her belt and wrote down his order with a stub of pencil. Her hands were very white and of a noble shape, her dress was worn but had obviously been bought at a good *maison*.

"Will you have some vodka?"

"Gladly. It's awfully raw out."

"Shall I bring some *zakouskas*? We have some wonderful Danube herring, red caviar that we've just received, and fresh-salted little Korkun cucumbers..."

He looked at her again. The white pinafore with the lace insets looked very pretty on her black dress, and beautifully shaped the breasts of this robust young woman. Her full lips were fresh and pink with no lipstick on them, her black hair was braided into a simple knot, the skin on her hands was white, the nails a pale shiny pink and obviously manicured.

"What *zakouskas* shall I order?" he asked, smiling. "If you don't mind I'll just have some herring with hot potatoes."

"And what wine will you have?"

"Red. The ordinary red wine you usually serve with dinner."

She jotted it down on her pad, and brought him the water carafe from another table.

"No, *merci*, no," he shook his head. "I never drink water or wine with water. *L'eau gâte le vin comme la charrette le chemin et la femme–l'âme.*"*

"What a nice opinion you have of us," she responded indifferently and went off to fetch the vodka and the herring. He watched her cross the room, walking very primly, her skirt swinging just a little. Yes, she was polite and indifferent, her manner and all her movements were those of a good, self-respecting waitress, but she was wearing very expensive shoes. Where from? Most probably she had an elderly rich *ami*... He had not felt so animated for a long time, it was thanks to her, and this last thought annoyed him somewhat. Year after year, day after day, in one's heart of hearts one waited for just one thing–a happy love encounter, in fact one lived only in hope of such an encounter, and it never came one's way...

The next night he came again and sat at the same table. She was busy, taking an order from two Frenchmen, and repeated aloud what she wrote down:

"*Caviar rouge, salade russe, deux chachlyks...*"

She went out, and when she returned she came to his table, smiling slightly as to an acquaintance.

"Good evening. I'm glad you liked it here."

He rose to his feet, smiling.

"How d'you do. I liked it very much. May I know your name?"

"I'm Olga Alexandrovna, and you?"

"Nikolai Platonich."

They shook hands, then she picked up her writing pad.

"Tonight we have a wonderful kidney soup. We have a marvel of a chèf, he used to work on the yacht of the Grand Duke Alexander Mikhailovich."

"Fine. Kidney soup it shall be... Have you been working long?"

"Two months."

"And before that?"

*Water spoils the wine as a cart ruins the road, and a woman–the soul.

"I was a saleswoman at Printemps."

"Staff reduction, I suppose?"

"Oh yes, I wouldn't have left of my own free will."

He was glad that his suspicions of an *ami* were unfounded, and asked:

"Are you married?"

"Yes."

"And what does your husband do?"

"He's working in Yugoslavia. He was an officer in the White movement. You too, probably?"

"Oh yes. I fought both in the First World War and in our civil war."

"I knew it at once. And, I suppose, you're a general," she said, smiling.

"An ex-general. And now I write the histories of those wars for various foreign publishing houses. So, you're all by yourself, I mean..."

"Yes, all by myself."

On the third night he asked:

"Do you like motion pictures?"

"Some are interesting," she replied, setting a soup bowl before him.

"There's a picture showing at the Etoile that's said to be remarkably good. Would you care to see it with me? You do have some days off, of course, don't you?"

"*Merci.* I am free on Mondays."

"Well then, let's go on Monday. What's today? Saturday? That means the day after tomorrow. Agreed?"

"Agreed. I take it you're not coming here tomorrow."

"No, I'm going out of town to visit friends. Why do you ask?"

"I don't know... It's strange, but I have already grown sort of used to you."

He glanced at her gratefully and flushed.

"And I to you. D'you know there are so few happy encounters in life..." And hastened to change the conversation. "Till after tomorrow then. Where shall we meet? Where do you live?"

"Near the Motte-Picquet metro."

"You see how very convenient–it goes straight to the Etoile. I'll be waiting for you at the exit at eight-thirty sharp."

"*Merci.*"

He bowed extravagantly, and said:

"*C'est moi qui vous remercie*. Put the children to bed and come," he said with a smile, wanting to find out if she had a child.

"I've been spared that blessing, thank God," she said, and floated away with his dirty plates.

As he walked home that night he felt both touched and sad. "I have already grown sort of used to you..." This may well be that long-awaited happy encounter, only it was too late, too late. *Le bon Dieu envoie toujours des culottes à ceux qui n'ont pas de derrière...*

It was raining on Monday evening, and the murky sky over Paris was hazily red. Hoping to have supper with her in Montparnasse after the show, he forewent his dinner, only stopping for a ham sandwich and beer at a cafe in Chaussasée de la Muette and then lit a cigarette and got into a taxi. He told the driver to stop at the exit of the metro and, once there, stepped out into the rain, while the driver–a corpulent man with purple cheeks–remained waiting trustingly. The metro exhaled a bath-house smell, a thick crowd of people came up the steps, opening their umbrellas as they emerged, and a newspaper vendor, standing close to him, yelled out the names of the evening editions in a low, quacking voice. He started when she appeared in the crowd, and went to meet her with joy in his heart.

"Olga Alexandrovna..."

She was fashionably and smartly dressed, the look in her darkly made-up eyes was uninhibited now, unlike her look when she waited at his table. She gave him her right hand with a perfect lady's gesture, and with her left hand picked up her long evening gown. He rejoiced even more, thinking: since she put on an evening gown she, too, expects us to go somewhere after the cinema. And, turning back her glove, kissed her on the wrist.

"Poor thing, have you been waiting long?"

"No, I've only just arrived. Let's dive into the taxi quickly."

He followed her into the dusky interior of the cab smelling of damp cloth, more excited than he had felt for a long time. The cab rocked when turning a corner, a street-lamp illumined the interior for a moment, he instinctively put a protective arm round her, smelt the scent of powder on her cheek, saw her knees outlined by the black evening gown, the gleam in her dark eyes, and her full painted lips: this was quite another woman sitting beside him now.

In the darkened cinema, as they looked at the radiant whiteness of the screen on which some loudly buzzing airplanes flew at a slant and fell into the clouds, they talked in whispers.

"Do you live alone or share a flat?" he asked.

"Alone. Actually, it's awful. It's a clean and warm little hotel, but you know it's the kind where a man can bring a woman for a night or even for an hour... I'm on the sixth floor, there's no lift, of course, and the red carpet runner ends on the fourth floor. At night, especially when it rains, it's terribly lonely. You open your window and there's not a soul to be seen, the town seems quite dead, and somewhere far below a solitary street-lamp soaking in the rain. And you are a bachelor, of course, and also live at a hotel."

"No, I've a small flat in Passy. I, too, live alone. I'm an old Parisian, you know. For a time I lived in Provence, I rented a farm there. I wanted to get away from everyone and everything and live by the toil of my hands, only the toil proved more than I could bear. I hired a Cossack to help me, but he turned out to be a drunkard, a gloomy, frightening man when in his cups. I tried breeding chickens and rabbits, but they kept dying, and once a mule nearly killed me—a terrible, vicious and clever beast... But the worst thing was the utter loneliness. My wife left me in Constantinople years ago."

"You must be joking!"

"Not at all. A very banal story. *Qui se marie par amour a bonne nuits et mauvais jours.** And I had very little of either. She left me when we were married a little over a year."

"Where is she now?"

"No idea."

She did not speak for a long time. On the screen meanwhile, one of Charlie Chaplin's imitators was running about idiotically in absurdly large, down-at-heel shoes and

*He who marries for love has good nights and bad days.

a bowler set at a rakish angle.

"Yes, you must be feeling very lonely," she said.

"Very. Oh well, grin and bear it, I say. Patience–*médicine des pauvres.*"

"Such a sad medicine."

"It is, indeed. Sometimes I feel so lonely that I even read the notices in *Illustrirovannaya Rossia*, you know there's a section in that magazine where they publish things like: 'A Russian girl from Latvia is lonely and would like to correspond with an understanding Russian Parisian and receive his photo...' Or else: 'A serious-minded lady with brown hair, not the modern type but nice-looking, a widow with a ten-year old son, would like to start a correspondence, with serious intentions, with a gentleman not under forty years old, of sober habits, a steady job–as a chauffeur, for instance–and one who liked the cosiness of home. He need not be high-born.' I quite agree with her here."

"Don't you have any friends or acquaintances?"

"No, no friends. And acquaintances are a poor comfort."

"But then who keeps house for you?"

"I've not much of a house to keep. I make my coffee myself and cook my breakfast too. A *femme de menage* comes in the late afternoon."

"Oh, you poor thing," she said and pressed his hand.

They sat thus, holding hands, united by the semi-darkness and the closeness of their seats, both pretending to be watching the screen at which a chalky-blue beam of light was directed over their heads from the projecting room at the back of the hall. Charlie Chaplin's imitator, whose smashed-in bowler had jumped off his head from fright, was driving a wreck of an antedeluvian car with a smoke-belching chimney at breakneck speed and going straight into a telegraph pole. The loudspeaker wailed musically in every manner of voice, from the stalls below veiled with cigarette smoke–they were sitting on the balcony–rose thunderous applause and shrieks of laughter. He leaned down to her and said:

"D'you know what? Let's go somewhere in Montparnasse or some place, this is terribly boring and it's so stuffy here."

She nodded and started pulling on her gloves.

In the darkness of a cab again, looking at the sparkling raindrops on the windows which flared up like precious stones from the light of the street-lamps and the neon advertisements, high up in the darkness, now blood-red, now shining like quicksilver, he again turned back her glove and lingeringly kissed her wrist. Her eyes, framed in thickly mascaraed eyelashes, sparkled strangely as she looked at him and with amorous wistfulness strained towards him, offering him her mouth that tasted sweetly of lip salve.

At the cafe Coupole they started with oysters and Anjou, then they had quail and red Bordeaux. Drinking their coffee with yellow Chartreuse, both felt slightly intoxicated. They smoked a lot, the ashtray was overflowing with her lipstick-stained cigarette stubs. As they talked, he looked at her flushed face and thought that she was quite a beauty.

"Now tell me the truth," she said, picking shreds of tobacco from the tip of her tongue with her fingers. "You must have had some affairs during all these years?"

"I have. But you can guess what sort. One-night stands in hotels... And what about you?"

"There was one very painful affair," she replied after a pause. "No, I don't want to talk about it. He was a mere boy, a gigolo actually... But how did you come to a parting of the ways with your wife?"

"Ignobly. There was a boy too, a Greek, a young Adonis, and extremely rich. And in a month or two no trace remained of that pure, touching girl who simply worshipped the White army and all of us. She started having supper with him in the most expensive nightclub in Pera, and he sent her enormous baskets of flowers. She said to me: 'Surely you can't be jealous? You're busy all day long, and I find him fun, he's just a sweet boy and nothing more.' A sweet boy! And she herself was only twenty. It wasn't easy to forget her, the girl she was before, in Ekaterinodar..."

When the waiter brought the check, she went through it carefully and forbade him to leave more than a ten per cent tip. After this it seemed very strange to part at once.

"Let's go to my place. We'll sit and talk a bit longer," he suggested wistfully.

"Yes, let's," she said, rising to her feet, taking his arm and pressing it to her side.

The driver, a Russian, brought them to a deserted side street and stopped in front of a tall house. In the metallic light of the gas street-lamp the rain could be seen falling onto the lid of a garbage bin. They entered the vestibule, then the small lift and slowly rode up, holding each other close and kissing tenderly. He succeeded in finding the keyhole with his latchkey before the light went out on the landing, and ushered her into the hall, and thence into the dining-room where only one lamp burnt bleakly in the chandelier. Their faces already looked tired. He offered her some wine.

"No, my dear, I can't drink any more," she said.

"Just one glass each, I've a bottle of excellent Pouilly."

"You have some, dear, and I'll go and undress and wash, and then sleep, sleep, sleep. We're not children, so I imagine you realized perfectly that since I consented to come to your place... And anyway why should we part at all?"

He was too overwhelmed to reply, and silently took her to his bedroom and switched on the light in the bathroom. The lamps were bright here, the heating was on, and the whole place was so nice and warm while the rain continued to drum rapidly on the roof. She immediately started pulling her long dress over her head.

He left her, drank a glass of the ice-cold bitter wine and then one more, and went back to the bedroom. The bathroom, with the door open, was brilliantly reflected in the large mirror on the bedroom wall opposite. She was standing with her back to him, completely naked, white-skinned and robust, bending over the wash-basin and soaping her neck and breasts.

"You mustn't come in," she said and, draping his bathrobe on her shoulders without bothering to cover up her full breasts, strong white stomach and solid white hips, came to him and embraced him as a wife would. He put his arms round her as if she really were his wife, embracing the whole of her cool body, kissing her wet breasts that smelled of toilet soap, her eyes, and her mouth from which she had already wiped off the lipstick...

Two days later she quit her job and moved in with him.

In the winter he persuaded her to take a strongbox in

her name at the Lyons Credit Bank and deposit in it all the money he had earned.

"Just to be on the safe side," he said. "*L'amour fait danser les ânes*,* and I feel twenty years old! But anything might happen..."

On Tuesday, in Holy Week, he died in the metro. He had been reading the newspaper, then suddenly he threw back his head and died...

It was a fair spring day when, in deep mourning, she was returning from the cemetery. Vernal clouds were floating here and there in the smiling blue sky over Paris, and everything spoke of young, everlasting life—and of her own finished life.

As soon as she got back home, she started tidying up the flat. In the hall closet she found his old army greatcoat, grey with a red lining. She took it down from the hanger, pressed it to her face, and pressing it ever closer sank on the floor, jerking and shuddering from her sobs, begging someone for mercy.

26 October, 1940

Galia Ganskaya

An artist and a former seaman were sitting on the terrace of a cafe in Paris. It was April, and everything delighted the artist: Paris, so beautiful in spring, and the Parisiennes, so charming in their new spring finery.

"But in my young days, Paris in spring was even more beautiful, of course," he said. "And not just because I was young—Paris itself was quite different. To think that there was not a single automobile! And then, did Paris live like it does now?"

"And I have remembered the spring in Odessa I don't know why," said the seaman. "You, being an Odessite, know its absolutely unique loveliness even better than I—that mixture of an already hot sun, the still wintry fresh-

*Love makes even the donkeys dance.

ness of the sea, the bright sky and the vernal clouds over the sea. And in Deribassovskaya, the women's springtime dressiness..."

Drawing on his pipe to get it going, the artist called: "*Garçon, un demi!*" and quickly turned back to the seaman.

"Sorry, I interrupted. Just imagine, when I spoke about Paris I, too, was thinking about Odessa. You are quite right—spring in Odessa is really quite unique. Only, I always recall the Paris and Odessa springs sort of inseparably, they alternated for me because you know how often I went to Paris in spring in those days. D'you remember Galia Ganskaya? You once saw her somewhere and told me you had never seen a sweeter girl. You don't remember? Well, never mind. Just now, speaking of Paris in those days I was, in fact, thinking of her and that spring in Odessa when she came to my studio for the first time. I expect every one of us has some especially precious love memory or perhaps an especially grave love sin. Well then, Galia, I believe, is my most precious memory and my gravest sin, but I swear it was unintentional, as God is my witness. This happened such eons ago that I can tell you about it without holding anything back.

"I knew her when she was a young schoolgirl. She was brought up by her father whom Galia's mother left when she was quite little. The father was a very wealthy man, a failure of an artist, an amateur but one so obsessed that nothing in the world interested him except painting, and all he did all his life was stand at the easel and clutter his house—he had an estate in Otrada—with old and new paintings, buying up everything that caught his fancy wherever possible. He was a very handsome man, tall and portly, with a wonderful bronze beard. He was half-Polish and half-Ukrainian; he had a lordly manner, he was proud, exquisitely polite, and very reserved by nature, though he played the part of a very open person, especially with us. At one time, for two years running, the whole crowd of us, young Odessa painters, came to Otrada every Sunday, and he always welcomed us with open arms, treated us quite as if we were his comrades, despite the difference in our years, talked tirelessly about painting and feasted us lavishly. Galia was thirteen or fourteen at the time and we admired her only as a pretty child, of course. She was sweet, gay, amazingly graceful, with the face of an angel framed in long, fair curls, but she was such a flirt that once, when she came running into the studio, whispered something in her father's ear and flew out again, he said to us: 'Oh dear, oh dear, what a minx I'm raising! I'm afraid for her, you know.'

"And then abruptly, with the rudeness of youth, we all stopped going there, every single one of us as if by mutual consent: we were sick and tired of something there in Otrada, probably his never-ending talk about art and his telling us that at long last he had discovered yet another wonderful secret of how one should paint. I had just spent two springs in Paris and fancied myself another Maupassant in matters of love, and when I came to Odessa I went about as the most vulgar of dandies in a knee-length pea green overcoat, top hat, cream gloves, patent leather boots with buttoned up felt tops, and carried a beauty of a walking stick. Add to this a wavy moustache *à la* Maupassant, and an attitude to women that was so irresponsible as to be utterly foul. And so, one fine day in April I was strolling down Deribassovskaya, I crossed Preobrazhenskaya and on the corner, near Liebman's coffee shop, I suddenly saw Galia. Remember the five-storey house where that coffee shop was? On the corner of Preobrazhenskaya Street and Cathedral Square, a building famous for the chirping starlings always perched close together along the cornices on sunny spring days. It was awfully nice and jolly. And so picture this for yourself: springtime, crowds of well-dressed, laughing and carefree people everywhere, those starlings whose incessant chirping sounded as if a sunny rain was sifting from the sky, and Galia. No longer a child, no longer an angel, but an amazingly pretty, slim girl dressed in an obviously very new, pale-grey spring suit. Her face was half-covered by the ash-grey nose veil coming down from the brim of her new grey hat, and her eyes shone through the veil like aquamarines. Well, naturally, there followed exclamations, questions, reproaches: 'You've all forgotten Daddy, you haven't been to see him for ages!' 'Ah yes, such ages that you became grownup in the time!' I immediately bought her a bunch of violets from a ragged little flower-girl, and with a swift grateful smile Galia thrust her face into the flowers, as all women always do. Shall we sit down somewhere, shall we have some hot chocolate? With pleasure. Lifting her nose veil she drank her chocolate, glanced at me gaily, plied me with questions about Paris, while I looked and looked at her. 'Daddy works from morning to night, and you, have you been working hard, or are you too enamoured with *les belles Parisiennes*?' 'No, no more, I do work and have done some decent things. Would you care to come to my studio and see? You may, being an artist's daughter, and besides it's only a step from here.' She was delighted. 'Of course I may! And then I've never been in an artist's studio, only Daddy's.' She pulled down her nose veil, picked up her umbrella, I took her arm and she immediately fell in step with me and laughed. 'Galia,' I said, 'may I call you simply Galia?' '*You* may,' she replied quickly and seriously. 'Galia, what has happened to you?' 'What do you mean?' 'You were lovely before too, but now you're really amazingly lovely!' She caught up in step with me again and said either in fun or in earnest: 'You haven't seen the best of me yet!'

"Do you remember that dark, narrow staircase going up to my garret from the yard? Here she suddenly became shy, and as she mounted those steps with her silk underskirt swishing, she kept looking behind her warily. She entered my studio with something like awe, and began in a whisper: 'It's wonderful here, so mysterious, and what a terribly big couch! What a lot of pictures you've painted, and Paris in all of them...' She went from one painting to the other, looking at them with quiet admiration, trying to be even too unhurried and scrupulous. When she had looked her fill she sighed and said: 'Yes, you have indeed painted a lot of beautiful pictures.' And I said: 'Would you care for a glass of port and some biscuits?' 'I don't know,' she said. I relieved her of her umbrella, tossed it on the couch, took her hand in the white kid glove and asked: 'May I kiss it?' 'But I've a glove on!' I unbuttoned the glove and kissed her palm. She pulled down her nose veil, glanced at me expressionlessly through it with her aquamarine eyes, and said quietly that it was time for her to go. 'No,' I said, 'let's sit and talk a little longer, I haven't looked at you properly yet.' I sat down on the couch and seated her in my lap—you know that delicious female heaviness, even in the slimmest women? She asked me somewhat enigmatically: 'Do you like me?' I looked her up and down, I looked at the violets which she had pinned to her new jacket, and laughed, feeling terribly touched. 'And do you like these violets?' I asked. 'I don't understand,' she said. 'What is there to understand? You yourself are like these violets.' Dropping her eyes, she laughed and said: 'At school we called it a scribe's style, comparing girls to different flowers.' 'Call it what you like, but how else could I put it?' 'I don't know,' she said. She sat dangling her pretty legs in her new dressy shoes, her childish lips were parted, her teeth glistened... I lifted her nose veil, tilted back her head a little, kissed her and she leaned a bit further back. I slid my hand up her slippery greenish silk stocking to her garter, undid the clasp on the elastic, kissed her warm, pink flesh above it, then her parted lips again, and she responded with gentle little bites..."

The seaman shook his head and said with a chuckle: "You old satyr."

"That's a silly thing to say, it hurts me terribly to remember," said the artist.

"Sorry. Carry on..."

"After that I did not see her for a whole year. One day, also in spring, I went at last to Otrada and Gansky welcomed me with such touching affection that I almost died of shame for having dropped him so callously. He looked much older, there was plenty of grey in his beard, but the animation with which he talked about painting was as keen as ever. Proudly he showed me his picture of enormous golden swans flying over some blue dunes—the poor old chap was trying hard not to fall behind the times. I praised the picture shamelessly: wonderful, wonderful, a great stride forward! He beamed like a child. 'I'm glad, so glad you like it, and now for some lunch,' he said. 'And where's your daughter?' I asked. 'She's gone to town. You wouldn't recognise her now, she's not the schoolgirl you knew, she's quite grownup and looks quite, quite different—tall and slender like a young poplar!'

"What rotten luck! I only went to Otrada because I terribly wanted to see her, and as ill luck would have it she'd gone to town. After lunch I took leave of my host, kissing his soft, perfumed beard and promising to come next Sunday for certain, and as I emerged from the house—there she was, coming back home. She seemed delighted, exclaiming: 'Is it really you? What brings you here? Have you been visiting Daddy? Oh, I'm so glad!' And I said: "I can't begin to tell you how glad *I* am! Your father told me I wouldn't recognise you, that you've grown like a young poplar, and you have indeed!' It was true, she was grown-up, and looked more like a young married woman than a girl. She was smiling and twirling her white lace parasol on her shoulder. White lace parasol, white lace dress, white lace picture hat, her hair a lovely reddish tint, the look in her eyes no longer naive, the face more oval now... 'Why, I'm even a little bit taller than you!' she said, and I only nodded, saying true, so true... 'Shall we walk down to the sea?' I suggested. 'Let's,' she said. We walked between gardens and I knew that she was aware that I was chattering at random and could not take my eyes off her. She moved her shoulders gracefully as she walked, she had folded her parasol and was holding up her lace skirt with her left hand. We came to the drop above the sea and breathed its freshness. The gardens were already donning their new leafage and basking in the sun, but the sea might have been an icy northern sea, rolling in tall green waves covered with white caps and merging with the bluish haze in the distance, that was the Pontus Euxinus, or the 'hospitable sea for you!' We stood gazing at the sea without speaking, as if waiting for something, and obviously she was thinking of the same thing as I—how a year ago she came to my studio and sat in my lap. I put my arm round her and crushed her hard to my body; she arched her back and struggled to break free, twisting her head and evading my lips seeking hers, but suddenly gave in and let me kiss her. And neither of us uttered a word, a sound. Then she pulled away from me abruptly and, straightening her hat, said in a simple and sober tone:

" 'Goodness, what a scoundrel you are, what a scoundrel!'

"She swung round and without a backward glance walked quickly away."

"Did you make love that time at the studio or didn't you?" asked the seaman.

"Not all the way. We kissed madly and all that, but then I took pity on her; her face burnt like fire, her hair was dishevelled, I could see that she no longer had control over herself, quite like a child she was terrified and desperately wanted to have that terrifying experience. I assumed an injured air: oh, alright then, never mind if you don't want to, it's alright, sort of thing. I kissed her hands gently and little by little she recovered her calm."

"But how come you didn't see her for a whole year after that?"

"I'm damned if I know. I was afraid that next time I wouldn't spare her."

"For a Maupassant you were a poor fish," said the seaman.

"Maybe. But let me tell you the whole story to the end. I did not see her for another six months or so. The summer was over, people started moving back to town although it was the very time to live in the country, for the Bessarabian autumn is truly divine with the calm monotony of hot days, the clean air, the beautiful smoothness of the blue sea, and the dry yellowness of the maize fields. I, too, moved back to town and one day, walking past Liebman's cafe again I met her coming from the opposite direction. She came straight up to me, as calm as you please, and exclaimed: 'Liebman's cafe again! What a fateful spot!' laughing and charmingly twisting her mouth. 'I'm awfully glad to see you,' I said. 'You're so happy, I wonder why?' And she said: 'I don't know. When I come back from the seaside I so love running about the town, it's heavenly! I'm sunburnt and taller still, right?'

"She had grown taller, but what impressed me most of all was her merriment and the freedom I sensed in her laughter, her talk, and her whole manner, as if she had just gotten married. And suddenly she asked:

" 'Have you any more port and biscuits?'

" 'I have.'

" 'I'd like to see your studio again. May I?'

" 'Good heavens, I should say so!'

" 'Well then, let's go. And let's go very, very quickly.'

"On the stairs I put my arms round her, she arched back as before and shook her head, but she did not really resist me. Kissing her face, I walked her to my studio.

"Once there, she whispered: 'Look, this is madness... I've gone out of my mind...'

"But she had already taken off her hat and tossed it on an armchair. Her reddish hair was upswept and held at the top of her head with a tortoise-shell comb, a curled fringe covered her forehead, her face was slightly and evenly sunburnt, and there was a senselessly elated look in her eyes. I started undressing her with mindless urgency and she hastily helped me. In a minute I got her white silk blouse off and, you know, I felt quite dizzy when I saw her pink body with sunburnt satiny shoulders, milky-white breasts uplifted by her stays, the pointed crimson nipples, and then, when letting her skirts drop on the floor she stepped out of them, I gaped at her slender legs in lacy flesh-coloured stockings and golden slippers, and her wide batiste bloomers with a slit, you know the kind women wore at the time. When I threw her brutally on the couch, her eyes darkened and dilated, her mouth opened feverishly—I can see it all now, she was inordinately passionate... But that is now beside the point. This is what happened two weeks later, during which time she came to my studio practically every day. She came rushing in one morning and asked before she had even crossed the threshold:

" 'I hear you're going to Italy? Is it true?'

" 'Yes, why?'

" 'But why didn't you say a word to me about it? Did you want to go away on the quiet from me?'

" 'Bless you, darling. I meant to go to your house today and tell you.'

" 'In Daddy's presence? Why not to me alone? You are not going anywhere!'

" I blew up like a fool.

" 'I *am* going.'

" 'No, you're not!'

" 'And I'm telling you that I shall go.'

" 'Is that your last word?'

" 'It is. But do try to understand that I'll be back in a month or at the most six weeks. And really, Galia, listen....'

" 'I'm no Galia to you! I understand everything, everything! And even if you swore to me now that you'd never go anywhere ever in your life, I wouldn't care any more. It no longer matters!'

"She flung open the door, shot out, slammed it shut, and flew down the stairs.

"I wanted to run after her but I controlled the impulse, thinking: let her come to her senses, I'll go to Otrada in the evening and tell her that because I did not wish to distress her I had decided not to go to Italy, and we would kiss and make up. But at about five in the afternoon, Sinani who was an artist friend of mine came in with a wild-eyed look on his face.

" 'You know, Gansky's daughter has poisoned herself. She's dead! She took some rare poison, the devil knows what, but something that acts instantly, she pinched it from her father, you remember that old ass showing us his collection of poisons, fancying himself another Leonardo. What a crazy lot they are, those damned Poles, both male and female. And what had suddenly made her do it—it's incredible!' "

"I wanted to shoot myself then," the artist said quietly after a pause, and stuffing his pipe added: "I nearly went insane..."

28 October, 1940

Heinrich

On a wondrous, frosty evening with lilac rime in the gardens, Glebov was whizzed along in his tall, narrow sleigh down Tverskaya to Loskutnaya Hotel, having stopped on the way at Eliseyev's for fruit and wine. It was still light in Moscow, the clear, transparent sky had turned a pale green in the west, the arches of bell-towers were silhouetted exquisitely against it, but down below, in the bluish frosty haze, it was already growing dark, the street-lamps had just been lit and glowed motionlessly and softly in the dusk.

At the hotel entrance, Glebov flung back the wolfskin rug, and ordered Kasatkin, his coachman who was thickly sprinkled with snow dust, to come for him in one hour.

"You'll take me to the Brest railway station."

"Yes, sir," replied Kasatkin. "Means you're going abroad then."

"Yes, abroad."

As Kasatkin sharply turned round his tall old ambler, scraping the snow with the runners, he shook his head with disapproval and grumbled:

"It's not as if he *had* to go gallivanting all over the world..."

Glebov entered the large vestibule, which badly needed smartening up, got into the spacious lift where Vassya, the uniformed lift-boy with speckled eyes and pale freckles, stood at the door politely, and as the lift rode up slowly, he suddenly felt sorry to leave this long familiar, habitual world. "And really what am I going for?" he asked himself, and glanced into the mirror; what he saw was a young, hale man, with a leanness that spoke of breeding, with lustrous eyes, rime on his handsome moustache, and good clothes—smart and light. It was heavenly in Nice now, Heinrich was a marvellous pal, and, most important of all, Glebov always imagined that somewhere far away something especially happy was in store for him, meeting *the* woman, perhaps ... he'd put up somewhere on his way and wonder who had been staying there before him, what had been hanging in the wardrobe, what was the woman like who had left her hairpins on the bedside table? Again there would be the smell of gas, coffee and beer at the Vienna station, the colourful labels on the bottles of the Austrian and Italian wines standing on the tables in the sunlit dining-car amid the snows of Semmering, the faces and clothes of the European men and women who filled this dining-car at lunch... And then night, and Italy... And in the morning, on the stretch along the seacoast to Nice, the train would roar through the smoking, reverberating darkness of the tunnels, the lamps would burn dimly on the ceiling of his compartment, there would be stops, and something ringing sweetly and continuously at the small stations, surrounded by flowering roses, beside the small bay, dreaming in the hot sun and shot with the sparkle of precious stones...

He walked quickly along the warm, carpeted corridors. His room was also pleasantly warm. From the transparent concave sky the sunset glow still shone into the window. The room had been tidied up and his suitcases packed. Again he felt a twinge of sadness, he was sorry to leave this familiar room, the whole of wintertime life in Moscow, he was sorry to leave Nadya and Lee.

Any minute now Nadya would come to say goodbye. He barely had time to put the wine and fruit in one of his suitcases, throw his hat and coat on the sofa behind the round table, when he heard her knocking urgently on his door. When he opened the door she came straight into his arms, sweetly fragrant and cold to the touch in her squirrel coat and small squirrel hat, in all the freshness of her sixteen summers, her pretty face rosy from the frost and her green eyes shining brightly.

"You're going?"

"I am, darling."

She sighed and flopped into an armchair, unbuttoning her coat.

"You know, I was ill in the night, luckily. Oh, how I'd love to see you off! Why won't you let me come with you to the station?"

"Nadya darling, you know very well that it's impossible. I'll be seen off by people you don't know at all, you'd feel out of it, all alone..."

"What wouldn't I give to go with you, I'd give my very life, I think!"

"And I? But you know it can't be, don't you..."

He squeezed himself into the armchair with her and as he kissed her warm neck he felt her tears falling on his cheek.

"Nadya darling, you're crying!"

She lifted her face and made an effort to smile.

"I won't, I won't... I don't want to tie you to my apron strings, you're a poet, you need your freedom."

"You're my clever girl," he said, touched by her seriousness and her childish profile—the purity, the sweetness of her hotly flushed cheek, the triangular shape of her parted lips, the innocence of her questioning look, and the tear sparkling on her eyelashes. "You're not like other women, you're a poetess yourself."

"Don't you dare speak to me about other women," she cried.

Caressing him with her fur and her breath, she whispered in his ear with a dying look in her eyes: "For just one minute... There is still time..."

The drive into the Brest railway station was aglow with lights in the blue darkness of the frosty night. As he entered in the wake of the porter quickly carrying his bags, he saw her at once: tall and slender in her oily-black, straight karakul coat and a large velvet beret, her black hair hanging in long curls down her cheeks, and holding her hands in a large karakul muff, she looked at him angrily with her black eyes, frightening in their magnificence.

"So you're going, you beast you," she said as if she did not care, taking his arm and hurrying after the porter together with him, stepping lightly in her tall grey felt overshoes. "You'll be sorry yet, you won't deserve another like me and will be left with your silly fool of a poetess."

"That silly fool is only a child, Lee, you ought to be ashamed of yourself thinking heaven knows what."

"Rubbish. I'm not a silly fool at all. And if this heaven knows what is really going on between you I'll throw vitriol in your face."

Hot, grey, hissing steam smelling of rubber poured from under the waiting train, illumined from above by opaque electric lamps. The yellowish panelling in the sleeper distinguished it from the rest. Inside the coach, in the narrow red-carpeted corridor with ground-glass doors and the resplendent sheen of stamped leather on the walls, it was already "abroad". The attendant, a Pole in a brown uniform jacket, opened the door into a small, hot compartment with the bed already made up and softly lit by a table lamp with a red silk shade.

"Lucky dog," said Lee. "You've even got a privy to yourself. And who's next door? Some companionable bitch, is it?" She tugged at the handle of the connecting door. "No, the door's locked. Well, thank your lucky stars. Kiss me quickly, the third bell is about to go."

She took an exquisitely thin, bluishly pale hand with long, sharp nails out of her muff, impetuously pulled his face close and kissed and bit him on the lips, on the cheeks, flashing her eyes extravagantly and writhing against him as she whispered:

"I adore you, adore you, you beast!"

Outside the black window panes large orange sparks flew back in a fiery witch's dance, the train's lights showed up the white snowclad embankments and the black thickets of the pine forest beyond, secretively glum in its immobility, living its mysterious nocturnal winter life. He shut off the heating under the small table, pulled down the blind over the cold window, and knocked on the connecting door next to the wash-stand. The door opened and in came Heinrich with a happy laugh. She was a very tall woman in a grey dress, her lemon-coloured hair dressed in the Grecian style, her features as delicate as an Englishwoman's, and her amber-brown eyes sparkling.

"Well, done your goodbye kissing? I heard everything. What I liked best was her trying to break into my compartment and calling me a bitch."

"Surely you're not starting to feel jealous, Heinrich?"

"Not starting, continuing. Had she not been so dangerous I'd have demanded her dismissal long ago."

"That's the whole point, she *is* dangerous, try dismissing someone like her without notice! But, after all, I do endure your Austrian, don't I, even knowing that you're going to sleep with him the day after tomorrow."

"I'm not going to sleep with him. You know perfectly well that I'm making this trip mainly to put an end to our affair."

"You might have done it in a letter, and you might have come openly with me too."

She sighed and sat down, swinging a foot in a grey suede shoe with a silver buckle as she carefully patted her hair in place.

"No, *mon ami*, I want to part with him nicely, so I'll be able to go on working for him. He is a man of business, so he'll consent to part peacefully. Where will he find another correspondent who will supply his magazine with all those titbits of scandal in the world of art in Moscow and Petersburg—theatres, literature, and everything else? Who is going to translate his short stories and get these masterpieces published? Today's the fifteenth. This means you'll be in Nice on the 18th, and I not later than the 20th or 21st. And let's not talk about it any more, after all you and I are good friends in the first place, we're pals."

"Yes, pals," he said, gazing happily at her delicate, faintly glowing face. "You know, Heinrich, I'll never have a better pal than you. You're the only person I always feel free and easy with, I can really talk with you as with a friend about anything under the sun, but you know what the trouble is? I'm falling more and more in love with you."

"And where were you yesterday evening?"

"Yesterday evening? At home."

"But who with? Oh well, never mind. And last night you were seen at the Strelnya, you were with a large party in a private room, with Gypsies. Now that is really in bad taste—all those Styopas, Grushas, and their black eyes..."

"And what of your Vienna drunks like Przybyszewski?"

"All incidental, *mon ami*, and not my cup of tea at all. And that Gypsy, that Masha, is she really as beautiful as people say?"

"Gypsies are not my cup of tea either. But Masha..."

"Come on, describe her."

"You are definitely becoming jealous, Elena Heinrichovna. What's there to describe, haven't you ever seen Gypsies? She's a bag of bones and not even pretty—flat, tarry hair, a rather coarse coffee-coloured face, a vapid look in the eyes with bluish whites, equine collar-bones adorned with a heavy yellow necklace, a flat stomach ... well, that goes very well with her long silk dress the colour of golden onion skin. And d'you know, when she picks up her shawl, made of some heavy old silk, and starts dancing to the tambourine, her little shoes flickering under the hem of her skirt and her long silver earrings swinging, you're done for! However, let's go and have dinner, shall we?"

She stood up, smiling faintly.

"Very well. You're incorrigible, *mon ami*. But let's count our blessings, shall we? Look what a nice place we have! Two lovely little rooms!"

"One too many."

She draped a fine hand-knitted woollen shawl over her head and shoulders, he put on his travelling cap, and they walked, swaying on their feet, through the countless cars, stepping over the jangling metal gangways in the cold, draughty and snow-sifting connecting passages that made one think of huge folding bellows.

Afterwards, he took her back to their compartment and returned to the dining-car alone, and sat there smoking. When he came back, he felt quite like a happily married man who was going to bed with his wife in the warm compartment: she had turned back a corner of the sheet and blanket, laid out his pyjamas, set out a bottle of wine on the small table and some pears in a woven basket, and was standing before the mirror over the wash-stand taking out her hairpins, her raised arms bare to the elbow, her full breasts thrust out, and already wearing only her nightgown and slippers, trimmed with blue fox. Her waist was slender, her hips were full, and her ankles beautifully chiselled. He kissed her for a long time, standing there with her, then they sat down on the bed and drank Rhine wine, kissing with lips, cool from the wine.

"And what about Lee?" she asked. "And Masha?"

Lying beside her in the darkness, he was saying with mock sadness:

"Ah, Heinrich, how I love these train nights, this darkness in the waggling coach, the lights of the stations flashing past, the curtained window, and you, you women, snares of temptation! There is truly something ineffable, divine and demonic in that concept of 'snares', but when I write about it and attempt to put it in words I am rebuked for shamelessness and base motives. Filthy-minded wretches! It was very well put in one ancient book: 'A writer has as much right to be bold in his verbal descriptions of love and forms of love as has been granted at all times to painters and sculptors.' Only the filthy-minded see something filthy even in the beautiful and in the terrible."

"And Lee, I imagine, has small pointed breasts, and wide apart too?" asked Heinrich. "A sure sign that she's hysterical."

"Yes."

"Is she stupid?"

"No... Or rather, I don't know. Sometimes she seems very intelligent, sensible, simple, easy and gay, grasping everything at a word, but sometimes she talks such highfalutin, vulgar, or vicious impassioned nonsense that it's an effort to listen to her, and I feel like an obtuse idiot, like a deaf-mute. But I'm sick of your talk about her..."

"You're sick of me because I don't want to be just your pal any more."

"Neither do I. I'm telling you once again: write to that Austrian blighter of yours and tell him you'll see him on your way back, that you're unwell and have to convalesce from your influenza in Nice. And then you and I will go not to Nice at all, but someplace in Italy."

"But why not to Nice?"

"I don't know. I don't want to go there, I don't know why. The main thing, let's go together."

"We've already discussed it, dear. And why Italy? You told me, didn't you, that you've grown to hate Italy?"

"Yes, I did. I'm angry with Italy because of our doltish aesthetes. 'In Florence I like only the trecento...' says one such aesthete who was born and bred in Belyovo, in the whole of his life spent less than a week in Florence. Trecento, quatrocento... I've come to hate all those Fra Angelico, Ghirlandajo, trecento, quatrocento, and even Beatrice and the dry-faced Dante in a woman's cap and a laurel wreath... Oh well, if not Italy, then let's go some place in Tirole, in Switzerland, in the mountains anyway, to a small stone village amid those granite devils piebald from snow sticking up into the sky... Just picture it: biting, damp air, those primeval stone cottages with steep roofs all clustered together beside a humped stone bridge, picture the swift noisy, milky-green little river under it, the jingling of sheep-bells from a flock that trots pressed close together, and right there there's a chemist's, a shop selling alpenstocks, a terribly warm little hotel with spreading antlers that might have been carved from pumice stone, mounted over the door... In short, the floor of a ravine where for a thousand years this mountain wilderness, alien to the whole world, has been living, multiplying, marrying, dying, watched since the beginning of time from above, from behind the granite rocks, by some eternally snowclad mountain, like a gigantic dead angel... And the wenches there! Oh Heinrich! Buxom, apple-cheeked wenches in black corsages and red wool stockings..."

"Oh you, poets!" she said with a gentle yawn. "It's

always wenches, wenches, and wenches with you... No, my dear, it's cold in that stone cottage. And I've had my fill of wenches..."

In Warsaw that evening, when they were driving to the Vienna train, a wet wind with rare, large, cold drops of rain blew into their faces, worrying the long whiskers of the wrinkled coachman who sat on the box of the wide carriage and angrily whipped on his pair of horses tossing his head as the raindrops trickled down the vizor of his leather cap. The streets had a provincial look.

At dawn that morning, he raised the blind and saw a plain that had a pallid look from the thin covering of snow and was dotted here and there with small red brick houses. The train stopped and was held up for quite a long time at a big station where, after Russia, everything seemed very small—the cars on the sidings, the narrow gauge railway, the metal lamp posts, and the black heaps of coal everywhere. A small soldier, wearing a tall cap with a truncated crown, a short mousey-blue coat and carrying a rifle, walked across the rails from the roundhouse; a lanky, bewhiskered man in a plaid jacket with a rabbit fur collar and a green Tyrolean hat with a pretty feather at the back, was walking up and down the wooden pavement under the windows. Heinrich awoke and asked him in a whisper to pull down the blind. He did as she asked, and crawled back under the blanket into her warmth. She laid her head on his shoulder and burst out crying.

"Why, Heinrich, what's wrong?"

"I don't know, dear," she replied softly. "I often cry at dawn. I wake up and suddenly I feel so sorry for myself... In a few hours you'll be gone, I'll be left alone, and I'll go to the cafe to wait for my Austrian... And in the evening there'll be a cafe again and a Hungarian band with heart-rending violins..."

"Yes, yes, and ear-splitting cymbals too... Well, haven't I been telling you to send your Austrian to hell and come with me?"

"No, dear, I can't. If I quarrel with him, what will I

live on? But I promise you I won't go to bed with him. You know, last time when I was leaving Vienna we had it all out with him in the street at night, under a gas street-lamp, and you cannot imagine what hatred there was in his face! From the gaslight his face looked pale green, olive green, pistacchio green... But the main thing is how could I now, after you, after this compartment which has brought us so very close?"

"D'you mean it?"

She held him tight and kissed him so hard that his breath caught.

"Heinrich, I don't recognise you!"

"I don't recognise myself. But come, come to me..."

"Wait, listen..."

"No, now, at once."

"Just one word. Tell me exactly when you will be leaving Vienna?"

"This very night, this very night!"

The train was already moving, they heard the soft footfall and the jingling spurs of the frontier guards walking past their door.

And there was Vienna, a smell of gas, coffee and beer, and Heinrich, smartly dressed and smiling sadly, got into an open landau with a red-nozed coachman in a cape and lacquer top hat. He removed the horsecloth from the nervous, delicate European nag with the tail cut short, which started twitching its long, aristocratic and wobbly legs as he urged it on and cracked his long whip, and then began running lopsidedly after a yellow tramcar... Then there was Semmering with all that foreign festiveness of a midday in the mountains; the left-side window in the dining car was hot, there was a bunch of flowers, bottles of Apollinaris and a bottle of red Veslau on the dazzlingly white table under the window, there was the dazzlingly white midday sparkle of the snowclad peaks, rising in their solemnly festive vestments into the heavenly indigo of the sky at an arm's reach from the train which went twisting and turning along the ledge above the narrow abyss where the early-morning wintry shadows lay blue and cold. And then there was a frosty, primordially incorrupt, chaste evening, a lifeless crimson turning blue for the night, on some mountain pass, immersed with all its evergreen firs in the great abundance of fresh, plump snows. Then came a lengthy stop in a dark ravine close to the Italian border amid a Dante's inferno of black mountains, with a feverishly-red, smoky light at the entrance into the maw of the tunnel. And then it was all very different, unlike anything that went before: an old, peeling pink Italian station, short-legged soldiers strutting with the pride of fighting cocks and with the feathers of fighting cocks on their helmets, and in place of a railway-station bar—a solitary urchin lazily pushing a trolley past the train with nothing but oranges and flasks on it. And after that the train went faster and faster down, down, and the warmer and gentler blew the breeze from the Lombardian plain in the distance, scattered with the welcoming lights of darling Italy. And late in the afternoon of the next, really summer day, there was the railway station at Nice with the seasonal crowds on the platforms.

In the blue twilight the countless shore lights stretched in a chain of diamonds all the way to cap d'Antibes, hovering like an ashen ghost in the west, and he stood without an overcoat on the balcony of his hotel room, thinking that in Moscow it was now twenty degrees below zero, and waiting for a knock on his door and a telegram from Heinrich. During dinner in the restaurant of the hotel, in the splendour of sparkling chandeliers and the crowdedness created by gentlemen in tails and ladies in evening gowns, he waited, expecting one of the bell-boys, wearing a short blue uniform jacket and white knitted gloves, to bring him a telegram on a salver; absently he spooned up his clear soup, drank red Bordeaux, and waited; in the lounge after dinner he drank coffee, smoked, and waited, growing more and more nervous, and wondering at himself: what's the matter with me? I haven't felt anything like this since my greenhorn days. Still no telegram came. The lifts went up and down, glittering and flickering, the bell-boys scurried about with cigarettes, cigars and the evening papers, the string band started up, and still there was no telegram although it was already past ten and she was to arrive on the Vienna train at midnight. He drank five glasses of cognac with his coffee, and feeling sick and tired of waiting rode up in the lift to his room, glaring at the uniformed lift-boy and thinking spitefully: "What a bad lot this sly, obliging and already thoroughly corrupt brat will grow up to be! And whose idea was it anyway to dress up these kids in all those silly caps and jackets, sky blue or brown, with all those shoulder-pieces, buttons, bindings and what not..."

No telegram came the next morning either. He rang, and a servant in a frock coat—a beautiful Italian youth with the eyes of a gazelle—brought him his coffee. "*Pas de lettres, monsieur, pas de télégrammes*." Glebov went and stood in his pyjamas in his open balcony door, squinting in the sun and, dazzled by the spiky golden glitter of the dancing sea, looked down at the crowds strolling on the promenade and listened to someone singing below his balcony, Italian lovesick singing, and finally said to himself, savouring his disgust:

"To hell with her then. It's all too clear now."

He went to Monte Carlo, played for a long time, lost two hundred francs, went back in a horse-driven cab to kill time—a whole three hours of clomp-clomp-clomp, a crack of the whip in the air...

The doorman told him with a happy grin:

"*Pas de télégrammes, monsieur.*"

He dressed for dinner, going through the motions dully and thinking:

"If suddenly there was a knock on my door and she came in, hastily and excitedly explaining why she had not telegraphed, why she had not come the night before, I believe I'd die of happiness! I'd tell her that I never loved anyone in all my life as I love her, that God would forgive me a lot of sins for a love like mine, He would even forgive me Nadya—take all of me, all of me, Heinrich! Yes, but at this very moment she is having dinner with her Austrian. God, how I'd love to give her the most brutal slap on her face and bash in his head with the bottle of champagne they are drinking together just now!"

After dinner, he strolled in the thick crowd up and down the streets in the warm air and the cloying stench of cheap Italian cigars, he went out to the quay, to the tarry blackness of the sea, gazed at the precious necklace of lights round the black curve of the bay, sadly vanishing in the distance to the right of him, he dropped into bars and drank now cognac, now gin, now whiskey. On returning to the hotel–his silk hat foppishly tilted, his face chalk-white, as white as his white tie and white waistcoat–he approached the doorman with a casually important air and mumbled through numbing lips:

"Pas de télégrammes?"

And the doorman, pretending not to notice anything wrong with him, replied with happy readiness:

"Pas de télégrammes, monsieur."

He was so drunk that he fell asleep at once, only taking off his silk hat, overcoat and tailcoat. He flopped down on his face and instantly dropped into a bottomless dark abyss, spangled with fiery stars.

On the third day, he fell fast asleep after lunch and, on awakening, suddenly saw his shabby, shameful behaviour in a harsh, sober light. He ordered tea brought to his room, and started packing his things, trying not to think about her or his senseless, ruined trip. Later in the afternoon he went down to the lounge, asked the clerk to prepare his bill, calmly went to Cook's and bought a ticket to Moscow via Venice on that night's train. He was thinking: "I'll stay in Venice for a day, at three the next morning I'll go straight home without stopping anywhere, home to my room at Loskutnaya Hotel... I wonder what he looks like, that Austrian?" From photos of him and Heinrich's description he is tall and wiry, with a glum and resolute look–affected, no doubt–on his slightly lowered face under his wide-brimmed hat... But why think about him? There is so much that life still holds in store for me! Venice tomorrow. Again the street singers would be strumming their guitars and singing on the promenade under his windows. Louder than the others would sound the harsh, impassive voice of a woman with loose black hair and a shawl on her shoulders, seconding a shrilling tenor that belonged to that short-legged man in rags and a pauper's hat who looked like a dwarf from above ... and there was the little old man who sometimes helped people into the gondolas. The year before he had helped Glebov in with a Sicilian woman who had swinging crystal earrings, fire in her eyes, and a cluster of yellow mimosa in her hair the colour of black olives... There would be the smell of the rancid canal water; the gondola varnished inside like a coffin having a jagged, rapacious pole-axe on the prow. The young gondolier with a red sash wound round his slender waist would be standing on the high, swaying stern, monotonously bending forward as he wielded the long oar, his left foot behind him in the classical pose...

Day was waning, the pale sea was calm and flat like some greenish alloy with an opaline sheen, the seagulls screamed angrily and pitifully above it, sensing bad weather on the morrow, the smokily blue western sky behind Cap d'Antibes was hazy and in it hung the dimming disc of a small sun, like an orange. He gazed at it for a long time, utterly crushed by his steady, hopeless anguish, and then, pulling himself together, walked briskly back to his hotel. *"Journeaux étrangers!"* shouted a newspaper boy, coming at a run from the opposite direction and sold him the latest *Novoye vremya* as he ran on.

He sat down on a bench, spread out the paper and in the dying light of the sun ran his eye down the still damp pages. And suddenly he sprang up, deafened and blinded, as if by an exploding magnesium flash. He read:

"Vienna. 17 December. In the Franzensring Restaurant today, Artur Spiegler, a well-known Austrian writer, shot a Russian woman journalist and translator of many modern Austrian and German authors, who used the pen-name 'Heinrich'."

10 November, 1940

Natalie

1

That summer I first put on a student's cap and was happy with that special excitement of starting upon a free young life which one can experience only at that age. I was brought up in a strict family on our country estate, and as a schoolboy, while passionately dreaming of love, I was still clean in body and soul, I blushed when the other boys talked smut, and they sneered at me: "You'd better go to a monastery, Meschersky!" But that summer I would no longer have blushed. When I came home for the summer holidays I decided that the time had come for me to be like everyone else, to shed my chastity and seek love without any romantic nonsense, and, prompted by this decision and a desire to show off my student cap, went visiting our friends and relations on the nearby estates in quest of amorous adventure. This brought me to the estate of my maternal uncle, a retired and recently widowed Uhlan, the father of Sonia, an only daughter and consequently my cousin.

I arrived late in the evening and there was only Sonia to meet me in the house. When I had leapt down from the tarantas and rushed into the dark entrance hall, she came in with a candle held high in her left hand and wearing a flannel dressing gown. She gave me her cheek to kiss and said in her usual mocking tone:

"Ah, here's the young gentleman who's always late!"

"Well this time it definitely wasn't my fault," I replied. "The train was late, not the young gentleman."

"Quiet, everyone's asleep. They waited for you all evening, quite dying of impatience, and then they gave you up. Daddy went to bed in a temper, cursing you for a featherbrain, and Yefrem who has obviously stayed behind at the station to meet the morning train—for an old fool. Natalie also went off in a huff, the servants drifted away too, and only I proved to be patient and true to you... Come on, take off your coat and let's go and have supper."

I replied, admiring her blue eyes and her raised arm, bared to the shoulder:

"Thank you, dear heart. To know that you're true to me is particularly pleasant now—you've become a perfect beauty, and I have the most serious intentions in regard to you. What a lovely arm and neck, and how tantalizing this soft dressing gown with nothing on underneath, I expect."

She burst out laughing.

"Almost nothing. But you, too, have become not bad-looking at all and very manly. A keen glance and a vulgar little black moustache... Only what's this new thing about you? In the two years that I haven't seen you, you changed from a shy and forever blushing child into a very attractive malapert. This would have promised us many amorous delights, as our grandmothers put it, if not for the presence of Natalie with whom you're going to fall head over heels in love no later than tomorrow morning."

"But who is this Natalie?" I asked, following Sonia into the dining-room where a lamp suspended from the ceiling was burning brightly and the windows were open into the blackness of the warm and silent summer night.

"Natalie Stankevich, my school friend who's come for a stay with me. Now that is really a beauty, no comparison with me. Just picture: hair of pure gold, as it is called, and black eyes. No, not eyes, black suns, as a Persian poet would say. Enormous eyelashes, of course, also black, and the skin on her face, shoulders and everything else with a wonderful golden tint."

"What do you mean—everything else?" I asked, delighting more and more in the flippant tone of our conversation.

"Natalie and I are going bathing tomorrow morning, and if you hide in the bushes you'll see what everything else. She has the figure of a young nymph too..."

Set out on the dining-room table was a plate of cold meat, a chunk of cheese and a bottle of red Crimean wine.

"I'm sorry, there's nothing else," she said, sitting down and pouring out the wine for herself and me. "No vodka either. Well, let's toast each other, if only in wine. Here's wishing!"

"What exactly do you wish?"

"To quickly find someone to marry who'll be willing to become a member of *our* family. I'm already twenty, you know, and I can't possible marry anyone who'll take me away from home, because who'll remain with Daddy then?"

"Well, to your wish!"

We touched glasses, she drained hers slowly and again looked at me with a strange little smile, watching me eat.

"No, you're not bad," she said as if speaking her thoughts aloud. "You look like a Georgian and are rather handsome. You were skinny before and had a greenish pallor. You've changed altogether, you're easier and nicer now. Only your eyes are shifty."

"That's because you unnerve me so with your charms. You're not quite what you were like before, you know, either."

And I looked at her with a merry twinkle in my eyes. She was sitting on the other side of the table a bit sideways to me, one leg drawn up and her plump knees showing; the even sunburn on her arm gleamed in the lamplight, her mocking lilac-blue eyes shone, and there were reddish glints in her soft, thick chestnut hair plaited for the night into a heavy braid; her dressing gown had slipped open to reveal her round sunburnt neck and the top of her breasts which were becoming full and also sunburnt in a triangular patch; on her left cheek she had a little mole with a pretty twist of black hair.

"And how's your Daddy?"

Still watching me with the same mocking smile, she took out of her pocket a small silver cigarette case and a silver matchbox and lit a cigarette somewhat too expertly, I thought, and shifted the leg she was sitting on to a more comfortable position.

"Daddy is all right, thank God. His bearing is as erect as ever, no flabbiness, he walks about rapping his cratch, fluffs up his grey quiff, dyes his moustache and sideburns with something brownish in secret from us, and gallantly eyes the parlourmaid... Only his head shakes worse than before, it gives him a stubborn air, as if he never agrees with anything... D'you want a cigarette?"

I took a cigarette, although I did not really smoke yet, she refilled our glasses and, glancing into the darkness outside the open window, said:

"Yes, so far everything's well with us, the Lord be thanked. And the summer is splendid this year too—what a night, eh? Pity the nightingales have done their singing. And I am truly very glad you came. I sent the carriage for you at six o'clock, afraid that Yefrem, who's in his dotage, would come late for the train. I waited for you more anxiously than anyone else. And I was glad that everyone went to bed, that you were late and that if you did come we'd sit here for a while by ourselves. Somehow I did expect to see you greatly changed, it's always like that with people of your sort. And you know it's wonderful to be the only one in the whole house sitting up on a summer night, waiting for someone to come from the railway station, and at long last to hear the bells and the carriage rolling up to the front porch..."

I reached across the table for her hand and held it in mine, already feeling drawn to her whole body. She sat blowing smoke rings with a gaily unruffled air. I dropped her hand and said with assumed lightness:

"You say Natalie, but no Natalie in the world can hold a candle to you... By the way, who is she, where from?"

"She comes from a splendid family, once very wealthy and now simply destitute. French and English is spoken in their house, but they have nothing to eat... She's a very touching girl, thin and fragile. She's brainy but so secretive that you can't tell at first whether she's intelligent or stupid. These Stankeviches are the nearest neighbours of your darling cousin Alexei Meschersky, and Natalie tells me that he's taken to visiting them very often and complaining about his lonely bachelor existence. But she doesn't like him. And besides he's rich, she'll be suspected of marrying him for his money and sacrificing herself for her parents."

"Let's get back to business, shall we?" I said. "Natalie this and Natalie that, but what about our love affair?"

"Oh, we'll have our love affair just the same," she replied. "You'll go crazy with love for Natalie, but it's me you'll kiss. You'll weep on my shoulder from her cruelty, and I'll comfort you."

"But you do know that I've been in love with you for ages?"

"That was just a boy's calf love for his cousin and it was too furtive, you were only ridiculous and boring then. Well, never mind, I forgive you your past stupidity and am ready to start our love affair tomorrow, in spite of Natalie. And now let's say good-night, I have to get up early tomorrow, since I run the house."

She stood up, wrapping round her dressing gown, picked up the almost burnt down candle from a table in the hall, and took me to my room. And on the threshold of this room, rejoicing and marvelling at my luck as in my heart I had rejoiced and marvelled all through supper that here, at the Cherkassovs', my amorous hopes were so unexpectedly luckily coming true, I kissed her long and hungrily, while she closed her eyes somberly, holding the dripping candle lower and lower. When she left me, her face flushed crimson, she shook a finger at me and said quietly:

"Only mind you, don't devour me with your passionate glances tomorrow, in front of everyone. God forbid that Daddy should notice something. He's terribly afraid of me, and I'm even more afraid of him. And then I don't want Natalie to notice anything. I'm very bashful, don't judge me, please, by the way I behave with you. And if you don't obey this order of mine, you'll become loathsome to me right away."

I undressed and flopped on my bed, and although my head was spinning I fell asleep at once, weak from happiness and physical tiredness, never suspecting that great unhappiness lay in store for me and that Sonia's jocular talk would turn out to be anything but a joke.

Later, I often remembered it as a sinister omen that when I entered my room and struck a match to light my candle a large bat darted silently at me. It darted so close to my face that even in the light of the match I clearly saw its horrible dark velvety body and its predatory little face, big-eared and pug-nosed, like an image of death, and then it fluttered nastily and dived into the blackness of the open window. But at the time I forgot it immediately.

2

The next morning I had my first fleeting glimpse of Natalie: she popped into the dining-room from the hall with her hair not yet done and wearing only a light morning wrap made of something orange, took one look and vanished with a flash of this orange thing, the bright gold of her hair and her black eyes. I was alone in the dining-room, I had just finished my coffee—my uncle had already finished his and left—and as I rose from the table, I turned round...

I had wakened rather early that morning when perfect silence still reigned in the house. There were so many rooms in that house that sometimes I lost my way. I awakened in a room at the back of the house facing the shady part of the garden, and after my very good sleep I enjoyed washing and dressing up—it was especially pleasant to put on my new Russian blouse of red silk. I carefully combed my wet black hair—I'd had a haircut in Voronezh the day before—went out into the corridor, then turned down another one and found myself before the door of my uncle's bedroom-cum-study. I knocked, knowing that in summer he got up as early as five o'clock. As no one answered I opened the door and looked in, and was glad to see that nothing had changed in this spacious old room with its bow window shaded by a hundred-year-old silver poplar; oakwood bookcases were spaced along the left wall, in one gap between them towered a mahogany grandfather clock, the brass disc of its pendulum now motionless; in the second was a stand holding a great number of different pipes with a barometer hanging on the wall above them; in the third, stood an ancient secretaire with a walnut flap, covered with green baize which had turned rust-coloured from age, let down to hold hammers, nails, a pair of pincers and a brass spyglass. On the wall behind a wooden sofa that must have weighed a ton was a regular gallery of faded portraits in oval frames; at the window stood a writing table and an armchair—both enormous in size; to the right, above a vast wooden bed, hung a picture that took up the entire wall: owing to the time-darkened varnish the smoky clouds and greenish-blue poetical trees in the background were hardly discernible, but in the foreground, gleaming like so much egg white turned to stone, was a stout nude beauty, almost life-size, standing half-turned to the viewer to show her proud face and all the curves of her hefty back, jutting behind and mighty legs, while tantalisingly covering the visible nipple of her breast with the widespread and elongated fingers of one hand, and the lower part of her belly, creased in great fat folds, with the other. As I ran my eye over all this I heard the powerful voice of my uncle, the Uhlan, as he came up to me from the hall tapping with his crutch:

"Oh no, my young friend, you won't find me in my bedroom at this hour. It's you, young people, who loll in bed until the three oaks."

I kissed his broad, dry hand and asked:

"Why three oaks, Uncle?"

"It's what the peasants say," he told me, shaking his grey quiff and surveying me with his still keen and clever eyes whose whites had yellowed with age. "The sun has risen three oaks high and you've still got your snout stuck in the pillow, they say. Come, let us go and have our coffee."

"What a wonderful old man, what a wonderful house!" I was thinking as I followed him into the dining-room, whose opened windows framed a view of the green morning garden and the whole summer well-being of a country estate. We were served by Sonia's old nanny, a small, hunchbacked little woman, my uncle drank strong tea with cream out of a thick glass in a silver holder, his wide thumb on the long, slender and coiled handle of an old golden, round teaspoon, while I ate piece after piece of black bread and butter and kept refilling my cup from the hot silver coffee pot. My uncle, who was interested only in himself, did not enquire after our family or anything at all and told me about his neighbouring squires, cursing and ridiculing them for all he was worth, and I, feigning attention, looked at his whiskers, his sideburns, the thick hairs on the tip of his nose, and longed for Natalie or Sonia to come in so terribly that I could hardly sit still. What was this Natalie like, and how would Sonia and I meet after last night? For Sonia I felt rapture and gratitude, I was thinking lasciviously about her and Natalie's bedrooms, about everything that went on in the early morning disarray of women's bedrooms... Had Sonia perhaps told Natalie something about our love that began last night? If so, then I felt something like love for Natalie too, and not because she was said to be a beauty, but because she had already become our secret partner, Sonia's and mine, and anyway why couldn't two girls be loved at the same time? In a moment they'd come in, glowing with their morning freshness, they'd see me, see my Georgian handsomeness and my red shirt, they'd start talking and laughing, they'd sit down and elegantly fill their cups from this hot coffee pot—youthful morning appetite, youthful morning excitement, eyes shining after a good night's sleep, a film of powder on cheeks that seemed even younger after sleep, and laughter after every word, not very natural laughter and all the more charming for it... And before lunch they would go through the garden to the river, they would undress in the bathing hut, their naked bodies lit from above by the blue of the sky and from below by a reflection of the clear water... I always had a lively imagination, and in my mind's eye I saw Sonia and Natalie holding on to the stair-rail and awkwardly going down the bath-hut steps, sunken in the water, wet, cold and slippery from the nasty green slime covering them, and Sonia throwing back her head, with her thick hair pinned round it, bravely flopping on the water with her upthrust breasts, and the whole of her chalk-blue body becoming strangely visible in the water, her arms and legs spread out just like a frog's...

"Well, until lunch then, lunch is at twelve, you remember, don't you," said my host, rising to his feet and shaking his head negatively—a tall, senilely stiff man with a shaved chin and brown moustache joining similarly dyed sideburns, wearing a loose raw-silk suit, stub-nosed boots, and leaning on his crutch with a broad hand covered with liver spots. He patted me on the shoulder and walked out with a swift stride. And it was then, when I had also risen to my feet meaning to go to the balcony through the next room, that she popped in and vanished, and I was instantly smitten with delighted admiration. I went out to the balcony in a daze—she really was a beauty!—and stood there, collecting my scattered wits. I had been waiting so anxiously for them to come into the dining-room, yet when I heard them there, I ran down into the garden—strangely shying in fear from both of them, with one of whom I already shared a lovely secret, but perhaps more from Natalie, from that fleeting magic with which she had dazzled me half an hour earlier. I walked about the garden, which, like the whole estate, lay in the river valley, and at long last I mastered my fear and, assuming a casual air, went into the dining-room where Sonia's greeting was gaily bold while Natalie gave me a sweetly humorous smile, looking me full in the face with her shining black eyes, so extraordinary with her golden hair, and said:

"We've already met!"

Afterwards we stood on the balcony, leaning on the stone balustrade, feeling the hot sun on our hatless heads with summery pleasure. Natalie stood beside me, and

Sonia, embracing her with one arm and pretending to gaze absently into the distance, was singing softly and mockingly: "I saw her by chance 'mongst the waltzers..." Then she straightened up and said:

"Now for a swim! We'll go first, you'll go in after us."

Natalie ran off for the bath towels, while Sonia hung back to whisper to me:

"As from today be good enough to pretend that you've fallen in love with Natalie. But if you find there's no need to pretend, beware!"

I almost replied with gay impudence that there already was no need, when she, glancing warily at the door, added softly:

"I'll come to your room after dinner."

When they returned from their bathe, I went down to the river, first along an endless birch-lined walk, then through the various old trees where there was a warm smell of river water and the noise of rooks screaming in the tree-tops, and as I walked I was again thinking about Natalie and Sonia with two entirely different feelings, and also that I was going to swim in the same water in which they had just been bathing...

After dinner, with the sky, the greenery, the sunlight, and all that was happy, carefree and serene looking into the open windows from the garden, after that long dinner of kvass soup, fried chicken, and raspberries with cream, during which I thrilled from Natalie's presence and from the anticipation of that hour when the whole household would retire for the after-dinner nap and Sonia (who had appeared for dinner with a dark-red rose in her hair) would slip into my room in order to continue in earnest and not just anyhow what we had begun the night before, I went to my room at once, closed the window shutters and lay down on the divan to wait for her, listening to the sultry quiet of the house, and the birds already singing languidly in their past-midday manner in the garden whence the air, sweetly scented by flowers and grasses, flowed in through the slats of the shutters, and thinking hopelessly: how was I to live now in this duality, holding these clandestine rendezvous with Sonia and being so close to Natalie, the very thought of whom already filled me with such pure amorous rapture, with a passionate wish only to look at her adoringly as I had looked at her slender body and sharp elbows when she stood leaning on the sun-heated old stone balustrade. Sonia, also leaning on the balustrade with one arm round Natalie's shoulders, had looked like a young matron in her flounced batiste peignoir, while Natalie, in her plain linen skirt and embroidered Ukrainian blouse, beneath which the young perfection of her body could be divined, appeared little more than a child. The supreme delight of all this was that I couldn't even dare to think that I might kiss her as desirously as I had kissed Sonia. I could see her slender arm with little reddish hairs on the lustreless golden skin in the wide sleeve of her blouse, embroidered with red and blue on the shoulders, and as I looked at her arm I wondered what would I feel if I dared touch it with my lips? And, sensing my stare, she had turned her bright-golden head, and flashed at me the brilliance of her black eyes. I walked away and quickly dropped my eyes, and saw her legs through the transparent hem of her skirt, and her slim, strong, blue-blood ankles in sheer grey stockings...

Sonia, still wearing the rose in her hair, opened my door, quickly closed it behind her and exclaimed in a low voice: "Were you sleeping?" I jumped up—heavens, no, no, how could I sleep?—and gripped her hands. "Lock the door," she told me. I dashed to the door, she sat down on the divan, closing her eyes,—"Come, come to me,"—and instantly we were lost to shame and reason. We did not utter a word in those minutes and she, in all the loveliness of her hot body, already let me kiss her everywhere, but only to kiss, closing her darkening eyes and flushing more and more brightly. And again, as she smoothed her hair on leaving me, she whispered threateningly:

"And as for Natalie, I repeat: beware of going beyond pretense. I am not as sweet-tempered as you might think!"

Her rose lay on the floor. I put it away in my table and by evening its dark-red velvety petals turned limp and drab.

3

Outwardly my life ran an ordinary course, but inwardly I did not know a moment of peace, on the one hand growing more and more attached to Sonia and the delicious habit of our passionate, strength-sapping nightly sessions—she now came to my room only late at night when the whole house went to sleep, and on the other stealthily watching Natalie, her every movement more and more tormentingly and rapturously. Life ran its usual summer course: breakfast together, bathing before dinner, then dinner, siesta, and then the garden—the girls did some embroidery, sitting in the birch-lined walk and ordering me to read Goncharov to them aloud, or else made jam on the shaded little glade under the oaks, not far from the house, to the right of the balcony; at half-past five tea was served on another shady glade to the left of the balcony, strolls in the garden or croquet in front of the house—Natalie and I against Sonia, or Sonia and Natalie against me—and at dusk there was supper in the dining-room. After supper, Sonia's father went off to bed, while we sat on in the darkness on the balcony for a long time, Sonia and I joking and smoking, and Natalie just sitting silently. And then Sonia announced: "Time to sleep!" I bid them good-night, and went to my room, and there waited with icy hands for that precious hour when the whole house grew dark and so quiet that I could hear the faint thread-like ticking of my watch, and thought with horror and wonder: how did I so err against the Almighty that he should punish me by granting me two loves at once, so different and so passionate, the tormenting ecstasy of adoring Natalie, and the sexual delights with Sonia. I felt that any night now we would be unable to endure our incomplete intimacy, and then I'd become quite demented from longing for our nightly rendezvous and reliving the sensation the whole of the next day, and all this with Natalie so close! Sonia already had fits of jealousy sometimes, flushing wrathfully, and at the same time she said to me when we were alone:

"I'm afraid that we don't treat each other casually enough at table and in Natalie's presence. Daddy, I think, is beginning to notice something. Natalie too, and as for nanny, she's quite certain, of course, that we're having an affair and probably carries tales to Daddy. Spend more time with Natalie alone in the garden, reading her that tiresome *Precipice*, and take her for walks in the evening sometimes... It's awful, I do see, you know, how stupidly you gape at her, I hate you at moments and feel like tearing your hair out in front of everybody like some operatic Odarka or someone, but there's nothing I can do, is there?"

The most awful thing of all was that Natalie, it seemed to me, was beginning to suspect that there was some secret between Sonia and me, and was either pained or resentful. Reticent by nature, she grew more reticent still, she played croquet or did her embroidering with too preoccupied an air. We had become used to each other, we had become close friends, but then one day, when we were alone in the sitting-room and she was leafing through some music as she reclined on the sofa, I said to her jocosely:

"I hear, Natalie, that you and I might become related."

She glanced at me sharply.

"What do you mean?"

"I mean my cousin, Alexei Meschersky who..."

She did not let me finish.

"Oh, I see. Your cousin, begging your pardon, that fattened giant with shiny black hair overrunning his face, with the overblown red lips and a slur... And who gave you the right to talk to me like that?"

"Natalie, Natalie, why are you so hard on me?" I cried, frightened. "I'm not even allowed to joke? Come, forgive me," I said, taking her hand.

She did not pull her hand away.

"I still don't understand you ... don't know you... But let's say no more about it," she said.

I got up and went to the balcony so as not to see her feet in white tennis shoes which she had drawn up sideways on the sofa and which attracted my gaze painfully. A raincloud was rising behind the garden, the air was dimming, a soft summer rustle was running through the garden, spreading ever wider and coming nearer, a rain-laden wind brought a sweet fragrance of meadow, and I was suddenly gripped with such a delicious, young, carefree, all-consenting happiness that I cried out:

"Natalie, come here a moment!"

She came to me and asked:

"What's the matter?"

"Just breathe this wind! How joyous everything might have been!"

She said nothing for a minute, and then replied: "Yes."

"Natalie, how unfriendly you are with me! Have you something against me?"

She shrugged her shoulders proudly.

"Why should I have anything against you?"

Late that evening, reclining in the wicker chairs on the balcony in the dark, all three of us were silent—the stars glimmered only here and there between the dark clouds, a lazy wind blew feebly from the river, where frogs could be heard purling drowsily.

"Rain is coming, I feel sleepy," Sonia said, stifling a yawn. "Nanny said that a new moon has been born and now it will wash itself for a week or so." After a pause, she added: "Natalie, what do you think of first love?"

Natalie responded from the darkness:

"Of one thing I'm convinced: the first love of a boy and a girl differ terribly."

Sonia thought this over, and said:

"Oh well, girls differ too..." She got up resolutely. "To sleep, to sleep, everyone!"

"And I'll stay and dream here a bit longer, I love the night," Natalie said.

Listening to Sonia's retreating footfall, I whispered:

"I'm sorry about the way our talk went today."

"No, it didn't go well..." she answered.

The next day we three met with seeming casualness. It had been raining a little in the night, but the morning dawned fair and by dinner-time the day was dry and hot. After four, before tea, Sonia went to her father's room to do some housekeeping accounts, Natalie and I sat alone in the birch-lined walk and tried to continue with our reading of *The Precipice*. Natalie was stitching something, her head bent over her work and the needle flickering in her right hand, while I read aloud to her, glancing every now and again with sweet longing at her left arm in the wide sleeve, at the flat reddish hairs on her forearm and identical little hairs on the back of her neck, and I read all the more excitedly without understanding a word.

"You read now," I said at last.

As she straightened up, the points of her breasts became outlined against her thin blouse; she put aside her sewing, bent her strange and lovely head low again, showing me the back of her neck and the beginning of her shoulder, placed the book on her knees and started reading in a quick, unsteady voice. I gazed at her hands, at her knees under the book, dying of insane love for her knees and the sound of her voice. Golden orioles cried out in flight in different parts of the garden, and exactly opposite us a red-and-grey woodpecker hung on to a pine growing lonesomely among the birches.

"How amazing is the colour of your hair, Natalie! And the braid is much darker, like ripe maize..."

She went on reading.

"Natalie, there's a woodpecker, look!"

She glanced up and said:

"I've seen it already, today and yesterday... Don't interrupt."

I kept quiet for a little, and then spoke again:

"I say, doesn't this look like dried grey worms?"

"What? Where?"

I pointed to some dried bird droppings on the bench between us.

"Doesn't it?"

I took her hands and squeezed them, muttering and laughing from happiness:

"Oh Natalie, Natalie!"

She gave me a long, grave look, and then said:

"But you're in love with Sonia!"

I blushed like a thief caught red-handed, but renounced Sonia with such passionate haste that she even opened her mouth a little.

"It's not true?"

"No, no, not true! I love Sonia like a sister, we've known each other since we were children together, you know!"

4

The next day Natalie did not appear for breakfast or dinner.

"Sonia, what's the matter with Natalie?" her father asked, and Sonia replied with a nasty sort of laugh:

"She's been lying all morning in bed in her morning wrap, her hair not dressed, and you could see from her face that she'd been crying. She didn't even finish the cup of coffee brought to her... What's the matter? I asked her. I have a headache, she said. She's fallen in love, I shouldn't be surprised."

"Quite likely," replied her father brightly, meaning to give me an encouraging nod, but shaking his head from side to side.

Natalie only appeared for afternoon tea. Her step was light and brisk, she smiled at me gaily and a bit contritely, I thought, surprising me with her briskness, her smile and a sort of dressed-up look: her hair was drawn back tightly and waved a little in front with a touch of curling irons, she wore a different dress made of some green stuff, very simple and smart, particularly at the waistline, her slippers were black and high heeled—inwardly I gave a gasp of new admiration. I had been sitting on the balcony leafing through the issues of the *Istorichesky vestnik* lent me by my uncle, when she suddenly appeared with that peculiar briskness and the rather embarrassed friendliness:

"Good afternoon. Let's go and have tea. I'll be pouring out. Sonia is not quite well."

"What? First it was you, and now Sonia?"

"I simply had a headache since early morning. I'm ashamed to say that I only just made myself look decent."

"This green colour goes amazingly well with your eyes and your hair!" I said. And then, flushing, suddenly asked: "Did you believe me last night?"

She blushed too—a delicate crimson—and looked away.

"Not at once," she said. "And not quite. And then it suddenly occurred to me that I have no reason not to believe you and that, actually, what business is it of mine what you and Sonia feel for one another. Shall we go now?"

Sonia appeared for supper and, finding an opportune moment, whispered to me:

"I'm unwell. This business always gives me a very bad time, I have to stay in bed for all of five days. It's still not so bad today, but tomorrow I'll be laid up. Don't do anything silly in my absence. I love you terribly and am awfully jealous."

"D'you mean you won't come for even a moment tonight?"

"Aren't you stupid!"

I felt both elated and disappointed: five days of complete freedom with Natalie, yet five nights without Sonia.

For a whole week the house was run by Natalie who, wearing a little white apron, went back and forth from the house to the kitchen across the yard, looking very business-like, as I had never seen her before. She obviously enjoyed the role of housewife very much, she seemed to be glad to relax her secret watchfulness over Sonia and me: how we looked at each other, how we talked. At the first dinner she ordered as Sonia's substitute she worried terribly that everything should go well. To her relief all indeed went well; the old chef and Khristya, the Ukrainian maid, brought in and served the dishes in good time, without irritating the master. The rest of the week, after dinner she went to be with Sonia in her room, where I was not allowed, stayed there till tea-time, and then again after supper. She tried not to be left *tête-à-tête* with me, and I felt bewildered, lonely and unhappy. Why had she become nice to me and yet avoided me? Was she afraid of Sonia, or of herself, of her love for me? I passionately wanted to believe that it was of herself, and I savoured the dream that was taking an ever stronger hold of my imagination—after all, I was not tied to Sonia for life, after all we, that is Natalie and I, were not going to stay here forever, and in a week or two I'd have to leave anyway, and that would be the end of my torments... I'd find some pretext to go and present myself to the Stankeviches as soon as Natalie returned home... It would be very painful, of course, to leave Sonia in this deceitful way with a secret dream of Natalie, of her love and the hope of winning her hand, because didn't I love Sonia as well, was lust all I felt when I was kissing her? But what could I do, sooner or later it would happen inevitably anyway... And constantly thinking these thoughts, in a constant state of nervousness and expectation of I knew not what, I tried to be as nice and as reserved as possible with Natalie, and in the meantime to be patient. I was bored and unhappy, and to make it worse we had three days of rain, pouring down steadily and tapping on the roof with a thousand clawed feet; the house was dusky, flies slept on the ceiling and the lamp in the dining-room, but I bore up, and sometimes sat for hours in my uncle's room listening to his stories.

Sonia began to come down for an hour or two in her dressing gown with a languid smile for her feebleness, she would recline in a canvas armchair on the balcony and, to my horror, talk to me in a petulant and unnecessarily affectionate tone, unembarrassed by the presence of Natalie.

"Come and sit beside me, darling, I'm in pain and miserable, tell me something to make me laugh... The new moon had really been washing itself, but I think it has finished now ... the weather is fair again, and the flowers smell so sweet..."

With irritation in my heart, I replied:

"Since the flowers smell so strongly they're going to get washed again."

She slapped my hand and pouted.

"Don't argue with me, I'm ill."

And now she started coming down to dinner and to afternoon tea still looking pale and ordering an armchair to be drawn up for her. She still did not come down for supper or to sit on the balcony afterwards. Once, after tea, when Sonia had gone to her room and Khristya had taken the samovar away into the kitchen, Natalie said to me:

"Sonia is angry with me for staying at her side all the time and leaving you all by yourself. She's not quite well yet, and you miss her."

"It's only you I miss," I replied. "When I don't see you..."

She paled but mastered her emotion and made an effort to smile.

"We did agree not to quarrel any more, didn't we?" she said. "You know what you'd better do: go for a walk until supper, you've been cooped up indoors too long, and then I'll come and sit with you in the garden, the omen about the moon has not come true luckily, and it seems it's going to be a fine night."

"Sonia is sorry for me, and you're not? Not a bit?"

"I'm terribly sorry for you," she said with a self-conscious laugh, stacking the teacups on the tray. "But Sonia's illness is over, thank God, and soon you'll stop feeling bored."

At the words: "I'll sit with you in the garden" my heart shrank with a dulcet, secret pain, but I told myself at once: no, she only meant it kindly, that's all. I went to my room and for a long time lay on my bed staring at the ceiling. Then I got up, took someone's cap and stick in the hall, and walked without conscious intention to the wide highway running between the estate and the Ukrainian village sprawling on a woodless knoll in the steppe. The highroad led to the fields, desolate at this hour of evening. The country was hilly but it was spacious and you could see far around you. To my left was a low-lying valley, the fields beyond it, also desolate now, sloped up to the horizon, the sun had just set there, leaving a fiery glow in the sky. To my right I saw an even row of identical whitewashed cottages, pink from the sunglow, but there was no sign of life in the village, as though the inhabitants had all died. Sorrowfully I looked now at the sunset, now at those cottages. When I turned homeward, warm and at moments hot gusts of wind blew into my face, the new moon was already shining in the sky, but it did not bode good weather: one half of it was shining brightly but the other half was visible too, as a sort of transparent cobweb, and the whole thing together made me think of an acorn.

At supper—supper was again served in the garden as it was too hot in the house—I asked my uncle:

"What do you think of the weather? I have a feeling that there'll be rain tomorrow."

"Why, my friend?"

"I've just been walking in the fields and thinking with regret that I'll be leaving you soon..."

"But why?"

Natalie also glanced at me and asked:

"You're leaving?"

My laugh was as artificial as it sounded.

"But, after all, I can't..."

My uncle started shaking his head with especial vigour, and this time quite aptly.

"Stuff and nonsense! Your papa and mama will endure the separation perfectly well! I won't let you go for another fortnight at the least. And she won't let you either."

"I have no right to forbid Vitaly Petrovich anything," she said.

"Oh, Uncle," I whined. "Do tell Natalie not to use that formal name!"

"I forbid you!" my uncle said, slapping his palm down

on the table. "And no more nonsense about your leaving. Now, as for the rain you're right, the weather will turn bad again very likely."

"It was somehow too bright, too clear out in the fields," I said. "And half of the new moon is very bright, it looks like an acorn, and the wind is coming from the south. And there, you see, the clouds are already gathering."

Uncle turned and looked into the garden where the moonlight dimmed one moment and shone brightly the next.

"You've the makings of a second Bruce*, my boy..."

After nine, she came out to the balcony where I sat waiting for her and thinking despondently: it's a lot of rubbish, even if she does care, it's not serious at all, just a passing, changeable feeling... The new moon, clear and without the cobweb, sparkled all the higher and brighter in the masses of gathering, smoky-white clouds that cluttered up the sky with majestic arrogance, and when it did emerge from behind them it looked like a man's deathly-white face in profile, and everything was lit up and flooded with a phosphoric light. Something made me turn round suddenly: Natalie was standing in the door, looking at me silently, her hands behind her back. I stood up and she asked indifferently:

"Not asleep yet?"

"But you told me..."

"I'm sorry, it was a very tiring day. Let's go up and down the walk, and then I'll go to bed."

I followed her. She paused on the balcony steps, looking at the tops of the trees from behind which the clouds were already rising in whorls with soundless lightning flashing across them. Then she entered the birch walk where the treetops formed a transparent canopy and the ground was dappled with spots of light and shadow. Walking beside her I said, simply for the sake of saying something:

"The birches in the distance glimmer so magically! There's nothing more strange and beautiful than the inside of a forest on a moonlit night with that satiny white sheen of the birch trunks in its depths..."

*Yakov Bruce (1670-1735)—a scholar and statesman in the reign of Peter the Great, who was credited with compilation of the famous *Bruce's Calendar* published in Moscow in 1709-1715.

She stopped and, her black eyes glowing in the semi-darkness, asked:

"Are you really leaving?"

"Yes, it's time..."

"But why so suddenly and so soon? I confess, I was startled when you told your uncle you were leaving."

"Natalie, may I come and present myself to your parents when you return home?"

She made no reply. I took her hands in mine and, in trepidation, kissed her right one.

"Natalie..."

"Yes, yes, I love you," she said hastily and expressionlessly, and turned back to the house. I followed her like a sleepwalker.

"Go at once, tomorrow," she said, without turning round, as she hurried on. "I'll return home in a few days' time."

5

When I came into my room I sat down on the sofa, without lighting the candle, and simply sat there stunned by that awesome and wonderful thing that had so suddenly and unexpectedly happened to me. I sat there, utterly lost to my surroundings and time. My room and the garden were already immersed in darkness brought on by the rain-clouds; beyond the open windows all was thrashing and shuddering and a swift instantly vanishing greenish-blue flame illumined me more and more brightly and at ever shorter intervals. The speed and strength of this thunderless lightning kept increasing, and then suddenly the room was lit up to an impossible degree of visibility, and a chill wind rushed in together with such a frantic din from outside as though the garden were howling in horror: the end of the world was at hand, the earth and the sky were on fire! I jumped up, with difficulty closed one window after the other, grabbing for the frames and struggling against the wind that buffeted me, and then ran on tiptoe along the dark corridors to the dining-room. Why should I worry in the state I was in that the windows in the dining-room and sitting-room were open and the panes could easily be shattered by the storm? But I ran there just the same, in great anxiety too. I found all the windows safely closed—I saw this in the greenish-blue flash of a truly unearthly colour and brilliance which illumined everything at once, with a keen-eyed look as it were, making the window frames appear enormous and visible down to the smallest pane and sash. In the next instant a dense darkness flooded everything, the flash leaving a fleeting trace of something metallic and red in one's blinded vision. I hurried back to my room, as though afraid that something might have happened there while I was gone, and from the darkness I heard an angry whisper:

"Where have you been? I'm frightened, light the candle quickly..."

I struck a match and saw Sonia, wearing only a nightgown and bedroom slippers on her bare feet, sitting on the sofa.

"No, better not, don't light it," she said fretfully. "Come quickly to me, take me in your arms, I'm frightened..."

I sat down obediently and hugged her cold shoulders. She whispered:

"Kiss me, kiss me, take all of me, I haven't been with you for a whole week!"

And she fell back on the pillows, pulling me down with her.

In that very moment Natalie appeared in the open door with a candle held high in her hand. She saw the two of us at once, but still she called out without conscious thought:

"Sonia, where are you? I'm terribly frightened..."

And vanished. Sonia rushed after her.

6

A year later she married my cousin Alexei Meschersky. They were wedded in Blagodatnoye, in an empty church, for none of his or her relatives or friends had been invited. Nor did the newlyweds pay the customary calls on anyone, and left for the Crimea after the ceremony.

In January of the following year, on St. Tatiana's Day, a ball was given in the Noblemen's Club in Voronezh for the local students. I was already studying in Moscow at the university and had come home to our estate for the Christmas and New Year holidays, but I could not miss this gala affair. I arrived in Voronezh late in the evening. The train was plastered with snow which rose in swirls like smoke when the blizzard swept it up; the street-lamps barely flickered through the snow screen as I rode in a sleigh from the railway station to the hotel. But after the quiet of the country this city blizzard and these city lights excited me, promising the pleasure soon to be enjoyed of entering a warm, even too warm room in that old hotel, ordering tea and starting to change for the ball that would go on late into the night, followed by student revels till morning. In the many months that had passed since that ghastly night in Sonia's room and then Natalie's marriage, I had gradually recovered, or in any case had become used to being a mentally ill person, which actually I was, but one who lived to all appearances like everyone else.

The ball had only just begun when I arrived, but the grand staircase and the landing at the top were already crowded, and more people kept arriving. From the main hall, from the musicians' gallery where the regimental brass band was seated, blared forth a wistfully-jubilant waltz that drowned out all other sounds. Because I was wearing my brand new uniform, I made my way through the crowd on the red-carpeted stairs with excessive care, overdoing the apologies; I plunged into the very thick and already hot throng before the doors into the dance hall, and then, for no reason, started elbowing my way through so insistently that I was probably mistaken for one of the officials who had urgent business in the hall. I stopped in the door, listening to the music rolling in waves from the musicians' gallery right above me, and looking at the rippling sparkle of the chandeliers and the scores of couples variously flickering in a waltz beneath them, and suddenly shrank back: in that whirling crowd all I saw was one couple, dancing with swift gliding steps and coming nearer and nearer to me. I recoiled as I saw him, tall and stout, waltzing with shoulders slightly hunched, a black figure, black shiny hair and black tails, dancing with that amazing lightness one finds in some stout people, and her—so tall with her hair piled up into an elaborate coiffure, in her white ball gown and pretty golden slippers, her body arched back a little, her eyes lowered, and her arm in a white elbow-length glove so gracefully placed on his shoulder that it looked like the neck of a swan. Suddenly she raised her black eyelashes and for a fleeting moment her black eyes flashed straight at me and so very close, but here her husband with a stout man's care swung her round smartly, her lips parted on a sigh at the turn, the hem of her gown gave a silvery flicker and away they glided. I squeezed through the press at the doors, struggled out of the crowd, and just stood there... In the open doors of the dining hall, as yet empty and cool, I saw two young student girls in Ukrainian dress—a pretty little blonde and a beautiful, swarthy and lean Cossack girl, almost twice as tall as the other—idly waiting for customers behind a champagne bar. I went in and with a bow held out to them a hundred-ruble note. They knocked heads as they reached for it and laughing merrily pulled out a heavy bottle out of the ice bucket under the counter, and exchanged baffled looks, as there were no opened bottles yet. I went behind the counter and had the cork shooting out with a sharp report in no time at all. I gaily invited the girls to have a glass with me—*Gaudeamus igitur!*—and drank the rest up alone. They watched me with amazement at first, and then with pity:

"You're so terribly pale!"

I finished the bottle and left. Back in my hotel room I ordered a bottle of Caucasian cognac and drank it in teacups hoping that my heart would burst...

Another year and a half passed. At the end of May when I was at home again for Easter, a messenger from the railway station brought us a telegram from her which said: "Alexei Nikolayevich died this morning from a stroke." My father crossed himself and said:

"God rest his soul. How awful! I never liked him, the Lord forgive me, but it's awful anyway. He wasn't even forty yet. And I'm terribly sorry for her—to be left a widow so early in life, and with a child too... I've never clapped eyes on her—he was such a loving nephew that he never once brought her over to meet us, but she is said to be charming. What's to be done now? Neither your mother nor I can undertake that trip in our old age—Blagodatnoye is a hundred and fifty versts away—and so you'll have to go..."

How could I refuse to go, what excuse had I? And then I did not want to refuse in the half-demented state I was plunged into by the unexpected news. I would see her, and that was all I knew. The pretext for us to meet was horrible but legitimate.

We telegraphed our condolences and my time of arrival, and the next day, on a warm May evening, the horses sent from Blagodatnoye to the railway station brought me in a mere half-hour to the estate. Driving up the slope along the water meadows I saw from afar that all the windows of the ballroom along the western wall of the house facing the still bright evening sky were shuttered, and was appalled by the thought: those were the windows of the room where he lay in state, and she'd be there too! In the yard, thickly carpeted with new grass, somebody's two troikas were outside the coach-house, their little bells jangling softly as the horses shifted their legs, but there were only the coachmen sitting up on their boxes and no other soul in sight. The arrivals and all the servants were already inside the house, attending the service. The quiet of a May evening in the countryside lay over everything, everything was vernally clean, fresh and new—the meadow and river air, the thick grass in the yard, the thickly flowering garden, pushing up close to the back of the house and to its southern side, while on the low front porch, propped against the wall beside the wide open doors stood an upended coffin lid, covered with yellow brocade. The delicately chill evening air smelled strongly of the sweet fragrance of pear blossoms clustering in milky white clouds in the south-eastern part of the garden against a sky that seemed opaque from this milkiness and empty save for Jupiter, shining rosily and brightly. And the youthfulness and beauty of all this, the thought of *her* beauty and youthfulness, and that once she loved me, suddenly tore at my heart with such anguish, happiness and need of love that, on leaping down from the carriage at the front porch, I felt as if I were standing on the brink of an abyss—how was I to walk into that house, see her face to face again after three years, and now already a widow and a mother! But I did step into the dusk and incense of that fearsome room, the darkness spangled with the tiny yellow flames of the candles which people held in their hands as they stood around the coffin, placed diagonally, the head towards the icon corner, illumined by the large red icon-lamp from above and the silvery, flowing sparkle of three tall church candles from below. When I came in the priests, with prayers and singing, were going round the coffin, swinging their censors and bowing, and I lowered my head at once so as not to see the yellow brocade on the coffin and the face of the deceased, but more than anything else not to see her. Someone handed me a burning candle, I took it and held it, feeling it trembling and lighting up my stiff, pale face, and listened with dull obedience to the priests' appeals and the jangling of the censor, seeing the cloyingly sweet smoke solemnly floating ceilingward, and suddenly lifting my head I saw her in spite of myself—she stood in front of everyone, in deep mourning, the light from the candle in her hand touching her cheek and her golden hair, and I gazed at her as at an icon now, and was unable to tear my gaze away. When the service was over and a smell of snuffed-out candles filled the room, everyone started moving cautiously and lining up to kiss her hand, I hung back, so as to be the last. When I came up to her I glanced with awed adoration at the nun-like simplicity of her black dress, which made her especially virginal, at the pure, young beauty of her face, eyelashes and eyes, which she dropped on seeing me, I bowed very, very low as I kissed her hand and in a barely audible voice said all the things I had to say as a relative, and begged her permission to retire at once and sleep the night in the old rotunda in the garden. I used to sleep there when I came to Blagodatnoye as a schoolboy, and Meschersky used it as a bedroom on hot summer nights.

She replied without raising her eyes:

"I'll have someone accompany you there and I'll order supper to be brought to you."

The next morning I left the minute the funeral was over.

As I took leave of her, we again exchanged only a few polite words, and again avoided looking into each other's eyes.

7

I finished the university, soon afterwards lost both my father and my mother almost simultaneously, settled down on our estate, became a busy country squire, and took for my unwedded wife the orphaned peasant girl Gasha who had grown up in the house and had been my mother's personal maid. And now she took care of me together with Ivan Lukich, our former serf, an old man with huge shoulder blades and hair so white that it had almost a greenish tinge. Gasha still looked rather infantile—she was short, skinny, black-haired, with expressionless eyes the colour of soot, enigmatically silent as if everything left her quite indifferent, and with a skin so fine and swarthy that my father used to say: "That's what Hagar* must have been like." She was infinitely dear to me, I loved carrying her about in my arms, and as I kissed her I thought: "And this is all that's left me in life!" She seemed to know what I was thinking, and understood. When she gave birth to a little black-haired boy and moved into my old nursery, I wanted to marry her, but she refused.

"I don't need it, I'd only be ashamed in front of everyone. Some mistress of the manor I'd make! And why should you want it? You'd only stop loving me the sooner. What you ought to do is go to Moscow before you're bored sick here, with me. And I won't be lonely now," she said, looking down at the baby she was nursing. "Go and enjoy yourself, only remember this: if you fall in love with someone in earnest and want to marry, I'll drown myself together with him, I won't hesitate a moment!"

I looked at her, and knew that she meant it. And I hung my head... After all, I was only twenty-six years old... I couldn't see myself falling in love and marrying, yet Gasha's threat reminded me once again that my life was finished.

In early spring I went abroad and spent about four months there. When I was returning home via Moscow I was thinking that I'd spend the autumn in the country, and again go away somewhere for the winter. On the way from Moscow to Tula I asked myself with resigned sad-

***Hagar—the Egyptian handmaiden of Abraham's wife Sarah who bore him a son named Ishmael.**

ness: "Here you're home again, but what for?" I remembered Natalie and thought: yes, that love "unto death" which Sonia mockingly predicted for me, did exist, only I had already become used to it, like people with an amputated arm or a leg eventually become used to their state. And while waiting to change trains in Tula, I suddenly went and sent her this telegram: "On my way home from Moscow will be passing your station at nine o'clock may I pay you a visit."

She met me on the front porch—a maid was holding a lamp high behind her—and stretched both hands out to me with a little smile.

"I'm awfully glad!"

"How very strange, but you've grown a bit taller!" I said, kissing her hands, poignantly aware of them already. I glanced at the whole of her in the light of the lamp which the maid raised higher and around which little pink moths were dancing in the rain-softened air. Her black eyes had a steadier and more confident look now, she was already in the full bloom of her feminine beauty, slender and quietly smart in a dress of green raw silk.

"Yes, I'm still growing," she said with a wistful smile.

The large red icon-lamp was hanging as before in front of the old golden icons, only it was not burning now. I hastily averted my eyes from that corner, and followed her into the dining-room. There, on the table covered with a gleaming white cloth, stood a spirit lamp with a kettle on it, and tea things for two of fine, translucent china. The maid brought some cold veal, pickles, a small decanter of vodka and a bottle of Lafite.

Natalie picked up the kettle and said:

"I never eat supper, I'll just have some tea, but do eat, please. You were in Moscow? Why? What's there to do there in the summer?"

"I am returning home from Paris."

"Oh! Were you there long? If only I could go somewhere! But my little girl is only three, you know... I hear that you're working hard, managing your estate..."

I drank a glass of vodka and asked permission to smoke.

"Oh please do!"

I lit up and said:

"Natalie, you don't need to entertain me with small talk,

or pay any special attention to me, I came only to take a look at you and disappear again. And you mustn't feel self-conscious–after all everything is past history now, gone beyond recall. You cannot help seeing that I am dazzled by you again, but my admiration must not discompose you in any way–it is now disinterested and calm..."

She dropped her head and her eyes–it was impossible to get used to the marvellous contrast between her golden hair and black eyelashes–and slowly her face began to turn crimson.

"It's perfectly true," I said in a firmer voice to convince myself that it really was true. "Everything passes, after all. As for my terrible guilt, I am certain that it stopped mattering to you ages ago, and that it must be much more understandable and pardonable than it was before. I was not entirely to blame, you know, and even at the time an allowance could be made for my extreme youth and the amazing web of circumstances in which I found myself. Moreover I have been punished enough with my whole wrecked life."

"But why wrecked?"

"Isn't it? Do you mean that you still don't understand me, don't know me, as you once said to me?"

She did not say anything for a minute or two.

"I saw you at that ball in Voronezh... How very young I was then and how amazingly miserable! But then can love be miserable?" she lifted her face and the question was written large in her wide-open black eyes. "Isn't the most mournful music in the world a happiness to hear? Better tell me about yourself, surely you haven't settled down for good in the country?"

"You mean you still cared then?" I asked with an effort.

"Yes."

I said no more, feeling the blood flooding my face.

"Is it true what I heard ... that you have a love and a child?"

"It's not love," I replied. "Heart-wringing compassion, tenderness, that's all."

"Tell me everything."

I told her the whole story, ending with Gasha's advice that I should go to Moscow and enjoy myself.

"Now you see how utterly wrecked my life is!"

"Come, come," she said, thinking some thought of her own. "You still have your whole life to look forward to. But marriage for you is impossible, of course. She's obviously the type of woman who won't spare even her child, let alone herself."

"Marrying doesn't come into this," I said. "Good God, me marrying someone!"

She looked at me thoughtfully.

"Yes, of course. But isn't it strange. Your prophesy came true, we *have* become related. Do you realise that we are cousins now?"

She placed her hand on mine and said:

"The journey must have tired you terribly, you haven't even touched the food. You look so wan, we've done enough talking for tonight, a bed has been made up for you in the pavilion, go now."

I kissed her hand meekly, she called the maid who led the way with a lamp, though it was quite light from the low-hanging moon, first down the main walk, and then along a side path to a large meadow in the middle of which stood the ancient rotunda with wooden columns. I sat down at the open window in an armchair standing next to the bed, smoking and thinking how stupid it was of me to act on the spur of the moment and come here, I shouldn't have trusted in my composure and my moral strength... The night was extraordinarily still, and the hour was very late. There must have been another short rainfall, for the air was even warmer and softer. And in charming harmony with this motionless warmth and quiet, the first cocks began to crow tentatively in different parts of the village. The bright disc of the moon seemed to hang still just opposite the rotunda, behind the garden, looking down expectantly as it shone amid the distant birches and the near apple trees, mixing its light with their shadows. Where the light fell it was glassily bright, while in the shadows it was motley and mysterious... And she, wearing something long, dark and silkily shiny, came up to the window as mysteriously and soundlessly...

Later the moon shone right over the garden and beamed straight into the rotunda, and we talked in turn—she, lying on the bed, and I, kneeling beside her and holding her hand.

"That terrible night with the lightning I already loved only you, there was no other passion in me, just the most rapturous and clean passion for you..."

"Yes, I understood everything little by little. But just the same, when I suddenly remembered those lightnings after I had just been remembering what came to pass between us in the garden a mere hour earlier..."

"There is no one like you in the world. When I was looking at this green dress and your knees under the dress, I felt I'd be willing to die for just touching the dress with my lips, just the dress..."

"Did you never, never forget me all these years?"

"I only forgot as one forgets that one lives and breathes. You're right: there is no miserable love. Ah, that orange morning wrap of yours, and all of you, so very young, flickering for a moment before me that morning, the first morning of my love for you! And then your arm in the wide sleeve of your Ukrainian blouse. Then your bent head when you were reading *The Precipice* and I was muttering: 'Natalie! Natalie!' "

"Yes, yes, yes..."

"And then you at the ball–so tall and so unapproachable in your already womanly beauty–how I wanted to die that night exulting in my love and in my ruin! And then you, holding a candle in your hand, your mourning dress and your look of virginity in it. I fancied that the candle became holy from mere closeness to your face."

"And here you are with me again, and this time forever. But we can only meet infrequently–can I, your secret wife, become your mistress openly, for all the world to see?"

In December she died in premature labour on Lake Geneva.

4 April, 1941

River Restaurant

At the "Prague" the chandeliers were sparkling, the Portuguese string band was playing amid the dinner-time hubbub, and there was not a single vacant table. I stood looking about the room for a little and was about to turn and go when I saw an army surgeon friend of mine who invited me to join him at his table beside the window opened into the warm spring night and Arbat Street, rumbling with tramcars. We had dinner together, drinking quite a lot of vodka and Kakhetian wine and talking about the recently convened State Duma, and then ordered coffee. The doctor took out his old silver cigarette case, offered me one of his gaspers and, lighting up, said:

"Ah yes, the Duma... Let's have some cognac, shall we? I feel so sad for some reason."

I thought he was joking, for he was not given to moods and was rather dryish and calm by nature (a big, strongly built man with stiff red hair, silvered at the temples, who looked very well in uniform), but he added seriously:

"It must be the spring that makes me sad. When you're getting on in years you become much more sentimental than you were in your youth, especially if you're a bachelor and a dreamer. Can you smell the poplars? Hear the jangling and rumbling of the tramcars? And let's close the window, it'll be cosier," he said, rising to his feet. "Ivan Stepanich, two glasses of Shustovsky..."

While Ivan Stepanich, the aged waiter, was fetching the cognac, he remained absently silent. When the cognac was brought and poured into our glasses, he kept the bottle on the table and, taking a sip, continued:

"There's something else too—certain memories. Just before you Valery Bryusov* came in with a girl, a small, skinny little thing who might be a poor student. He said something harsh and angry in his nasal bark to the headwaiter who came running and obviously apologetic—a table must have been booked by telephone, but had not been kept for the poet—and then he haughtily walked out. You know him well, but I know him a little too, we meet in

*Valery Bryusov (1873-1924)—a Russian symbolist poet, an active figure in the country's cultural life after the Revolution of 1917.

circles that are interested in ancient Russian icons, I'm interested in them too, and have been for a long time, ever since serving for some years in Volga towns. And besides, I've heard quite an earful about him, about his love affairs, so much so, in fact, that I felt rather sorry for that girl, undoubtedly his current worshipper and victim. She was terribly touching, gazing in confusion and rapture at all this restaurant splendour, probably quite unfamiliar to her, and at him as he barked out his displeasure, making a demonic play with his black eyes and eyelashes. All that aroused certain memories in me. I'll tell you about one stirred up by Bryusov, seeing that the musicians are leaving and we can sit here in peace and quiet..."

Alcohol always brings a flush to the faces of red-haired people, and although his colour was already high from the vodka, wine and cognac he had drunk, he re-filled our glasses again.

"I remember," he began, "how twenty years ago or so a certain young army surgeon, or to put it plainly, myself, was walking along the street of a Volga town. I wasn't going anywhere in particular, simply to drop a letter in the mail-box, and I was walking along with that carefree contentment in my heart which one sometimes feels for no reason at all when the weather is fine. And the weather was excellent in fact, it was a windless, dry, sunny evening in early September when the fallen leaves rustle so nicely underfoot. I was lost in thought and, happening to raise my eyes, saw walking with quick steps in front of me a very slender, graceful young girl in a grey suit, a grey hat with the brim beautifully curved, and carrying a grey umbrella in a grey-gloved hand. I looked at her and felt that something in her appealed to me terribly, and for another thing the swiftness of her walk struck me as rather curious: where and why was she going in such a hurry? Though, to think of it, why not? After all, people do have all manner of urgent matters, don't they. Still, I was intrigued, I don't know why. I hastened my own step and almost caught up with her, and it was a good thing I did. On the corner ahead was a squat old church, and she made straight for it, although it was a weekday and too early for evening service. She ran up the porch steps, with difficulty pulled open the heavy door, slipped inside and I followed her in and stopped there. The church was empty, she did not see me and walked with a light, quick step to the front of the church, crossed herself, knelt down with lithe grace, threw back her head, clutched her hands to her breast, dropping the umbrella on the floor, and looked at the altar with that insistent plea with which people pray the Lord to sustain them in grief or to grant them their heart's desire. From the narrow barred window to the left of me poured a yellowish evening light, a serene light that seemed also to be ancient and pensive, while in the low vaulted depths of the church it was already dusky, with only the glitter of the gold robes of the saints on the altar-wall icons hammered with wonderful ancient crudeness, and there she knelt, gazing fixedly at the images. Slender waist, a lyre-shaped behind, high-heeled smart shoes, the toes stuck into the floor... And then she quickly dabbed at her eyes with a handkerchief, picked up her umbrella with a resolute gesture, got up to her feet lissomely, ran to the door, and I saw her face, and was startled by the fear that flashed in her eyes, glistening with tears."

The lights were dimmed in the room next to ours, the restaurant was emptying of diners, and the doctor looked at his watch.

"Oh, it's still early," he said. "It's only ten. Must you hurry away? No? Then let's sit here a little longer and I'll finish telling you this rather strange story. The strangest thing about it was that I met her again that evening, or rather night. I was at the river restaurant where I'd only been two or three times in the whole of that summer, and I only went there to breathe some river air after the hot day in town. Heaven knows what made me go there on that particular night when it was already quite cool, it was as if something were guiding me. One might call it a simple coincidence, of course: what's so remarkable about meeting someone by chance at a restaurant one went to for lack of anything better to do? Very reasonable, of course. But it wasn't as simple as that, I mean I met her there of all places and suddenly my vague suspicions were justified, I mean the presentiment I had when I first saw her and was stirred by her preoccupation, by the secret and troubled purpose that was compelling her to go to church and there pray so tensely and silently, begging the

Lord with all her heart for something, pleading with all that is most genuine and important in us. I had forgotten all about her when I came to the restaurant, I sat there for a very long, dull time all by myself in that dive, a very expensive one, by the way, notorious for the all-night revels often running into thousands of rubles when the big merchants went on a spree. I sat there and listlessly drank the Zhiguli beer, remembering the Rein and the Swiss lakes where I'd been the summer before, and thinking how vulgar were all the provincial Russian amusement places, the out-of-town restaurants, the ones on the Volga among them. Have you ever been to our Volga towns and to those river restaurants, standing on floats or piles?"

I replied that I did not know the Volga well and had never been to those river restaurants but could easily imagine what they were like.

"Well, naturally," he said. "Russian provincial towns are more or less the same everywhere. The only difference here was the Volga itself, which is unlike anything else. From early spring till winter it is wonderful everywhere and always, in any weather and at any hour of the day and night. For instance, sitting at night in one of those river restaurants, gazing out of the windows which comprised three of the walls—and on a summer night they'd be wide open—gazing straight into the dark, into the blackness of night, you'd have a special awareness of the untramelled grandeur of the river's expanse: you'd see thousands of different-coloured scattered lights, hear the splash of the passing rafts, the men calling out to each other from the rafts and barges, yelling their warnings, you'd hear the multitonal music, now resonant, now low, of the steamers hooting in the dark and blending with it the treble of the swift little river tugs, you'd remember all those highway robbers' and Tatar words like Balakhna, Vasil-Sursk, Cheboksary, Zhiguli, Batraki, Khvalinsk and the frightening hordes of stevedores on the wharves in these towns, and then you'd remember the inimitable loveliness of the old Volga churches, and you'd only shake your head thinking: how really incomparable with anything else is this Russia of ours! But when you look about you, you ask yourself: what sort of restaurant is this anyway? A timber barn standing on piles with windows in crudely made frames, cluttered with little tables with white but not clean tablecloths, laid with cheap, heavy covers, a restaurant where the salt is mixed with pepper in the salt-cellars and the napkins smell of kitchen soap, where a platform has been nailed together from boards, a parody of a stage for the balalaika and accordion played and the women harpists, the rear wall hung with kerosene lamps equipped with blinding tin reflectors; flaxen-haired waiters scurrying about; the owner, a man with a peasant background, little bear's eyes and coarse hair—how reconcile all this with the thousand-ruble worth of champagne drunk practically every night? All that is Russia too, you know... Am I boring you?"

"Not at all!" I protested.

"Well then, let me finish. The point I'm trying to make is to show you the sort of disreputable place where I suddenly saw her again in all her pure, noble loveliness, and with what an escort! Towards midnight the restaurant began to come awake and fill up: lights were lit, a huge and terribly hot lamp under the ceiling, lamps on the walls, the lamp on the wall behind the stage, a whole army of waiters came out, and crowds of guests poured in—gilded merchant-class youth, of course, officials, contractors, ship captains, a troupe of actors on tour... The waiters, twisting their bodies obscenely, started rushing about with trays, the parties at the tables grew noisy, yelling and laughing, cigarette and cigar smoke hovered in a cloud, balalaika players in operatically-peasant shirts, clean cloth hose and brand new bast sandals, appeared on the stage and sat down in two rows on either side, and after them appeared a chorus of powdered and painted young whores who, standing in line, all put their hands behind their backs and to the strumming of the balalaikas began to sing in shrill voices with stony faces a plaintive, wailing song about some poor warrior who had long been a captive of the Turks and had at last come home: 'His parents did not recognize him, and asked him: 'warrior, who art thou?' ' Then someone, announced as the 'famous Ivan Grachev', came out with a huge accordion, sat down on a chair on the very edge of the platform, and tossed his thick flaxen hair worn with a central parting in the typically plebeian fashion. He had the mug of a bouncer, and wore a yellow blouse with embroidery in red silk on the high collar and hem, belted with a red sash twisted into a thick rope with long shaggy ends, and brand new tall boots with patent-leather legs... He gave his hair a toss, settled the accordion with black and gold bellows on his raised knee, fixed his vapid gaze on something overhead, played a short rollicking passage and then got the accordion to roar and to sing, breaking, bending and stretching the bellows into a thick snake, his fingers running over the keys with amazing intricacy, his playing grew all the louder, sharper and with more variations, and finally he threw back his head, closed his eyes and shrilled in a woman's voice: 'I went walking in the meadow for my sadness to forget...' And it was at precisely that moment that I saw her come in and, obviously, not alone. I had stood up to call the waiter and pay for my beer, and was struck speechless: the door behind the platform was pulled open and in she came in a khaki-coloured sort of cap, and a belted raincoat of the same colour–I must say, she looked lovely in those clothes, like a tall boy–and behind her, holding her by the elbow, came a short man with a swarthy and already wrinkled face and restless eyes, dressed in a *poddyovka* and a peaked nobleman's cap. And you know I saw red! The man was an acquaintance of mine, a wastrel of a landlord who had squandered all he had, a drunkard and a profligate, a former Hussar lieutenant who had been kicked out of his regiment, and blindly, with my thoughts in a whirl, I ran so quickly between the tables that I was on them just inside the door. Ivan Grachev was still screaming: 'For a flower I looked there, to send to my sweetheart...' When I rushed up to him, he glanced at me and shouted gaily: 'Ah, doctor, hello!' while she turned deathly, bluishly pale as I pushed him aside and whispered furiously to her: 'You, here, in this den! At midnight, with this depraved drunkard and card-sharper, known to everyone in town and throughout the district!' I grabbed her by the hand, threatening to break every bone in his body if she did not leave the place with me at once. He was stunned–but then, what could he do knowing that I could break horseshoes with my bare hands! She turned and, dropping her head, walked out of the door. I overtook her under the first streetlamp on the cobbled embankment, and took her arm–she did not lift her head or shake off my hand. She stopped at a bench past the second street-lamp and thrusting her face into my shoulder began to tremble and cry. I made her sit down on the bench, holding her dear, tear-wet delicate girlish hand in mine, and embracing her shoulders with my other hand. She was saying inarticulately through her sobs: 'Not true, not true, he's good ... he's unhappy, but he's kind, big-hearted and carefree...' I kept silent, for dissuading her would be senseless. I called a cabby driving past. She stopped crying, and in silence we drove to town. At the square, she said in a low voice: 'Now leave me, I'll walk, I don't want you to know where I live', and suddenly kissed my hand, jumped down from the cab, and without looking back went stumbling across the square... I never saw her again, and till this day I do not know her name or who and what she was..."

We paid the waiter, put on our coats in the cloakroom downstairs, the doctor walked with me to the corner of Arbat Street, and we stopped for a moment to say goodbye. The street was empty and quiet until it would come to life again towards midnight with people pouring out of the theatres and wanting supper in the restaurants both in town and out of town. The sky was black, the street-lamps under the young, fresh leafage in Prechistensky Boulevard shone with a clean light, and the air smelt sweetly of springtime rain which had sprinkled the streets while we were at the Prague.

"D'you know what," the doctor said with a glance about him. "I was sorry afterwards that I had, so to speak, rescued her. There had been other incidents of this kind in my life... And now I ask you, why did I meddle? What's the difference what makes a person happy? The consequences, you say? But consequences always exist just the same. After all, everything leaves cruel traces in one's soul, I mean memories which are especially cruel and tormenting if one remembers something happy... Well, goodbye then, I am very glad we met tonight..."

27 October, 1943

The Beginning

And I, gentlemen, fell in love for the first time, or, to be more correct, lost my innocence when I was twelve years old. I was going home to the country for the Christmas holidays from the town where I went to school, and it was one of those warm, grey days we often have about that time. The train ran through pinewoods deep in snow, and I was childishly happy and untroubled, delighting in the mellow winter day, the snow and the pines, dreaming of the skis awaiting me at home, and there I sat all by myself in the overheated first-class coach of the old-fashioned "mixed" kind which was sort of divided into two sections, I mean there were four red-plush couches—the plush seemed to enhance the hotness and the stuffness somehow—and four smaller matching couches along the windows on the other side with a passage between. I was there all by myself for more than an hour, and I didn't have a care in the world. But then, at the second stop from town, the door from the vestibule was pulled open, admitting a welcome whiff of the wintry air, and in came a porter carrying two suitcases in cloth covers and a plaid hold-all, followed by a very pale dark-eyed young lady in a black satin bonnet and a black astrakhan coat, behind the lady came a tall gentleman with yellow hawk eyes wearing a deerskin hat with the earflaps raised, lambswool felt hip boots, and a shiny deerskin coat. Being a well-bred boy, I naturally got up from the big couch near the door, moved to the second section and sat down on one of the small couches along the window from where I could watch the lady and gentleman. Children, you know, are as curious about new people as dogs are about strange dogs. Well, then, it was there, sitting on that couch, that I lost my innocence. When the porter had placed the luggage in the net above the couch on which I had been sitting before then, wished a happy journey to the gentleman who had thrust a ruble note into his hand and hurried out as the train began to move, the lady immediately lay down on that couch with her head on the plush bolster, while the gentleman clumsily got down the hold-all from the net with hands that were unused to any kind of work, pulled out of it a small white pillow and handed it to the lady without looking at her. She said softly: "Thank you, *mon ami,*" tucked it under her head and closed her eyes, and he, throwing his coat on to the hold-all, went to stand at the window between the small couches and lit a thick cigarette, the aromatic smoke trickling through the stuffness in the car. He stood towering there, the earflaps of his deerskin hat sticking up, and seemed to be staring intently at the pines running back, and I stared intently at him at first, hating him terribly for completely ignoring my presence, never glancing at me once as if I wasn't there at all, and because of this for everything else: for his lordly calm, his hugeness that was somehow both a prince's and a peasant's, his round hawk eyes, his carelessly untrimmed chestnut moustache and beard, and even for his thick, loose brown suit and his light and velvety felt boots that reached above his knees. But in less than a minute I forgot all about him, for suddenly I remembered the deathly but beautiful pallor which had amazed me when the lady, now lying on the couch, first entered the car. I shifted my gaze to her, and until the next station when I had to get off I saw nothing else, only her, her face and body. She sighed, found a more comfortable position by shifting her body a bit lower down, without opening her eyes unbuttoned her fur coat, to reveal a flannel dress, kicked off her warm overshoes, worn over open suede slippers, removed her satin bonnet and dropped it beside her—to my great surprise her black hair was cut short like a boy's—then undid something holding up her grey silk stockings, first on her right leg, then on her left, lifting her skirts as she did this so that I caught a glimpse of the bare flesh above the stockings and then, pulling down her dress, she fell into a doze. Her heliotrope lips with a dark fluff above them that were yet so young and feminine became slightly parted, her pale face, almost transparently white, with the eyebrows and eyelashes very black against it, became completely expressionless. A sleeping woman desired by you, a woman to whom your whole being is drawn—ah, you know what it is! And here for the first time in my life I saw and felt the magic—until then I had seen only my sleeping sister or my mother—and I stared and stared with a parched mouth at the boyishly feminine black head, at the immobile face against whose pure whiteness the thin black eyebrows and thick eyelashes stood out so beautifully, at the dark fluff above her slightly parted lips, too agonizingly tormenting in their loveliness, already appreciating and relishing all the inexplicable lure there is in the body of a woman when she is lying down, in the fulness of her hips and the slimness of her ankles, and with frightening vividness I kept seeing in my mind's eye that incomparable feminine colour of her flesh under her flannel dress which she inadvertently showed me when she was undoing her garters or something. The jolt of the train as it stopped at my station brought me to my senses, but coming out into the sweet wintry air I swayed on my feet. Behind the timber railway station building there was a sleigh, meant for a troika but with two horses harnessed into it, their bells jingling, and a raccoon greatcoat was held out for me by our old coachman who told me grumpily:

"Your mama ordered you to put this on for sure."

Obediently, I got into grandfather's old coat with a huge, already yellowing and balding collar, smelling of fur and winter freshness, sprawled low in the soft and spacious sleigh, and went rocking pleasantly along the deep and soundless snow road cut through the pinewood, with the little bells muttering hollowly, my eyes closed, still tingling from what I had just experienced, and thinking with a bitter-sweet vagueness only about that and not about the joys I used to love before and which now awaited me at home: the skis and the wolf cub, taken from the den of his mother, killed in a hunt last August, and kept in a deep hole in our garden from where, only two months afterwards, when I came home for two days for the Intercession of the Holy Virgin, he already spread such a savage and wonderful wild-beast smell.

23 October, 1943

Young Oaks

At the time, my friends, I was only twenty-two, so you see how long ago this happened, back in the days of Tsar

Nicholas,* bless his memory. That memorable winter I had just been promoted to cornet in the Guards and given a fortnight's furlough to go home to our Ryazan estate where my mother lived a lonely life after the death of my father. And soon after I arrived, I fell madly in love. One day I thought I'd have a look at my grandfather's long unlived-in estate in Petrovskoye, a small village next to ours, and after that started going there more and more often under any pretext I could find. Russian village life is dismal till this day, in winter especially, and how much more so it was all those years ago when I was young! Such was the village of Petrovskoye and the unlived-in estate there called Young Oaks because of the few oaks growing at the head of the drive, which in my day were already ancient, powerful trees. Under those oaks stood a crude old cottage, behind it were the remains of stables and barns demolished by time, beyond these stretched the snow-drifted waste of the felled park, and the ruins of the manor house with dark, gaping window holes. And it was in this cottage under the oaks that I sat for hours almost every day, talking all sorts of rot that was supposed to sound like estate business with our bailiff Lavr who lived in that cottage, cadging for his friendship quite basely, and furtively darting lovelorn glances at his silent wife Anfissa, who looked more like a Spanish lady than a plain Russian peasant woman and who was half the age of her husband, a big man with a brick-red face and a dark-red beard who could easily pass for a chieftain of a band of highwaymen. In the morning I read whatever came to hand or tinkled on the piano, singing with passionate longing: "And when my heart demanded: must I love or perish..." and after dinner I rode off to the Young Oaks in spite of the biting winds and blizzards that assailed us from the Saratov steppes without let-up. Thus passed the Christmas holidays, and the day of my departure, of which I informed Lavr and Anfissa with studied casualness, was drawing close. Lavr replied quite reasonably that the tsar's service came first, naturally, and went out of the cottage to fetch something or other. And Anfissa, who was doing some needlework, suddenly dropped her sewing in her lap, watched her

*Tsar Nicholas I (1796-1855).

husband go out with her Castillian eyes and the moment the door banged shut behind him threw me a glance full of urgent passion and whispered hotly:

"He's going to town for the night tomorrow, master, come and spend a farewell evening with me. I wouldn't let on, but I'll tell you now: it will be hard to part with you."

I was naturally smitten by such a confession and could only nod in agreement before Lavr returned.

After that, you'll easily appreciate, I could hardly wait for the next evening to come, I was in such a dither of impatience I didn't know what to do with myself, and all I could think about was that I'd give up my career, resign from the regiment, settle in the village, marry her as soon as her husband died, and so on and so forth... After all, he was already an old man and would die soon, I was thinking, ignoring the fact that Lavr was not fifty yet. The night passed at long last–I did not sleep a wink, I sat smoking my pipe or drinking rum without getting the least drunk, becoming more and more inflamed by my silly dreaming, and then the short winter day passed too, darkness gathered. A furious snowstorm was raging. How could I leave the house in that weather, what could I say to my mother? I was at an utter loss, when suddenly the simplest solution dawned upon me: to slip out on the quiet, that's all. I excused myself from supper, saying that I was not feeling well and wanted to turn in early, and as soon as my mother finished supper and retired to her room–the early winter night had already fallen–I dressed with great haste, ran down to the stables, ordered a horse to be harnessed into a light sleigh, and was off. I could not see a thing in the whirling snow but since the horse knew the road well I gave it its head and in less than half an hour I saw the oaks darkling through the white obscurity, and the light in her window. I tied the horse to one of the oaks, threw the horsecloth over it, and in a frenzy of excitement plunged through the snow to the dark porch. I groped for the door handle in the darkness, stepped into the room and there she was, all dressed up, rouged and powdered, sitting on the bench beside the table, covered with a white cloth and with food and drink set out on it, eagerly waiting for me. She seemed to be wavering and trembling in the smoky reddish light of the burning splinter, but even through this haze I could see her eyes and their wide, intense look. The splinter, stuck into the holder on the stove above a basin of water, crackled, blinded me with its spurting, dark flame, and dropped fiery sparks that hissed as they fell into the water below; on the table stood plates with nuts and mint biscuits, a decanter with home-made brandy and two glasses; and she was sitting with her back to the window plastered with snow on the outside, wearing a purple silk sarafan over a white blouse with wide sleeves, and a string of corals round her neck, her pitch-black hair that any society beauty would have been honoured to possess was smoothly dressed with a central parting, and in her ears were dangling silver earrings. When she saw me, she sprang to her feet, quickly pulled off my snow-laden hat and my fox-lined coat, and pushed me down on the bench, acting as in a frenzy, negating all my former thoughts about her proud aloofness, sat in my lap, and embraced me, pressing her hot cheeks to my face...

"Oh why did you hide your feelings," I said to her, "keeping them until we've got to part!"

"But what could I do!" she cried in despair. "I fair swooned every time you came, I saw you hankered after me, but I didn't give myself away! And how could I open my heart to you? I was never alone with you for a minute, and I could not even tell you with a glance, he's keen-eyed like an eagle, if he noticed something he'd kill me, his hand would not quaver!"

And she embraced me again, squeezed my timid hand and laid it on her knees... Through her thin sarafan I felt her body against my legs, I was already losing control when suddenly she straightened up, alert as a wild thing, sprang up and, looking at me with the eyes of a Pythia, said:

"Hear it?"

I could not hear a thing, only the snowstorm howling outside.

"Someone has driven up! I heard a horse neighing. It's him!"

She ran round the table, sat down, and trying to calm her heavy breathing said in a loud, ordinary voice as she poured out the wine with a shaking hand:

"Take a drop of our brandy, sir. It'll warm you on the way back..."

And here he walked in, his sheepskin hat and coat shaggy with snow, gave us one look and said: "Good-evening, sir." He laid out his sheepskin coat on the plank-bed deliberately, took off and shook his hat, wiped his face and beard with the skirt of his coat, and spoke unhurriedly:

"My, some weather this! I somehow got through to Bolshiye Dvory, but no, I said to myself, I'll never get to town, I'll get lost, so I drove into an inn, put my mare under the shed in the lee, gave her plenty of feed, and went straight in just in time for a plateful of good hot cabbage soup; and so there I sat all day, till nightfall. And then I said to myself–no, I'd better go home, come what may, maybe with God's help I'd get there safely, never mind town business–the way it is blowing. And so here I am, the Lord be thanked..."

She and I were sitting there stunned speechless, horribly embarrassed, realising that he had understood everything at once. She never raised her eyes. I glanced at him now and then. He did look picturesque, I must say! Big and broad-shouldered, his coat with a coloured Tatar design tightly belted with a green sash, his legs in sturdy Kazan felt boots, his red-brick face flushed from the wind, his beard glistening with melting snow, and his eyes burning with fearsome intelligence... He lit and put a new splinter in the holder, sat down at the table, picked up the decanter with his thick fingers, poured a glassful, downed it, and said without looking at me:

"How will you ever get home now is more than I can tell, sir. And yet it's time you went: you horse is drifted over with snow, standing there all hunched and bent... You won't mind if I don't come out to see you off, will you, I've had a hard day, and then I haven't seen my wife all day and there is something I want to talk with her about..."

Without a word in answer, I got to my feet, dressed and left...

Early the next morning a mounted messenger came from Petrovskoye with the news that Lavr had strangled his wife with his green sash leaving her to hang from the iron hook in the door jamb, and himself came to the village and announced:

"A terrible thing has happened, good neighbours. My wife has hanged herself—from distress of mind, I reckon. I woke at dawn and there she was hanging, her face already blue, her head drooping down. All dressed up, painted and powdered no knowing what for, and there she hangs her feet just off the floor... Come and bear witness, like good Christians."

The men looked at him and said:

"God forbid, doing herself in like that! And why is your beard all torn out in clumps, who clawed your face like that, and why is your eye bloody? Grab him and tie him up, men!"

He was flogged and sentenced to hard labour in the mines in Siberia.

30 October, 1943

Hotel Madrid

Late one evening, in the pale light of the new moon, he was walking up Tverskoy Boulevard, and she was coming from the opposite direction: she sauntered along, her hands stuffed in a small muff, and hummed something, slightly nodding her head in the smart little astrakhan hat set at a jaunty angle.

She paused when she neared him and asked:

"Would you like to keep me company?"

He looked at her: she was a smallish girl with a retroussé nose, rather high cheekbones, eyes shining in the moonlight, a sweet, timid smile, and a voice that had a pure sound in the frosty air.

"Why not? With pleasure."

"And how much will you give me?"

"A ruble for love, and a ruble pin money."

She thought it over.

"D'you live far from here? I'll come if it's not far, because after you it still won't be too late to walk some more."

"It's only a step. It's right here in Tverskaya, the Madrid rooming house."

"Oh, I know it. I've been there four or five times. One card-sharp took me there. A Jew, but an awfully kind man."

"I'm kind too."

"That's what I thought. You're nice, I liked you right away."

"Let's go then."

As they walked he kept glancing at her—what an amazingly sweet girl!—and asked:

"Why are you all by yourself?"

"I'm not by myself, the three of us always come out together—Mura, Anelia and I. We live together too. Only this is Saturday, and they've been taken by salesmen. And no one wanted me the whole evening. Men don't take me much, they like plump girls better, or else someone like Anelia. She may be skinny, but she's tall and saucy. She drinks something terrible, and can sing like a Gypsy. She and Mura hate men, they're terribly in love with each other and live like man and wife..."

"I see... I see... And what's your name? Only don't fib."

"Nina."

"I told you not to fib. Tell me the truth."

"Oh all right, I'll only tell you. It's Polia."

"You must be new at this, aren't you?"

"No, quite a long time. Since spring. But why d'you keep asking and asking? Better give me a cigarette. I guess you smoke the best, look at the posh cape and hat you're wearing!"

"I'll give you a cigarette when we get there. Smoking in the cold is bad for you."

"Oh, as you wish, only we always smoke in the cold and are none the worse for it. True, it's bad for Anelia because she's got consumption... Why d'you wear neither beard nor moustache? He didn't either..."

"Still on about that card-sharp of yours? You certainly remember him."

"That I do. He also has consumption, but he smokes terribly. Burning eyes, parched lips, sunken chest, cheeks sunken too and dark..."

"And horrible hairy wrists..."

"That's right! Why, d'you know him?"

"Now really, how could I know him?"

"And afterwards he went to Kiev. I came to see him off

at the Bryansk railway station, and he didn't know I'd be coming. The train had already started when I came. I ran after it, and just then he poked his head out of the window, he saw me, waved and shouted that he'd be back soon and would bring me some candied fruit and berries from Kiev."

"And he never came back?"

"No, I guess he was caught."

"And how did you find out that he was a card-sharp?"

"He told me himself. He had too much port, he got weepy, and told me. I'm a card-sharp, he said, it's the same as a thief, but what can I do, he said, if sleight of hand is my living... And you, are you an actor perhaps?"

"Something like that. Well, here we are."

A small lamp was burning above the reception desk just inside the front door, but there was no one there. The room keys hung on a board nailed to the wall. He took his, and she whispered worriedly:

"How can you leave your key here? Thieves will get in!"

He looked at her, and feeling jollier all the time said:

"If they rob me they'll be marched off to Siberia! What a darling little face you have!"

"You're laughing at me," she said in embarrassment. "Let's go up quickly, for Christ's sake, it's not allowed to bring in anyone so late, you know..."

"It's all right, don't worry, I'll hide you under my bed. How old are you? Eighteen?"

"You know everything, don't you? I'm in my eighteenth year."

They walked up the steep staircase, stepping on the narrow threadbare carpet, then turned down a narrow, dimly lit and very stuffy corridor, he stopped to stick his key into the key-hole and she rose on tiptoe to see the number of his room.

"Number five! And he stayed in number fifteen on the third floor..."

"If you tell me one more word about him I'll kill you."

She puckered her lips in a pleased smile and swaying her hips slightly stepped into the ante-room of his apartment, unbuttoning her coat with the small astrakhan collar.

"You forgot to put out the light when you left."

"Small matter. Where's your hankie?"

"What d'you want it for?"

"Your cheeks are rosy but your nose is chilled..."

She got the hint, quickly took her balled-up hankie out of her muff and wiped her nose. He kissed her cold cheek and patted her on the back. She took off her hat, gave her hair a toss, and standing started pulling off her overshoes. The overshoe stuck, she gave it a hard tug and, loosing her balance, clutched at his shoulder and laughed merrily.

"Ouch, I almost fell!"

He took off her overcoat, which left her in a simple black dress that smelt of cloth and her warm body, and pushed her gently towards the sofa in the room.

"Sit down and give me your foot."

"Oh no, I'll manage..."

"Sit down, I tell you."

She sat down and stretched out her right foot. He went down on the knee, placed her foot on his other knee, and she bashfully pulled down her skirt over her black stocking.

"Aren't you a one, honestly! They're really terribly tight, you see..."

"Keep quiet."

Quickly he pulled off her overshoes together with her slippers, threw back her skirt, planted a hard kiss on the bare flesh above her stocking, and rose with a red face.

"Be quick now... I can't..."

"You can't what?" she asked, standing on the rug in her small stocking feet, looking touchingly small without her heels.

"Silly little fool! I can't wait–understand?"

"Shall I undress?"

"No, dress!"

He walked away to the window and nervously lit a cigarette. Behind the double windows, encrusted with ice at the bottom, the street-lamps were glowing palely in the light of the new moon, and bells jingled merrily on the sleighs-for-two whizzing past along the Tverskaya...

"I'm already in bed," she called out a minute later.

He turned off the light, hastily pulled off his clothes and got into bed with her. And she, trembling all over, clung to him and whispered, laughing happily:

"Only for Christ's sake don't blow at my neck or I'll scream the house down, I'm ever so ticklish..."

Afterwards she slept for about an hour. Lying beside her, he gazed into the semi-darkness of the room diluted by the dim light coming from the street, thinking in hopeless bewilderment: how can it be that in the morning she'll go away somewhere? Where? To think that she shares a room with some whores, over a laundry or something, walks the streets together with them every evening as though she were going to work, in order to earn two rubles under some swine, and she's so childishly carefree for all that, simple-hearted to the point of idiocy! When she gets ready to go in the morning I believe I, too, will scream the house down...

"Polia," he said, sitting up and touching her bare shoulder.

She started up in fright.

"Oh, mercy! Forgive me, please, I didn't mean to fall asleep... I won't be a minute..."

"What are you talking about?"

"I won't be a minute, I'll dress and go..."

"Ah no, we're going to have supper. I won't let you go until morning."

"No, no! What about the police?"

"Nonsense. And my Madeira is just as good as your cardsharp port."

"Why d'you hold him against me all the time?"

Suddenly he switched on the light, it dazzled her and she thrust her face into the pillow. He pulled off the bed covers, started kissing the back of her neck and she kicked happily, shrieking:

"Ouch, you're tickling me!"

He fetched the bottle of Crimean Madeira and the paper bag with apples standing on the window-sill, then two tooth glasses from the wash-stand, and sitting down on the bed told her:

"Here, eat and drink. Or I'll kill you."

She bit deep into an apple and chewed it, washing it down with the wine and speaking:

"And what do you think? Maybe someone *will* kill me one day. Ours is that kind of job. You go you don't know where and you don't know who with, he may be drunk or crazy, he'll turn on you and either strangle or knife you... My, what a nice, warm room you have! Here I sit with never a stitch on, and I don't feel a bit cold. Is this Madeira? I love it. There's no comparing it to port, port always smells of the cork."

"Oh well, not always."

"It does smell, honestly it does, even if you pay two rubles for a bottle, it's all one."

"Here, let me fill your glass again. Let's touch glasses, drink up and kiss. Bottoms up!"

In her haste she choked on the wine, and coughing and laughing dropped her head on his chest. He lifted her head and kissed her wet, primly compressed lips.

"Will you come to the railway station to see me off?"

She gaped at him in surprise:

"You are also going away? Where to? When?"

"To Petersburg. And not very soon."

"Thank God. I'll only come to you now and no one else if you like."

"I do. Only to me. Promise?"

"I won't go with anyone else not for all the money there is."

"Mind you don't. And now, let's sleep."

"I must go some place for a sec..."

"It's right here, in the bedside table."

"I'm ashamed ... with you here to see. Turn off the light for a sec..."

"I'll turn it off for good. It's after two o'clock."

Back in bed, she lay on his arm, clung close to him again but with affectionate tenderness now, and he said:

"Tomorrow you and I will have lunch together..."

She raised her head eagerly:

"Where? I've been to the Terem once, that's behind the Arch of Triumph, and it was so cheap, it cost almost nothing and they give you such a lot for the money you simply can't eat it all."

"Well, we'll see where to go. And after lunch you must go home so your bitchy friends won't think that you'd been murdered, and I'll be busy too, but come back here at seven and we'll go and have dinner at Patrikeyev's, you'll like it there, there's an orchestrion and a balalaika band..."

"And after dinner we'll go to the Eldorado, shall we?

There's a wonderful picture showing there now, it's called 'The Fugitive Corpse'."

"Splendid. And now, sleep."

"In a minute... No, Mura is not a bitch, she's ever so unhappy. And if it wasn't for her I'd come to ruin."

"What do you mean?"

"She's my father's cousin, you see..."

"Well?"

"My father was a coupler at the freight station in Serpukhov and he got his chest crushed by buffers, and my mother died when I was only a baby, and so I was left all alone in the whole wide world and went to Mura in Moscow, but it turned out that she no longer worked as a chambermaid in a rooming house, and I got her address from the address bureau, and I came to her place with my basket in a cab, and here she was living together with this Anelia and walking the boulevard together with her in the evenings... Well, she took me in, and afterwards talked me into walking the boulevard too..."

"And you told me that if it wasn't for her you'd come to ruin?"

"But where would I go in Moscow if I had no one? Of course she made me go wrong, but she didn't mean me harm, did she? Oh well, what's the use of talking about it. Maybe, God willing, I too will find some sort of work in a rooming house, only I'll never quit my job and I won't let anyone near me, no fear, because the tips I'll get will do me fine, what with free board and lodging too. Now, if I could get a place like that here in your Madrid. I couldn't wish for anything better!"

"I'll think about it. Maybe I can get you a job like that somewhere."

"I'd kiss your feet for that..."

"Ah yes, to make the idyll perfect..."

"What did you say?"

"Nothing, I was dozing off... Sleep now."

"In a minute... I somehow got to thinking about things..."

26 April, 1944

The Second Coffee Pot

She was his model, his mistress and his housekeeper living with him in his studio in Znamenka—yellow-haired, rather short but nicely built, quite young still, sweet-faced and affectionate. In the mornings now he painted her as the "Bather": she stands on a small platform, as though beside a forest stream and is afraid to go into the water from where pop-eyed frogs are ogling her completely naked well-developed peasant's body, her golden hair down below covered with a hand. After working for an hour or so, he drew away from his easel, squinted at the canvas from various angles and absently said:

"We stop at this station. Heat up the second pot of coffee."

She sighed with relief and, padding in her bare feet over the floor mats, ran to the corner of the studio and lit the gas-cooker. He stood scraping something from the canvas with a thin knife, the gas-cooker made a hissing noise, spreading a sour smell of its green burners and the fragrant smell of coffee, and she burst into carefree song in a loud, ringing voice:

On the shoulder of a giant cliff
Slept a little golden cloud...

Turning her head to the artist she told him happily:

"Yartsev, a painter, taught me this song. Did you know him?"

"Slightly. A tall, lean man?"

"The very one."

"A gifted chap he was, but a proper blockhead too. He's dead, isn't he?"

"Dead he is, drank himself to death. No, he was good and kind. I lived with him for a year like I'm living with you. It's he who ravished me too, and already at the second sitting. He sprang away suddenly from his easel, flung down his palette and brushes and knocked me off my feet on to the carpet. I was so scared I couldn't even scream. I clawed at his chest, at his coat, but there was no stopping him! His eyes were crazy, laughing sort of..."

"Yes, I know, you already told me. Good girl. And still you loved him?"

"Naturally I loved him. Terribly afeared of him I was. The things he did to me, when he was drunk, God forbid! I didn't make a sound and he'd yell: 'Quiet, you!' "

"Nice man!"

"Drunk he'd be. Yelling to bring down the roof: 'Quiet, you!' when I was quiet as can be anyway. And then he'd start singing at the top of his voice: 'To the shoulder of a giant cliff clung a little golden cloud...' and change the words at once to: 'clung a bitchy golden cloud,' meaning me, that is. You could die laughing. And next thing he'd stamp his boot and yell: 'Quiet, you!' "

"Nice man! But wait a minute, I've forgotten, wasn't it your uncle or someone who brought you to Moscow?"

"My uncle it was. I was in my sixteenth year when both my father and mother died, and so he brought me to Moscow. He brought me to my other uncle, who owned a pub for cabmen. I was dishwasher and laundress there, and then my auntie decided to sell me to a brothel. And she would have, too, but God saved me. Once, in the early hours, Chaliapine and Korovin came there from the Strelnya restaurant to clear their heads with some hot tea, and when they saw me together with Rodka, our waiter, heaving the huge, boiling samovar on to the counter, they started shouting and roaring with laughter: 'Good morning, Katia darling! We want you and not this son of a gun to serve us!' How did they ever guess that my mane was Katia! Uncle woke up, he came out yawning and scowling—she can't serve you, he said, that's not her job. And Chaliapine roared at him: 'I'll put you in irons, you'll rot in Siberia if you don't obey my orders!' Here my uncle got good and scared and I, too, was scared to death, and hung back, but my uncle hissed at me: 'Go and serve them or I'll skin you alive, they are the most famous people in Moscow!' So I went to them, Korovin looked me all over, gave me ten rubles and told me to come to his place the next day, he wanted to paint me, you see, and he gave me his address. So I came to his place, but he had already changed his mind and sent me to Doctor Goloushev, a bosom pal of all the artists he was, he worked at the police certifying the drunks and the dead, and also painted a bit. Well, he put me up for hire, he wouldn't let me go back to the pub, and so there I was in just the clothes I stood up in."

"What d'you mean, he put you up for hire?"

"To painters. At first I posed fully dressed, a yellow kerchief on my head, and all for lady painters, to Kuvshinnikova who was Chekhov's sister you know, but truth to tell she was no good at all in our business, and amateur she was, and then Malyavin himself took me on. He made me sit back on my heels, stark naked, with my back to him, holding a shift over my head as if I was putting it on, and painted me like that. My back and buttocks came out fine, powerful molding it was, only he spoilt the picture with the heels and soles of my feet, turning them in in quite a nasty way..."

"Alright, quict you! The second bell has gone. Bring the coffee."

"Oh Lordie, talking my head off like that! Here it is, here it is..."

30 April, 1944

A Cold Autumn Evening

In June that year he was staying with us in the country—he was always regarded as almost one of the family, for his late father had been a close friend and neighbour of my father. On June 28th Francis Ferdinand was assassinated at Sarajevo. The next morning, after the newspapers had been delivered to the house, my father came into the dining-room where he, mother and I were still sitting at the breakfast table, and holding the Moscow evening paper in his hand, said:

"Well, dear friends, it's war! The Austrian Crown Prince has been assassinated at Sarajevo. It means war."

On St. Peter's day, July 12th, which was my father's nameday, we had a great many guests, and at dinner our engagement was announced. But on August 1st Germany declared war on Russia.

In September he came for just one day to say goodbye

before going to the front (everyone believed that the war would soon be over, and our wedding was to take place in early spring). It was our farewell evening. After supper a steaming samovar was brought in as usual, and my father, looking at the misted window panes, said:

"What an amazingly early and cold autumn!"

That evening we all sat very quietly, only now and again exchanging a few random remarks, comporting ourselves with exaggerated nonchalance to hide our secret thoughts and feelings. Father's remark about the autumn had also been spoken with shammed simplicity. I went to the french window and wiped the misted glass with my handkerchief: clean, icy stars shone with a brilliant, sharp light in the black sky above the garden. Sitting back in his chair, my father was smoking and absently looking at the hot lamp hanging low over the table, while my mother, wearing spectacles, was busily stitching a small silk sweet-bag under the lamp—we knew what it was for—and it was both touching and chilling.

"D'you still insist on leaving early in the morning, and not after lunch?" my father asked him.

"With your permission, yes," he replied. "It's very sad, but I haven't quite arranged everything at home."

My father sighed shallowly.

"Oh well, as you wish, my dear. Only in that case Mother and I will turn in because we simply must see you off tomorrow morning."

Mother stood up and made the sign of the cross over her future son-in-law, who then kissed her hand and after that my father's. The two of us, left alone, stayed a bit longer in the dining-room—I started playing patience and he paced the room silently.

"Would you like to come for a walk?" he asked.

My heart was growing heavier and heavier, and I answered indifferently:

"Very well."

As we were putting on our coats in the hall, he continued to think some thought of his own and with a dear little smile remembered these lines of Fet's:

Oh, what a very cold autumn!
Do put on your shawl and pelisse...

25—904

"I've no pelisse," I said. "How does it go?"
"I don't remember. Something like this:

Look, there's a fire burning,
Those tall darkling pines amidst!

"What fire?"
"The rising moon, obviously. There's a peculiar charm in this poem—autumn in the country. 'Do put on your shawl and pelisse...' The days of our grandfathers and grandmothers... O Lord, O Lord!"
"What is it?"
"Nothing, my dear. It's sad, you know. Sad and good. I love you very, very much..."
With our coats on, we walked across the dining-room to the balcony, and down into the garden. At first it was so dark that I had to clutch at his sleeve. And then black branches, sprinkled with minerally sparkling stars became etched against the paling sky. He stopped, and turning to the house said:
"Look at the lighted windows, it's quite a special, autumnal glow. If I live, I'll always remember this night..."
I looked at him and he took me in his arms. I pushed my shawl back from my face and tilted my head a little for his kiss. He kissed me, and looked into my face.
"How your eyes shine!" he said. "Not cold? The air is quite wintry. If I'm killed, you won't forget me at once, will you?"
And I thought: What if he's really killed? And will I really forget him after some time—after all, everything becomes forgotten in the end? And horrified by this thought, I answered urgently:
"Don't talk like that! I shan't survive your death!"
He did not speak at once, and then said slowly:
"Oh well, if I am killed, I'll wait for you there. And you must live a little longer, rejoice in life on earth, and then come to me..."
I wept heartbrokenly...
In the morning he left. My mother hung the little bag she had been stitching the night before round his neck—sewn into it was the small golden icon which her father and grandfather had worn to war—and we all made the sign

of the cross over him with something like nervous despair. We watched him out of sight standing on the porch in that state of stupefaction which always comes when someone dear is seen off for long, and all we were aware of was the amazing incompatibility between us and the radiance of the sunny morning and the rime sparkling on the grass. At last, we went back into the house that seemed deserted now. I walked about the rooms, my hands behind my back, not knowing what to do with myself—to sob my heart out or sing at the top of my voice...

He was killed—what a strange word!—a month later in Galicia. A whole thirty years have passed since then. I have gone through so much, so much, in those years which seem so very long when you think carefully about them, and go over in your memory all that was so magical, inexplicable, and incomprehensible to either the mind or the heart and that is called the past.

In the spring of 1918, when both my father and mother had died, I lived in Moscow, in a basement room of a Smolensk market fishwife, who was always taunting me: "How's trade, your ladyship?" I also peddled things, like many others at the time I sold whatever I still had left to soldiers in fur Cossack hats and unbuttoned greatcoats—a ring, my baptismal cross, a moth-eaten fur collar—and it was there, peddling my things on the corner of Arbat Street and the market, that I met a man with a rare, beautiful soul, an elderly retired officer, whom I married soon afterwards and with whom, in April, I left Moscow for Yekaterinodar. I went there with him and his nephew, a boy of seventeen who had also been trying to make his way to the White Volunteer army for some time. I was dressed as a village woman with bast sandals on my feet, and my husband had let his beard grow—black with streaks of white—and wore an old Cossack coat. We reached the Don, and lived for more than two years in Kuban. On a day in winter, in hurricane weather, we boarded a ship in Novorossiisk, together with a vast crowd of other refugees, and sailed for Turkey, and on the way there my husband died of typhus. I had no one in the whole wide world now, only my husband's nephew, his very young wife, and their seven-months-old baby daughter. Before long, however, the nephew and his wife went back to the Crimea, to join Wrangel's army, and left the baby with me. They were never heard of again. And I went on living in Constantinople for a long time after that, earning our daily bread for the child and myself with back-breaking toil. Afterwards, like many other emigrants, we trailed through—Bulgaria, Serbia, Czechia, Belgium, and finally came to Paris and Nice...

The girl has long been a grownup woman now, she chose to remain in Paris and has become quite a Frenchwoman, very pretty and completely indifferent to me. She works in a chocolate shop near the Place de la Madeleine, where with her well-kept hands, the nails glittering with silver enamel, she wraps the boxes of chocolate in satin paper and ties gold string round them. And I am still living in Nice, always from hand to mouth... I came to Nice for the first time in 1912, and could I have thought in those happy days what this town was going to be for me!

And so I have outlived him, even though I once said recklessly that I would not survive his death. But, remembering everything I have lived through since then, I always ask myself: what has there really been in my life? And I answer myself: only that cold autumn evening. Has it really been? And that is all that there has been in my life—the rest was dispensable and unreal. And I believe, I passionately believe that he is waiting for me somewhere, as loving and young as on that cold autumn evening. "Live a little longer, rejoice in life on earth, and then come to me." I have lived enough, I have rejoiced in life on earth, and soon I'll come.

3 May, 1944

S/S Saratov

In the dusk, a brief May-time shower drummed outside the window and passed. The pock-marked orderly who had been drinking tea in the kitchen in the light of a tin oil-lamp, glanced at the clock, ticking on the wall, rose to his feet and, stepping clumsily in his new boots so that they should not squeak, went to the dark study and, approaching the divan, said:

"It's after nine, Your Honour."

He woke up with a start:

"What? After nine? Can't be..."

Both his windows were open into the street, a quiet street hemmed in by gardens, and the fresh smell of springtime dampness and poplars came pouring into the room. With that peculiarly acute sense of smell that comes after a good, wholesome sleep, he became aware of these scents at once and quickly swinging his legs down from the divan, ordered his man:

"Light the lamp and fetch a cabby quick. Find one who has a fast horse..."

He went to wash and change, poured cold water over his head, touched his short curly hair with eau de cologne and combed it, and then took another look at himself in the mirror: his face was fresh and his eyes were bright. From one o'clock until six he had been lunching with a large party of officers; when he returned home he fell instantly asleep, as one does after several hours of drinking, smoking, chatting and laughing, and he felt fine now. In the hall, his orderly handed him his sabre, cap and light summer overcoat, and flung wide the front door. He leapt nimbly into the cab and shouted a bit hoarsely:

"Make it quick! I'll tip you a ruble!"

The clear light of the street-lamps flickered through the thick oily leafage of the trees, the smell of the wet poplars was fresh and spicy, and the horse flew on, cutting red sparks with its shoes. Everything was splendid—the leafage, the street-lamps, the foretaste of the rendezvous, and the flavour of his cigarette which he had managed to light in the breeze. And all this became fused into one happy feeling—a readiness for anything. The effect of the vodka, the benedictine, and the Turkish coffee, perhaps? Rubbish, it was simply spring and everything was wonderful...

The door was opened by a small and very depraved-looking maid on high wobbly heels. He quickly took off his overcoat, unhitched his sabre, threw his cap down on the hall table, fluffed up his hair a little, and, with his spurs clanging, walked into the small room, cramped from an excess of boudoir furniture. She came in the same instant through another door, also wobbling on the high heels of her backless slippers worn on bare feet—a long, undulating figure in a tight-fitting gown patterned like a grey snake, with long loose sleeves slit to the shoulder. Her somewhat slanted eyes were also long. In her pale, long hand she had a smoking cigarette in a long amber holder.

As he kissed her left hand, clicking his heels, he said:

"Pray forgive me, I was detained through no fault of mine..."

From her tall height she looked down at the wet sheen of his short curly hair, at his bright eyes, and caught his wine-laden breath.

"The same old story..."

She sat down on a silk pouffe, holding her cigarette high in her right hand, cupping the right elbow in her left hand, and crossed her legs, revealing her thigh in the side slit of her gown. He sat down facing her on a small silk sofa and, pulling his cigarette case out of his trouser pocket, said:

"Now this is what happened, you see..."

"I see, I see..."

He lit his cigarette smartly, waved the match to put it out and threw it into the ashtray on the little Oriental table beside the pouffe, settling down more comfortably on the sofa and looking with his usual immodest admiration at her bare knee showing in the slit of the gown.

"Oh well, if you don't want to listen, don't... What's the programme for tonight? Shall we go to the Merchants' Garden? They have a 'Japanese Night' or something on tonight, you know all those pretty little lanterns, geishas on the stage, 'for my beauty I received first prize', and all that..."

She shook her head.

"No programmes. I'm staying at home tonight."

"As you like. That's not a bad idea either."

She let her gaze wander about the room.

"My dear, this is our last rendezvous."

"What do you mean, our last?" he asked in smiling astonishment.

"Just that."

His eyes danced all the more merrily:

"I didn't quite get it, but it sounds amusing."

"I didn't mean it to sound amusing."

"Splendid. But just the same I'm curious to know what this is all about? What's bitten you, as my sergeant says?"

"I'm little interested in what sergeants say. And, truth

to tell, I don't quite understand what you're so happy about."

"I'm always happy when I see you."

"That's very nice, but *malapropos* this time."

"But damn it all, I still don't understand anything! Has something happened?"

"It has, and I ought to have told you about it long ago. I'm going back to him. Our breakup was a mistake."

"Oh my sainted aunt! Are you serious?"

"Perfectly serious. I was criminally guilty, but he is willing to forgive and forget."

"My, how very, very generous of him!"

"Stop clowning. I saw him two months ago, during Lent..."

"You mean clandestinely, while continuing to..."

"To what? Oh, I see, but it doesn't matter. I saw him, clandestinely of course, because I did not want to cause you any suffering, and it was then I realized that I had never stopped loving him."

He narrowed his eyes,

"You mean his money?"

"He's no richer than you. And what's your money to me! If I wanted I'd..."

"Forgive me, but only cocottes talk like that."

"And what am I if not a cocotte? Am I not kept by you?"

"When there's love money doesn't mean anything," he muttered with an officer's fastidiousness.

"But I do love him!"

"And I was only your temporary plaything, something to amuse yourself with when you were bored, or one of the better paying bidders?"

"You know very well that you were not an amusement and not a plaything. Yes, of course, I am a cocotte, but throwing it in my face is foul just the same."

"Easy, madam, easy! Choose your expressions well, as the French say."

"And I'd advise you to do the same. In short..."

He stood up, feeling a fresh upsurge of that readiness for anything with which he had sped to this rendezvous, walked up and down the room, collecting his thoughts and still unable to believe the absurdity and unexpectedness which had suddenly smashed all his happy plans for this evening, kicked out of the way the yellow-haired doll in a red sarafan lying on the carpet, sat down again on the small divan and, looking her straight in the face, asked:

"I ask you once again: are you not joking?"

Closing her eyes she waved a negation with her long-dead cigarette.

He thought over her answer, lit another cigarette, and said, weightily dropping the words:

"And do you really imagine that I'll just simply give him these hands and legs of yours, and that he's going to kiss this knee here which only yesterday had been mine to kiss?"

She raised her eyebrows.

"After all, I'm not a thing, my dear, which can be given or not given. And what right have you anyway..."

Hastily he put his cigarette down in the ashtray, and bending forward took his small, slippery and hefty Browning out of his back pocket, and balanced it in his palm.

"Here is my right."

She glanced at it obliquely and said with a bored smile:

"I'm not keen on melodrama." Raising her voice, she called the maid dispassionately: "Sonia, please give Pavel Sergeyevich his overcoat."

"What's that?" he asked, aghast.

"Nothing. You're drunk. Go away."

"Is that your last word?"

"Yes."

She stood up and straightened the side slit on her gown. He stepped close to her with elated resolve.

"Mind that it isn't really your last word!"

"Drunken clown!" she said with distaste, and fixing her coiffure at the back of her head with her long fingers, started from the room. He gripped her so hard by her bared shoulder, that she bent backwards, swiftly turned round and with eyes more slanted than ever took a swing at him. And he, ducking agilely and with a virulent grimace, fired.

In December that same year the S/S *Saratov* was sailing along the Indian Ocean headed for Vladivostok. On the deck, under the tent stretched above, in the motionless sultry air, the hot half-light, and sparkling reflections from the water, sat and lay the convicts, stripped down to their white duck pants, half of their heads shaven, and chains round the ankles of their bare feet. His body, like the others', was also lean, brown from sunburn and bared to the waist. Like the others, he also had short-cropped hair only on one half of his head, while the other half was shaved. His hollow cheeks bristled with reddish-black stiff hairs, and his eyes glittered feverishly... Leaning on the railing, he peered intently at the densely blue sea speeding in humps far down below along the tall side of the ship, and from time to time spat into it.

16 May, 1944

The Raven

My father looked like a raven. It had occurred to me when I was a child: one day I saw a picture in the *Niva* showing a rock with Napoleon standing on it, pot-bellied, in buckskins and short black boots, and suddenly I laughed joyfully as I recalled a picture in Bogdanov's *Travels in the Arctic* because Napoleon looked just like a penguin, and then the sad thought struck me: "And Papa is like a raven."

My father held a very prominent post in our town, which was a gubernia centre, and this had an even more ruinous effect on his character. I do not suppose that even in that society of civil servants to which he belonged, there was anyone more overbearing, gloomy, taciturn and coldly cruel in his ponderous words and actions than he. He was really like a raven—short, thickset, slightly round-shouldered, with coarse black hair and a long big-nosed face, clean-shaven and dark-skinned—and he looked particularly like one when, in his black dress-coat, he attended one of the charity balls sponsored by the Governor's wife and stood hunched and immobile close to a booth, decorated to look like a Russian *izba*, moving his large raven's head, staring obliquely with his bright raven's eyes at the dancing couples, at the people who came up to the booth, and at the lady in the booth who, with a charming smile, served the cheap yellow champagne in shallow glasses with her large hand, sparkling with diamonds. She was a tall woman, wearing a boyar head-dress and a gold brocade gown, and her nose was so pink and white with powder that it looked like a false one.

Father had been a widower for a good many years, he only had us two children—my eight-year-old sister Lilya and myself—and the huge, highly polished rooms of our apartment gleamed with cold, unlived-in splendour. The apartment was on the first floor of one of the buildings belonging to the Department where my father was employed, and its windows faced the poplar-lined avenue between the cathedral and the main street. Fortunately, I spent most of the year in Moscow, where I was a boarder at the Katkov Lycée, and I only came home for Christmas and the summer holidays. But something quite unforeseen awaited me on my arrival home for the summer when I had finished school.

When I arrived home from Moscow I was simply astounded: it seemed as though the sun had suddenly come to shine in our apartment which had been so funereal before—it was aglow with the sunny presence of a lively young girl, who had just been taken on to replace my sister's old nurse, a tall, flat old woman who looked like a mediaeval wooden statue of a saint. Being a poor girl, a daughter of one of Father's subordinates, she was exceedingly happy to have found such a good position immediately upon leaving school, and that now I had arrived she would have someone of her own age in the house. But goodness, how timorous she was, how shy in my father's presence at our stiff dinners as she anxiously watched our black-eyed Lilya, who was taciturn like Father, but this very taciturnity of hers was brusque, as was her every movement, for she sat twisting and turning her black head about with an air of defiance, as if she was for ever on the lookout for something. Father was quite unrecognizable at dinner now: he no longer threw sullen looks at old Gury, serving at table in white knitted gloves; he talked a little now and then—dragging out the words, it's true, but it was talking anyway—addressing no one but her, of course, calling her "dear Elena Nikolayevna" most ceremoniously—and he even attempted to joke and smile. And this so embarrassed her that she merely smiled miserably in reply and blushed, her delicate thin face crimsoning in spots—the face of a slight, fair-haired girl in a soft white blouse, dark under the arms with hot young sweat, with small breasts, barely outlined. At dinner she never dared to raise her eyes to mine, for then I was even more frightening to her than Father. But the harder she tried to avoid looking at me, the colder became the oblique looks Father darted at me: I felt we both realized that her painful efforts to ignore me and listen instead to Father or attend to the ill-natured, restless though silent Lilya, concealed quite another fear—tremulous fear for the happiness we both felt in being together. I remember Father always had his evening tea served to him in a large gold-rimmed cup on his desk in the study, but now he had it with us in the dining-room, and she poured it out for us, presiding at the samovar—Lilya would already be in bed by then. He would come out of his study dressed in a long, loose smoking-jacket, lined with red, settle down in his armchair and pass his cup to her. She would fill it to the brim, the way he liked it, and hand it to him with shaking hand, then she poured mine and hers and, dropping her eyes, took up her sewing, while he talked, taking his time, of things that were very strange indeed:

"Women with fair hair, dear Elena Nikolayevna, look their best in either black or crimson... Now, for instance, a black satin gown with a high pointed collar like Mary Stuart's, sewn with small brilliants, would become your face very well ... or a mediaeval gown of crimson velvet with a small *décolleté* and a little cross of rubies worn with it... A fur-lined wrap of blue Lyons velvet and a Venetian beret would suit you too... All this is daydreaming, of course," he would say, smiling. "We only pay your father 75 rubles a month, and he has five children besides you to support, all of them young—therefore, it's more than likely that you'll have to live in poverty all your life. But then I always say—what's the harm in daydreaming? It cheers you up, it gives you strength and hope. And then again, it does happen sometimes that a dream suddenly comes true, doesn't it? Very rarely, of course, very rarely indeed, but it does. Take that cook at the Kursk railway station, for instance, the one who drew a two hundred thousand lottery ticket—an ordinary cook, mind you!"

She tried to pretend she was taking all this for kindly banter; she forced herself to look up at him and smile, while I sat playing patience as if I wasn't listening to any of it. As for Father, he went even farther on one occasion. He suddenly said, indicating me with a nod:

"Now this young man here probably has his dreams too. He's thinking his dear papa will die one day and then he'll have more gold than he can count. And, indeed, he won't be able to count it, for there will be nothing for him to count! It goes without saying that his papa does have certain holdings—that little estate, for instance, of a thousand acres of black soil in Samara Gubernia—but I very much doubt that the son will inherit it, he's not too affectionate with his papa, and then, as far as I can judge, he'll develop into a first-class wastrel..."

This last conversation took place on the eve of St. Peter's Day, a very memorable day for me. Father started off early the following morning to attend service at the cathedral first and afterwards to lunch with the Governor whose birthday it was that day. But Father never had lunch at home except on Sundays anyway, and so the three of us were alone as usual. Towards the end of the meal, when Lilya was given some cherry jelly instead of her favourite sugar cakes, she started screaming at Gury at the top of her voice, banged her fists on the table, flung her plate on the floor, her head began to jerk and shake and angry sobs choked her. We carried her to her room with some difficulty because she kept biting our hands and kicking, but we entreated her to calm down, promising her we would punish the cook severely for this, and at last we managed to placate her and lull her to sleep.

And even this alone—our hands touching as we carried Lilya to her room—was like a tremulous caress, filling us with untold tenderness for one another. Rain was falling heavily outside, lightning pierced the darkening rooms again and again, and the window-panes rattled with the thunder claps.

"It's the thunderstorm that has affected her so," she said in a happy whisper when we came out into the passage, and suddenly she stopped, listening.

"Oh, there's a fire somewhere!" she said.

We ran to the dining-room, threw open the window and saw the fire brigade rushing past our house, rumbling down the avenue. Rain was pouring down swiftly on the poplars—

the thunderstorm was over, just as though the rain had put it out—and we heard the firemen's bugle sounding a soft and impishly playful warning amid the clamour of the rushing long-shafted carts loaded with hoses and ladders, with brass-helmeted firemen standing up in them, amid the jingling of the bells fixed on the bows above the manes of the black draught horses; and the metallic clatter as the horses drew the carts over the cobble-stones at a gallop. Then came the very, very rapid peals of the alarm bell, clanging in the belfry of St. John the Warrior's. We stood close to each other at the window, breathing in the fresh smell of water and the rain-beaten street dust, and we seemed to be straining, with all our senses stirred to a pitch of excitement, only to see and to hear. And then the last of the carts, with a huge red tank on it, rumbled past, my heart beat faster, the skin felt tight on my forehead—I took her hand as it hung limply at her side, I gazed at her profile beseechingly, and she blanched, parted her lips, and took a deep breath that raised her bosom. There were tears and a plea in the eyes she turned to me. I caught her shoulder with my hand and for the first time in my life tasted the exquisite coolness of a girl's lips...

After this not a day, not a single hour passed without our meeting, accidentally as it were, either in the drawing-room or in the dining-hall, or in the passage and even in Father's study—he never came back until late. They were short meetings with desperately long, insatiable kisses, already unbearable in their inconclusiveness. And Father, sensing something, again stopped coming to the dining-room for evening tea with us, and grew morose and taciturn once more. But we no longer took any notice of him, and her manner at the dinner-table became more serene and poised.

At the beginning of July, Lilya fell ill from eating too many raspberries, and was in bed recuperating slowly, spending all her days drawing pictures with coloured crayons of some fabulous cities on large sheets of paper tacked on a board, and therefore Elena had no choice but stay beside Lilya's bed, embroidering a Ukrainian blouse for herself—she could not possibly leave her post because Lilya demanded constant attention. And I, alone in the empty, silent house, was tormented with a ceaseless desire to see her, kiss her and hold her in a close embrace. I would go and sit in my father's study trying to read, picking books at random from his bookcases. And that is what I was doing on that particular day too. It was already close on evening. Suddenly I heard the sound of her light, swift footsteps. I threw down my book and jumped up.

"Has she fallen asleep?"

She made a hopeless gesture.

"Oh no! You don't know her–she doesn't care if she stays awake two nights running, like all mad people! She made me come here to hunt for some yellow and orange pencils on her father's desk..."

And, bursting into tears, she came up to me and dropped her head on my breast:

"Oh God, when will it all end? Tell him at last, tell him that you love me, that nothing in the world can keep us apart!"

Raising her face, wet with tears, she threw her arms about me impetuously and clung to me in a breathless kiss. I pressed her whole body to mine, I drew her towards the sofa–could I remember or think of anything at a moment like that? But then I heard someone clearing his throat in the doorway: I looked over her shoulder and saw Father standing there, watching us. Then he turned about and, hunching his shoulders, walked away.

We none of us appeared at dinner that night. Later, Gury knocked on my door and said: "Your father requests you to come to his room." I went into the study. He was sitting in the armchair facing his desk and, without turning round, he began to speak:

"Tomorrow, you will leave for my Samara estate and stay there for the rest of the summer. In the autumn you are to go to Moscow or Petersburg and look for a post. If you dare disobey me I shall disinherit you for ever. What's more, I shall ask the Governor to have you banished into the country immediately and taken there under escort. Now go, and don't let me see you again. Your train fare and a certain amount of pocket money will be delivered to you by my man in the morning. I shall write to my estate office in due course to give you a sum of money for your first days in the capitals. You need entertain no hopes of seeing her before you leave. That is all. Go."

That same night I left for the province of Yaroslavl and

remained there all the summer, staying with one of my school friends. With the help of his father I secured a post that autumn at the Ministry of Foreign Affairs in Petersburg, and wrote to my father telling him that I not only renounced my rights to his inheritance for ever, but also refused any assistance from him. The same winter I learnt that he had retired and had also moved to Petersburg "with his charming young wife", I was told. And one night, as I walked into the stalls of the Mariinsky Theatre, a few minutes before the curtain went up, I suddenly saw them. They were in a box close to the stage, sitting in the front seats with her mother-of-pearl opera-glasses lying on the barrier before her. Looking like a raven in his dress-coat, hunched and squinting with one eye, he sat reading his programme intently. And she, gracefully poised, her fair hair piled up on top of her head, looked eagerly about her at the warm, brilliantly lighted, softly murmuring house below, at the evening gowns, dress-coats and uniforms of the people in the boxes. A little cross of rubies glowed darkly on her breast, her slender but already rounded arms were bare, and something like a peplum of crimson velvet was caught with an agraffe of rubies on her left shoulder...

May 18, 1944

Camargue

She boarded the train at a small station between Marseilles and Arles, walked down the car with her whole Gypsy-Spanish body moving sinuously, sat down at the window on a single seat and, as though seeing no one around, started shelling and eating roasted pistachios, lifting the hem of her black skirt and dipping for more nuts into the pocket of her white, grimy underskirt. This car, filled with common folk, was not divided up into compartments but simply had benches set back to back, and many of the passengers who sat facing her kept glancing at her intently.

Her lips, moving above her white teeth as she chewed, were dove-coloured, and the bluish fluff on her upper lip deepened in hue above the corners of her mouth. Her fine, swarthy face, lit up by her sparkling teeth, was antiquely heathenish. Her elongated, golden-brown eyes, hooded by dark brown lids, were turned in upon herself with a dull, primordial languor. Her pitch-black hair, that seemed to be made of brittle silk, was parted in the centre and fell in curls on her low forehead; long silver earrings glittered against her smooth dark neck. A faded blue shawl, draped over her sloping shoulders, was beautifully knotted on her breast. Her hands, thin and dry, Hindu hands with mummy-like fingers and lighter nails, kept shelling the nuts with the swiftness and nimbleness of a monkey. When she had eaten all the nuts she had, she brushed the shells off her skirt, closed her eyes, crossed her legs and leaned back on the bench. Her hip bones stood out in hard yet rounded knobs under her gathered black skirt which emphasized that special womanly grace of her lissome waist. On her thin, bare, sunburnt feet she wore black sandals woven from rags and secured with criss-crossed red and blue ribbons.

She left at Arles.

"C'est une camarguaise," said the man sitting next to me, a Provencal, strong as an ox, with swarthy, ruddy cheeks covered with a network of capillaries. He said this very sadly, unnerved by her beauty as he followed her with his eyes.

23 May, 1944

A Hundred Rupees

I saw her one morning in the courtyard of the hotel where I was staying—an ancient Dutch house standing in a cocoanut grove on the shore of the ocean. And after that I saw her there every morning. She reclined in a reed deck chair in the thin and hot shadow cast by the house, within arm's reach of the veranda. The Malayan servant, a tall, yellow-skinned man with too-narrow eyes, dressed in a white duck jacket and trousers, brought her a cup of golden tea on a tray, set it down on the small table beside her deck chair, said something to her deferentially without moving his dry, pinched lips, then bowed and went back to the house, his bare feet rustling on the gravel. And there she reclined in her deck chair, slowly fanning herself with a straw fan, and fluttering her extraordinary black velvet eyelashes... What breed of earthly creatures did she belong to?

Her small, tropically strong body could be seen in its partial coffee-coloured nudity—neck, shoulders, arms and legs from the knees down, while her torso and hips had some bright green stuff wound round them. The red-varnished toe-nails of her small feet peeped between the red straps of her wooden-soled yellow sandals. Her coarse tar-black hair, dressed in a tall coiffure, clashed strangely with the sweetness of her childish face. Golden rings swung gently from the lobes of her tiny ears. Her black eyelashes were unbelievably long and magnificent, like those gorgeous butterflies that hover so magically over exotic Indian flowers... Beauty, intelligence, stupidity—all these words were as ill-suited to her as any other human quality. She may have come from another planet. The only word that suited her was muteness. And there she reclined in her deck chair mutely, slowly fanning herself and radiating a steady glow from her black eyes framed in butterfly eyelashes...

One morning, when the rickshaw I usually employed to take me to town came at a run into the courtyard, the Malay servant met me on the veranda steps and, with a bow, said quietly in English:

"A hundred rupees, sir."

24 May, 1944

Revenge

In the pension in Cannes, where I came at the end of August to bathe in the sea and paint from nature, this strange woman drank her coffee in the morning and ate her dinner at a small table to herself with a look that was invariably glum and preoccupied as though she did not see anyone or anything about her, and after breakfast she always disappeared until evening. I had already been living there for about a week but I still watched her curiously, intrigued by this woman with thick black hair, plaited into a heavy braid pinned round her head, a strong body in a red cotton dress patterned with black flowers, a handsome, somewhat coarse face—and that sombre look... We were served by an Alsace girl, she was only fifteen or so but she had big breasts and wide hips, a very plump girl, her plumpness amazingly young and fresh, singularly stupid and sweet, who blushed with fright and broke into a smile at every word addressed to her. Well then, coming across her in the corridor one day I asked:

"Dittes, Odette, qui est cette dame?"

With a readiness to flush with fright or smile, she stared at me with her blue eyes.

"Quelle dame, monsieur?"

"Mais la dame brune, là-bas."

"Quelle table, monsieur?"

"Numéro dix."

"C'est une russe, monsieur."

"Et puis?"

"Je n'en sais rien, monsieur."

"Est-elle chez vous depuis longtemps?"

"Depuis trois semaines, monsieur."

"Toujours seule?"

"Non, monsieur. Il y avait un monsieur."

"Jeune, sportif?"

"Non, monsieur... Très pensif, nerveux..."

"Et il a disparu un jour?"

*"Mais oui, monsieur..."**

* "Tell me, Odette, who is that lady?"
"Which lady, sir?"
"That brunette, over there."
"At which table, sir?"
"Ten."
"That's a Russian lady, sir."
"What else?"
"I don't know anything else, sir."
"Has she been here long?"
"Three weeks, sir."
"Always alone?"
"No sir. There was a gentleman."
"Young, athletic?"
"No sir... Very pensive, nervous."
"And one day he disappeared?"
"Yes, sir..."

"Well, well," I thought. "It's a bit clearer now. But where does she go every morning? Is she still looking for him?"

The next morning, breakfast over, from the open window of my room I heard crunching footsteps on the pebbles in the pension's flower garden below and, looking out, saw her, hatless as usual and with a sunshade the colour of her dress, going somewhere in a hurry, striding swiftly in her red sandals. I grabbed my walking stick and straw hat, and hastened after her. From our side street she turned down Boulevard Carneau—I did the same, hoping that in her perpetual preoccupation she would not feel that she was being followed and turn round. And indeed she did not turn round once all the way to the railway station. Nor did she turn round as she entered the compartment of a third-class coach. The train was going to Toulon, I bought a ticket to St. Raphael just in case, and took a seat in the next compartment. Obviously she was not going far, but where? I poked out my head to see in Napoule and in Theoulle... Finally, poking my head out in Fréjus where the train stopped for one minute, I saw her already on her way out of the station. I jumped out of the train and again followed her, keeping a safe distance. It was a long walk—along the highway which followed the curves of the precipitous coast above the sea, up steep stony paths through a thin pine forest which made a short cut to the little bays which bit into this rocky, wooded and desolate shore at the foot of the mountains. It was almost noon, the air was hot, motionless and thick with the smell of sun-drenched pine needles, there was not a soul about, not a sound to be heard save the grinding, rasping noise made by the cicadas; the sea, open to the south, sparkled and danced in large silver stars. At last, she ran down a path to the tiny green bay between the red cliffs, threw her sunshade on the sand, kicked the sandals off her bare feet and began to undress. I lay down on the overhang of rock under which she was taking off her red dress with the sombre pattern of black flowers, and watched her, expecting her swimsuit to be as gruesomely coloured. But there was no swimsuit under her dress, only a short pink slip. She pulled off this slip and walked over the pebbles to the clear, transparent water, her strong, firm body sunburnt all over, her beautiful feet stepping tensely, her taut buttocks twitching, and her sunburnt hips gleaming in the sun. She stood for a minute at the water's edge, perhaps dazzled by the sparkle, then splashed her feet in it, squatted down shoulder-deep, and then lay down on her stomach, stretched out, her elbows and dark head on the sandy beach, and her legs splayed. In the distance the great expanse of water shimmered with silvery needles, the enclosed little bay and the whole of its rocky cosiness was becoming hotter and hotter, and the silence in this sultry wilderness of rocks and thin southern forest was so complete that I could hear the waves running over the body lying face down beneath me and receding from the gleaming back, the buttocks, and the large splayed legs in small glassy ripples. And I, lying behind the rocks and peeping out again and again, was growing more and more disturbed by the sight of this magnificent nudity, and forgetting the absurdity and impudence of my behaviour rose a little to light my pipe nervously, and suddenly she too raised her head and stared up at me inquiringly without, however, shifting her position or making a movement. I got on to my feet, not knowing what to do or say. She spoke first.

"All the way here I heard someone following me. Why did you come after me?"

I decided to answer frankly.

"From curiosity, forgive me..."

She cut me short.

"Yes, you are obviously curious. Odette told me that you questioned her about me, I happened to hear that you are Russian and so I wasn't surprised—all Russians are far too curious. Still, why did you follow me?"

"Driven by curiosity, professional curiosity in particular."

"Yes, I know. You're a painter."

"And you're paintable. Besides, you went away somewhere every morning and it intrigued me—where, what for?—you always missed lunch, which boarders rarely do, and then you always had such a preoccupied look, which wasn't quite usual. You don't mix or talk with people, there is something secretive in you... Well, and as to why I didn't go away the moment you started undressing..."

"That can be understood," she said, and added after a

silence: "I'll get out now. Turn away for a minute, and then come down here. You interest me too."

"I shan't turn away for anything in the world!" I replied. "I'm a painter, and we are not children."

She shrugged.

"Oh, all right, I don't care."

She rose to her full height, confronting me boldly in all her womanly might, then walked unhurriedly over the pebbles, slipped her pink slip over her head, and pulled it down on her wet body. I ran down to her and squatted beside her.

"Perhaps you have some cigarettes, too, besides your pipe?" she asked.

"I have."

"Give me one."

I gave her a cigarette and struck a match.

"Thanks."

Inhaling, she gazed into the distance, twiddling her toes and never once turning round. And suddenly she asked ironically:

"So I can still be attractive?"

"And how!" I cried. "You've a beautiful body, wonderful hair, eyes... Only the expression on your face is ever so unkind..."

"That's because I really am preoccupied with one unkind thought."

"I knew it. You have recently parted with someone, someone has left you..."

"Chucked, not left me. Ran off from me. I knew that he was a bounder, but I loved him after a fashion; and now it turns out that I loved a downright cad. I met him in Monte Carlo about a month and a half ago. That evening I was playing at the casino. He was standing next to me, also playing and watching the little ball with insane eyes and winning again and again, once, twice, three, four times... I was also winning, he saw it and suddenly said: 'Enough. *Assez*!' and turned to me: '*N'est-ce pas, madame?*' Laughing, I replied: 'Yes, enough.' 'Ah, you're Russian?' 'Obviously.' 'Then let's make a night of it!' I looked at him—he was much the worse for wear, but a gentleman by the look of him. The rest is easy to guess."

"I know. Over supper you felt you were kindred souls,

you talked without end, and when the hour came to part you wondered why you had to part at all..."

"Quite right. We did not part, and started squandering our winnings. We lived in Monte Carlo, in La Turbie, in Nice, we had lunch and dinner in restaurants on the road between Cannes and Nice–you probably know what all that cost–for a while we even lived in a hotel in Cap d'Antibes, playing at millionaires... The money dwindled away, the trips to Monte Carlo, gambling with the little we had left, ended in fiasco... He began to disappear I don't know where and return with some money again, but it was just chicken feed, fifty francs, or perhaps a hundred... And then he sold my earrings, my wedding ring–I was married once, you see–and my baptismal gold cross..."

"And, of course, he assured you that a huge debt was going to be paid back to him any day now, and that he had a lot of high-standing and prosperous friends and relatives."

"Exactly. I still don't know just what he was, he never spoke clearly or in detail about his past, evading the issue, and somehow I didn't pay much attention to it. After all, he had the usual past of many emigrants: Petersburg, service in an elite regiment, then the war, the revolution, and Constantinople... In Paris, he said, he always had and always could find decent employment thanks to his old connections, but in the meantime there was Monte Carlo or else Nice where, he said, some titled friends of his would never let him down... I was already losing heart, I knew moments of despair, but he only smiled and said: 'Don't worry, leave it all to me, I have already taken some serious steps in Paris, but it's not the little woman's business to worry her head about such things...' "

"I see..."

"What do you see?" She swung to me suddenly, flashing her eyes and flinging her cigarette far away. "D'you find all this amusing?"

I gripped her hand and held it tight.

"Shame on you! If you're not careful I'll paint you as a Medusa or Nemesis!"

"That's the goddess of retribution?"

"Yes, and a very vicious one."

"Nemesis! Some Nemesis I am!" she smiled ruefully. "But you're a good sort, you know... Give me another cigarette, will you. He taught me to smoke... He taught me everything!"

And again she sat smoking and staring into the distance.

"I forgot to tell you how surprised I was to discover that you came here to bathe—why make that long trip every day? But I know the answer now: you want to be alone."

"Yes..."

The heat was growing more and more intense, the cicadas on the hot, fragrant pines were grinding and chirring all the more insistently and furiously, and I felt how burning hot her black hair, bare shoulders and legs must have become.

"Let's move into the shade out of this scorching sun, and you'll finish telling me your sad story," I said.

She started, and said: "Yes, let's."

We walked round the semicircle of the little bay and sat down in the pale and sultry shade of the red cliffs. I took her hands again and held them in mine. She did not seem to notice.

"What's there to tell?" she said. "You know, I no longer feel like remembering this really very sad and sordid story. I suppose you think that I'm used to being kept now by one scoundrel, now by another. Nothing of the sort. My past is very ordinary too. My husband was in the Volunteer Army, first with Denikin, then with Wrangel,* and when we ended up in Paris he, naturally, became a chauffeur, but he took to drink and drank himself into such a state that he lost his job and turned into a proper tramp. I could not possibly go on living with him. The last time I saw him was in Montparnasse at the door of Dominique—you know that small Russian restaurant, of course? It was a rainy night, he was shod in what were once tall boots with the

*The Volunteer Army was formed in the South of Russia in December 1917 for the purpose of fighting the Revolution. In 1918, command of it was assumed by Anton Denikin (1872-1947), who organised a crusade against Soviet Russia. A counter-offensive of the Red Army ended in an almost complete routing of Denikin's army, the remains of which were evacuated from Novorossiisk to the Crimea, where Baron Pyotr Wrangel (1878-1928) replaced, in April 1920, Denikin as Commander-in-Chief.

In November 1920 the Red Army advanced to the Crimea, while the disbanded remains of Wrangel's forces, to which many civilians opposed to the Revolution had attached themselves, fled to Constantinople and subsequently drifted through Europe.

legs cut off and was shuffling about in the puddles, bent over and holding his hand out for alms, clumsily handing people out of taxis, or rather getting in their way... I stood and looked for a minute, and then I went up to him. He was startled and embarrassed—you can't imagine what a splendid, kind and tactful man he is!—he stood there, looking at me in confusion: 'Masha, you?' Small, ragged, unkempt, his face covered with a reddish bristle, drenched in the rain and shivering from the cold... I gave him all the money I had in my handbag, he grasped my hand with his wet, icy fingers and started kissing it and weeping, shaking all over. But what could I do for him? Only send him a hundred or two hundred francs two or three times a month—I have a hatshop in Paris, you see, and I make quite a decent living. I came here to rest from my labours and swim in the sea—and here I am. In a day or two I'll return to Paris. I longed to meet him, slap his face and make a scene—a very silly dream, and d'you know when I realised how really silly it was? Only just now, thanks to you. I started telling you my story and understood..."

"But anyway, how did he run off?"

"That's the whole thing, it was much too mean and shabby. We took up residence in this small pension—and that, mind you, after the splendiferous hotel in Cap d'Antibes!—where you and I happen to be fellow boarders, and one evening, only about ten days ago, we went to a tea dance at the casino. Well, there was a band, of course, several dancing couples, but I simply could not take it any more, I've seen all I could stomach!—but anyway I was sitting there, eating the cream cakes which he kept ordering for me and for himself and laughing sort of strangely all the time—look, look, he said, look at those musicians, proper apes aren't they, stamping their feet and grimacing! He opened his empty cigarette case, called the *chasseur*, told him to bring some English cigarettes, thanked him absently when he brought them and said he'd pay after tea, and then, looking at his finger nails, said to me: 'What awfully dirty hands! I'll go and wash them...' He got up and left..."

"And never came back."

"No. I sat and waited. Ten minutes, twenty, half an hour, an hour... Can you imagine what it was like?"

"I can imagine it very well..."

I pictured it clearly: the two of them sitting at a small table, looking at the dancing couples without speaking, each one thinking differently about the hateful situation they were in. Behind the large windows there was the evening sky, the gleam of the calm sea, and the dark fronds of the palms; and here there were the musicians stamping their feet, blowing their trumpets, striking metal discs, more like dummies than living people, and the gentlemen dancers were shuffling and swaying in time to the music, pressing on at their ladies, as though pushing them towards a very definite finale... The *chausseur* in leggings and a sort of green uniform jacket doffed his cap deferentially and handed him a packet of "High-Life"...

"Well, and then? There you were sitting..."

"I was sitting there and dying by the minute. The band left, the place became deserted, the lights were switched on..."

"And the windows turned a dark blue..."

"Yes, and I still sat there, frozen to my chair. What was I to do, how save myself? All I had in my purse was something like six francs and some small change."

"And he really did go to the men's room, did what he needed there, thinking about his crooked life, then he buttoned himself up, ran on tiptoe down the corridors to the other exit, and jumped out into the street... For the love of God, whom did you love, just think! You want to find him, to take revenge on him? What for? You're not a schoolgirl, you ought to have seen what he was and the mess you had landed in. So why did you go on with that existence, horrible in every respect?"

She thought it over, and shrugged.

"Whom did I love? I don't know. I had a need of love, you see, which actually I had never really experienced before... As a lover he did not and could not give me anything, having long lost his male abilities... I ought to have seen what he was and the mess I had landed in, you say? Of course I ought to have, but I did not want to see or think–for the first time in my life I was having a sinful holiday with all its pleasures, and it was like a spell. Why did I want to find him and revenge him in some way? That too was a spell, an *idée fixe*. D'you think I did not realise that I wouldn't be able to achieve anything except a nasty, sordid row? And you ask me: what for? Why, for falling so low and living that crooked life thanks to him, and mainly for that horror, that disgrace I had to go through that evening at the casino when he ran off out of the WC. When I, beside myself, babbled something to the casino manager, trying to wiggle out and begged him to take my handbag in security until the morrow, and when he refused to take it and contemptuously forgave me the tea, the cream cakes and the English cigarettes! I sent a telegram to Paris, received a thousand francs two days later, went to the casino and there the manager, averting his eyes from me, took the money I owed and even gave me a bill... Oh, my dear, I'm no Medusa, I'm simply a woman and a very sentimental, lonely and wretched female besides, but do try to understand me—after all, even a hen has a heart! I have simply been ill all this time since that cursed tea dance. And you have simply been sent down to me by the Lord God Himself, to make me come to my senses... Let go of my hand, it's time to dress, the train from San Rafael is due soon..."

"Forget the train," I said. "Better look around you, look at these red cliffs, this green bay, the crooked pines, and listen to this heavenly grating... From now on we're going to come here together. Right?"

"Right."

"And to Paris we'll return together too."

"Yes."

"And let the future take care of itself."

"Yes, yes..."

"May I kiss your hand?"

"Oh yes, yes..."

3 June, 1944

On the Swing

On a summer evening he sat in the drawing-room tinkling the keys of the piano, and on hearing her footfall on the balcony he brought both hands down in a crashing chord and sang out in a tuneless shout:

I don't envy the gods,
And the kings I don't envy,
When my love I behold—
Blue-eyed, dark-haired, and slender!

She came in wearing her blue sarafan, a string of coral beads round her throat, and her dark hair hanging in two long braids down her back. The blue eyes in her sunburnt face were smiling.

"And all that is about me? The aria personally composed by you!"

"Yes!"

He banged the keys again and yelled:

I don't envy the gods...

"Heavens, how can anyone be so tone-deaf!"

"But then I'm a famous painter, so there! And as handsome as Leonid Andreyev.* It's to your woe I turned in at your gate!"

"He tries to frighten me and I'm not afraid, as Lev Tolstoy said about your Leonid Andreyev."

"That remains to be seen!"

"And what about grandfather's crutch?"

"Your grandfather, though a hero of Sevastopol, only looks ferocious. We'll elope, get married, then fall at his feet and he'll weep and forgive us."

In the dusk before supper when a mouth-watering smell of meat balls fried with onions came from the kitchen, and it was growing chilly in the dewy garden, they went flying high on the swing, standing on the board face to face, the iron rings squealing, and her skirts streaming in the wind they raised. He pulled at the ropes, half-squatting to give stronger momentum to the board and goggling to make it more frightening, while she, flushed and thrilled, looked intently at him with vapid, happy eyes.

"Hello there! The first star and the new moon are out, and the sky above the lake is so very, very green, look, painter, look at that thin crescent! New moon, new moon... Ouch, we'll fall off!"

*Leonid Andreyev (1871-1919)—a Russian writer.

Descending from that great height, they jumped down to the ground and then sat down on the board, looking at each other and trying to control their excited breathing.

"There you are! I told you, didn't I?"

"What did you tell me?"

"That you're already in love with me."

"Maybe I am... Listen, they're calling us to supper... We're coming, coming!"

"Wait a minute. The first star, the new moon, the green sky, the smell of dew, the smell from the kitchen—must be my favourite meat balls in sour cream again—your blue eyes, and your beautiful happy face..."

"I have a feeling that there'll be nothing happier than this evening in my life ever..."

"Dante said about Beatrice: 'In her eyes is the beginning of love, and the end in her lips.' And so?" he said, taking her hand.

She closed her eyes and inclined her head to his shoulder. He put his arm round her, soft, thick braids and all, and lifted her face.

"The end in her lips, yes?"

"Yes."

Walking back to the house, he stared under his feet as he spoke:

"What are we to do now? Go to grandfather, fall at his feet and beg him to give us his blessing? Can you see me as a husband?"

"No, no, only not that!"

"But what then?"

"I don't know. Let everything remain the way it is... It can't be bettered."

10 April, 1945

Chaste Monday

The greyness of Moscow's bleak winter day was darkening, the street-lamps began to glow with their cold gaslight, the shop windows were warmly lit, and the life of the town, shedding its daytime cares, accelerated its pace—the sleigh-cabs came thicker and faster, the crowded tramcars rumbled more laboriously—it was already dark enough to see the green stars fall hissing from the overhead wires—and along the snow-covered pavements hastened the vaguely darkling figures of the pedestrians. Every evening, at this hour, my coachman drove me in the sleigh pulled by my streaking trotter from Red Gate to the Church of Christ the Saviour: she lived exactly opposite the church. Every evening I took her out to dinner at the Prague, the Hermitage, or the Metropol, after dinner we went to a recital or to a play, and then to the out-of-town Yar or the Strelnya. What all this was going to end in I did not know, and I tried not to think about it, not to construe anything, for it would be as useless as talking to her about it after she had once and for all refused to speak about our future. She was an enigma that I could not understand, and our relations were strange too—our intimacy was still not complete, and this kept me in a constant and frustrating state of suspense, in an agony of waiting, and yet every hour I spent with her was sheer bliss.

She had become enrolled at the Higher Courses for Women, for no reason that I could see, and rarely attended the lectures, but still did not drop them altogether. I asked her once: "Why go at all?" She shrugged and said: "And why do people do what they do in the world? Can we understand our actions or explain them at all? Besides, I'm interested in history..." She lived alone, her widowed father, an enlightened man who belonged to a distinguished merchant-class family, lived in retirement in Tver, and like all such merchants was a collector. She rented a corner flat on the fifth floor of the house opposite the Church of the Saviour simply for the view it offered of Moscow. There were only two rooms in the flat, but they were large and well-furnished. In the first room much of the space was taken up by a wide ottoman; there was an expensive upright piano on which she was always learning to play the slow and somnambulistically beautiful beginning of the "Moonlight Sonata"—just the beginning alone—and on top of the piano and on the table under the mirror stood cut-glass vases with ornate, bright flowers—I had a flower shop deliver fresh flowers to her every Saturday—and when I arrived on a Saturday evening she would slowly hold out her hand for me to kiss, as she lay on the ottoman on the wall behind which for some odd reason hung a portrait of a bare-footed Lev Tolstoy, and absently acknowledged the gift: "Thanks for the flowers..." I brought her boxes of chocolates, new books–Hofmannsthal, Schnitzler, Tetmajer, Przybyszewski–and all the gratitude I received was the same absent-minded "Thanks", her warm hand to kiss, and sometimes an order to sit down beside the ottoman, still in my overcoat. "I don't know why," she would say dreamily as she stroked my beaver collar, "but I think there can be nothing better than the smell of winter which one brings into the room from out of doors..." I had a feeling that she had no use for anything: not the flowers I sent her, not the books I brought, not the dinners, plays, or midnight suppers in the out-of-town restaurants I took her to, but at least she did have a preference in flowers, some were her favourite while others she did not like, and she always read all the books I brought her, finished a whole box of chocolates in one day, and ate as much as I did at our dinners and suppers, and loved pies with fish soup and pink-fleshed hazel grouse fried in sour cream. "I really don't understand how can people eat dinner and supper every day of their lives and not get tired of it!" she sometimes said, while she herself enjoyed her dinner and supper with a Muscovite's knowledgeable relish. What she definitely had a weakness for was clothes–velvets, silks, costly furs...

We were both rich, healthy, young, and so good-looking that people turned their heads to look at us in restaurants and concert halls. I come from Pensa Gubernia, but at the time, oddly enough, I was handsome with a hot, southern beauty, I was even "indecently handsome" as I was once told by a certain famous actor, a monstrously fat man, a great glutton and a paragon of intelligence. "The devil knows what you are, a Sicilian or something," he said sleepily to me. My temperament, too, was sanguine and southern, I loved a good joke and was always ready to break into a happy smile. And she had an Indian or Persian kind of beauty: a dark amber face, magnificent softly shining hair with something sinister in its very thickness and blackness, eyebrows that had a sheen like the fur of black sable, eyes like velvety coal; the lovely crimson mouth was outlined with a line of dark fuzz on the upper lip. For going out she mostly wore her garnet coloured velvet gown and matching shoes with gold clasps (yet to the Higher Courses she always went dressed as a poor student girl and ate a thirty-kopeck lunch at the vegetarian lunchroom in Arbat Street). She was as fond of silence as I was of simple-hearted fun and chatter, she was always deep in thought, as if she were mentally trying to fathom something; lying on the ottoman reading, she often put down her book and stared before her as if seeking an answer to something that puzzled her. I saw this when I sometimes dropped in in the daytime during those three or four days every month when she did not leave the house at all, lay reading most of the time and made me sit in an armchair beside her ottoman and read something without uttering a sound.

"You do chatter and fidget terribly," she'd tell me. "Let me at least finish this chapter in peace..."

"If I wasn't such a chatterbox and fidget I'd probably never come to know you," I'd answer, reminding her of the way in which we met. One evening in December, I went to the Art Group* to hear a talk by Andrei Bely** who actually sang it, dancing and running about the stage, and I laughed and fidgeted so terribly that she, who happened to have the chair next to mine and glanced at me with disapproval at first, finally also burst out laughing and I quickly took my chance to start a conversation with her.

"That's true," she would say. "But do keep quiet for a bit, read something, or smoke..."

"I can't keep quiet! You cannot imagine how terribly I love you. And you don't care for me!"

"I can imagine it. You say I don't care for you, but you know perfectly well that my father and you are all I have in the world. In any case you are my first and last. Isn't that enough? Let's say no more about it. Since you won't let me read, let's have tea..."

I would get up, boil the water in the electric kettle

Moscow Art Group to which Ivan Bunin and his brother Yuly belonged.
**Andrei Bely (1880-1934)—pen name of Boris Bugayev, a leading symbolist poet.

which stood on a small table at the foot of the ottoman, took the cups and saucers out of the walnut cabinet in the corner, and said the first thing that came to mind.

"Have you finished reading 'The Fiery Angel'?"*

"I've finished glancing through it. The style is so grandiloquent that you feel ashamed for the author."

"And why did you suddenly leave midway through Chaliapine's concert last night?"

"He was too boisterous. And then I don't like flaxen-haired Russia as such."

"There's so much that you don't like!"

"Yes, very much..."

Waiting for the water to come to the boil I stood gazing out of the window and thinking how strange our love was. The room smelt of flowers, and for me she was combined with that smell; one of the windows offered an enormous view of the town sprawling low on the opposite bank of the Moskva river and now clad in bluish snow; from the other, left window I could see a part of the Kremlin, and facing me, too close somehow, was the too-new white bulk of the Church of the Saviour, the golden dome reflecting in bluish blurs the magpies that were forever wheeling round it. What a strange town, I said to myself, thinking of Okhotny Ryad, of the Church of Our Lady of Iviron, of the Church of Basil the Beatified. The Chruch of Basil the Beatified, the Church of the Saviour on the Hill, the Italian cathedrals, and something Kirghizian in the pointed tower-tops on the Kremlin wall...

When I came at dusk I sometimes found her lying on the ottoman wearing only her silk house-robe trimmed with sables–inherited from her Astrakhan grandmother, she told me. I sat beside her in the semi-darkness, without putting on the light, and kissed her hands, her feet, and her amazingly smooth body... She accepted my caresses without protest, in utter silence. I sought her hot lips, and she let me kiss them, with already a catch in her breath, but still in utter silence. And when she felt that I could control myself no longer, she pushed me away, sat up, calmly asked me to switch on the light and went off to her bedroom. I switched on the light, sat down on the

*A novel by Valery Bryusov.

revolving chair in front of the piano, and gradually came back to my senses, cooling off from the hot blinding spell. A quarter of an hour later she appeared from her bedroom fully dressed and ready to go out, as composed and unself-conscious as if nothing had happened at all.

"Where to tonight? The Metropol perhaps?"

And again all night long we talked about everything under the sun, only not us. Soon after we had become close and I broached the subject of marriage she told me:

"No, I'm not made to be a wife. No, no..."

I was not discouraged. "We'll live and see," I said to myself then, hoping that she'd change her mind with time, and did not talk about marriage any more. At moments our incomplete intimacy was unbearable, but here again, what could I do except hope and leave it to time? Once, sitting beside her in the dusk and quiet, I cried out in despair:

"It's more than human flesh can bear! And why must you torture yourself and me so cruelly?"

She did not say anything.

"No, this isn't love, no..." I said.

"Perhaps," she replied calmly from the darkness. "But does anyone know what love is?"

"I do, I know!" I cried. "And I'll wait until you also come to know what love is, and happiness!"

"Oh, happiness, happiness... 'Happiness, my friend, is like water in a fishing-net: when you start pulling it in it seems full, and when you've pulled it out there's nothing there.' "

"What does this mean?"

"That's what Platon Karatayev said to Pierre."

"Oh, let's forget it," I said with a gesture of dismissal. "Never mind all that eastern wisdom."

And again all that night we talked only about extraneous things—the Art Theatre's new production, Leonid Andreyev's new story... And for me it was again happiness enough to be sitting so close to her in the swishing, gliding sleigh, holding her and feeling the smooth fur of her coat, and then entering the crowded restaurant with her to the sounds of the march from *Aida*, eating and drinking with her, hearing her slow voice, looking at her lips which I had been kissing only an hour earlier, yes, yes, I had been kissing

27—904

them, I told myself with rapturous gratitude as I looked at them, at the dark fuzz on her upper lip, at the garnet velvet of her gown, the slope of her shoulders and the roundness of her breasts, smelling the slightly spicy perfume of her hair and thinking–Moscow, Astrakhan, Persia, India! In one of the out-of-town restaurants, towards the end of supper when the place grew noisier and hazier from cigarette smoke, and she had also been drinking and smoking, she sometimes, a bit drunkenly, took me to a private room and asked me to call in the Gypsies, and they would enter, playing up their loud-voiced, free and easy familiarity. At the head came an old Gypsy carrying a guitar on a blue ribbon over his shoulder and wearing a kaftan trimmed with gold lace, his face blue and bloated like a drowned man's, his bald head a cast-iron ball, and behind him came the principal songstress with a low forehead under a tar-black fringe... She listened to the Gipsy songs with a strange and languid half-smile... At three or four in the morning I took her home, and as we drove up to her house kissed the snow-sprinkled fur collar of her coat, closing my eyes from happiness, and then in a mood of rapturous despair flew home to Red Gates. It will be the same tomorrow and after tomorrow, I was thinking, the same torture and the same happiness! Oh well, but it was happiness anyway, enormous happiness!

Thus passed January, February, and then Butter Week. On the Sunday before Lent, Forgiveness Sunday, she ordered me to be at her place soon after four in the afternoon. When I arrived she met me already dressed for the street in a short astrakhan coat, a small astrakhan hat, and black felt overshoes.

"All in black today!" I exclaimed in my usual cheery manner.

Her glance was gentle and meek.

"Tomorrow is Chaste Monday, you know," she replied, giving me her hand in a black kid glove. "Would you like to come with me to the Novodevichy Nunnery?"

"Oh, yes!" I answered eagerly, although I was a bit nonplussed.

"For a change from all those restaurants and night clubs," she added. "Yesterday morning I went to the Rogozhskoye cemetery..."

I was even more dismayed.

"To the cemetery? What for? That's the famous Old Believers' cemetery, isn't it?"

"Yes, the Old Believers! Russia before Peter's time. It was the funeral of an archbishop. Can you picture this: the coffin was a hollowed-out oak, like in ancient times, the gold brocade may have been hammered metal, the face of the deceased was covered with a white pall, embroidered in large black writing, beautiful and frightening. And at the coffin stood the deacons with *ripidas** and *trikirias**..."

"How d'you know all those things? *Ripidas, trikirias* and what not..."

"It's you who don't know me."

"I didn't know that you were so religious."

"It's not religiousness. I don't know what it is... You see, very often in the morning or in the evening when you don't drag me off to one of those restaurants, I go to the Kremlin cathedrals, and you never even suspected it... Let me go on then. The deacons—and what deacons! Peresvet and Oslyabya** in the flesh! And there were two choirs singing, and all the men Peresvets again: tall, powerful men in long black kaftans, now one choir singing, now the other, always in unison, and the music before them had ancient notations, not our notes. The inside of the grave was lined with shiny fir branches and the day was frosty, sunny with blinding snow... Ah no, you can't understand this! Let us go..."

The afternoon was serene and sunny with rime on the trees; magpies were chattering in the quiet on the blood-red brick walls of the nunnery, and the clock on the belfry chimed every quarter of an hour delicately and sadly. In the silence the snow creaked under our feet as we entered the cemetery and walked along the paths—the sun had just set, it was still quite light, the rime-covered tree branches were wondrously etched as grey coral against the gold enamel of the sunset, and all around us glimmered the lit-

**Ripida*—a round icon mounted on a staff; *trikiria* —a three-branched candlestick.—*Tr.*

***Peresvet and Oslyabya*—two stalwarts, monks from the Trinity Monastery, of St. Sergius, are remembered as heroes of the Kulikovo Battle (1380). Peresvet's single combat with the Tatar Chelubei, in which they killed each other, gave the start to the great battle in which the Tatar Golden Horde army was routed.

tle icon lamps above the graves mysteriously, serenely and sadly. I walked behind her, looking at the touchingly small footprint her new felt overshoes left in the snow, a star where her heel trod, and suddenly she turned round, sensing my mood.

"You do really love me!" she said with something like bewilderment, shaking her head.

We stood for a minute or two beside the graves of Ertel and Chekhov. Holding her hands in her muff she looked at Chekhov's tombstone and said with a shrug:

"What a nasty mixture of pseudo-Russian and Art Nouveau styles."

It was growing dark and cold, and we slowly walked to the gates where my coachman Fyodor was patiently waiting for us with the sleigh.

"Let's drive about a little," she said. "And then let's go to Yegorov's for our last *blini* this year... Only you won't drive too fast, Fyodor, will you?"

"No, ma'am."

"Somewhere in Ordynka there's a house where Griboyedov* lived once. Let's go and look for it..."

And so we went to Ordynka, we drove about for a long time up and down some side streets where the houses were set back in gardens, we also came to a side street that bore Griboyedov's name, but no one could point out to us the house in which the writer once lived. There was not a soul about, and even if there had been could anyone have cared? It had long grown dark, and rosy lights glowed in the windows behind the rime-silvered trees.

"There's also a St. Martha and St. Mary Nunnery here," she said.

"Are we going to one more nunnery?" I asked, laughing.

"No, I didn't mean anything..."

The ground-floor rooms of Yegorov's restaurant in Okhotny Ryad were crowded with shaggy, bundled-up coachmen, who sliced through their stacks of *blini*, drenched in melted butter and sour cream, and ate them in huge forkfuls. It was as hot here as in a steam-bath. In the upstairs rooms, low-ceilinged and also very warm, stolid

*Alexander Griboyedov (1795-1829)—Russian writer, author of the famous play *Wit Works Woe*.

merchants were eating piping hot *blini* with black caviar and drinking iced champagne. We passed on into the second room where in the corner, an icon lamp was burning before the image of a three-armed Virgin painted on a black board, and sat down on a black leather sofa before a long table... I could not tear my admiring gaze from her face—the fuzz on her upper lip had rime on it, her amber cheeks had taken on a rosy tint, her dilated pupils almost merged with the blackness of her irises. Taking a handkerchief out of her scented muff, she said:

"Lovely! Gorgin savages downstairs, and here—*blini* with champagne and the three-armed Virgin. Three arms! Why, that's India! You're a nobleman, you can't understand Moscow and all of this as I do."

"Oh, I can, I can," I protested. "And let's order a mighty feast."

"Why mighty?"

"Don't you know? 'And spake Gyurgi...' "

"How lovely! Gyurgi!"

"Yes, Prince Yuri Dolgoruki. 'And spake Gyurgi to Svyatoslav, the Seversky prince: Come to me, brother, to Moscow, and he ordered a mighty feast to be prepared.' "

"How lovely! And *that* Russia is only left in some northern monasteries. And also in church singing. The other day I went to the church of the Miraculous Conception monastery—you can't imagine how beautifully they sing there! And at the Miracle monastery it's even better. Last year I went there everyday in Passion Week. Ah, it was so lovely! Puddles everywhere, the air already soft, a sort of tenderness, a sadness in your heart, and that awareness of mother-country all the time, of her antiquity... All the doors of the cathedral stood wide open, people came and went all the time, common people I mean, services held all day long... Oh my, I'll go and take the veil at some nunnery somewhere, the most remote there is, in Vologda or Vyatka gubernia."

I wanted to tell her that I'd go to a monastery too, or else would cut someone's throat and get marched off to Siberia, and lit a cigarette forgetting in my agitation that smoking was not allowed here, but just then a waiter in white pants and a white shirt belted with a raspberry-red sash, deferentially reminded me:

"I beg your pardon, sir, but smoking is not allowed here." And immediately changing to a waiter's usual patter, said with particular obsequiousness: "What will you have with the *blini*? Herb-flavoured vodka? Caviar, salmon? We have some exceptionally good sherry to go with the fish soup, and for the sturgeon we have..."

"We'll have sherry with the sturgeon too," she said, gladdening me with her good-natured readiness to talk which did not desert her all evening. And I was already listening absently to what she was saying. But she was speaking with a soft light in her eyes:

"I love Russian chronicles and legends so much that passages I like especially I read over again and again until I know them by heart. 'There was a town named Murom, and the sole ruler in that town was a God-fearing prince, Pavel by name. And the devil caused his wife to be possessed by a winged snake for sin. And this snake appeared to her in human guise, and very beautiful indeed...' "

"Oh, how terrible!" I said, with a comically horrified look.

She ignored my jocularity, and continued:

"Thus God put her to the test. And when the time came for her to die, this prince and princess begged the Lord to allow them to come to Him on one and the same day. And they were to be buried in one coffin. And they ordered a vault for the double coffin to be hewn out of a single rock. And together and at the same time he donned a monk's habit and she a nun's..."

I had been listening absently, but now I wondered, surprised and even alarmed: what was the matter with her?

And that night, when I brought her home at a quite unusual hour, just after ten, and said goodbye to her at the door, she suddenly called me back when I was already getting into the sleigh:

"Wait a minute. Tomorrow night come and fetch me not earlier than ten. The Art Theatre is giving a *kapustnik**."

"So what? D'you want to go?"

"Yes."

**Kapustnik*—a party given by a theatrical company or the staff of an enterprise with dancing, refreshment and, above all, a show of humorous sketches, parodies, songs, etc., specially devised for the occasion.—*Tr.*

"But you told me that you couldn't think of anything more vulgar than these *kapustniks*!"

"I still can't. But I want to go just the same."

Mentally I shook my head—nothing but whims, Moscow whims—but responded brightly:

"Alright!"

The next evening, at ten o'clock, I rode up in the lift to her floor, opened her door with my key, and hung back in the dark hall: the rooms beyond were strangely brilliant with all the lights burning—the chandeliers, the candelabra on each side of the pierglass, and the floor lamp with a silk lampshade behind the headboard of the ottoman—and she was playing the beginning of the "Moonlight Sonata", the music sounded more and more stirring, more languorous, more alluring its somnambulistically blissful sadness. I banged the front door shut, the music stopped at once, and I heard the rustle of movement. When I walked into the sitting-room I found her standing rather theatrically erect beside the piano in her black velvet evening gown which enhanced her slenderness, a radiant beauty with her elaborately dressed pitch-black hair, the amber swarthiness of her bare arms, shoulders and the beginning of her soft, full breasts, the diamond earrings sparkling against slightly powdered cheeks, the coal-black velvet of her eyes and the velvety crimson of her lips. Thin braids of gleaming black hair were looped down the sides of her face, curving up to the corners of her eyes, which made her look like one of those Oriental beauties one sees on boxes of sweets.

"Now if I was a singer and sang on the stage," she said, looking at my distrait face, "I'd respond to the applause with a pleasant smile and slight bows to right and left, up and down, while I'd be carefully and unnoticeably kicking aside my train lest I should trip on it."

At the *kapustnik* she smoked a lot, took sips from her champagne glass all the time, and looked intently at the actors who with short, vigorous shouts and snatches of song were performing something that was supposed to be Parisian, at the big Stanislavsky with white hair and black eyebrows and the thickset Moskvin with a pince-nez on his trough-shaped face who very painstakingly and, with comic seriousness, falling over backwards, were doing a hilarious cancan while the audience roared with laughter.

Kachalov, pale from drink, with large drops of sweat on his forehead over which fell a strand of his fair hair, came up to us, raised his glass and, somberly and theatrically devouring her with his eyes, said in his low actor's voice:

"To you, Queen of Shemaha!"

She smiled slowly and touched glasses with him. He took her hand and kissed it drunkenly, bending so low that he nearly lost balance. Righting himself, he clenched his teeth and glared at me.

"And who's this pretty boy? I hate him!"

And then a barrel organ began to wheeze, squeak and blare, with the jumping and stamping of a polka, and Sulerzhitsky*, a small, forever hurrying and laughing little man, came flying to us with gliding steps, bent over double, miming a shop assistant's gallant manner, and muttered:

"Allow me to ask you for a polka."

Smiling, she stood up and went off to dance with him between the tables, sharply and smartly tapping her feet, her earrings, gleaming black hair, bare shoulders and arms flashing, followed by admiring looks and applause, while he, tilting back his head, bleated like a billy goat:

Come and dance this polka with me,
Come and dance with me, sweetheart,
I will tell you of my love, dear,
As we turn this way and that...

It was past two in the morning, and half-closing her eyes she rose to go. When we had put on our coats in the cloakroom, she looked at my beaver hat, stroked the beaver collar of my coat, and started for the door, saying either in fun or in earnest:

"You really are a pretty boy, Kachalov was right... And the snake appeared to her in human guise, and very beautiful indeed..."

She did not speak at all as we drove home, bending her head low from the pale, moonlit whirls of snow flying in our faces. A full moon was diving in and out of the clouds

*Leopold Sulerzhitsky (1872-1916) was a notable figure in Moscow's literary and theatrical circles and from 1905 he was Stanislavsky's right hand at the Art Theatre.

above the Kremlin, and she said: "It's like a luminous skull." When the clock on Spasskaya Tower chimed three, she said:

"What an ancient sound, it's tinny and there's cast iron in it too. And to think that in the fifteenth century the same sound announced that it was three o'clock. The chimes have exactly the same sound in Florence, and there it made me think of Moscow..."

When Fyodor reined the horse in at her house, she ordered me in a lifeless voice:

"Tell him not to wait for you..."

I was staggered–she never let me come up to her flat at night.

"I'll walk home, Fyodor," I mumbled.

We rode up in the lift without speaking, and entered the nocturnal warmth and quiet of her flat where tiny hammers seemed to be knocking in the radiators. I helped her out of her fur coat, slippery from the snow, she took off her wet, fluffy shawl, letting it fall into my arms, and quickly walked to her bedroom, her silk underskirt rustling and swishing. I took off my overcoat and hat, went into the sitting-room with a sinking heart, as if I were standing on the brink of an abyss, sat down on the ottoman. The door into the brightly lit bedroom stood open, I could hear her walking about there, I heard her dress getting caught in her hairpins as she pulled it off over her head... I got up and went to the door: wearing nothing but her slippers, trimmed with swansdown, she stood in front of the mirror, with her back to me, combing the long strands of black hair hanging down the sides of her face with a tortoise-shell comb.

"Here you were always saying that I didn't think enough about you," she said, dropping the comb on the dressing table, and tossing the strands of hair on to her back. She turned to face me: "No, I have been thinking about you..."

At daybreak I felt her moving. I opened my eyes–she was staring fixedly at me. I half-rose from the warmth of her bed and her body, she leaned over me and said in a quiet, level tone:

"This evening I'm leaving for Tver. For how long, God alone knows..."

She pressed her cheek to mine, and I felt her blinking her tear-wet lashes.

"I'll write you everything as soon as I reach there. I'll write you everything about the future. And now, please leave me, I'm sorry but I'm very tired..."

And she laid her head down on the pillow.

I dressed quietly, timidly kissed her hair and tiptoed out of the flat to the landing, already illumined with a pale light. The new snow was sticky under my feet as I walked home; the snowstorm had passed, all was peace and quiet, I could already see far ahead along the streets, the air smelt both of snow and of freshly baked bread. Taking off my hat I entered the Church of Our Lady of Iviron hotly blazing with veritable bonfires of candles, and went down on my knees on the floor tramped with snow amid a crowd of old women and beggars. Someone touched me on the shoulder, I turned round and saw a little old woman, the poorest of wretched beggars, looking at me and wrinkling up her face from tears of pity for me.

"Don't go breaking your heart like that, it's a sin, a sin!"

The letter I received from her about two weeks later was brief, just an affectionately worded but firm request not to wait for her any more, not to try and find her or see her. "I shall not come back to Moscow. For the time being I'm going to be a lay sister, and then perhaps I'll decide to take the veil... May God give you the strength not to write to me—there's no sense in dragging out and increasing our agony..."

I obeyed her request. I took to drink, spent my nights in the filthiest of dens, and sank lower and lower, wallowing in my misery. And then I began to recover little by little, indifferently and hopelessly... Nearly two years passed thus since that Monday, the first day of Lent...

On New Year's eve in 1914 the afternoon was as still and sunny as that unforgettable one. I left the house, took a cab and drove to the Kremlin. There I went into the empty Archangel Cathedral, stood for a long time in the semi-darkness without praying and just looking at the faint shimmering of the old gold on the iconostasis and the tombs of the Moscow tsars; I stood, as though in expectation of something, in that peculiar silence of an empty church when you do not dare to even breathe. When I came out I told the cabby to take me to Ordynka; like that time I had him drive me at a walk up and down the dark streets with the lighted windows of the houses seen through the trees in the gardens, then down Griboyedov Street, and I was weeping and weeping all the time...

I told the cabby to stop at the gates of the St. Martha and St. Mary Nunnery*: I saw several dark carriages in the front court, I saw the open doors of a small church and heard the nuns' choir singing sorrowfully and sweetly. I felt I simply had to go inside, but the gate-keeper barred my way, saying in gentle, pleading tones:

"You mustn't go in, sir, you mustn't!"

"Why ever not? Why can't I go into the church?"

"You can, sir, of course you can, only I beg you for the love of God not to go in now, because the Grand Duchess Elizaveta Fyodorovna and the Grand Duke Dmitry Pavlovich are there now..."

I thrust a ruble note into his hand, and with a grievous sigh he let me go in. But just as I stepped into the front court, a procession emerged from the church–icons and gonfalons, and then the Grand Duchess, a tall woman all in white, on her head a white veil with a gold cross sewn on it in front, the eyes on her fine-featured face kept low, walking slowly with a large candle in her hand; behind her came a long file of nuns or lay sisters, I don't know which they were or where they were going, all in white too, holding lighted candles in front of their faces and chanting. I looked at them very intently, myself not knowing why. And suddenly one of the nuns walking in the middle of the file lifted her head, covered with a white veil, and screening her candle with a hand peered into the darkness, staring straight at me, I thought... But what could she see in the darkness, how could she sense my presence there? I turned away and slowly went out of the gates.

12 May, 1944

***At the St. Martha and St. Mary Nunnery the famous architect Alexei Schusev built the Church of the Intercession in 1908-1910 with paintings by the no less famous artist Mikhail Nesterov. The church was patronized by the royal family.**

The Chapel

The summer day is hot. Beyond the garden of the old estate lies a long neglected graveyard, humps of earth sprouting flowers and grasses, a collapsing brick chapel, overrun by a tangle of flowers, grasses, stinging nettles and thistles. Children from the estate come here to squat beside the chapel and with their keen eyes peer into the long, narrow and broken window at ground level. Only a chill breath comes from the darkness, where nothing can be seen. Everywhere else it is light and hot, and inside it's dark and cold; lying there in iron boxes are somebody's grandfathers and grandmothers, and also some uncle or other who shot himself. It's all very curious and fascinating: here there's sunshine, flowers, grasses, flies, bumblebees, and butterflies, we can run about and play, it's creepy, of course, but exciting to be squatting beside the chapel and peering in, while they must always lie there in the dark, as if it's night all the time, in their thick, cold metal boxes. All those grandfathers and grandmothers were old people, but the uncle was still a young man.

"But why did he shoot himself anyway?"

"He was terribly in love, and when people are terribly in love they always shoot themselves."

Beautiful white clouds appear as islands in the sea of blue above; from the fields a warm wind carries the sweet fragrance of flowering rye. And the hotter and brighter shines the sun, the colder the breath from the darkness, from that window.

2 July, 1944

One Spring in Judaea

Those long ago days in Judaea which left me lame and crippled for life belong to the happiest time of my youth, said a tall, slender man with a yellowish face, brilliant brown eyes and short frizzy silver hair who always walked with a crutch because of his unbending left knee. I was a member of a small expedition whose purpose was to explore the eastern shores of the Dead Sea, the legendary sites of Sodom and Gomorrah, and I lived for a time in Jerusalem waiting for my companions who had been detained in Constantinople, and sometimes going to one of the Bedouin camps on the road to Jericho to see Sheikh Ahid, who was recommended to me by the Jerusalem archeologists and who had undertaken to provide our expedition with all the necessary equipment and personally lead it. For my first talks with him I went with a guide, but the very next day he came to Jerusalem himself to see me. After that I started going to his camp all by myself, riding a wonderful young mare I had bought from him, and, in fact, I started going too often... It was spring. Judaea was bathed in radiant sunlight, and the *Song of Songs* came to mind: "The winter is past, the rain is over and gone, the flowers appear on the earth, the time of the singing of birds is come, and the voice of the turtle is heard in our land ... the vines with the tender grape give a good smell..." There, on that ancient road to Jericho, in the stony Judean desert everything was lifeless as always, bare and desolate, just the blinding sun and sands. But even there, during those bright spring days, everything seemed infinitely joyous and happy to me: it was my first time in the East, I was seeing an entirely new world, and in that world– something quite fabulous–Ahid's niece.

The Judean desert is a whole country that steadily descends to the Jordan valley, a hilly country, now rocky, now sandy, here and there covered with a bristly growth, inhabited only by snakes and partridges, and locked in eternal silence. Winter there, as elsewhere in Judaea, is a time of pouring rains and icy winds; in spring, summer and autumn, there is the same graveyard serenity and monotony, sweltering heat and lethargy. In the hollows where water-wells occur you can see the traces of Bedouin camps–the ashes of their fires, the stones laid in circles or squares on which they anchor their tents... And the camp where I went and where the sheikh was Ahid comprised a small number of flat and square black felt tents, their blackness sombre against the yellow sand, set up in a wide sandy dale surrounded by the hills. Every time I came there I saw small heaps of smouldering manure briquettes in front of the tents, and the space between the tents was crowded with dogs, horses, mules, goats—I still cannot understand what they fed on and where—and multitudes of naked, swarthy, curly-haired children, men and women, some of them looking like Gypsies, others likes Negroes, except that their lips were not thick. And it was strange to see how warmly the men were dressed in spite of the heat—a dark-blue cotton shirt down to the knees, a padded jacket, and on top of that an *aba*, that is, a very long and heavy, wide-shouldered robe made of woollen cloth with white and black stripes, and on the head—a *kaffiyeh*, that is, a yellow scarf with red stripes falling down the cheeks onto the shoulders, and held in place by a double circlet of two-coloured twisted wool. All this was in complete contrast to the clothing of the women who wore just a long shirt of dark-blue cotton with sleeves falling almost to the ground, and on their heads—a square of the same cloth which left their faces uncovered. The men wore crude boots with metal heel taps, while the women went barefoot, and all of them had lovely feet, very quick and burnt quite black by the sun. The men smoked pipes, and the women did too.

When I came to the camp the second time and without a guide, I was already received like a friend. Ahid's tent was the largest of all, and in it I saw a whole assemblage of elderly Bedouins sitting round the black felt walls with the entrance flaps raised. Ahid came out to welcome me, he bowed and touched his lips and forehead with his right hand. As I entered the tent ahead of him, I waited for him to sit down on the carpet in the middle of the tent, and then I did what one is always supposed to do there—bowed and touched my lips and forehead with my right hand just as he had done in greeting me, and repeated this according to the number of men sitting there. Then I sat down beside him and, sitting, performed the salaam all over again and was naturally answered likewise. Only the host and I talked—briefly and slowly. That, too, was in keeping with custom, and for another thing I was not very fluent in Arabic at the time. The others sat smoking and saying nothing. In the meantime, a repast for the guests and me was being cooked outside the tent. As a rule the Bedouins eat *khybyz*—maize flat cakes—and cooked millet with goat's milk. But guests are always treated to *kharuf*—this is a sheep roasted in a hole dug in the sand with layers of smouldering manure briquettes heaped on. After the sheep, coffee is always served, but never with sugar. And so everyone sat there eating with relish quite unaffected by the truly infernal heat and stuffiness inside the felt tent or finding it as frightening as I did to look out of the wide-open flaps at the sands sparkling so dazzlingly in the distance that they seemed to be smelting before one's very eyes. After his every word the sheikh called me *khavadja*, or sir, and I called him *sheikh bedavi*, that is a son of the desert, a bedouin. By the way, do you know what Jordan is called in Arabic? Very simply Shariat, and all it means is a watering place.

Ahid was about fifty years old, not very tall, big-boned, spare and very strong; his face was the colour of baked brick, his eyes were grey, transparent and piercing; his coarse copper-red beard streaked with grey and his moustache were neatly trimmed as is always done by the Bedouins; and on his feet, like everyone else, he wore heavy metal-tipped boots. When he came to Jerusalem to see me he had a dagger hanging from his belt and carried a long rifle.

I saw his niece the day of my second visit when I was sitting in the tent as already a friend: she walked past the open flap, holding herself erect and carrying on her head a large can filled with water, supporting it with her right hand. I do not know how old she was, no more than eighteen I thought, and later I found out that she had been married for four years, that she had been widowed that year, never having borne a child, and being an orphan and very poor besides had been given a home by her uncle. "Return, return O Shulamite!" I thought. (Shulamite, you know, must have looked like her: "I am black but comely, O ye daughters of Jerusalem"). As she walked past the door flap she turned her head slightly and glanced at me: her eyes were unusually dark, mysterious, her face was nearly black, her lips purple and big—they amazed me more than anything else in that moment... However, was it only her lips! Everything amazed me: her beautiful arm raised to support the water can and bared to the shoulder, the slow, undulating movements of her body under the long cotton shirt, the full breasts that lifted up that shirt... And it so happened that shortly afterwards I met her in Jerusalem at the Jaffa gate! She was coming from the opposite direction amid a crowd of people, and this time she was carrying something wrapped in linen on her head. She stopped when she saw me and I rushed to her.

"Do you recognize me!"

With her free left hand she patted me on the shoulder lightly and smiled:

"I do, *khavadja*."

"What's that you're carrying?"

"Goat's cheese."

"To whom?"

"To everyone."

"You mean you're selling it? Then bring it to my place."

"Where?"

"Why, right here, to the hotel."

I was living next to the Jaffa gate in a tall, narrow house which was part of the solid wall of other houses in this street, to the left of a small square from which started King David Street, a dark passage, in places roofed with canvas and elsewhere with ancient stone vaults, going down in broad steps between equally ancient workshops and shops.

Without the slightest hesitation she started up the steep, narrow stone stairs of my house ahead of me, her shoulders thrown back a little, easily tensing her undulating body, and so completely baring her right arm which held the round of cheese wrapped in a linen on her head on top of the dark-blue square of cotton that I could see the thick tuft of black hair in her armpit. She paused at one turn of the stairs: seen through the narrow window far down below was the ancient pool of the prophet Ezekiel, its greenish water lying as in a well in the square space formed by the solid walls of the houses with narrow latticed windows—the very same water in which once bathed Bathsheba, Uriah's wife, who captivated king David with her nudity. Pausing, she looked out of the window and, turning, glanced at me with happy wonder in her amazing eyes. I could not help myself and kissed her bare arm, and she looked at me in dismay—kissing is not practised among the Bedouins. Upon entering my room, she placed her bundle on the table and held out her right hand to me, palm up. I put several coins in it and then, too overwhelmed to speak, took out a gold sovereign and showed it to her. She understood and humbly inclining her head covered her eyes with the inner side of her arm, bent at the elbow.

"When will you bring me some cheese again?" I asked, taking her to the stairs a half hour later.

"I can't come soon," she said, slightly shaking her head, and held up five fingers—meaning five days.

About two weeks after this, as I was riding away from Ahid's camp and had already gone quite a distance, I heard a shot behind me and saw a bullet hit the stone lying in the road before me and send up a spurt of smoke. Bending low, I whipped my horse to a gallop and heard a second shot and felt the bullet hit me under my left knee. I galloped all the way to Jerusalem, now and again glancing at my boot down which the blood was pouring, frothing... Till this day I wonder how Ahid could have missed twice. I also wonder how he could have found out that it was I who bought the goat's cheese from her.

1946

Mistral

"All thy waves and thy billows are gone over me."
"Behold, thou hast made my days as handbreadths;
"And my age is as nothing before thee."

Lying in the black darkness of the bedroom amid the noise and droning outside, I lose track of time. Dozing off, I think: "Day must break soon..." But then again one sees the same black darkness, one hears the mad rushing of the mistral outside, and one realizes that this darkness, this noise and this droning of the wind are still nocturnal, midnight things. With a habitual gesture I reach for the light switch above my head, illumine the room, and look at my watch: it is the deadest hour of the night. With the light on, everything suddenly appears much more ordinary: the noise and the droning disattach-themselves from the house, all is calm in the cube of my brilliantly lit bedroom, and facing me is the mirror gleaming dispassionately above the mantlepiece. A second bedroom, similar in everything to the first, save that it is lower and smaller, recedes into the depths of the mirror; there, too, a lamp is burning above an old oakwood bed, on which for so many years now I've been sleeping in this old, alien house, and lying on a slightly raised pillow on this bed is a thin face, with dark eye hollows seen in the light falling from above, a pale forehead, and a side parting in the silvery hair... Again I reach for the light switch, and again there is only the humming and the darkness in which something phosphorescent seems to be hovering here, there, and everywhere...

"You boarded a ship, you made a voyage, you reached harbour: time to disembark."

And so, it seems there was a time when I "boarded a ship", a carefree youth with no thought of any harbours... That time, where has it gone? There is only my thought about it left! "The life of each is paltry. And paltry is every end of the world... You have not long left now. Live as on a mountain top. And as from a mountain top survey the earthly happenings: gatherings, campaigns, battles, sowing and harvesting, weddings, births, deaths..." And in my mind's eye I see Provence, across which sweeps the mistral with a savage longing to destroy everything human and temporary, and I see the whole of this ancient land, sleeping now and empty, I see it with all its mountains and valleys, with the roads flickering whitely in the feverish sparkle of the stars, just as it was then, in those legendary Roman times, when the world was ruled by the one who in some "land of the Quadi", during his lonely nights in a camp tent wrote about the paltriness of all human lives, countries and ages... In remote Provencal villages, primordially beautiful in their unsophistication, smelling of smoke from shepherd's fires, a smoke that has soaked into the stone and clay of the houses and hearths, people say that the mule is a prophetic creature, with a secrecy of feelings and intentions rarely found, also intelligence and sensitivity to all that is secret and wondrous with which the world is filled, and that on nights like this he stands till daylight in his dark, cold and draughty shed with his eyes open, never for a minute relaxing his alertness and attention to the "work" of the mistral. Probably he, too, sees and feels that empty, endless flight into space of those ancient Roman times which to me seem to be also my own...

Again I came to my senses in the same darkness, but in a state of unexpected profound composure: all is mute, silent, the windstorm may never have been. I get up, run down quietly into the hall and open the outside door: there is the freshness of the night air, the terrace and the tubbed palms on it, the tiered garden below, and the sky—already motionless and scattered with white stars... Predawn nothingness everywhere. Behind the house, above the dark wooded mountain, there is already something secret, promising, glowing transparently and disappearing in the vault of sky. But as yet there is no sign of life anywhere. From the top of the palms, the round fronds, spreading this way and that, hang like dead black claws. Lower down, over the garden at my feet planted with modestly greyish olive trees, the enormous stone-pines stretch their far-spreading branches to form a black canopy. In the distance beyond them, barely discernible through the darkness is the dale, wrapped in nocturnal sadness; still further, is a cold, sleepy haziness—the whitish frozen breath of the sea. To the west, the ranges Esterol and Mort are outlined as a dark cloud in the sky. To the east darkens the hump of Cap d'Antibes. And there, on that hump, the lighthouse with its keen white eye winks secretively and clearly at regular intervals...

But suddenly this light goes out. The sky behind the cape has become pale and weightless. And somewhere far down below, at a farm, the first cockerel cries cock-a-doodle-doo, as yet through its sleep, unconsciously, but already cockily with a husky, strenuous two-voices scream...

It is yet another morning of mine on earth.

1944

Notes

Ivan Bunin was born on October 23rd 1870 in Voronezh into a family of the old landed nobility which had known better days. As a child Bunin lived at Butyrki, the family homestead in Orel Gubernia. In 1881 he was enrolled in the grammar school in Yelets, but dropped out after less than four years and continued his education at home, taking instruction from his eldest brother Yuli, an exiled revolutionary, a member of the Narodnaya Volya. Bunin's name first appeared in print in 1887, and in 1891 his first collection of poems was published in Orel.

In December 1895 Bunin became acquainted with Chekhov, and in 1899 he met Gorky who drew him into the work of the *Znanie* publishing house. Bunin's place in Russian literature was stabilized when he received the Pushkin Prize for his book "Fallen Leaves" (1901). And in 1909 he was elected honorary member of the Russian Academy of Sciences.

Bunin was hostile to the Revolution of 1917, and in 1920 he emigrated to France. There he wrote the novel *The Life of Arseniev*, a book of stories about love entitled *Shadowed Paths*, and the philosophical treatise "The Liberation of Tolstoy". In 1933 he was awarded the Nobel Prize.

Bunin died in Paris on November 8, 1953.

APPLE FRAGRANCE

"Apple Fragrance" was the finest of Bunin's early stories, confidently promising greater things to come. However, after this story readers and critics firmly affixed to Bunin the label of "bard and mourner of the gentry's ancient nests" whose decline and impoverishment he poeticised. In 1915, surveying his first ten years in literature, Bunin wrote: "Most of the people who wrote about my first books not only hastened to docket me once and for all, but also, with enviable competence, characterised my very nature. According to them, I was the quietest of men (a singer of autumn, melancholy impoverished country estates, and so on), and also that there was no one more settled in his manner and resigned than I. But, in actual fact, I was anything but quiet by nature. I felt everything acutely, be it sorrow or joy, I took a passionate interest in the world about me, and altogether I lived a far more complex and intense life that was reflected in the little that I published then."

Maxim Gorky highly assessed Bunin's intimate knowledge of the landed gentry's way of life, and admired the consummate skill with which he described it in his stories, writing in the unhurried rhythm peculiar to this provincial life and perfectly attuned to it. He said: "Here Bunin sings like a young god! Beautifully, eloquently, and stirringly!"

SUKHODOL

Bunin here speaks about the decline and the degeneration of the country squires, living an abnormal, insulated life. The characters in this story are fictitious, but they and their passions are taken from real life, from family legends. Thus, in Aunt Tonia the author portrayed his paternal aunt who also lost her mind after refusing the proposal of marriage made to her by an officer friend of her brother, and was treated by both doctors and sorcerers. In Pyotr Kirillich he embodied the characteristics and fate of his own grandfather, who grieved so terribly over the death of his young wife that he actually went off his head. "However, it is said that during the Sevastopol campaign, when he lay down for a nap under an apple tree, a great windstorm arose, shaking the tree and hurling big apples down on his head, as a consequence of which he became 'not all there'." As for the carefree and charming head of the family, Bunin leant him certain features of his father, who was to appear later in the novel *The Life of Arseniev.*

LIGHT BREATHING

"I wrote this story in the country, in Vasilyevskoye, in March 1916. *Russkoye slovo* had asked me to produce something for the

Easter issue, and how could I have refused? This newspaper paid me two rubles a line at the time. But I had nothing new to send in. And suddenly I remembered that winter day in Capri when my ramblings brought me to a small cemetery and I chanced upon a grave with a convex porcelain medallion set in the cross and bearing the photograph of a very young girl with amazingly lively, happy eyes. I picked up my pen, instantly made this girl into a Russian, called her Olga Mescherskaya, and started making up a story about her, writing it with that delicious fluency which came to me in the happiest minutes of my work."

MITYA'S LOVE

It is the most important of Bunin's stories written in the 1920's and only second in length to "Sukhodol". Before Bunin, no Russian author wrote about love as he did. The boldness with which he describes love is combined with a classic clarity and perfection of verbal form, a style which was entirely novel and Bunin's own. In many respects the story is autobiographical and tells of young Bunin's infatuation with Varvara Paschenko. This is confirmed by his wife who says, however: "There is nothing autobiographical in the development of the plot, of course, but Mitya's love and suffering were truly those of young Bunin. Nowhere more frankly than in this story did he ever disclose his feelings, which he camouflaged so carefully." To Katya in this story Bunin ascribed some of the traits of Varvara Paschenko's character and her actions—she was as fickle and stage-struck, and had also dropped Mitya for another man.

SUNSTROKE

This story is a prelude to the book *Shadowed Paths* where the tragic philosophy of love was to be presented in variations, dictated by the circumstances of life and the nature of the characters involved. One of the critics wrote: "In literature I do not remember anyone else so powerfully communicating that almost physical sensation of sunlight, as achieved only in painting by the genius of Manet and the impressionists. This very short story is indeed a marvel with its emotional tension, sunlight, happiness and heartache of love, and its life-like poignancy."

The book *Shadowed Paths*

Compiled of disconnected short stories which are yet united into a single whole by the theme of love, life, and death, *Shadowed Paths* held a place apart in Bunin's work. He treated this book with special tenderness, and continued to make amendments and improvements in the text even after it had been published.

On July 24, 1953, shortly before he died, Bunin sent a copy to a friend as a gift and wrote: "I think *Shadowed Paths* is probably my best book as regards conciseness, vigour, and craftsmanship in general."

BALLAD

"I have not much longer to live anyway," wrote Bunin. "And as I was putting my writings in order, to the best of my already very poor ability, in the hope—also rather feeble—that some day they will be published, I re-read almost all my stories and realized that I did not give them their due before, because actually they are wonderful in many respects: originality, variety, conciseness, impact, inner and outer beauty. I am saying this without any embarrassment, without any vanity, simply as an artist. Some of the stories are especially precious to me, they seem delightful, and 'Ballad' is one of them. And yet what prompted me to write this and many other stories was a driving need of money. One morning—this was in Paris—I saw that my purse was quite empty, and so I had to write something quickly for the newspaper, to make up a story at once. I started remembering Russia, the country estates where I stayed in different seasons almost every year, I pictured an old country house on the eve of a holiday in winter, and inspiration came to me in the shape of this perfectly beautiful story."

STESHA

Bunin wrote: "Once, in pouring rain, I was driving to Boborykino from my brother Yevgeny's estate, and as I passed an inn, which stood just off the road, I saw a man, obviously just arrived there, standing on the porch and scraping the mud off his tall boots with the handle of his whip. The rest of the story took shape in my mind without premeditation, shall I say, and when I began to write it I had no idea how it was going to end.

"It is always happening to me—a face, a landscape, the weather momentarily fire my imagination, the vision flashes before me and vanishes at once, but lingers at the back of my mind, troubling me and vaguely urging me to develop it and materialise it.

"Most of my stories originate like that."

MUSE

Bunin recalled: "There was an estate some three versts away from ours in Ozerki, a small village in Yelets Uyezd, which had once belonged to my mother, then to a Mr. Logofet, and in my youth to his down-and-out son, a red-haired, skinny drunkard. I went to see him occasionally, once on a night when there was a full moon and the whole house was illumined only by moonlight. And then one day, I don't know why—one never knows why—I remembered a moment of that evening and desperately wanted to enlarge upon it, to put it into a story which simply refused to be written. All this came back to me suddenly in the last days of September 1938 in Beausoleil, near Monte-Carlo, and as suddenly I had the plot of 'Muse' complete in my head—why and how it occurred to me I have no idea, it was simply there. The only true thing in this story is that once I stayed for long spells at a time in the 'Stolitsa' rooming house in Arbat Street.

"I remembered that rooming house and, to my own surprise, saw myself as someone who wanted to become a painter, but for the life of me I cannot remember wherefrom and why this strange girl, Muse Graf, came into it. I've never had such an encounter in my life. The description of the artist's nights and days at the summer place near Moscow is a much romanticised version of my own brief stay at the dacha of the writer Nikolai Teleshov."

THE HOUR WAS LATE

The story was inspired by memories of Varvara Paschenko whom Bunin knew in Yelets. The belief that Varvara Paschenko was the prototype not only of Lika in the novel *The Life of Arseniev* but also of the girl in this story is confirmed by the entry which Bunin made in his diary on May 7th, 1940: "I wrote 'The Hour Was Late' after I had conclusively reconsidered the story I had so ineptly called 'Lika'... I have gone over my stories to be included in the new book, and I think the best are 'The Hour Was Late', followed, perhaps, by 'Stesha' and 'Ballad'."

VISITING CARDS

Bunin called this a "piercing" story. He recalled: "In July 1914 my brother Yuli and I boarded a steamer in Saratov to sail up the Volga to Yaroslavl. On the first night out, after supper, when my brother was taking a stroll on the deck and I was sitting alone outside the window of our cabin, a lady came up to me—a slight, sweet, shy and inconspicuous woman, quite young but already wilted, and told me that she had recognized me from photographs and was 'so happy' to meet me. I invited her to take a seat, asked her the usual questions—who she was and where she was from—in reply she said something very provincial and insipid, I don't remember what, and in spite of myself and without any ulterior motive I started talking pleasantries with her. But here my brother came up, gave her a silent glare, reducing her to utter embarrassment and making her hurry away, and said to me: 'I heard your mating call—disgusting!' "

HEINRICH

V. N. Muromtseva-Bunina says that "Heinrich" was really Max Lee, a journalist who, together with her husband, wrote novels which were printed in *Vestnik Yevropy*. Bunin thought this story one of his greater successes. On December 11, 1940, he wrote in his diary: "Late last night I finished 'Heinrich' (I started it on the 6th, and continued on the 7th and 9th). I read it over this morning, crossing things out and putting things in. When I finished I ran up and down in front of the house in my excitement because it seemed so good."

NATALIE

"What gave me the idea was the thought of Gogol inventing Chichikov who travelled about buying up 'dead souls'," recalled Bunin. "And I thought, why shouldn't I invent a young man who started out in quest of amorous adventures? At first I thought it would be a series of rather amusing stories. But it turned out quite differently. The young hero of my story first goes for a short stay at the estate of his uncle, a retired Uhlan. For a prototype I took Alexei Alexeyevich Muromtsev, my wife's uncle once removed, who was nicknamed the 'tetchy Uhlan'. My hero's uncle was the kindest of men and his only likeness to the 'tetchy Uhlan' was his size and build. I placed his estate in a river valley, like Muromtsev's."

In his diary Bunin wrote about this story: "No one wants to believe that I made it all up, every word of it, as I had done in practically all my stories, the old and the new. But then I marvel at myself too—how could I have made it all up, if only in 'Natalie'? And I'm afraid I won't be able to make things up and write like that any more." (The entry was made on September 20, 1942).

THE SECOND COFFEE POT

In "The Origin of My Stories" Bunin wrote: "It's all pure fiction. I often thought about writing something like 'Notes of a Painter', and bits of this and bits of that flickered disconnectedly in my imagination. It was from one of these flickering bits that I made up 'The Second Coffee Pot'." The people mentioned here are the Russian painters Grigory Yartsev (1858-1918), Konstantin Korovin (1861-1939), Sofia Kuvshinnikova (1847-1907), Fillip Malyavin (1869-1940), and the journalist and theatrical critic Sergei Goloushev (1855-1920), pen-name Glagol.

Bunin agreed with people who called his "Hotel Madrid" and "The Second Coffee Pot" very humane stories. He said: "When I was writing about the girl in 'Madrid' and about the artist's model, I caught myself laughing fondly all the time, and was on the point of weeping tender, joyous tears." And on October 1, 1945, he wrote: "In these stories, too, there is the appealing charm of the Russian woman's soul. The two stories have not lost their power to move me..."

A COLD AUTUMN EVENING

Bunin wrote: "Early in July 1914, my brother Yuli and I went by steamer from Saratov up the Volga; on the 11th of July there was a long stop at Samara, so we made a trip to town and on our way back to the ship late in the evening saw several young boys running along the embankment waving batches of telegrams and yelling in shrill, cheery voices: 'Urgent telegram, the Austrian Crown Prince has been assassinated in Sarajevo, in Serbia!' My brother snatched a telegram from the hands of one of the boys, read it through again and again, and said: 'Well, it's the end of us! Russia will go to war for Serbia, after that there'll be a revolution in Russia, and the end of our old life!' "

On January 1, 1943, Bunin wrote in his diary: "A *Cold Autumn Evening* is a very moving story."

REQUEST TO READERS

Raduga Publishers would be glad to have your opinion of this book, its translation and design and any suggestions you may have for future publications.

Please send all your comments to 17, Zubovsky Boulevard, Moscow, USSR.